HEART'S PRISONER

DARK WORLD MATES

OLIVIA RILEY

CHAPTER ONE

The bar was like any other in the city. On Tanis, base L3Z, home to hundreds of military recruits, and just as many students, the city was filled with them. Lana had lived on the base for a solid four years now and she never much cared to visit the generic, blue-lit bars with small tables and bare white walls. Not even when colleagues offered to buy her a drink if she joined them. She preferred time researching in her lab. Or working in her study. There was always something that needed to be looked over... re-worked... analyzed.

But tonight was different. Tonight, she searched the bar with hopeful anticipation, craning her neck to peer around a pair of servicemen, her eyes straining to see through the dimly lit room.

At the back, Lana saw the figure of a tall, dark man seated in the corner. They locked eyes and his bright smile pierced the dark corner of the room. He waved to her, and Lana smiled and waved back. She slipped through the crowd easily, her gaze never leaving his.

"Jacob." Lana let out a breath. "God, it's been...forever."

Jacob's smile widened. "Lana." He rose and hugged her, patting her softly on the back. "Or should I say, Dr. Lana Hart." He drew away to look at her carefully. "You've certainly earned the title."

Lana shrugged indifferently. "It comes with its perks." She looked down at Jacob's uniform and caught the badges on his chest. "And you, Base General, it's almost hard to believe."

Jacob laughed. "Yea, whose bright idea was that, right? It's hard for me to wrap my head around, too."

They sat down and Jacob shook his head. "Four years. Who would've guessed? It still seems like a lifetime ago we were on Prominus together. With you working on your thesis..."

Lana smiled, remembering. She looked around the bar and caught sight of a few Gyda standing nearby, their blue scales shimmering against the neon lights as if they could glow in the dark. Jacob followed her gaze over to them.

"You did great work, Lana. I always knew you would."

The Gyda turned their heads in Lana's direction and caught her stare. They bowed their heads slightly. Lana returned the gesture, then looked back at Jacob.

"How long did it take? You know...to get through to them?" Jacob said, gesturing toward the fish-like men.

"Two years and eight months," said Lana. "The Gyda thankfully aren't a very hostile race."

"And that's a damn good thing. Real surprising they didn't declare war on us as soon as your lab started testing."

Lana's eyes dropped. "I made sure to communicate perfectly that the research was completely by choice. It took a lot more to convince the head of research that then it was to convince the Gyda that we only wanted to study them to learn their ways; to learn how they evolved through communication, not dissect them like lab specimens."

Jacob nodded, understanding. "Well, I'm glad the convincing worked. They were lucky to have the best behavioral and biological therapist this side of the solar system on their team. Regarding that, I'm betting you're wondering why I called you here."

Lana went to answer until Jacob stopped her.

"But first, let me get you a drink." Jacob winked. Lana didn't stop him as he got up and went over to the bar then a few minutes later came back with two white spritzers. Lana took hers without complaint. She took a sip, watching Jacob drink half of his before setting his glass down.

"I called you here because I want to make you an offer," Jacob began.

Lana raised her brows. "An offer?"

Jacob nodded.

"For?"

"A job."

Lana's eyes widened and she straightened in her chair.

"And I know what you're thinking. What could I possibly offer that's better than what you got going on here? I know your research and time spent with the Gyda is important, trust me, it's history in the making–bringing our kind together. But..." Jacob glanced around, then leaned closer. "You and I both know they aren't the only ones...you know...the only *alien* race we encountered. Sure, the government tries to keep things all hush hush. But with the Gyda melding into our society so well, thanks to you and your team, there arc others that the government wants to understand better, and needs to learn about, so we can know that what happened with the Gyda can be done with others."

Lana studied Jacob seriously. "Or to find out if they are a threat to society, am I correct?"

Jacob shrugged. "More or less."

Lana was speechless. She'd heard her share of rumors around the base about other encounters through the military's exploration and research team–those who went to other worlds and studied them extensively. The government didn't care to share this with the population, but Lana had a strong feeling the Gyda hadn't been the first nor the last alien race they had come into contact with. And now Jacob was not only telling her that her theory was correct, but that he wanted her to...

"You want me to try to communicate with these new beings like I did with the Gyda, don't you?"

Jacob nodded. "But it won't be like the Gyda, Lana. The ones we got are...well, let's just say we already have a basic understanding that they aren't so 'peaceful' and 'willing' like the Gyda."

"They are hostile?"

"Some we aren't certain. Others...have been threatening," Jacob said and drank down the rest of his glass.

Lana brushed a hand through her hair. "This is...I would have to think..."

Jacob dragged his chair closer to hers, then put a hand on her shoulder. "If you need time to think it over, no problem."

"It's just..." Lana fixed her eyes with his. "I know a lot about the Gyda. I was lucky to be one of the head therapists when we first discovered them. I've studied them for years now. It gave me an edge on the best ways to interact with them. With a new...species, and more than one by my guessing, it could take me a lot longer, and I can't guarantee any sort of cooperation."

"Hey, yea, trust me, we understand the risks," said Jacob. "But also trust me when I say you are our best choice. I've reviewed your work, Lana, plus I know you. I can't think of anyone more qualified for the job."

Lana turned her eyes away from him to gaze back around the bar. The two Gyda were now talking with a few human men and women, speaking in broken, yet still impressive, English. Their mannerisms and gestures were clearly human, not their own.

"You said you have them, these new beings," Lana said. "I take it I won't be going to their home planet or interacting with them in a separate community?"

"No. They are housed at the base on LV012."

Lana turned back to Jacob, stunned.

"Lazris?" she breathed.

Jacob nodded. "The one and only."

Lana sat back, staring at him firmly. "How dangerous are these individuals, Jacob?"

Jacob took up his glass, swirling the remaining ice around. "Dangerous enough that Lazris is the only place for them."

Lana watched him for a considerable time, thinking. Lazris was one of the military's top security and research facilities. Built below ground on a terraformed world, it was made to be one of their most confidential bases. No other place was more secure and heavily guarded than LVo12.

If the government had other alien races housed at Lazris, then they could only be of high risk to humanity.

At least for now.

If Lana agreed to go, she could see these aliens for herself, discover a way to communicate effectively and efficiently enough to allow them to interact in human society. Just like the Gyda. If she could do that, she'd finally have the means to begin her one private research and exploration program, perhaps still backed by the government, but still hers nonetheless; and not stationed on some base, but rather traveling to various communities all through the galaxy.

The Gyda, after all, had only been the beginning. They had been successfully introduced into their society–true–but there was so much more to be done. With more races being discovered, human society could quickly be on its way to a vast global federation not unlike the kind dreamed of in the oldest sci-fi books and movies.

Lana closed her eyes and breathed deep. "How long?"

"The contract starts at two years. Can be made longer, pending on if more testing needs to be done..."

Lana opened her eyes and saw Jacob giving her a look she had seen many times back when they studied together.

"What aren't you telling me, Jacob?"

Jacob sighed, setting down his glass. "I'm gonna level with you, Lana. I almost didn't want to recommend you for this."

"Oh?"

"Not because I don't think you couldn't do the job. It's just that..." Jacob glanced at the Gyda then back at her. "The team currently assigned to LV012 have been working with these aliens for a few months now. Even our most advanced and qualified therapists have been struggling to understand them. Some of these beings are very intelligent, we think maybe more intelligent than they are letting on. That's why I knew we needed you to come in. I had been directed to ask you sooner–way sooner–but I kept it off."

Lana arched her brows. "Why?"

"I know you won't care when I say it's dangerous work. But that's beside the point. Cole, the head of the department, wants you to help study these aliens... but there is one in particular he wants you to work with specifically...personally."

Lana frowned. "Just one?"

"Yea." Jacob's face darkened. "Don't even have a name for his kind yet, but he's been...challenging."

Lana tilted her head slightly. Strangely, a more Gyda gesture.

"Alright, more bluntly, he's a real pain in the ass. Made two other therapists quit in a span of two weeks. And he's just straight evil-looking, in my honest opinion, really off-putting. Not that there aren't a few others there that would ever win beauty contests. But still, I know how stubborn you can be, how determined. I feared how this could affect you psychologically, you know?"

"This alien. Does he have a name?"

"From what they could render, he goes by Xerus."

Lana went quiet for a moment, thinking. She took one last sip of her drink then offered it to Jacob, who took it gladly, finishing off the rest.

"And he is...different from the rest?" she asked carefully.

Jacob grunted. "In a way, yes."

Lana's eyes traveled around the bar and over the crowd of people. If she could get through to this Xerus, if she could successfully gain his cooperation and integrate him into society just like the Gyda...

"I know it's a lot to think about, Lana. I'll give you a week or two to decide if you think—"

"No need." Lana looked back at him and smiled. "I'm in."

Jacob raised his brows in surprise. "Seriously?"

Lana nodded, her smile growing wider. "Yea. I want this. In fact, I think I *need* this."

Jacob snorted. "I hate to say I knew I could count on you, Lana." For a second Lana thought she caught a dark glint in his eyes until he smiled and it was gone. He offered his hand, and Lana took it. "Welcome to the Lazris team, Dr. Hart."

CHAPTER TWO

It took Lana two months total to complete her transition from base L3Z to LV012. Despite having all her credentials and necessary "paperwork" in order, she still had to undergo several tests and background checks before she was approved for her transfer. Once complete, she had her personal things shipped to the base, then waited several days at the flight port for the ship to take her to her new home away from home.

LV012 was only a system away from her old base, but still far enough away she would have to go into a sleeper-unit for at least a few hours. She hated the things. But understood their necessity. She swallowed the sleeping pills a half hour before needing to enter the unit and took the little time she had beforehand to once again look over some of the data Jacob had sent to her from Lazris' database. On her sleek laptop, she pulled up the files for each 'asset'. No pictures popped up, so she still had no idea what they looked like. There was a short description as well as status, containment procedures, and threat levels, but nothing too in-depth. She'd get the full files once she was secured at the base.

Her eyes traveled over the data, looking at each file carefully. The first asset seemed pretty commonplace:

LAZRIS Project 30001B

Asset C
Dog-like quadruped. Six feet, long sharp nails, whip-like tail
Status: active contained
Containment procedures: monitor regularly, keep in the secured cell. Only to be taken out for lab testing.
Threat status: medium

Nothing unusual. And the next three—though different in appearance—had nearly identical information save for one that needed to be fed before it could be taken out to be tested.

It was the next few that really caught her attention. They all had a high threat status. Their containment procedures were also longer and more descriptive. And they were only allowed out of their holdings for very special circumstances.

The first of these was a Raptor-like species as tall as her waist. One individual raptor only had a threat status of medium but all together they raised that to high. Lana theorized they were social creatures with a high pack mentality, bred to survive as a group.

After them came a creature that—based on the description—Lana could only imagine looking like a mix between a mangled werecat and the monster from The Thing. It walked on two legs but apparently ran on four. It was to be monitored frequently and only allowed out for special testing but must first be put under and kept in its cell for at least twenty minutes until deemed safe to move, otherwise—as the procedure specifically read—"it very well might not be asleep and will easily drag the nearest unfortunate soul into its cage and eat them alive. Slowly."

Then, lastly, came what she could only assume was her new patient.

Asset X

Seven feet, two inches. Biped. Reptilian(?). Sharp spikes along the head, back (spine), and tail (poisonous?). Red eyes

Status: active contained

Containment procedures: monitor constantly, keep in a secured cell. Asset must not leave its holding under any circumstances. Any testing (if possible) must be done within the unit and must have an active weaponized military team on standby. SPECIAL PROCE-DURES: Cell must be under UV red light only. Window must be closed when not in use. Individuals should not stay within the unit for longer than an hour to avoid any extreme mental and emotional distress.

Threat status: high

Lana shifted in her seat. The dull ache of self-doubt suddenly pressed against her chest. If this Xerus was so dangerous, could she really get through to him enough that he'd ever be allowed out of Lazris? What if it was his plan all along to harm them?

Lana tapped her finger on the side of her computer, thinking. With all the background checks, testing, and packing the last couple of months, she had little time to prepare herself for how she planned to work with this being. She could try the same methods she used on the Gyda and hope they proved successful. After all, she was confident in those methods. They worked well for her for many years. She had to believe they could work now.

Her alarm went off, letting her know it was time to move to the sleeper-unit. Lana closed her laptop and placed it in a secured bag then stepped over to the pod. She could feel the pills starting to take effect as she laid herself out on the bed and let the door close on top of her.

* * *

Lana drowsily awakened, hearing the soft beeps of her sleeper-unit and the swish of the door opening above her. She blinked several times, then slowly rose to a sitting position.

"Docking in twenty minutes, please step from the sleeper-unit and prepare for landing," came a voice over the intercom.

Lana stretched and gritted her teeth as she obeyed the voice, her body stiff. She dressed carefully, then sat back in her seat, buckling herself in. She peered out the window next to her and could see the bright tan and green planet coming into view.

LV012 was a desolate planet with shallow lakes and near barren seas and more deserts and wastelands than forests. It had once been much worse, but years of terraforming had made it habitable to a minimal degree. There was nothing truly unique about the planet save for the advanced human tech orbiting its atmosphere and the ships entering and exiting from a patch of brown land. Though the rolling, chaotic storms that passed by—more wind, dust, and lightning than rain—were nothing to scoff at. LV012 was no paradise. But inside Lazris, its base, it was said to be much more hospitable.

Lana's grip tightened on her seat as the ship broke through the atmosphere, shaking slightly as it dropped down, gaining momentum. She took a deep breath and closed her eyes, laying her head back. She heard the gears turning and the roar of the wind. She felt her stomach drop as it approached the land. She jumped when the ship made ground and remained tense until it slowed. When she opened her eyes and peered back toward the window, she caught a glance of the outside before the ship rolled into the docking port. The light of day slipped away into darkness and neon lights as the docking doors slid closed.

As soon as the ship came to a smooth stop, Lana quickly unbuckled and readied her things, swinging one bag over her shoulder and picking up another. Lights flickered off and on and the engines slowed to a dull hum as she slunk out of the room and rushed down the aisle. The exit doors slid open and bright light beamed across her face, catching her off guard.

Lana raised her hand, squinting her eyes and reaching for the rail of the steps when she nearly bumped into someone.

"Dr. Hart, welcome!" came a sweet, feminine voice. "Oh, please let us get those for you. Your items will be waiting for you in your personal unit." Lana felt her bags being taken from her and a hand on her elbow to help guide her down the steps. When the light passed her eyes, Lana blinked carefully, then looked around, coming to a dead halt just as she made it onto the bottom landing. She took in the sight of the port first: a large and impressive space with several docked ships and cargo lined up to be taken in and out of the base. Bots of all sizes marched by, carrying equipment and placing them in the necessary holdings. Then she looked over to her left and saw the cheerful, smiling face of a young, well-kept, blond.

"Dr. Hart," said the blond in that sweet voice. "I am Officer Kinsley. But you can call me Nicole. I will be directing you today."

Lana glanced at Officer Nicole's attire, noticing the gray and blue suit with the Lazris' insignia on her right breast–a black star with eight points. Above this star was a red badge with an ID. She looked back at Nicole's face and smiled, holding out her hand. "Lana."

Nicole's smile widened, and she took Lana's hand, shaking it firmly. "Lana. You've got a lot to see today. Let's get you settled in."

Lana followed Nicole out of the dock to a security clearance midpoint located just before the terminal that would lead down into the center base. She presented her IDs and credentials to various stoney-faced officers before going through one last routine exam. With all required vaccinations in order and her background confirmed, she was presented with her own official Lazris ID, badge, and keycard. Once securing each to her shirt, Lana followed Nicole past the checkpoint to the main terminal where an elevator-car was already waiting for them. Nicole pressed a button with her polished finger and the doors parted. Inside, white seats were secured to both sides, each fitted with a seat belt. Blue lights flowed around the upper half of the car like waves. Nicole took a seat on the left side, gesturing for Lana to take hers on the right. Lana sat facing her and grabbed at the seat belt.

"No need for that." Nicole smiled. "It's just a precaution."

'A precaution for what', Lana thought and almost let the words slip out. Instead, she shrugged, letting the belt fall.

"There have been a few tremors," Nicole said, as if hearing her thoughts, anyway. "Nothing too serious, but can't be too safe either."

"Have they been happening often?" Lana asked curiously.

"No, only maybe a few a month. But you can be assured Lazris and everything within was built to withstand any planetary or natural event. The storms, the tremors, are just slight inconveniences at best."

A loud bell rang and the doors of the car shut tightly. A second later, the car began to move downward at a smooth pace. A few seconds after that, an image on the back of the car popped up as if the wall had now turned into a screen. On the screen, a woman with her hair knotted back and her smile just as pristine as Nicole's began speaking.

"Welcome to Lazris," the woman said in a polite tone, "home to human advancement and discovery. Here we create and innovate." The woman grew smaller in size and, to her right, sprung an image of LV012. "Lazris was built on the planet known as LV012 approximately 2 miles under its surface. Made from thick titanium steel, Lazris is the most secure base in our governing system." The woman disappeared and images of Lazris took her place. "Here a total of twelve thousand three hundred and twenty-two military and civilian employees work and live. Each level is built to hold each unique facility and sector. A map can be found beside each elevator, emergency stairway, and accessed through a Scibot or a computer. The levels are as follows: Level One, City, and Welcome sector, where this terminal arrives and departs. Also, the location of specialized shops and entertainment. From here, you will take the elevator to other levels. Level Two, Agriculture, and Natural Resources. Level Three, Armory, Supply Warehouse, and Mechanics Bay. Level Four..."

The levels were listed off, twelve in total. The very last one, by no margin of surprise, was her own facility.

"Level Twelve, Center for Bio-scientific and Specimen Research. Access to this level is prohibited unless given special authorization. All Levels have emergency stairs. A keycard will be needed to access certain floors and rooms and will be used to enter your unit."

The car shook slightly, and the screen glitched, making the woman's smiling face distort briefly. The car began to slow.

"Thank you for joining us." The woman gave a salute, and the screen disappeared. The car came to a stop and Nicole stood up as the doors slid open.

"Follow me."

Lana carefully exited the car. She followed Nicole, turning left and then around to a set of doors behind the terminal. When they approached, the doors opened and Lana paused, eyes widening.

"Jesus...Jacob really hadn't been joking," she whispered. She followed Nicole into the bright, vast foyer that was the base city welcome sector. A several-stories tall, football-field-long strip that held a fountain at its center and a digitally enhanced ceiling above that portrayed light like the sky.

It was flawless.

To each side were various stores, restaurants, and bars, almost like she was stepping through a mall or resort. The walls and ceilings were white and gray, the floor was a colorful mosaic of green and blue, and the Lazris star was displayed as a piece of floating metal within the fountain beyond. Banner-screens hanging from the ceiling displayed ads for the various stores; one looked like a luxurious spa—

another, a fine-dining restaurant. Trees and plants had been planted in various pots along the sides of the walkway and Lana could see they were real, not the fake, cheap kind she had seen in her old base.

As they walked, they passed groups of other personnel, most making their way to the glass elevators between the shops that would take them up to other floors within the city sector. Nicole passed them by without a glance, while Lana watched them curiously. Something caught her eye from above and, when she peered upward, she caught sight of several drones hovering silently, several feet from the ground.

'Interesting method of security,' she thought. She had seen no standing guards either. Lazris didn't seem to want to waste bodies by having them just standing around watching.

As they approached the end of the great hall, they came to a set of much larger, metal elevators, at least eight in total. Nicole brought out her keycard, swiped it, then pressed the button on the side, going down.

"I'll take you down to your unit first so you can get situated and comfortable, then we can start our tour of each level and..."

Lana couldn't hide the impatient grimace on her face, which Nicole seemed to notice, and stopped.

"Is it really necessary?" Lana said hesitantly. "I think I got the gist while heading down here..."

Nicole's mouth turned up. "Ready to get to work, huh, Doctor?"

"It's been a long two months of waiting. Can you blame me?" 'And I've been waiting for this chance for even longer,' she thought.

Nicole glanced around, then looked back at Lana. "It's usually protocol but..." She gave a little shrug. "Well, I guess an exception could be made for you. Though I ask that at some point you do make your way through the levels. You'll want to become familiar with them."

Lana placed a hand to her heart. "Promise I will."

The elevator doors opened, and they stepped inside. "We will make a quick stop to your unit and while you're inside, I will call in on level twelve and let them know you are coming down," Nicole stated and hit the button for level nine. The elevator doors closed, and it immediately began its descent.

"Thanks, Nicole," Lana said gratefully.

Nicole slipped another smile. "In truth, Dr. Kingsley has been pretty impatient to see you, too. He'd be grateful to hear that you're ready to go. It's been pretty wild down on twelve..." Nicole cleared her throat. "At least so I've heard."

"Kingsley..." Lana looked at her curiously. "You are related?

"My uncle. And the head of the department."

"Ah," Lana said. "Well, if he is as nice as you have been, then I have nothing to fear."

"Unfortunately..." Nicole's eyes turned on Lana. When Lana looked at her with slight concern, she laughed. "Don't worry, he's no drill sergeant, but he can be...intimidating when he wants to be."

"I guess it comes with the territory."

Nicole let out a breath. "Yes, you'll definitely get the serious ones around here. The stiff-necks I like to call them."

"Do they mostly run security?" Lana joked, thinking of the officers running the security clearance.

"Mostly. I'm sure you know how it can be on base."

"Oh, do I."

The two laughed and Nicole glanced at her, bright-eyed. "We are glad you're here. It goes without saying that I'm a fan of your work. I studied a little about interspecies communication and neo-biology back in the day. Fascinating stuff. I read your paper on the Gyda. Got to meet a few myself."

"So you know what I'm up against now, then?"

Nicole's smile dropped slightly, and she nodded. "It's been challenging. But they are confident you can help."

"I hope so."

The elevator doors opened and Lana stepped out with Nicole into a hallway lit by soft blue light trailing along the walls. To each side were sets of doors with keypads similar to that of some hotels.

Numbers ran along each side, starting from twelve hundred. Nicole took Lana down toward the middle and stopped at room twelve sixty-three. Lana used her keycard to open the metal door, which slid open just as she slid her card through the pad.

"I'll wait out here and call twelve," Nicole said as Lana stepped inside. Lana nodded to her just before the door slid closed and locked soundly. She turned to look around and take in the sight of her new home.

It was a small apartment really, but comfortable none-the-less. A bed at the back with a makeshift window above, making it look similar to daylight. A kitchen area with a table to the left, a desk, and a computer to the right, along with a small closet. Through another door beyond, she could see a shower. It wasn't much, but it was enough. Her bags, just like Nicole said, were already placed alongside the bed. On the bed itself was her uniform. Gray and blue with a black star.

Lana changed quickly and met Nicole back outside. With her arrival now expected, they made their way back to the elevators. This time, when the doors opened, they found a Scibot waiting inside. The humanoid, faceless robot, with a computer screen mounted on its chest, turned towards them.

"Hello, please let me know if you need assistance." It spoke in a male voice.

"Did you have Scibots on your base?" Nicole asked.

"They were only just being introduced."

"They can be handy when they want to but, oh, how I hate seeing one loping around in the dark." Nicole seemed to shudder.

The elevator moved down, and it was then Lana noticed her heart begin to race. When the elevator stopped and the doors opened, they stepped out to a small, yet long, foyer where a large, thick steel door sat at the end, guarded by two soldiers. To one side of the foyer, a window looked into a security office where an officer sat within.

"Hello David, I'm here with Dr. Hart," Nicole said as they approached.

David looked up at Lana with icy blue eyes and nodded. He typed in a code into his computer and a loud beep responded. The door at the far end began to slide open and the soldiers before it stepped aside.

"This is as far as I go," Nicole said. "Good Luck, Doctor. If you are ever in need of...well, anything, don't hesitate to contact me."

"Thank you, Nicole." Lana's heart thumped harder, but she gave her a confident smile. "I know I'll be seeing you."

Lana watched Nicole step back into the elevator before she turned around. She took a deep breath, kept her head up, and walked on alone. The soldiers said nothing as she walked past and when she entered through the wide door, one turned to follow behind her.

Beyond the door revealed an impressively large, hexagonal room, carved and smoothed out of the very rock. Vertical lights melded along the walls, lighting the chamber in dim white light that cast a yellowish glow on the walls. To each side of the hexagon was a thick metal door similar to the one she had just entered through. Lana could only assume behind each was one of the alien species Lazris kept contained within its compound. Her assumptions were correct when she glanced upward and saw several monitors hanging from the ceiling, each showing video feed into the different cells. She didn't linger on them long enough to see the aliens in detail. Instead, her focus turned to the mix of computers and lab equipment that had been placed in the center of the room. Several men and a few women gathered around the machines, too caught up in their work to take notice of her approach. The soldier who had been following her now took the lead, directing her around the equipment. A containment pod to her left gave her a glimpse of an unidentifiable plant growing within, purple and veiny. Past the pod, she spotted a water tank holding strange lime-green crustaceans with some kind of coral growing on their backs.

"Doctor Hart," she heard the soldier say. Lana forced her gaze away from the tanks to steer her eyes over to the two men before her. One got up from his seat at a long desk with several monitors and pinned her with a blue-eyed gaze, his lips twitching up into a smile.

"Miss Hart, Cole Kingsley." Cole extended his hand and Lana took it, squeezing gently. She was forced to lift her head up to the towering figure in order to meet his eyes. Despite his graying hair, Cole was much younger looking than she had anticipated; no wrinkles or facial scars to be seen, his face perfectly shaved and clean. His smile turned into a grin, showing perfectly white teeth. "It's a lot to take in at first, isn't it? You're not the first to come walking in here with an awestruck stare."

Lana blinked and shook her head. "It's just hard to believe I'm really here."

Cole released her hand. " It can seem daunting, but I think you'll feel right at home in a few days." His eyes shifted over to the second man wearing a military guard's uniform sitting beside the desk, his feet propped up on its edge. His black eyes regarded Lana as Cole gestured to him. "This is Officer Justin Torrence, head of security and defense, on level twelve."

Torrence didn't move to stand or extend his hand, nor did he smile. His eyes flickered down Lana's form then back up. Lana noticed his hands moving in a circular motion and saw the flash of a wrapper. His jaw moved in a similar motion as he chewed on what she could only assume was some kind of gum or perhaps tobacco. He gave her a single nod and a low grunt of acknowledgment.

"Nicole told me you were ready to get started as soon as possible," Cole said, turning back to her. "I'm glad to hear. We've been impatient to have you. Can I assume rightly that you have been given all the necessary information about what you'll be working with?"

"General Hartin sent me a few files and gave me the run-down but only the barest of details on the...specimens within. And what is required of me exactly."

Cole nodded. "Makes sense. There's already been talk of information getting leaked. Thankfully nothing serious enough but we can never be too cautious." Cole gestured beyond Lana, pointing to the doors along the walls. "As I'm sure you guessed, behind each door contains the assets, all contained within their own unit. Yours"–he pointed to the door opposite the one she had come through–"will be within unit three. I assume General Hartin has already warned you of its nature."

Lana stared down the door of unit three. "He mentioned it was aggressive, yes."

Officer Torrence laughed low behind her. Lana turned to look at him and watched as he set his feet on the ground and leaned forward. "Aggressive is an understatement, Miss Hart. Try violent and offensive. Hostile."

Lana frowned. "Jacob…General Hartin, mentioned that too."

Torrence fixed his eyes with hers. "Then you won't take offense when I say that I think you being here is a fuckin' waste of time."

"Careful now, Officer Torrence," said Cole.

Torrence shrugged. "I'm just telling it like it is." He slowly unwrapped the crumbled wrapper in his hands and dropped the gum he had been chewing into it, then wrapped it back up. "Did Jacob mention what happened to the last two 'behaviorists' that tried to work with that thing?"

Lana glanced at Cole then shook her head.

"One lasted two weeks then stormed out without a word and never came back. The other only lasted four days and went as far away from here as possible."

"It is unfortunate," said Cole. "However, none had your unique kind of expertise."

"This also isn't some docile land fish like your–what were they called? Gida?"

"Gyda," Lana corrected.

"Yea, that." Torrence threw his old wrapper then fished for a new one out of his pocket. "This one's more like a demon if you ask me. Straight out of hell itself. And if it were up to me?" He unwrapped his gum and popped it in his mouth, chewing slowly. "I'd send it right back to where it came from. With a single bullet."

Lana shifted uncomfortably on her feet.

"Officer Torrence, always the dramatic one." Cole laughed softly. "He doesn't exactly share our views on the preservation and discovery of these new species."

"Your little discovery nearly killed four of my men just to transfer it here," Torrence growled.

"Regardless, you needn't worry," Cole said, ignoring him. "The asset is contained in a state-of-the-art cell enforced with titanium steel and thick electro-charged glass. Guards are stationed nearby and we have security lock-down measures just in case. Safety is always of great importance."

"I'm not worried," said Lana. She forced a confident smile just to show Torrence he hadn't gotten to her (even if he had a little).

Cole nodded. "As for the rest, in time you can be introduced. Understand we'd like you to get settled in first."

Lana understood. Better to make sure she could handle it; that she didn't go running after only one encounter. She gazed over the other doors and noticed each had a number corresponding to their unit. Only the last door on the far right had no number, just a containment sign that read 'virus and disease lab personnel only'.

Cole clapped his hands. "Good. With that, how about we introduce you to your new patient?"

* * *

Before they entered the room, Lana was given the proper protocols and procedures, this time more in-depth. The room was to stay low lit and would only brighten in an emergency. She was under no circumstances to give the asset information about its surroundings or anything about Lazris and its facilities, no matter how much it tried to push the subject or bribe its way into getting her to spill. She was warned heavily not to let it get too close despite her duties. To not let it learn too much about her. Clearly they didn't trust this Xerus and, though she could understand why, it also bothered her. The more she was told the more it seemed she was there not to study and learn and teach, but to interrogate.

"This ISpad has all the complete information you need to know about the asset. Or at least what we've learned so far." Cole handed her the tablet and on its screen popped up an assortment of different apps and files. "The files on the subject are under Asset X. The Envision app will give you access to controls in the room. You can make the room brighter or darker, pause and start recordings, control the QS translator..."

Lana, whose eyes had been drifting over the sleek little tablet in her hands, paused and looked up at Cole. "You use a QS translator?"

"Have to currently. We have yet to completely learn its language by traditional means." Cole began to make his way to the door marked "Unit 3" and Lana followed. Her eyes fell on Torrence briefly enough to see his black gaze still watching her before she pulled her attention back to Cole. "You can thank our quantum computer engineer, Dr. Hoffmen, for even being able to use the program. He took the recordings of the subject's conversations then threw them into our most advanced computer installed with the translator. We used the video feed we had and the very few instances of the creature using body language and other means of communicating certain information. It wasn't a lot at first but, after a few more conversations, there was enough to give us something to work with. Took the translator a few weeks to finally work out some sort of language." Cole nodded back to Torrence and pointed to the door. Torrence hesitated only for a moment before he passed a code into the computer beside him and the door began to slide open. Guards near the walls moved closer in and placed hands on the guns at their sides.

"Granted the translator still isn't perfect. Some things still get lost in translation," Cole continued.

Lana watched the door slowly slide up into the wall, the sound of thick metal grazing over smooth stone filling her ears. When she looked back at the central lab, she saw other employees stopping conversations or other menial tasks to take positions at nearby computers and monitors. A flashing yellow light signaled the opening of the door and a feminine voice snapped over an intercom.

"Unit three opening, code white." A harsh ring followed until the door opened completely. As soon as it locked in place, guards stationed themselves on each side.

"There's a few other things, Dr. Hart," Cole said, his eyes never leaving her, " Once the door closes behind you, it will automatically lock back in place. But you needn't worry, someone will always be monitoring. Once you are finished with your work, just use your ISpad to communicate with us that you are ready to end the session. Either I or Officer Torrence will be watching from the monitors should anything happen." Cole stepped closer to her, his head falling near to hers. "I know you have been warned enough of the many disturbing things about this creature but there is something else about the asset not yet mentioned. Even without a clear means of communicating, it seems to have a way to...throw its voice. The creature may use this trick to toy with you."

Lana frowned with confusion. "What do you mean?"

"The QS translator not only translates the sounds into words that we can understand, it also tries to mimic the pitch and tone of voice. The subject can change its tone and pitch to sound completely different from its own. Think like a natural ability at ventriloquism or mimicry. It may be unnerving at first." Cole placed a warm, heavy hand on Lana's shoulder. " But I trust you'll be able to handle it. If at any time you need to talk with one of us, don't hesitate." Cole lifted his hand and stepped away. "We will be recording so we will hear everything. You'll have fifteen minutes inside just to get acquainted. Good Luck, Doctor." He placed his hands in the pockets of his lab coat and walked back toward the central lab.

Lana nodded and gave him a brief smile before turning toward the door. She paused to breathe before stepping inside.

Beyond was a short hallway drenched in deep red light. As soon as she stepped inside, the door behind her began to close. She nearly stopped and looked back but caught herself, forcing her gait to slow to a calming pace.

'Don't let them see you hesitate, Lana, or they'll see your fear.' she thought. Because despite her best efforts she was afraid. Or at least uncomfortably anxious. Funny how she hadn't really paid attention to her body's response until now. Her racing heart, her skin turning hot, her shaking limbs; she had ignored them before, keeping her composure cool in front of the others. But now that she was alone and heading into what looked like the den of a dragon, her composure was slipping.

The end of the hallway met with a simple sliding door which opened as she approached, giving her a view into an even darker red room.

Lana did hesitate this time, but only for a moment. She had been waiting for a chance like this for so long, she wasn't going to let her fear ruin it for her now. With her tablet clutched tight in one hand, she walked into the room.

The first thing she noticed oddly was the smell. It smelled like someone had just brewed a fresh pot of coffee. Lana frowned looking around the room but saw no steaming pot or cup anywhere. The only things she saw were a single chair and table in the center of the darkened room, seated perfectly in front of a huge glass window that stretched from floor to ceiling (though the ceiling was rather low) and was as wide as two armored cars. The glass, she noted, looked as if it had some sort of milky film covering it and she realized it was a screen meant to hide the contents within...or keep the contents from seeing out.

Lana slowly brought herself up beside the chair and stared at the screen. Beyond the milky cover, there was only a bright red. She shivered thinking it reminded her of a pool of blood.

Her eyes flitted to the side where two monitors hung next to the window. One monitor showed a video feed which was black currently. The other showed...

Lana's brow furrowed. She crept closer to observe until she realized it was vitals. Some program was monitoring the subject's heart-rate and energy level. The pulse didn't change, never going above 40 bpm.

"Interesting scent." Came a voice filling the room.

Lana jumped but quickly recovered. She looked down at her tablet and saw the QS translator blinking on; when she tapped on it, the program brought up a window that showed two separate wave-lengths pulsing slightly. The voice had been deep, like a man's. The translator was working to mimic the tone and pitch like Cole had said.

"Different," came the voice again. "What new little toy have they brought me to play with this time?"

Lana tapped back to the home screen of her ISpad and found the controls for the room. As she searched for the options that would lift the screen from the window, a large shadow passed by. Lana glanced up in time to see the silhouette of the subject glide by and then disap-pear. She had to quickly sit down before her knees gave out.

He was huge. With long limbs and a slender mid-frame. She could make that out enough. His tail slithered and weaved behind him as long as the window was wide. Horns along his head twisted upward from the top and down the back of his neck. The sensation Lana felt seeing his shape pass the screen was akin to the time she had seen a massive great white shark swim past her cage as a tween back when her father had taken her cage diving off the Pacific.

Lana sat motionless, trying to gauge exactly what she just saw. If his shadow could produce such a reaction from her, then she feared what his true form might do. Jacob had warned her.

No, she needed to focus. Whatever he looked like, she must remember what she was here for and to keep her mind calm; to approach the situation as a professional scientist and doctor should. Leave personal feelings aside.

Lana cleared her throat. "Hello, Xerus. I am Dr. Hart."

There was no response. Lana pursed her lips and glanced back down at her ISpad. She could see the QS translator working to translate her voice for the alien to understand on his end, so he could clearly hear her. "Forgive me, I am trying to pull up the screen so that I can better see you but it seems I am having trouble with finding the...ah, here we are." Lana tapped through to the windows controls and slid her finger upward. In response, the milky film along the window began to slowly fade. When she peered up again she had to stifle a gasp. Swallowing it down was painful. Immediately her body went cold as she stared into the cell.

Xerus stood in the center of the room and all Lana could think was what Jacob and Torrence had told her was true.

He was evil-looking.

Lana had seen her share of horror films and sci-fi art depicting the horrifying creatures man's imagination could conjure. To these artists, Xerus may well be a true masterpiece.

Xerus cocked his head slightly as he watched her through the glass. His tail, which had been motionless only a second before, began to lazily sway behind him. A tail, Lana noticed, covered with purplish-red spikes all the way down to the sharp dagger-shaped tip. Those very spikes started small then grew in size as they reached further up his backside, all along his spine and to the nape of his neck where they merged with long twisted horns that formed the base of his skull. It reminded her almost of a mohawk only instead of hair there were solid, deadly points with two main horns that grew on each side of it. Long and curved like an african impala's antlers.

The room beyond was colored red. But Lana could tell even then that Xerus' skin was the same color only a shade darker. It was not soft skin like a person's but rather more like a lizard's. Scales that started smooth underneath but turned increasingly rougher to the outer parts of his arms and torso. Her eyes drank him in until they rose to finally look on his face. She flinched when she saw his eyes cutting into her. They were red, bright red, like hellfire. And around the iris was black.

Lana looked away and cleared her throat again. She didn't want to seem rude by staring at him and nothing else. Her hand shook slightly as she tapped on her ISpad to bring up her work files and the program she'd use for her notes. She was silently grateful to have noticed they let him keep on a pair of what looked to be armored leggings to cover himself so that he wasn't housed like a complete animal.

"I'm here to...communicate with you," Lana said carefully. "To hopefully–"

"I know why you're here."

Lana looked up. Xerus still leered down at her. He turned his body slightly but didn't move a step. "They'll keep sending your *kind* until they think they can reach some agreement with me."

Lana found herself focusing on his mouth as he spoke. A mouth that was wider than a human's. She caught a glimpse of shiny black teeth as sharp and long as the rest of him. When his mouth moved, she could see him speaking his own language but obviously couldn't hear it. The QS translator spoke over him.

He began to slowly walk alongside the window, his movements smooth and agile like a cat's. "Or when you've learned all you need to. Then I can be cut up so you can take a look at my insides."

Lana frowned. "No, actually that isn't true." She paused. "Well, the learning part, yes, but we aren't here to dissect you."

Xerus stopped and turned toward her. "Is that what they told you?"

"I was given this job solely to help you."

A strange clicking and growling noise escaped him, catching Lana off guard.

"To help me..."

Before Lana could speak, Xerus stepped closer to the window, closer to where she sat. "That's what the others said too. I tried to understand that meaning; really put effort into trying to decipher exactly why I was in need of it from the likes of your kind. Unless by which you mean to free me?"

Lana licked her lips and swallowed but said nothing.

Xerus bared his teeth. His hand rose to the window and, with one long, clawed finger, he tapped on the glass. "I didn't think so."

"I'm here to learn more about you, but also to help teach you about the human race and our society," Lana said.

Xerus seemed to sneer. Letting his hand fall, he turned away.

Lana nearly leaped from her seat but she remained cool. "You have to understand. We just want your cooperation."

Xerus kept his back to her, his tail flicking like an agitated cat's. "You are a female of your species."

Lana shifted in her seat, realizing it wasn't a question. "Yes."

"I knew you seemed different. Looked different. Smelled different." Xerus turned his head to the side to eye her. "I have yet to see a female of your kind. I thought the males looked weak. I could only assume they were the weaker sex." Xerus' eyes flickered down Lana's body. "Looks like I was wrong. You look even more fragile–breakable really."

Lana went rigid in her seat. She noticed her hands clasped tight around her ISpad, sweat forming on her palms. She placed the ISpad flat on her lap and carefully wiped her hands on her pants. "You would be surprised," she said softly.

"Would I?" Xerus turned back to face her. "Perhaps so. The last two who came here...were like whimpering *shila* with their tails between their legs. Though one developed a spine eventually. The other ran away. Fight or flight is a basic instinct all living things have knowledge of." Xerus moved closer towards her. "I wonder... which you'll choose."

In a flash of movement Lana barely caught, Xerus whipped his tail around and hit the glass. He hit it with such violent force that a sharp crack echoed through the room and the window vibrated.

Lana leaped from her seat, her ISpad falling from her lap to ground with a *thunk*. She inhaled sharply, heart jumping. She turned cold as she saw Xerus bare his teeth at her in a sort of cruel grin.

She stared wide-eyed unable to move, her jaw clenched, fingers clamped at her sides.

"Interesting. I've yet to see 'frozen in fear' as an instinctual reaction."

Lana brushed a hand over her mouth so as to not give away her frown of displeasure. She bent down and retrieved her ISpad off the ground. 'He's just trying to scare you,' she told herself. 'And you are scared.' She carefully wiped at the ISpad's screen. 'But you don't have to show it.'

When she faced back up, she forced herself to smile.

"That was impressive," she said. "You must use that tail as a weapon. And judging by *your* looks, you must be quite the fighter. I don't think any here could stand a chance against you. In fact," Lana clutched the tablet to her, "I'm surprised they were able to get you here at all. It must have been some amazing feat."

Xerus hissed sharply. "Don't think I don't understand human sarcasm, female, I've experienced plenty of it from your *risshet* soldiers."

Lana's smile dropped and her face heated. "I'm sorry, that wasn't...I didn't mean to..."

Xerus began to pace again, his face turned up in a snarl. Lana cursed herself for her words. The last thing she needed was for him to be angry and start to hate her already. 'Great introduction this is turning out to be, Lana,' she thought.

"You have no idea how I got here. You have no idea of anything," he snapped. When Lana peered over at his vitals, she saw his heart rate go up but only slightly. Then quickly it began to lower back down.

Xerus stopped his pacing and gazed back at her. He let out a short grunting hiss and Lana realized he was sort of chuckling.

"So the females have back-bones. What a surprise," he said in a soft, higher-pitched voice. Xerus distanced himself from the window. "For now. We will see how long it takes before you go running. I'd say longer than the others...but not by much."

Lana opened her mouth to respond when a soft beep from a speaker interrupted her, followed by a short click.

"Time's up, Lana," came Cole's voice.

Lana bit the inside of her cheek. She caught Xerus' eyes. "We will talk again soon."

Xerus' pupils narrowed slightly and the slits that were his nostrils flared. Lana tapped on her tablet and the milky screen from before began to spread across the glass. Xerus glared at her and Lana held his stare until the screen blocked him out entirely and all that was left was his shadow.

<h1 style="text-align:center">CHAPTER THREE</h1>

Lana's composure had nearly slipped while inside the room with Xerus but as she came out from the tunnel and back into the central lab, she made to keep her cool. The soldiers stepped away from the door as it closed behind her. Cole seemed to observe her carefully as she walked back toward him.

"How are you feeling?" he asked.

"She looks a little pale," said Torrence.

Lana gave him a sharp glance then turned to Cole, clearing her throat. "I'm fine."

Cole placed a hand on her shoulder. "Quite the specimen, yes? Disturbing. But intriguing."

Lana nodded. "I guess I shouldn't have been so surprised. I'd been warned. I should have prepared better..."

"Very little would have prepared you for that. You did well."

Lana looked back at the door to unit three and frowned. "He tried to scare me," she said softly. She looked back at Cole. "I think I might have angered him. So much for a good first impression."

Cole chuckled. "I wouldn't worry about it. The creature already hates us. But that's why you are here, to hopefully remedy that."

Lana heard Torrence make a noise behind her. When she looked over at him he was smiling.

"I think you've had enough for today. You can be shown the rest of the facility tomorrow. Go and get some rest." Cole patted her, turning back to his desk before she could speak. Lana frowned but decided against arguing. Her hands were still cold and clammy. She nodded to Torrence and went to leave.

"Ah, one thing, Lana," Cole said. He brought out his own ISpad and began sifting through files until he swiped his hand toward her and she heard her ISpad ring. She brought it up and saw the files he had sent her pop up.

"That's the rest of the confidential files about the asset I had forgotten to send. Not much still I'm afraid, but you can go over it before your next meeting." Cole sent another file over. "And that one is your appointment."

"Appointment?"

"You'll have to go to level six before you come back."

Lana opened the file and saw it was a required appointment with Dr. Ramstine and his associates. Signed by Cole.

"This isn't necessary," she said. "I'm fine."

"Sorry, standard procedure."

Lana wanted to argue but Cole's stern gaze quieted her.

She was completely fine! Sure a little shook up, but who wouldn't be after seeing a creature that might have come out of a nightmare dimension. It didn't mean she was scared, or in trouble of gaining PTSD...

"Also," Cole continued without glancing back at her, "in your room you will find your new work cell. I'm afraid your old one won't work here. Your computer should be up to date as well. See you tomorrow, Doctor."

That hollow dismissal didn't go unnoticed by her, but Lana shook it off. She eyed the other doors, her gaze falling last on the door to unit three, before turning away.

* * *

Lana didn't finish working despite Cole's orders to rest and get herself situated in her new home away from home. Instead, she poured over Xerus' files, organizing and studying each carefully. She didn't even bother to unpack, only taking a moment to use the bathroom and eat a small meal before turning on the computer at her small work desk where she remained late into the night.

Several of the files were just notes from the other Doctors, each describing their encounters with the creature; trying to decipher every movement, every sound, word, gesture. One–a Dr. Grimmer–mentioned in his theories that the way Xerus moved and the way he was built showed evidence of what he believed to be the "perfectly evolved predator", unequaled by any other. He even believed that Xerus' species could withstand bites or stab wounds of even the most critical nature. That the species' skin was so tough he wondered even if it was bulletproof. Course, there was no way of knowing any of this for sure unless one tested the theory. His notes mentioned his and Officer Torrence's discussions on the matter.

The other Doctor–Dr. Cronberg–had other ideas. He believed Xerus was far more than just some top predator. That he was highly intelligent. Much more than what they were led to believe. Though Xerus had given them little information or background on himself (and there had only been reports of a few others of his kind being sighted on the hellish planet where he had been captured), Dr. Cronberg firmly believed Xerus' kind were more than just some primal community like those groups seen and studied in the amazon; that they came from a vast civilization, with technology beyond anything they currently held. Sadly, most of his theories and remarks were shot down or slighted, and he made very clear his frustrations on the matter.

Though, even Lana couldn't help wondering too how he came up with the theory. As she searched through the report on the day of his capture, it showed no indication that Xerus came from any such civilization; no equipment had been found, no tech, no ships. And by the information given, Xerus had never mentioned or even hinted about others of his kind. Granted, Lana reminded herself that the last behaviorists didn't exactly stick around long enough to gather a well-spring of data on the subject.

As the digital clock on her computer ticked at 2 AM, Lana sighed and sat back, biting her nails as she stared at the screen. Lost in thought, she searched the folders, thinking she'd found everything and just needed to go to bed when she clicked on one folder and found several undiscovered videos. She perked up, leaning forward in her chair.

The videos were feeds from previous sessions.

Lana could clearly see Xerus in the still and the other doctor sitting behind the large window looking into his cell. She clicked on the first video and it instantly started playing.

"Asset X, analysis 3," came the voice of a man clipped with static. "Hello, Xerus."

The room was bright red. Within, Xerus paced as she had seen him do before. He didn't look at the man, only ahead. He was irritated.

"Tell us about your world, Xerus. Tell us where you are from."

Xerus said nothing, though she caught the flash of teeth in a quick snarl.

"We only wish to help you. We want to understand."

Lana's face heated. The words—a near repeat of her own session—made her realize her folly. How could she think Xerus would have cooperated with her when all he heard was the same thing over and over from another scientist just trying to coax information from him? Then she remembered his own words and wished she had listened.

When Xerus said nothing, the man only looked down at his tablet, made a note, and continued. "If you don't cooperate, we will have no choice but to keep you locked in here. We don't want that. And I'm sure you don't want that either. Just tell us why you were in the forest. Is that your home?"

Xerus growled. With clenched teeth, he looked over at the man and hissed something in his language–something the translator couldn't pick up. He got real close to the window, his tail swaying furiously.

"Is that your home?"

The doctor stilled, his face turning pale. He stared at Xerus in wide-eyed wonder. Confused, Lana paused the video and went back a few seconds.

"Is that your home?"

The doctor's lips hadn't moved. The question came from Xerus, clear English, and in the exact tone of the doctor's voice.

Nothing in the files stated he understood their language yet...at least what they believed. The video was dated several months ago meaning Xerus couldn't have been able to communicate in English; the QS translator could be softly heard within the cell speaking in his own language to show proof of that. He must have insanely good hearing to make out the doctor's voice over the translator.

'He isn't communicating', she thought. 'He's mimicking.'

So Cole's warning hadn't been an exaggeration.

The doctor in the video (who she figured then to be Dr. Cronberg) stared at Xerus, speechless. He opened his mouth to say something then closed it several times.

"W-what did you just..." The doctor finally stammered out. Xerus repeated him.

The doctor, clearly disturbed, ended the session early, and the video ended.

Lana's throat felt dry, and she took a sip of water before starting the next video. This time it was of Dr. Grimmer.

"Asset X, analysis 12," the doctor said in a monotonous, almost bored voice. "Asset appears agitated, did not take food or water for the fifth day."

Xerus sat as far from the window as possible, his body facing the opposite wall. He didn't look back at the man. His tail swayed.

"Asset X..."

Xerus' head only turned slightly.

"We just want your cooperation. Tell us where the others are."

Xerus said nothing.

"Tell us why you attacked the camp on planet 421. What were you doing there?"

Xerus' head turned back to the wall. The doctor sighed.

"If you don't talk, we will be forced to make you."

The alien didn't move. His face was too dark for Lana to make out.

'This is more of an interrogation than a conversion,' Lana thought annoyingly. 'How could they think this would ever work?'

The doctor wrote something down in his tablet, his mouth set in a deep frown. "Asset refuses to cooperate. May need to prepare shock-induced thera–"

The QS translator interrupted in a low, sharp tone, translating Xerus' words. "There's blood on your breath."

The doctor stopped, his frown deepening into confusion. "What was that?"

Xerus didn't turn to look at him when he said, "The scent of blood. I can smell it."

The doctor paused. His hand raised to his mouth where he breathed into his palm and then sniffed. "I smell nothing."

Xerus looked around at him. "I do. You're going to die soon. You're too weak."

The doctor stiffened at this but seemed to keep his composure. "I was just checked in the medical bay and I assure you I'm just fine." He paused and his frown turned to a scowl. "Are you threatening me, Asset X?"

Xerus lifted his lip, exposing his teeth in a strange smile. "Do you really want to know what I was doing in your camp?"

The doctor shifted forward in his seat. "Yes."

"I was on a mission."

The doctor's brows raised. "To do what?"

Xerus turned away. "To kill."

The video went black. Lana leaned back in her seat, feeling a wave of cold hit her spine. A knot started to form in her stomach as she sat staring at the blank screen as if in a trance. She closed out the files and turned off the computer but didn't leave the desk right away. Instead, she remained deep in thought.

Getting through to Xerus wasn't just going to be difficult. It might very well be impossible. If what he said was true, that he intended to kill them, then the chances of converting him into human society were very low.

A waste of time Officer Torrence had said. And her worst thoughts were that he might be right.

Still, Jacob had believed she could somehow do it. That meant he thought there must be a chance. Perhaps Xerus was only tasked to kill them; maybe his intentions were not his own. He'd said he was on a mission—from who no one knew but him. There was the chance he could be convinced otherwise. That he could be swayed to change his mind.

Unfortunately, based on what she just saw in the videos, he had very little cause in his current situation to do that. Even a human being would have perfectly good reason to resent, even hate, the very people keeping them locked up and questioning them, even threatening them. With an alien species, it would be no different, in fact, it would be much worse.

Lana finally rose from her seat and made her way to the bathroom. As she turned on the shower with a press of a button and began to unclothe, she thought about the way the other doctors had treated the alien. As a specimen or as a prisoner, it didn't matter. Xerus had reason to be enraged.

If she wanted to get through to him, she couldn't use the same tactics as the others. She wasn't here to pose as an interrogator. He would push her away like the others if she tried.

As the hot water poured over her skin, Lana began to form her plan.

* * *

"Blood pressure seems fine so far, and no abnormalities have been seen yet in your brain scan, I'd say you're doing fairly well, Ms. Hart," Doctor Ramstine said, flipping through her medical files on his tablet as Lana sat on the Doctor's table. She clasped her hands tightly in her lap, chewing on her lip to keep from shouting at him.

Obviously, she was perfectly fine. But she didn't think that would get her out of these tedious tests and appointments. They had to study her just as much as they studied everything else.

"Now that the physical evaluation is over, I'll let my associate take over from here," said the doctor with little interest. "Just a few more moments, Ms. Hart, and you'll be good to go. Have a nice day, we will see you soon." He placed his tablet under his arm and shut the door behind him. Lana stared at the door, burning as much disdain as she could muster, imagining melting a hole right through the steel.

Every other week she was to visit the medical bay on level six for these physical and emotional evaluations. Exactly twice a month. It was too much. She would have a serious talk with Cole that if he wanted her sane and compliant he'd do well to free her from these appointments altogether, though, in reality, her best bet would be to cut them down to once a month.

It wasn't that she didn't understand the severity of the situation. Being close to a new, otherworldly species held the risk of becoming exposed to unknown, possibly deadly diseases and viruses. But she knew they had already tested for that based on Xerus' files and found nothing they deemed harmful to people. Though testing was always being done to discover anything they missed, she had no reason to fear being contaminated by the alien (unless, of course, she were to be sliced by his tail which was found to be poisonous after all, but that risk only came if he somehow got out, and by then she'd probably be dead before it mattered).

So the tests were really just precautions. The physical side she might be able to deal with once in a while but having to see a therapist as well seemed pointless. If she couldn't deal with the work, then she would just leave as the others had.

The door opened and Lana straightened, her eyes widening as a familiar blond-haired woman stepped into the room.

"Hello, Lana." Nicole smiled her dazzling smile. "How did things go yesterday?"

Lana gave the girl a questioning look but smiled back. "It was fine. Why are you..." Lana almost began to ask Nicole what she was doing in the room when she looked down and saw that Nicole no longer wore the officer's uniform as before, but now a doctor's coat. "You work in the medical bay?" Lana asked instead.

"Yes, I double as one of the therapists as well as a nurse and medical assistant in various departments." Nicole placed her tablet on a table nearby and sat opposite Lana. "So just fine?"

Lana pursed her lips. "It was probably one the most thrilling and terrifying experiences I've had so far," then she said quickly, "did you know before or after you sent me down to twelve that they were going to send me up here to be evaluated every other week?"

Nicole gave her a pitying look. "No. At least not so consistently, and I didn't think I would be assigned to do it. Unfortunately, they keep me in the dark about certain things just as they have you. The joys of military life I suppose."

"I guess I'm not used to it like I thought," Lana said. "My research might have been on a base, but we were separate in a way."

"Nothing is separate here, I'm afraid," said Nicole.

Lana eyed her wearily. 'And I didn't exactly have a boss watching my every move, either.' she thought. 'How I miss it already.'

Lana was thankful for Nicole's friendly, cheerful demeanor. Without it, she might not have cooperated so easily. Nicole asked her questions about how she was feeling and if anything were bothering her but Lana had little to say in such a short time so Nicole released her quickly from any more prodding, making short notes about their session.

"I will talk to my uncle and see about cutting back to once a month. I can see it will do little good to do more than that," Nicole said as she finished writing on her tablet.

"And I promise if I need to talk more for any reason, I'll come to you," Lana said as she rose from her seat.

Nicole opened the door for her. "You'll likely find me here most of the time. As I said before, I help in many departments and most on this level."

Lana stepped out of the room then paused and turned back to Nicole. "How much can I say about my work to you next time we meet?"

"As far as I'm concerned anything we speak of is confidential."

Lana eyed her seriously. "And if I have questions of my own?"

Nicole smiled. "If I can answer them I will."

"May I ask you one now?"

Nicole raised her eyebrows. "Of course."

"The other behaviorists working with...the asset. Do you know where they went?"

A flicker of something passed over Nicole's eyes, something Lana barely caught. "They left the base. We didn't keep track of their whereabouts after," she said.

"Yes, I understand, but do you know if they are both alive?"

Nicole looked at her confused. "Why do you ask?"

"Some of the old sessions I found in my work files seemed to hint that one was ill," Lana said. "Dr. Grimmer."

Nicole frowned. "I see."

"I was just curious if he recovered. Maybe I could even get in contact with them, get some personal insight about their work."

"I'm afraid I can't say," Nicole said stiffly. "Dr.Grimmer and Dr. Cronberg left very quickly. Any medical records we have on file are of course confidential."

Lana nodded. Of course they would be. Though she couldn't help wondering what happened to the doctor; If he really did have a sickness as Xerus had said or if the alien had only been trying to scare him.

Nicole didn't look comfortable giving out any information though Lana couldn't understand why. Surely she would at least be able to tell her if he had passed away. Unless she really knew nothing about it.

"My uncle might be able to get you their contact info, but I'm afraid I know nothing about one being sick. I'm sorry."

Lana forced a soft smile. "It's alright. Maybe I'll ask Cole at some point; when I'm not stressing over my work."

Nicole gave her another bright little smile. "And I suspect that feeling won't end. And we'll have much more to discuss."

CHAPTER FOUR

Before her next session with Xerus, Lana was taken through to the other units, giving her a glimpse at the other alien species Lazris had discovered and continued to study. She was surprised to find that, unlike Xerus' lone unit, there were many more containment rooms beyond each of the thick, metal doors, housing more extraterrestrial creatures than she had first thought. Some were not very threatening but Lana could still understand the need for caution. One pair was huge. At least twice the size of an elephant with sharp green shells on their backs and horns on their heads. The pair of 'Arothidons' she heard them called, were stuck in one large tank filled partially with water and moss. Others had likenesses to creatures back on earth, only larger or with more aggressive features. Asset C, for instance, looked like a huge dog with a sleek, near shiny coat as black as oil and a tail as long as its body that, when whipped around, could slice through thick wood like a knife. It seemed pretty timid but, when she and the others got near, it growled and snapped its tail in their direction, leaving a temporary mark on the nearby wall.

As they moved through the units, the aliens turned increasingly more intimidating. She encountered the pack of raptor-like creatures with blue skin and red eyes who were contained in their individual cells, none facing each other and separated by thick, soundproof steel. "It's to make sure they can't properly communicate with each other," one lab tech had said. Because once communication was established they'd work together to find a way out and hunt every living thing they saw.

The last unit she visited held what everyone on level twelve considered to be the second most dangerous asset (though whether it was an actual close second to Xerus was still yet to be determined). One mishap had proven its placement when it had been put under for testing only to wake up and make a meal of a pair of the unfortunate lab workers trying to move it. It was a nasty-looking specimen for sure. With mangled fur on its back and two long, hooked claws for hands. What unnerved her was that its face was like a spider's with eight pupilless eyes and a pair of pincers on either side of its mouth. It had four arms and two short tails, one white and one red. Lana was convinced it had to be some Lazris experiment gone bad, but the other scientists assured her that it wasn't and had been found in one of the caves on the same world where Asset X had been discovered.

It had even built a web on the ceiling of its unit and was currently curled up in a corner, watching her. Lana shuddered as she looked at Asset T and wondered which disturbed her more, the spider above or the devil next door.

* * *

Lana went through every door in the facility except for the un-numbered one. When she inquired about it, Cole mentioned it was merely a separate lab for testing bacteria and viral diseases and that she needn't worry about stepping foot into that part of the facility. She'd yet to see anyone entering or exiting but could guess they'd have to wear proper gear like hazmat suits and safety masks, either of which she didn't care to put on just to walk around and take a look-see.

She'd seen enough and was ready to get back into unit three. Even if her heart was starting to pound faster at the idea.

"Well, Dr. Hart, I believe your patient is impatient to see you," Cole said as he leaned against the corner of his desk.

Lana found that hard to believe. Cole laughed when her expression gave away her feelings.

"You find that unlikely, but I think he is curious about you." Cole shrugged. "You're not like the others after all. And you gave off a much more effective first impression than you think." Cole pointed up to the ceiling, up at the monitor showing an image of Xerus' room looking down on it from above. Lana saw the alien crouching at the back of the room, crushing himself into the corner as best he could to hide a part of himself from the camera that he somehow knew was watching him from one end. His head, however, was not hidden and it was turned toward the window as if he was watching for something. Or waiting.

"A subtle but still noticeable change from the usual pacing back and forth. Or sitting and staring at the wall." Cole's mouth turned up slightly. "Haven't seen this much interest in the window since we first brought him."

"And what makes you think that has to do with me?" Lana asked.

"Well." Cole moved off the desk to stand beside her, placing his hands in his pockets. "He has rarely moved from that spot since you left."

The door rose slowly. Lana clutched her tablet, her knuckles going white. She ignored Officer Torrence beside her with his handgun drawn, his black stare cutting into her, making her uneasy. He didn't so much as nod at her when she said hello, chewing his gum and glaring at her as he yelled at his subordinate to open door three. As soon as the door was level, Lana walked on down the hallway without looking back.

She heard the door closing behind her as she came to the sliding door at the end which opened instantly as she approached. She entered the room and the smell of coffee hit her just like before. Still, there was no cup or pot. She stood in the middle of the room, breathing in the scent and realized it wasn't entirely like the smell of coffee but only very similar. There was an offness to it that she couldn't place but for some reason reminded her of a fresh cup of that wonderful black liquid.

"Come to try again, Doctor?"

Lana turned her head toward the window and saw a massive shadow before her, just behind the milky screen. She drew closer to it and hesitated only a beat before tapping on her ISpad and lifting the screen.

Xerus looked down at her, this time not looking entirely annoyed or pissed off. Lana had to quickly remind herself not to hold her breath as she quickly inhaled at the sight of him, her heart doing a little flip. She told herself the fear would lessen and she would get used to him. Eventually.

"Hello, Xerus," she responded as calmly as possible. She even braved a little smile. She caught his eyes briefly but found she couldn't hold them. Instead, she looked behind him and around the room, noticing a small dip in one corner with a drain. On the other side, stuck to the wall, was a raised bed. On the bed were the remains of a barely touched slab of meat.

Xerus watched her looking around. Seeing her eyeing the meat, he went over and picked it up. "Care for some?" He took four steps with his long stride, slinking over to the opposite side of the room beside the window. From there Lana noticed a transfer box, crafted to send items between her room and his without the possibility of him being able to grab her. Xerus wrenched the thing open and flung the meat inside then slammed the thing shut with such force she flinched at the loud bang. The stench of meat wafted into her room and Lana had to keep herself from gagging.

"What? Don't like it? Pity." Xerus shrugged and moved away from the box. " I assumed humans thought it a pleasant enough meal if they considered I'd care to eat it also."

Lana wiped a hand over her mouth. "No. We prefer our meat cooked."

If Xerus had eyebrows, she imagined he'd be raising them. "I see. And I, being a mere beast of some sort to you, must rightly like it still bleeding."

"I don't think you are a beast."

Xerus laughed at that. "Yes, you do." He paced slowly alongside the window, his eyes never leaving her. They flickered over her face. "You say you don't, but everything about you tells me otherwise." He stopped and cocked his head. "The racing of your heart. The erratic breathing." His eyes swept over her body. "The tension in your form. Like you are about to bolt at my slightest movement. A small, trembling *Mimnii.*"

Lana didn't care for the sound of that. Though the translator didn't pick up the word she had a feeling it wasn't something she cared to be compared to. Likely equal to something like a mouse or maybe a child.

"I am a beast to you because I am not like you," he continued. " I figured it was because humans were xenophobic but its more than that. I look like something from your homeworld. Something that might have preyed on you or something you feared."

Lana wasn't sure how to respond to that. But from her silence, he could guess enough that it was true. Though lizards weren't known to exactly prey on humans, some were deadly and feared, as were mythical beasts, to which Xerus could have resembled.

"I'm sorry. I will tell the others to give you something else to eat," was all Lana could think to say.

Xerus gave her an odd look, maybe something close to confusion. Then he snorted and turned away, his tail flicking back and forth.

Lana went to her chair and sat down. She placed her tablet on her lap and watched Xerus with caution before saying, "Is it alright if we talk?"

Xerus turned his head. "Is this not talking to you?"

"I meant seriously talk. I'd like to ask you a couple of questions."

Xerus moved back toward her, stopping an inch from the glass. "You're asking me?"

Lana shrugged. "You don't have to answer if you don't want to."

Xerus observed her extensively and Lana let him even if it felt like an eternity. Slowly, he lowered his body till he crouched before her, now nearly eye level.

"And what do I get in return?" he asked, his breath lightly fogging the window.

Lana didn't know why but she couldn't fully meet his gaze. The heat of his eyes made her squirm in her chair. In a low voice she asked, "What do you want?"

She caught his strange smile, the flash of silvery black in his grin. "Besides wanting to be free and to rip out the entrails from more than a few of your soldiers? Not much. But..." he tilted his head in a sort of shrug and sat back. "Since I take it that's not an option, then...I'll think about it. For now, I'll allow you to speak."

Lana let slip a little smirk. Such arrogance for someone in a cage. She opened her files and notes on the work pad, trying her best to ignore Xerus' stare.

Thinking carefully over her words, Lana began with "When the military men brought you here you were put on a ship..."

Xerus waited for her to say more.

"...what was your reaction when first seeing it?" Lana asked.

Xerus flicked his tail. "What do you mean?

"I mean what did you think of it? Did it frighten you?"

"Did what frighten me?"

"The ship."

"Why would a ship frighten me?"

Lana began typing on the pad. "So you knew what it was?"

When Xerus didn't respond Lana glanced up to see him glaring at her with narrowed eyes and a tight mouth. "The ship didn't frighten me."

Lana nodded, continuing to type. "Were you curious then? About what you saw? or what you were seeing when put on the ship?"

"Not really."

"So you've seen technology before?"

Xerus clicked his claws on the ground. "Your technology did not surprise or fascinate me or make me curious."

Lana observed his expression which she gauged impossible to read. It wasn't like he wasn't answering her questions but why did they seem...dodgy?

Lana tapped her ISpad. "I want to show you a few images and I'd like you to tell me what you think of them." From her ISpad, Lana brought up a picture and, with the window controls, sent the image to be displayed before both of them on the glass. The picture was of fire.

"I know what fire is," Xerus said.

"Right but does it mean anything to you?"

"What do you mean?"

"As in, do you see it as a tool, or a god; or maybe as some kind of resource, like fuel?" Each question Lana asked she noticed Xerus' mouth growing tighter.

Xerus grunted. "It is useful when it needs to be."

Lana frowned. These questions seemed to be going nowhere. Still, she pulled up the rest of the images to gauge his reaction. A lightbulb, a spear, a mirror, and a military-grade handgun.

"What is the first one?" Xerus asked.

"A lightbulb, a glass container that holds electricity to create light. It's how we light our rooms like you can see above, though they are much more advanced here."

"Why is this one the color of the sun," Xerus pointed at the image, "but the one in this room the color of blood?"

Lana's brows furrowed. "I...I thought...the bulbs in your unit use UV light. It's supposed to give necessary vitamins to keep you–"

She could see Xerus had no idea what she was talking about and Lana realized the use of the red light was another clueless theory among the other scientists about Xerus being some kind of lizard;

even though they still were uncertain about that notion since they weren't able to perform tests.

"Nevermind," Lana said.

Xerus eyed her curiously then looked back at the images. "The bulb is strange, the stick-knife looks useless, what is the third image?"

"A mirror," Lana said. "To see your reflection."

"...Mm doesn't seem useful either."

"It works like this." Lana pulled up the camera on her ISpad so that she saw herself on the screen. She stood up from her chair and got closer to the window, turning the ISpad around so Xerus could see himself. She watched his reaction with great care. When the alien saw himself, he didn't jump or lunge at the glass or even hiss. He instead looked himself over, scratched at his jaw, then grunted.

"Maybe something a *Dirraa* would use." Xerus stood up and turned away and seemed no more interested. Lana turned the ISpad back toward her and turned off the camera.

The image of himself hadn't scared Xerus which to Lana meant he was at least self-aware, but whether his kind actually used something like mirrors was still a mystery.

Lana deleted all the images off the screen except for the last. "And this one?"

Xerus glanced at the gun then looked away. "Useful. If you aren't in close range."

When he said nothing more, Lana deleted the image and silently wrote down her thoughts on the workpad. She didn't get as much information as she liked but it was to be expected.

"So do you think you have me figured out now?"

Lana looked over at him. "Have you...figured out?"

Xerus came back to the glass to look down at her seriously. "You think you have some idea about me."

It wasn't a question but Lana still paused to consider her answer. "I have...theories, yes."

"Tell me." When Lana gave him a look of uncertainty he gave her a nod. "I'm curious."

Lana didn't see the harm in it. After all, if she was wrong he might tell her and she could cancel out any incorrect assumptions.

"Based on what you've told me so far...you have some technology. And you aren't completely primal, living out in the woods."

Xerus tipped his head up. "What makes you think that?"

"You know what fire is but you don't consider a spear a useful weapon. My guess is you might be living in the caves. You either can see in the dark or use flame for light or maybe another source that isn't like our own," Lana said. When Xerus said nothing, she continued. "I also think that you don't use weapons much at all, except for maybe something long-range. But I don't think it's a gun. I think you only discovered their usefulness from when you were captured."

Xerus' tail swished beside him. "Interesting theories. And what makes you think I don't use weapons?"

This time it was Lana's turn to size him up. She looked him over and Xerus tilted his head at her as he watched her observing him.

"You don't need weapons because you were built to be one yourself," Lana said. "Others theorized this already. But from what I can see myself, I also agree. Your scales are thick, maybe thick enough that they are hard to cut or penetrate. Horns and spikes like what you have are usually used for defense by animals...at least from my world...but your tail and claws and teeth are easily those of a predatory species. Your gait shows the power in your limbs giving you the ability to strike fast and hard or to move with great stealth. You have little competition in surviving or perhaps none at all."

Xerus dipped his head low, his eyes narrowing. "Careful, Doctor. Too much of this flattery and I might...what's that strange thing humans do? Blush?"

Lana smiled. "Don't think too highly of yourself just yet. I also know that you have vulnerabilities. One made obvious to me now."

"Oh?"

Lana gestured toward the strange, scaly armor leggings Xerus still wore. "You wear clothes, on your bottom half at least, to cover and protect your...more sensitive parts. The scales along your lower stomach are less thick and are smaller which means you're vulnerable to any strikes in those areas."

Xerus' mouth twitched slightly. "A sound theory," he said smoothly. " Or maybe..." Xerus placed his hands on the glass, "I'm just hiding my best weapon."

Lana looked away from him and cleared her throat. The room seemed a little warmer than before. Whether he was playing with her or not, she couldn't tell. She half hoped that maybe the translator was being faulty.

"As for another vulnerability that I noticed," Lana continued, ignoring his sly eyes. "Is the large pores on the side of your neck and along your chest."

"Pores?"

Lana pointed at his upper body. "The narrow holes just under the scales. I'm not sure yet what they are...Maybe scent glands or gills? but I judge that they could easily become clogged or infected."

"Scent glands...gills." Xerus laughed, tugging at one of his horns. "Ah, you humans can be entertaining when you're not completely infuriating." Xerus eyed her. "Or maybe it's just you and your 'theories'."

Lana frowned and cursed silently. Judging by the way he said it, she had a feeling she was going to have to cross off a lot from her list. Still, he didn't dispute all of it. Though he didn't exactly tell her she was right either. And she didn't expect him to tell her otherwise.

Sighing, Lana put her ISpad on the table next to her. "Alright, fine then. Since I told you mine, let's have yours."

Xerus' eyes lit up. He lowered himself so that they were once again eye level. "About humans in general or about you?"

Lana knew this could be a perfect opportunity for him to mess with her. But she had to play fair. And, regardless, she was curious to know what he thought.

"Both," she said.

Xerus' tail swayed back and forth. His eyes, like twin flames, assessed her with a cold, unblinking stare.

"'The human race, from what I've gathered, think highly of themselves. They think they have everything figured out...as if they know how the universe works and have the astounding arrogance to believe it revolves around them." Xerus' face inched closer to the glass. "But they are naive and confused. They have no idea of anything. Blind to the massive truths that float in the darkness beyond the scope of their bright little sphere. They think they are wise and strong but they are in fact the very opposite. They use their machines to gain knowledge, but only accept the kind of knowledge that benefits them while the rest they turn a blind eye and pretend it doesn't exist. They use weapons to gain power and control over whatever they see fit as if the universe is theirs by right, ready for the taking. This idea, this *need* for conquest, doesn't surprise me; it is not a rare concept, certainly not among my kind. But the way humans strive for it is messy and ill-planned." Xerus scratched the side of his neck with indifference. "Like they are newborns playing war games by themselves, having yet to be challenged by a real opponent. This is why they are so afraid. They have yet to discover the very thing that could obliterate them off the map. They have yet to encounter something larger than themselves, something that could dismantle their whole world."

"And you think that something is you?"

Lana barely noticed his mouth twitch. "Yes...but your kind weren't even on our radar. At least not until you made yourself a target for..."

"For?" Lana leaned closer.

Xerus' head tilted to the side, and he eyed one corner of the room. Then he turned back to her. "You fear death," he said. "But you will welcome it when you learn that there are things far worse. Death is your bright sphere now, and the darkness moves ever closer."

Lana sat back, confused. "I don't understand." What had they made themselves a target for? And was he threatening them? Or was it a warning?

"In time you will. When it's too late."

"Xerus," Lana tried to plead, wanting straight answers, but Xerus provided her none.

"As for you," Xerus said, his voice growing deeper, his eyes darkening. "I admit you are an enigma compared to the other so-called 'doctors' forced on me, but I haven't decided if it's because it's my first encounter with a human female or if it's just...you. You try to act like them but you are different from them. You want to earn my trust but you want to follow the rules they've placed on you. You trust too easily."

"Ah, I was unaware we were theorizing personality traits," Lana mumbled.

"Physically," Xerus continued, standing up and beginning his usual pace along the window, "It's obvious you are weaker than the males, but you act like you are not, which is good. It shows you aren't timid or meek. You keep up a brave persona despite your fear."

"Because you can smell it, right? My fear?" Lana asked.

Xerus stopped to look over at her as if it were obvious. "Yes. And by the pounding of your heart," he said.

Lana nodded. "Anything else?"

Xerus seemed to think about it. He edged over to the side near his bed, looking down at it curiously, then his eyes flicked over to her. "You are alone."

There was a hint of uncertainty in that theory and Lana herself didn't know what he meant by it.

"Sound theories," Lana said, forcing her expression blank. She wouldn't admit how true some of them were. "Maybe more will come to light the next time we meet."

Xerus grunted, turning back toward her. "Yes, we shall see."

CHAPTER FIVE

After her first couple of days, Lana started to fall into a simple but effective routine. At night she worked on new methods to reach Xerus, organizing her notes, and writing journals about the sessions she had. She knew Cole recorded everything but she wanted to have her own personal take on the situation, in her own words.

She didn't see Xerus every day for several reasons. Some days Cole wished her to work with other biologists on studying the different assets in the facility. But deep down Lana knew it was to give her time away from the devilish alien. Cole didn't want her exposed to him too often in fear she would lose her mind and leave as the others had. She couldn't blame him for that and, in a way, she knew it was for the best. Because, when she did see Xerus, she was never sure what sort of day they were going to have.

Some days went better than others. On the good days, Xerus would cater to her whims, if barely. Allowing her to ask him simple, non-invasive questions by showing him basic objects as images displayed on the window. His answers were always vague but sometimes she was able to gauge what he did and didn't know. The more she showed him the more she suspected he had at least some modern tech of his own though different than a human's. She still couldn't decipher what his home was like; if it was even on planet 421. But she stuck to her theories that it was some place dark and some place warm.

Eventually, Xerus ran out of patience with her "amusing little picture game" and refused to do any more.

"I tire of these meaningless questions," he had hissed. "If I have to look at one more of your damnable images and play a guessing game one more time, I might claw my eyes out."

This was their fifth session together. As much as she had expected him to cut her short, she was at least surprised and grateful that she had gotten any answers out of him at all even if they revealed almost nothing.

With that method out the window, Lana had to weigh out other options to get through to him.

She planned out these few options on his worst days; when Lana dared not go to him at all. His moods were always ever-changing and, though most session days he was in a decent enough mood (His usual cranky demeanor calming briefly when they talked), some days he would go into the blackest temper imaginable, one that she couldn't even quell. She would watch him on the monitors on these particular days, sit and watch in terrified, tight-lipped silence as the intelligent being she had been talking to for several days turned into a savage beast before her very eyes.

Like a monster on a rampage, he roared and snarled, his tail whipping around, slamming into the walls. He clawed and ripped and bit at anything and everything, leaving marks she hadn't noticed before over every surface.

It was when he began to attack the window and received an electric shock from hitting it so hard that she sprung from her chair and implored Cole to let her see him.

"I'm sorry, Lana, but it isn't safe for you to go near him right now." Cold had said, shaking his head.

"But maybe I can calm him if just a little."

"I don't think he's even there right now. It's best to just let the storm pass on its own."

"But he might hurt himself," Lana had nearly shouted.

"He will recover," Cole had said calmly.

Fuming, Lana had no choice but to return to her lab desk and watch helplessly. By the door to Xerus' unit, Officer Torrence and his band of guards kept close with guns drawn, laughing and joking as they watched Xerus rage.

"Fuckin animal, ya think it needs a muzzle to shut that thing up," one of the guards had said, wheezing. "Look at it go." He started to mimic Xerus, making shrieking noises and crouching low as if ready to pounce.

The others had laughed, all except for Officer Torrence whose lip only curled up slightly, and Lana was a breath away from snapping at them to be quiet.

Eventually, the storm did pass and Lana was safe enough to go back into unit three. When she did, she did so with extra caution.

"Will you play a game with me?" She asked Xerus after sitting quietly for a long moment just to observe him and gauge his emotions. She was beginning to learn some of his body language which helped her better understand his moods, more so than watching his face.

Xerus paced slowly alongside the window, his tail barely moving, his body upright. He was calm. For now. His eyes traveled over to her. "You are fond of games aren't you?"

Lana shrugged and Xerus looked away and exhaled a long breath. "Well seeing as I'm filled with nothing but free time. I'll indulge you. But it better not involve any more images."

Lana smirked. "Promise it won't be anything like that." She opened an app on her tablet and used the controls to have the game be displayed on the window between them. Xerus gazed at the checkerboard with the little figurines on either side with a blank stare.

"It's called Chess," Lana said. She explained the mechanics of the game to him and showed him how to move the pieces on the board. Using the controls for the window, Lana was able to allow the alien to move his pawns on his side of the glass.

"Seems simple enough," he said.

They played a couple of games as a sort of tutorial and Lana was pleased with how quickly he picked it up, asking very few questions. He seemed entertained enough by the game, at least for now.

"Let's play again but I would like to raise the stakes," Lana said. "If I win I get to ask you a question—any question I like. I promise it won't pertain to the whereabouts of your people or anything too revealing about yourself."

Xerus tilted his head down and flared his nostrils. He thought about it, then locked his eyes with hers. "And if I win?"

Lana smiled. "You can ask me anything you like as long as it doesn't endanger myself or those around me or," Lana said, "you can request something from me."

Xerus seemed to perk up at that. "Request something?"

Lana nodded.

"Like what?"

"Like...a favor."

Xerus snorted. "And how exactly are you supposed to perform favors for me from beyond my holdings?"

"Well..." Lana said. "Firstly, I hope that someday you will be free."

Xerus' expression looked a little stunned, as if to say 'You honestly want that? Are you so sure?'

"And secondly," Lana continued. "I can perform favors even with you here. I know we already talked about changing your...diet. But maybe there's something else you want? At least something I can give you to make your time here better. Or it can be something I can do for you when you're free."

Xerus gave her a doubtful look. "There's nothing you could give me that I want except to be free. And, anyway, how could I trust you to keep your word?"

Lana thought it over. "Well, humans usually shake on it as a promise. But since we can't shake hands...perhaps something your people do to tie a deal?"

Xerus scratched his jaw, thinking. "Come to the glass." He gestured.

Lana hesitated, then rose from her chair. She walked cautiously up to the glass, standing before him. Xerus lifted one hand and placed it on the glass and motioned for her to do the same. Lana did as told, placing her hand in position with his.

"Repeat after me," Xerus said. "By *Rikasha* and *Veradis* I take this vow and if I should break it may they who I chose to serve take from me what is owed. By blood or by life as is the *exari* of this vow. By their strength let it be so."

Lana paused, looking at him wearily. Then slowly repeated the words. The vow sounded much more serious then what she was offering, but she made do. Hoping she didn't just agree to some lifetime vow of servitude, she released her hand from the glass and cleared her throat, turning back to her seat.

"Ready to play then?" she asked.

Xerus dipped his head, and she noticed his mouth widen a little.

The first serious game they played, Lana won, but only barely.

"So I get to ask my question," she said, straightening in her seat, trying not to smile. Xerus' tail swayed lazily behind. "Fine," he said.

Lana looked down at her lap thinking for a long moment, then her gaze drew back to him. "What position do you hold amongst your kind?"

Xerus clacked his nails against the ground. "Position?" he said.

"Like...what do you do for your people? Are you a hunter? A gatherer? Or do you specialize in something? A farmer? An Engineer?"

Xerus let out a low breath, closing his eyes then opening them again slowly. "My position is...complicated."

Lana arched a brow. "How so?"

"Because it is ever-changing."

"Oh..." Lana frowned. "Well, what is it currently?"

"A Destroyer."

Lana's frowned deepened and pursed her lips. "I take it then that your job goes with the namesake?"

Xerus tilted his head in a sort of shrug. "It is given to warrior castes when they are at war."

Lana's eyes widened. "So you are a warrior?"

"For now..."

Lana tapped her fingers against her workpad. "And what will you be after this...war?"

Xerus' mouth widened. "That is more than one question."

Damn, but she was so close. Finally she was gaining some traction. But she had to play fair.

"Let's play again." Lana refreshed the board.

This time the game took longer and Xerus won.

"The first thing I want is the lights changed. It's giving me head pain."

Surprised, Lana brought up the controls for the light but hesitated before changing them. "I'll have to verify it's alright with the others first."

Lana called Cole from the lab. He discussed it over with others then agreed to let her change the lights but only from red to a mild orange. The orange light made Xerus shake his head and blink several times revealing a second set of white transparent lids that covered his eyes briefly, opening and closing from his outer eye to his inner. Lana jotted down a few notes on her pad while he adjusted.

"Better?" she asked.

"A little," he said.

They played two more games. The first Lana won (and again only barely) and the second went to Xerus.

"What will be your position after the war?" Lana asked again.

Xerus locked eyes with hers. "If we win and I go through my Rite. I will become a *Predomis*."

"What is a..." Lana cut herself off when Xerus' eyes narrowed at her. Right, too many questions.

"My next request is I wish to not be recorded," Xerus said abruptly.

Lana stiffened. "How do you know we are–"

Xerus growled loudly, making Lana jump. "If I give you any more answers while we play your games they will be between you and me."

Lana sat back in her chair, her heart doing a quick little flip as Xerus' anger rose to the surface.

"Alright," Lana said softly. "I will...see what I can do."

CHAPTER SIX

It took a great deal of time and convincing to get Cole to allow her to stop the recordings at any given interval. Lana implored Cole to see that if they were going to get any information from Asset X, they needed to gain his trust. Eventually, they agreed that for five minutes only Lana was allowed to shut off the recorder. Any information she gathered was to be put into a report. The video feed, however, would not stop. Under any circumstances.

Lana was slowly beginning to find out that getting through to Cole with anything was a challenge in itself. Despite his polite and calm demeanor, he really could be a hardass at the worst times. Any sort of negotiating was hardly that, making her feel more like a little girl trying to beg her stubborn father for a toy.

"You're learning quickly on how things roll here," Dahlia, one of the biologists, told her. "If you wanna get anything outta the big man you'll need at least half the staff on your side. And even then good luck."

If there was anyone he seemed to listen to more, it was the engineers and Officer Torrence for some unfathomable reason.

Obtaining certain information was also equally frustrating. If it didn't pertain to her work, Cole seemed to think she didn't need to know. He would put his hands in his pockets and give her that irritating smile and tell her with the most indifferent air possible that she just needed to focus on her work and not worry about the rest. And when it did pertain to her work, it wasn't serious. When she finally confronted him about contacting the previous behaviorists, he merely shrugged, saying there was no point in finding and talking with them and that all the information she had was what they kept.

His aloofness and disregard for her interests were infuriating and, quite frankly, offensive.

The more time she spent in the facility and fought him the more she was beginning to realize that her level of importance wasn't as high as she thought. And the way Cole ran the place and his methods for dealing with the specimens within, made her deeply suspicious that his goals may not be aligned with her own. The aliens were subjects and experiments to him and he regarded them as such just like Torrence regarded them as merely animals and nothing more. If she didn't know any better, she would have believed that their mission to have Xerus or any of the other aliens converted into their society was just some kind of front. Level twelve wanted to learn about these beings but they didn't seem particularly interested in actually understanding them. With this depressing prospect, Lana began to feel very much alone, wondering why they had her there in the first place.

She voiced her concerns with Nicole. Meeting her this time at one of the fancy bars in the city sector per Lana's request.

"I'm beginning to feel like a joke," Lana said, taking a sip of her vodka tonic.

"You can't say that. It's only been two weeks," Nicole said. "You can't know that they don't care about what you're trying to do. We do have you here for a very important reason, Lana. It's just that everyone's caught up in their own work is all."

Lana peered down at her glass, swirling the contents. "It's just...I thought their whole goal was to convert these beings. But I feel like just some odd side project. Even when I'm helping the others, I don't get what they are trying to find."

"There are many things they are trying to discover. These projects take time," Nicole said.

"Or maybe they are so sure I'm going to fail. That I'll give up just like the others had, so they don't want to bet all their chips on me," Lana said.

"You've been doing great work, Lana." Nicole's eyes were sympathetic.

Lana laughed. "I'm not so sure. Getting anything out of your uncle is one thing. It's frustrating, sure. But it doesn't compare to..."

Nicole looked at her squarely. "Asset X is giving you a hard time."

Lana pursed her lips and nodded. "No surprise, I know, but..." Lana shook her head. "It's like when I feel like I'm so close to getting through, Xerus surprises me and then I feel like I've gotten nowhere."

"But you have made it so far, Lana. Cole mentioned you've gotten the alien to open up more in that last few days then most of the other behaviorists did in their whole time working with him."

Lana shrugged. "I might not make him as angry as the others did. And for some reason, he finds me amusing. But it's like he's toying with me. And he won't take my questions seriously, always giving some cryptic response." Lana crossed her arms and watched the people around the bar. "And now I think I made a big mistake in making any sort of deal with him..."

"What deal?" Nicole asked, looking a little concerned.

Lana gave her an apologetic glance. "I..." Lana sighed. "I was trying a new method to get him to tell me...well anything really. We play these games and if I win he has to answer my questions honestly, and if he wins..."

Nicole's eyebrows rose. "Yes?"

"Well he can either ask me any question–which he, of course, hasn't–or he can ask me for a favor."

When Nicole gave her an even more concerned look, Lana put up her hands in defense. "Nothing that would put anyone in danger or compromise the facility, I promise. Anyway...I won a few times, but once he got a knack for the game, well..."

Nicole frowned. "How many favors do you owe him, Lana?"

Lana looked down as if embarrassed. "More than I'd care to admit. And I won't go into detail about what they are."

She could see Nicole wanted to know but was polite enough not to push her on it and Lana was thankful. After the first day of their games, for every one match Lana was able to win, Xerus won at least three. The favors had started innocent enough at first. He learned quickly that being stubborn just for the sake of it wasn't any reason he couldn't use her offer to his advantage. Sure she wouldn't free him obviously. But why reject the chance to have someone under your thumb?

And he certainly took the chance every time he got. There was even a point when Lana truly believed he was only making up favors just for fun, or maybe just to rile her up.

Some involved bringing him food—he didn't want any of the others to do it. It had to be either her or a Scibot. Since the Scibot wasn't made to do the sort of task, she had to coax one of the engineers to reprogram it. Xerus only wanted cooked meat and only the finest parts (thighs were especially good for some reason).

Other strange favors were to have her brighten the lights on her side of the room, to have her sit closer to the window, to have her clean the window (that one she was sure was just for a laugh) and to give him a lock of her hair because he was 'curious at how it felt'.

Cole allowed these small favors at least, seeing them as naturally harmless. Even the use of the Scibot he authorized, seeing it more a benefit now that he didn't have to force anyone but Lana to go inside Asset X's unit.

When Xerus started asking serious favors, like turning off the lights for a brief time, that's when they were forced to draw the line.

And once he knew he couldn't get much farther with any more requests while he was in his cell, he began to think up favors to give her when he was out. At some point she had to catch him something called a *drednat* (whatever the hell that was), had to prepare some special dish for him called *Vala*, and even had to assist bathing him once he was free, polishing his horns and filing his nails; grooming him like some kind of servant.

Lana took another sip of her drink then set it aside, rubbing her forehead. "Honestly, I would have stopped the games way sooner," she said to Nicole. "But every time I got at least one victory and was rewarded with some kind of answer, I couldn't stop myself from trying for another."

Nicole gave her a sad smile. "Did you find out anything at least?"

Lana looked around making sure no one was in hearing distance. "Not much but some things, yes. I know now he was a highly ranked soldier of a special class and he was the leader of his team, fighting a war that had been spanning many years. When I tried to ask who his enemy was, however, he only replied with 'They are all around.' He was tasked with one mission and that was to destroy."

Nicole straightened in her chair, looking tense. "You think...it's to destroy us?"

Lana shrugged, uncertain. "I don't know honestly. But whoever his enemy is, they were on planet 421."

Nicole nodded, her brows furrowing. "I know you'll figure it out, Lana. In time. Maybe just lay off the games for a while?"

"Maybe..."

"And I know this wasn't meant to be a therapy session or anything but how have you been feeling otherwise? Sleeping okay?"

Lana's eyes fell to her lap and she clasped her hands together. "I...ah...I've been having these dreams."

Nicole leaned forward. "Oh?"

Lana closed her eyes. "Okay, more like nightmares."

When Lana opened her lids, she saw Nicole staring back at her. "Tell me," she said.

Lana sighed. "I'm in the room where I do my sessions with Xerus. It's like any normal day. We are talking...or I am talking and Xerus is just...watching me. Then suddenly he is speaking but I don't understand him and his tone changes and it sounds like..." Lana's eyes met Nicole's. "It sounds like my father's voice. And when it changes, I can understand him and suddenly I am crying. No, I am weeping. Then the glass just disappears. I scream and run for the doors but they won't open and I can feel Xerus right behind me. When I feel his breath on my neck, that's when I wake up."

Nicole reached out and placed her hand on Lana's. "When did they start?"

"About four days into my sessions."

"I can prescribe a sleeping agent that might help dispel the dreams."

Lana shook her head and smiled. "Those always give me a raging headache when I wake up. It's okay, I'll manage. It hasn't affected my work."

'At least not yet,' Lana thought.

Nicole's lips tugged up in a little smile as she released her hand and sat back. "Just keep at it, Lana. You've got this."

* * *

Lana decided to take Nicole's advice and pause any more games with Xerus for the time being. At their next session, she entered the room carrying a bag over one shoulder and a box in her hands. She set the box down on the table and dropped the bag next to her chair. Xerus was by the window just as she turned off the screen.

"No games today I take it?" he said, eyeing the box and bag.

"Not today. I'm...holding off on playing anymore for a while," Lana said.

Xerus' mouth twitched. "Pity. I was really enjoying all the favors."

Lana gave him a tight smile. "I'm sure." She went to the box and opened it. "Since you've been too shy to talk about yourself. I thought today would be about me." Lana took several items from the box and set it aside then she took her laptop out from the bag and set it on the chair. Xerus gazed at the items curiously.

"What are those?" He pointed to the items on the table.

"Those are gifts I am giving to you," Lana said. She went to pick one up but hesitated when she caught Xerus` confused stare. "You do know what a gift is right?"

Xerus' eyes flashed over to her. "Yes, I know. I just don't know why you are giving them to me."

"Because I want to. Does there need to be any other reason?"

Xerus looked at her suspiciously. "Gifts are not usually given without just cause."

"Well, where I come from it can be." Lana hid her smile while she picked the first item. She turned back to the window and held it up for Xerus to see. "This is a mango. It's my favorite fruit."

Xerus looked down at her to gauge how serious she really was. Then he glanced back at the fruit. "It's...edible?"

"It sure is, see?" She took one bite from it and showed off the dark orange innards. "It's sweet and tangy. Care to try?"

When Xerus didn't say anything but didn't look completely disgusted either, Lana took out a non-bitten mango and went over to the transfer box by the wall. She opened it and dropped the fruit inside then closed it back up. She stepped away and observed Xerus carefully while taking another bite of her mango.

Xerus didn't move right away. He watched her eat hers for a moment then decidedly made his way over to the box. He took up the fruit with his claws and Lana imagined if he cared to, he could easily crush it with his hand, seed and all. Instead, he held it with surprising gentleness and lifted it to his mouth where he sniffed at it.

After a long pause, he opened his jaws and, with one whole bite, devoured the fruit completely. Lana froze with mango raised to her mouth, her eyes wide with shock as she just watched the alien eat the fruit without even savoring it, noticing his sharp teeth only clamp down once, like some kind of shark eating its meal whole. His long tongue came out and licked around his jaws and mouth where some of the juice had slipped through his teeth.

Lana lowered her mango. "Ah...um...you weren't really supposed to eat the seed."

"What seed?" Xerus asked.

Lana's mouth thinned. "Nevermind. So what did you think?"

"Mmm...texture is strange." He thought about it some more. "But the taste was...nice."

"Nice? really?" Lana couldn't help smiling a little, feeling relieved. She figured he was going to hate it. "Do you have sweet fruit where you come from?"

"If by fruit you mean the edible growths from the ground then, yes, there are some but they are uncommon. And they are not...sweet as you call it. They taste more like the earth from which they come from and they are darker in color."

Interesting. She would have to make a note of that later.

Lana set her mango aside. "I will bring you another fruit when I get a chance." Lana took up the next item. "This is another sweet food, but it's also one of my favorites." Lana turned and showed him the bar of chocolate in her hands. "It's called chocolate."

Xerus leaned closer to the glass. "It looks awful."

"Maybe it doesn't look appetizing, but it's a big hit among humans." Lana went over to the box and broke off a piece of the bar then tossed it inside. Xerus took the piece between two claws and sniffed.

"They use it in a lot of different items too, to make different kinds of treats." Lana bit off a piece, letting the chocolate melt on her tongue. Xerus watched her with acute interest. He opened his mouth and, this time, let it slide in. He clamped down and Lana saw his mouth work and his throat move as he swallowed.

"And what did you think of that?"

Xerus' tongue flicked out and he blinked. "A little too sweet for my taste but the texture was better. Not sure about the aftertaste."

"It's a little bitter I admit but that's because it's dark chocolate."

Xerus' head tilted. "Dark?"

"It's... just got more flavor than the regular kind."

"Hm..."

Lana went back to the table again and this time picked up items that were not edible.

"This is soap and a scrubber. I'm not sure how you clean but considering you've mentioned bathing..."

Xerus bared his teeth in an odd grin and she had a feeling it was because he remembered she was going to have to 'serve' him in the endeavor, eventually. "Yes," he said.

"...I assume your skin doesn't just magically clean itself or that you use your tongue to do it. And since you have yet to be provided with anything, I thought...well, here." Lana placed the bar of soap and cloth in the box along with a canister of water.

When Lana turned back to the glass she was caught off guard by seeing Xerus pressed close to it, looking at her. His tail swaying calmly from side to side.

Lana cleared her throat. She went over to her laptop and signed in. "Anyway. Something else I want to show you." Lana pulled up a playlist and synced it to the speakers within the room. She pressed start and music began to play.

Lana turned to the glass and saw the Xerus still hadn't moved. That he had been watching her. Though once the music began, his head tilted back and his eyes flickered upward.

The piano music was soft and delicate, filling the room with its sweet sound. Lana put her hands behind her back and swayed a little. She observed Xerus as he turned from the glass and stood in the middle of the room, listening.

"It's Clair de Lune."

When Xerus looked back at her, confused, Lana pointed up. "The music. This piece. That's what it's called."

"Is this what most humans listen to?" he asked.

Lana shook her head. "No, not all. Everyone has different tastes."

"And this is yours?"

Lana closed her eyes, continuing to sway. " I like it, yes. But I like other kinds too." When she opened her eyes, Xerus was watching her again. His expression was dark, but his eyes were bright. When she looked back at him squarely, they stared at each other for a few seconds before Lana had to look away.

She cleared her throat. "Sorry, maybe it's not your thing."

"It's not."

Lana nodded her head and went to turn the music off.

"But it is beautiful."

Lana paused and turned back to him and saw his eyes still on her. She smiled weakly and laughed. "You recognize beauty?" she asked, half-joking.

Xerus' mouth widened. "Yes. I can tell when something is beautiful."

Lana's smile turned to a grin. Xerus lifted his head and some emotion passed over his eyes but Lana didn't catch what it was. She did catch herself staring at him and quickly turned away.

"Let's try something different. How about this?" Lana selected another song. This one was nearly the opposite of the previous with a fast beat and heavy synths.

Xerus seemed indifferent to it. Though he recognized it as dancier music. Lana tried several other pieces of different musical genres that she liked and most of his reactions remained the same.

"Curious..." Lana glanced at the alien then went to the search bar and looked for a genre she didn't like as much but was interested to see if he would. "How about this?" Lana pressed play and heavy metal blasted through the room.

Xerus tensed up at the noise and bent forward, crouching like a predator. His lips lifted in a snarl and his eyes narrowed into fiery slits. A low growl escaped him and he looked ready to attack.

Panicking, Lana quickly shut the music off. "Xerus?" she called to him nervously.

Xerus didn't seem to hear her at first. He huffed and grunted like an animal for a few seconds, his heart jackhammering in his chest. She was about to call to him again when he let out a long breath and straightened his body.

He shook his head and blinked then looked at her. "What the hell was that?"

"Heavy metal."

"...I wouldn't play that again if I were you."

Lana made a big mental note on that one. "Let's try one more. This one's not so heavy." Lana found a song that was worldly in its essence, focusing on drum beats and bass instruments. When it began to play, Xerus seemed to perk up.

"Mm. This is better."

"Is this the kind of music your people listen to?" she asked.

When Xerus gazed at her, Lana put up her hand. "Ah. Forgot. No, questions."

Xerus sank to the ground, placing himself in a crouching position. "It is similar to certain songs among my kind, yes."

Not wanting to bother moving her laptop, Lana sat down on the ground next to the glass. "This one derives from the desert and tropical regions in my world."

Xerus listened, his eyes fogging over as if recalling something. "This reminds me of *Yersha's* dance."

Lana leaned in slightly, her forehead nearly touching the window. "Who is Y*ersha?*"

Xerus' eyes flickered over to her then looked away. "She was *Veradis'* sons' mate."

Lana recalled that name and remembered it was a name mentioned in that vow she took when she and Xerus began to play Chess with the high stakes.

She was about to ask who *Veradis* was but decided she better not push it. "What's the dance like?" she asked instead.

Xerus gave her a sly look. "It's not for me to perform if that's what you are wondering."

"Oh, come on, I know you aren't self-conscious," Lana said playfully.

Xerus snorted. "No, it's not that. I literally mean it is not meant for me to perform. It is a dance by females for their mates."

Lana straightened. "Oh." Shifting a little, she was itching to ask more but, instead, decided to sit quietly and just listen with Xerus. It was a lovely song and she could imagine the kind of dance performed.

When it ended they sat for a moment in silence. When Lana glanced back at Xerus, she smiled.

"Did your mate perform the dance? Is that how you know it?" the question just slipped out of her without thought and her face heated, bracing herself for Xerus to snap at her. Before she could take it back, however, Xerus grunted low.

"No, I learned of it as a fledgling. I have no mate as of yet." Xerus stood up and Lana followed. "...but once I become a *Predomis*, that will change."

Lana was about to blurt out yet another personal question when Xerus suddenly hunched over and groaned, clutching his stomach.

"Xerus? Xerus, what's wrong?" Lana moved to the glass with concern.

Xerus growled and began to dry heave. Then without warning, he vomited brown and orange liquid. The juice splashing against the ground.

Shocked, Lana's hands clamped to her mouth. He vomited several more times and all Lana could do was watch in horror. When his stomach finally quieted, Xerus groaned and looked at her.

"I don't think I like chocolate."

CHAPTER SEVEN

Lana smoothed out the top of her uniform and brushed off her pants before stepping over to the door with the Lazris star and pressing the button on the intercom. She took a step back as a screen on the intercom lit up and a Scibot's faceless head came into view.

"Please state your name and business," it said in a monotonous voice.

"Lana Hart. Here to see Jacob Hartin," Lana said, clasping her hands together.

"One moment..." The screen went black and a few seconds later a buzzing sound indicated the door was unlocked. The door slid open and the Scibot greeted her on the other side.

"Please follow me." The bot turned away and began to lope over to another door. Lana stepped into the small foyer and followed quickly behind. A muffled echo of music and laughter seeped past the inner door and when the bot placed in a code and the door opened, the noise blasted out into the hall. The Scibot stood to the side and Lana moved past it into the room beyond.

People gathered around a lush living area, drinks in hand, sitting on long white couches, or standing near a small bar in the corner. A few heads turned to her as she entered, curious eyes watching her as they took in the color of her badge, indicating she was from level twelve.

Lana couldn't help checking other's badges as well. Every color was different, representing each level. There was green for level two, red for level six, and silver for level four, the general's headquarters and apartments. These were the main ones she saw but there were a few blues for level five, the security and tech center, and one orange for the mechanics bay. From what she could tell, she was the only one wearing a purple badge.

"Lana!"

Jacob's booming voice made her jump slightly. Her eyes shot over to the far end of the room, by a pool table, where a few other men congregated. Jacob's smiling face broke from them to greet her.

"Jacob." Lana grinned and met him in the middle to accept his embrace. Jacob hugged her tightly, practically lifting her off the ground. He swung her around and released her.

"I'm so glad you could make it. Let me get you a drink."

Before Lana could protest, Jacob went over to the bar and came back with martinis for them both. Lana took it but didn't taste. Jacob drank half of his before saying another word.

"So tell me how everything is going, I've been dying to hear." Jacob directed her over to a free space on the couch and they sat down.

Lana looked around as she situated herself and Jacob must have seen her hesitance because then he said, "Don't worry about anyone hearing anything. In truth, most have some idea of what's going on down in twelve, just not anything in detail."

"Well the devil is in the details," Lana said, laughing softly. When Jacob looked at her a little confused, she shook her head. "Nevermind. Everything has been...good actually. Better now."

Jacob raised his brows. "Oh, yea? Well, that's great, Lana, really.

You know I would have gotten a hold of you sooner to see how you were settling in but with tours and work..."

"It's totally fine, I get it. I've been really busy too."

Jacob nodded his head and took another swig of his drink, placing the glass on a table next to him. "It's been almost a month now and you haven't run. So that's a really good sign."

Lana smiled. "It was a rocky start for sure. But guess that was to be expected."

Jacob's face moved closer to hers. "And the asset. He hasn't scared you too bad? Given you any trouble?"

Lana looked down at her drink, fingering the edge of the glass. "He did...and sometimes still does scare me when he's in his bad moods. As for trouble," Lana took one sip of her drink. She put her glass next to Jacob's and let slip a little laugh, shaking her head as she thought about Xerus' silly favors and his way of playing with her when he was in a good mood. "Yea...he gives me plenty of trouble."

Jacob's dark eyes assessed her curiously. "You two are getting along?"

Lana shrugged. "He tolerates me much more than he did the others now that's for sure." Lana frowned. "Let's just hope he doesn't become bored with me too quickly."

Jacob nodded. He didn't speak for a long moment as if considering his thoughts. "You should know," he said finally. "I've read the reports and spoken with Dr. Cole Kingsley. He says you've been making clear progress but that your methods are unusual."

Lana's eyes caught his. "Unusual?"

"He's concerned that you are exposing yourself too much to the asset."

"That's absurd," Lana said. She felt the heat of anger simmer in her belly. "He doesn't understand. If I am to get close to Xerus, I have to...to show he can trust me."

"Yeah, I totally get that, Lana. But you have to remember what you are dealing with."

Lana's eyes widened. "This is my job. You brought me here in hopes of gaining Asset X's cooperation and bring his kind into our society. If I am to do that..."

Jacob put up his hands. "Hey, I know. But I'm just saying I wouldn't get too friendly. I mean I hear you have to perform favors for him now? And you've been giving him things?"

Lana opened her mouth then closed it. "I just want him to experience what the human race has to offer."

"Cole said you tried to give him books the other day and they had to stop you."

Lana's face heated. She was still recovering from that fight. Who would've thought books would have been too dangerous to give the alien. She certainly didn't. But Cole seemed to think otherwise. Their argument started off professional enough until Torrence got involved.

"What the hell does it need books for. It can't read them," the security guard had said at his usual seat by the desk, chewing on his gum. "He'd sooner eat them and make a mess in the cell and we sure as shit ain't gonna clean it up."

"I was hoping that I could start having him learn how to read and write English," Lana had countered.

Torrence had laughed. "You think that thing wants to learn anything from us."

Lana put up her hands in defeat. "Then why am I even here?"

"Beats the hell out of me."

"That's enough," Cole had said. He looked to Lana then, his stare grave. "I'm sorry, Dr. Hart, but for security purposes, we can't allow those in his cell. If you want to teach him something that is what the ISpad is for."

"He hates when I use the images," Lana had murmured.

"Well, he will just have to get used to it."

Lana had been speechless then. How could something so innocent as a book be considered a risk? She had sat in her room for some time trying to figure it out and the only conclusion she could come up with is that they didn't want Xerus to know certain things.

They didn't trust him, that was obvious. But they wanted information from him. They needed someone who could find a way to open him up, not necessarily teach him anything.

And Xerus was no fool. He knew this from the start. Hell, even she had to admit some of the ways she tried to gain his trust had also been to find out his secrets. The games had been one clear way. But she suspected it wasn't just any random piece of information they wanted. They were seeking something specific. Something they hoped she would be able to make him reveal.

This thought had put her in a dark mood but she was determined not to let it keep her from her own personal goal.

"You're right, some of those things were careless," Lana said, not meeting Jacob's eyes. "Maybe I am getting too close."

Jacob put his hand on her knee. "We, of course, want his cooperation and that is what you are here for. But trust takes time and we need to know more about him and his kind first. You did well revealing his identity. And this war he spoke of definitely sounds like something to be looked into further."

Lana nodded, her throat tightening.

"Look, I'm gonna tell you now before they mention it down at twelve. In a month's time, other top generals and myself will be coming together to assess the projects and work of each level. If you can gain Asset X's trust enough in that time and show he is capable of being trusted by us, we will be able to talk over the next phase. Which could be to give him more freedom."

"You'd let him out of the cell?" Lana barely breathed.

Jacob shrugged. "Maybe give him some time out of it. Or maybe even move him out of twelve altogether, into something more accommodating. It all depends on how convinced the others and myself are. And that will be up to you to decide."

Lana's dark mood finally began to lift.

"But that still means you need to be careful. He's still considered hostile. But if he starts cooperating, we can try to reward him for good behavior, you understand what I'm saying?"

"Yes, of course, you got it." Lana took up her drink and offered it to him. "Thank you, Jacob."

Jacob gave her a quick little smirk, took the glass, and drank it down.

CHAPTER EIGHT

The room was red again. Lana stood rigid in the center, her chair and table gone. She couldn't remember changing the lights.

The glass window loomed before her, it seemed oddly larger than usual. Oddly unnerving. With the pool of blood rippling over it like water. Then, like a shark drifting closer to the surface, a giant shadow of a monster appeared.

Lana lifted the screen and came face to face with...

"Xerus," Lana spoke the name but it sounded muffled, like an echo.

The alien looked down at her with a cold, unfeeling stare. His face dark, his eyes like fire being sucked into a black hole. There was darkness there. So much darkness.

"Seefri rishak iridis."

Lana shook her head, not understanding him. Xerus growled low, baring his sharp teeth at her. His spiked tail curled and weaved behind him. He tilted his head.

"Drifa xeris refadi nimadin."

Lana shook her head again.

"Why are you here?"

The voice and tone made Lana's heart turn cold. It was her father's. Why, why did he speak like him?

"Why are you here?" Xerus repeated.

Lana let out a soft whimper. She wrapped her arms around herself and shivered. She began to cry.

"I don't know...I don't." Lana couldn't think why.

Another growl ripped through the room and Lana winced.

"Run."

Lana's eyes shot up and terror welled in her as she watched the glass melt away. Xerus bent his head low and stepped out of the cell. Unable to even scream, Lana turned and fled for the door.

It wouldn't open. She banged her fists and cried but it was sealed. She felt Xerus' breath on her neck and her terror turned wild.

She turned and his hellfire eyes met hers.

"Xe lathari Nikara," He hissed. He raised his sharp hand toward her and Lana trembled so bad she bit her lip, tasting blood. Xerus' taloned finger grazed her cheek. It felt like a blade brushing against her skin.

His hand slipped lower and gripped her jaw, tilting her head up to him. His face edged closer to hers and Lana caught the smell of dark coffee.

"Erradis xi nilla," Xera whispered as his thumb grazed her bottom lip. In her terror, Lana felt a spark light deep within her, warming her. He released her jaw and brought his hand away and Lana saw her blood smeared on his thumb. He brought it to his mouth and licked the blood away.

"So sweet. Just like I imagined." Xerus' hand slipped back down, this time to encircle her throat. *"You will be perfect...my prey."*

He bared his black fangs at her in a grim smile and his face shot down towards her.

Lana screamed.

Everything was dark and all she could hear was the huff of someone gasping for air. It took her several seconds to realize that someone was her. She blinked several times and found she was sitting up in her bed, her blankets and sheets drenched. Shivering, Lana wiped at her face, brushing away damp hair. She sat for a long moment trying to catch her breath and when she was finally able to calm down, she leaped from her bed and went straight for the bathroom.

Going to the sink, Lana washed her face, letting the icy water wake her. As she became more alert, she realized she could still feel pangs of terror washing through her. It was like her intuition had kicked into overdrive and was setting off an alarm.

Something was wrong.

She tapped at the mirror and an LED display appeared. A digital clock on the surface read 4 am.

Washing up quickly, Lana threw on her uniform and took up her keycard. Not bothering to even bring her workpad, she slid out the door and raced down the hall.

* * *

As soon as the elevator doors opened, Lana was faced with at least twelve security guards all standing by the door as if barricading it. They all had semi-automatics in their hands and were talking quietly, some looking tense.

Lana stepped out into the hall and, without hesitating, made for the door.

"Hey, Lana, hold up," came a voice to her right. Lana looked over and saw Ben, one of the engineers, standing off to the side. She had been so focused on getting to the door, she somehow missed him. He nodded his head to her and Lana paused, thinking whether to ignore him and keep going or stop.

He gestured to her and Lana frowned, approaching him. When she got closer, she noticed the e-cigarette he hid in one hand.

"What's happening?" she asked quickly.

Ben shook his head. "A big fuck up. You'd better brace yourself."

Lana's heart felt like it might jump out of her chest. "Did he...did one of the assets get out?"

When Ben shook his head, Lana had to stifle a deep sigh. He laughed. "You think any of us would be out here in the open if they did? I sure as hell wouldn't be. Nah. No escape, thank christ. But you'd better be careful." Ben took a hit from his cigarette. Lana noticed his hand shaking. "I got here at three and saw... shit, you'll see. Everything was recorded. I told them I'd be back but..." He shook his head again.

Lana thanked him for the warning and turned away. She headed to the security window and asked David to let her in. He gave her one of his icy stares.

"The level is in lockdown, Doctor," he said. "You will have to get permission from the head."

She cursed silently. "Please tell Dr. Kingsley then."

David made the call and Lana was forced to wait nearly fifteen minutes before she was allowed to enter.

When the doors finally opened, the guards stepped aside to let her pass. Inside the facility was under low yellow lights which meant they were in a code yellow lockdown. As she approached the central lab, Lana instinctively glanced up at the monitors, seeking unit three's. She saw Xerus inside, lying in the center of his cell, motionless. Not even his tail flicked from side to side. For a clear instant, panic shot through her chest as she thought he might be dead. But, to her relief, she saw next to the feed his vital signs moving, albeit dangerously low.

When Lana's eyes shot back down, she froze and her stomach dropped. On one of the equipment tables, a Scibot was laid out. Its neck was crushed, its head almost separate from its body, one arm was ripped to shreds, wires spilling out, the hand gone. The computer on its chest was cracked. It was completely dismantled, its body a jumbled pile of metal. Next to it was a piece of bone, cracked on one side.

Lana stared at the table for a long moment before she heard

someone call her name. She blinked as if coming out of a trance and turned her head toward the sound.

Cole, along with Dahlia and another biologist, Dr. Yanlin, huddled around a set of computers. Cole waved her over and Lana approached like a sleepwalker.

"What did he do?" Lana asked.

Cole straightened, placing his hands in his lab coat pockets. He swept his eyes around the room before he locked on to her. "Asset X attacked the Scibot that was distributing his meal."

Lana shook her head in disbelief. "How...how is that possible?"

"The bot went to put in his food and found the transfer box jammed. It put its hand in to fix it and Xerus...he got to it. The engineers were able to shut the bot down remotely but Xerus had the bot crushed against the box for three minutes, who knows what information he got." Cole shook his head.

Lana raised her brows. "Are you honestly telling me he was somehow able to hack it?"

"See for yourself," said Dahlia beside them. Lana went over to the monitor as Dahlia brought up the footage.

Xerus was pacing as usual. It was rare they ever caught him sleeping and it usually looked more like meditation than sleep. The Scibot entered the room carrying a boxed tray. It set the tray down on the table and took up a plate of cooked meat and sliced mango, carrying it over to the transfer box. Xerus watched it intently, creeping beside the glass. When the bot opened the box, it slid out halfway but no more. The bot pulled at it several times in a repetitive movement but the box was stuck and would neither open more or close. Pausing to think over the issue, the bot placed the tray down then went back to the box and, without hesitation, slipped its hand inside. Xerus moved closer to the box as the Scibot rifled through it, reminding Lana of a cat stalking its prey. She watched in horrified fascination as Xerus slipped his tail through the slim opening made by the jam and whipped his tail out to encircle it around the bot's throat. Quick as a snake, Xerus wrenched his tail back and the bot slammed into the wall, being crushed instantly against the box. It struggled pitifully, not programmed to react quickly to such an attack.

Xerus moved swiftly then. Lifting the bot up, he twisted his arm through the opening and, though the bot blocked their view to see it, Lana could tell he was playing with the computer on the bot's chest, his head bent low into the box so he could see. For three whole minutes she watched the bot shaking and seizing, like a fly entrapped by a spider. Sparks flew and the bot went limp. Just as Xerus wrenched his hand out and released the bot, six armored soldiers with guns entered the room. There was some yelling and one soldier dragged the bot away. They tried to order Xerus back against the wall and he hissed at them, mocking them. Torrence was there giving commands. He took out a device that looked similar to Lana's ISpad. He went through several controls and the window began to brighten. Electric currents rippled and danced along the glass and the lights flickered. Xerus stood in the center of his cell and moved back a step as the current struck him. He roared but didn't move away. He hardly moved at all.

A soldier was ordered to fix the box. He moved toward it, his eyes never leaving the alien. He fumbled through it and took out the bot's dismembered hand. Working fast, he rifled through it some more until a piece of bone was discovered. Xerus lunged at the box and Torrence immediately amped up the electrical defense to its max, causing Xerus to stumble and freeze. Xerus bared his fangs and the soldier by the box jumped and nearly fell back at the alien's closeness. Xerus' tail whipped around, slamming against the glass. The electricity hit him continuously but, as painful as it must have been, he didn't yield.

The lights went out completely and the only light was the electric currents in Xerus' cell. Like lightning, they flashed and struck everywhere until they eventually stopped and the lights came back on to reveal an unconscious alien on the cell floor.

Soldiers moved around, one carrying the bot, the others assessing the damage. Only Torrence stared down at the alien, not so much to make sure he was okay Lana was sure, but that he was out for real. When he deemed it safe, he ordered the others to leave. The video ended there.

Lana watched it all in stunned silence. When the video stopped, her eyes scanned back over to the table with the Scibot and the shard of bone.

"Where did he get it? The bone?" Lana asked softly.

"Where do you think?" Dr. Yanlin replied, crossing his arms, his face red. "It was in his food. A cooked ribeye. Someone didn't think to check it." His eyes purposefully looked to her, but she ignored his criticizing gaze.

"Do we know what data he might have gotten from the bot?" Lana asked.

"We aren't totally sure as of yet," said Cole, "but engineers will be scanning the bot here shortly trying to work it out."

Lana's gaze flicked up to the monitor above, watching Xerus intently. "I want to talk to him," she said and looked back down at Cole. "Let me talk to him."

Cole leaned against the table. "I don't know if that's a good idea, Dr. Hart."

Lana went over to the computer connected to the intercom and opened the controls to each room.

"Lana..."

She selected unit three's and tried to access the speakers but an alert popped up saying she wasn't authorized. She hit her fist against the desk in frustration.

"You can't do that, Ms. Hart." A voice yelled out to her, echoing around the lab. Lana looked up and saw Torrence emerge from the entrance to the facility. Accompanied by two other guards, he approached the central lab, looking squarely at her, his gun drawn. "Why don't you back away from the computer now. You don't have permission to access the controls."

Stunned, Lana straightened, turning her body toward him. "I have every right to speak to my patia—"

"Not in this situation you don't." Torrence kept moving toward her till he was standing inches away from her. Lana backed up a step. Her eyes shot over to Dr. Yanlin and Dahlia who said nothing, then to Cole who merely watched.

Lana's eyes turned back to Torrence, her jaw clenching. "I have to assess that he is okay."

"He will be just fine." Torrence brought up his gun and, using the handle, touched the side of her arm, gently pushing her away from the computer. "Why don't you go back to your room, eh? It'll be safer that way."

Lana stepped aside and looked to Cole, but Torrence blocked her view.

"Are you ordering me out, Officer Torrence?" Lana asked through clenched teeth.

"That I am." Torrence nodded to one of his men who came forward. "Donny here will escort you back."

Shaking her head in disbelief, she didn't move until the guard put a hand on her shoulder. She jumped back. "Don't..." She snapped. She put up her hands and began to walk. "Cole, please I just need to see him."

"I think it's best if you take a few days off, Dr. Hart. For your health," Cole said.

The guard touched Lana's back to keep her moving forward. Lana turned and took one last look up at unit three's feed. Xerus still hadn't moved.

"He could be really hurt," Lana pleaded.

"He will be taken care of," was Cole's only reply.

Lana cursed silently. Seething, she turned away, tugging her arm away from the guard.

CHAPTER NINE

Lana wasn't allowed back into the lab for nearly a week. In that time she made at least a half a dozen requests to be let back in, all which were ignored. Feeling defeated, Lana sulked in her room but didn't stop her work. Frustrated by their disregard for Xerus and by their need to not let her get too close, Lana accessed the QS data as well as all information that they had on Asset X so far and began studying diligently. She watched every video, again and again, watching Xerus movements, his body language, learning how he expressed himself in ways that didn't always show clearly on his face.

When there was finally hope that she would be able to return, she was told she must first go through several psychoanalysis and evaluations before she was deemed proper to continue her work on level twelve. Lana accepted and was even happy to walk up to level six to complete them, knowing it was her chance to vent to the one person who might hear her out.

"It's a total disregard for my work," Lana said to Nicole as they sat in Nicole's study. "I had every right to be there just as anyone. The situation involved my patient so I should have been able to tend to him. Officer Torrence had no right to keep me from him. And another thing..."

Nicole sat quietly and just listened. Patient and bright as always.

"I'm truly sorry that happened," she said when Lana had finished. "Did you ever find out what happened to Asset X?"

"Dr. Dahlia Gray was kind enough to give me an update. He did wake up eventually and seems...stable. But whether there was any lasting damage from the shocks, she couldn't say."

Nicole nodded her head, thinking for a moment. "Well, I don't blame your frustrations at all, Lana. I will speak to my uncle and let him know you should be allowed back. But as a warning, I would be careful going against any more orders. Not just saying this as your therapist but as a friend. Be careful. I know my uncle. He puts on a face for professionalism. But..." Nicole looked away and frowned. "He finds ways to get what he wants."

Lana stepped out of the elevator and walked straight for the door, nodding her head at David who let her through. The usual guards huddling by the door gave her cold glares as she passed. As she entered, she looked up and saw on the monitor that Xerus was awake. He sat facing the wall, his eyes closed as if meditating.

"Welcome back, Lana. Feeling better?"

Lana skimmed her eyes down and smiled at Cole with a fake grin. "I am."

"Good. That's good to hear."

Lana clutched her ISpad in both hands. "And if it's not too much trouble I'd like to get started right away if you–"

"So this is the lady who works with the thing, huh?"

Lana turned toward one of the unit doors and saw a group of guards standing near the edge of the lab. They were unfamiliar to her save for Torrence. The one who spoke smiled at her; a large, beefy man with a mustache and shadow of a beard. The smile was somehow off putting. He waved her to come over.

"Come here, sweetheart, let's take a look at you."

Lana looked at Cole. "Who are they?" she asked.

"After the incident, it was Officer Torrence's request to bring in a new security team. I was inclined to agree with the decision."

Lana looked back over and the smiling guard shrugged as Torrence whispered something to him. Then the man laughed. The group moved into the lab and as they approached, Lana caught the red stars with a golden eagle above them on their uniforms. She'd seen those badges before.

"This is S division SEAL team 6," Cole said. "Officer James Galger is their leader."

Lana stiffened. Jesus, how did Torrence acquire the most advanced tactical team within the system's registry. *The* military's top soldiers.

Officer Galger's eyes drifted down her body. "You guys let a cutie like this near that lovecraftian horror?" He shook his head. "Awful I tell ya." He put out his hand and gave her another ear to ear grin.

Lana took his hand hesitantly. "I'm Dr. Lana Hart, I work exclusively with Xer–with Asset X."

"Lucky bastard." Galger gripped her hand firmly when she tried to pull away. "Well, you take care, Lana." His steel-gray eyes seemed odd somehow like they saw beyond her or through her. They didn't shine. With his buzzed head and his tattooed neck (twin knives in the shape of a cross), he looked almost criminal.

Lana tugged her hand away. "Nice to meet you," she murmured, turning away. The others in the group watched her carefully but she paid them no attention. "Officer Torrence if you don't mind, I'd like to get into the unit now."

Torrence glanced at Galger, who shrugged. Slowly the team of soldiers drifted off to take positions near the unit's door as Torrence went to the controls.

Lana didn't hesitate. As soon as the door slid open enough, she slipped through and made her way down the hall. When she made it to the sliding door, she was forced to wait until the main door closed shut. Once it did, she hurried into the room.

As the screen was lifted Lana saw Xerus had his back to the window, head bowed. Placing her ISpad on the chair and stepping over to the glass, he lifted his head.

"So...you didn't run."

A chill went down Lana's spine as if she were remembering something. "No. I didn't," she said softly.

Xerus twisted around and his hellfire gaze caught hers. "When you didn't come back after...I could only assume."

"I wasn't allowed back. They forced me to leave."

Xerus grunted and looked away. "I theorized that as well."

"Are you hurt?"

Xerus' tail flicked beside him. He looked back at her and for a moment all he did was stare. "Nothing *they* do could hurt me."

Lana frowned. She placed her hand gently on the glass. "Xerus, why did you do it?"

Xerus turned away. "You know why," he said in a low rumble.

Lana shook her head. Then she thought about it and looked down at the ground. "You want to be free."

"No."

Lana looked up at him in shock. He stood up slowly and turned around to face her.

"Yes, I want to be free, but that wasn't the reason."

"I don't under..." Lana's brows furrowed. Then she gazed at him and somehow knew. "Your mission. You're still trying to find a way to..." Lana's throat tightened and she thought she might be on the verge of tears. "Damn you" She hit her fist against the glass. "Damn you!"

Xerus straightened, his nostrils flaring, pupil's narrowing. Lana took it as a sign of surprise.

Lana whipped around and picked up her ISpad from the seat. She brought up the record controls and hit the button to speak to

Cole. "I need five minutes, " she said quickly. Before he could answer she shut off the recorder. Turning back to Xerus, she couldn't stop shaking.

"You have no idea what you did cost you. They will *never* let you go, do you understand, Xerus? Does...does anything I've done mean anything to you? I'm the only one who wants you free, *the only one!*"

Xerus remained quietly still and Lana laughed.

"They brought in a SEAL team. That's the best soldiers we have. They intend to stay for as long as you remain here, I guarantee it." Lana shook her head. "Everything was working out, we had a chance..."

"We?"

Lana closed her eyes. "You...You had a chance. But now I don't..." Lana opened her eyes. She remembered what Jacob had told her. "You may only have one last chance. I know your mission is important, whatever it is and I know you won't say. But be honest with me, just tell me one thing just this once, that you don't intend to harm anyone here."

Xerus came closer to the window, to stand near her. He placed his arm on the glass and leaned against it. His head lowered so that she was made to lock eyes with his.

"I must destroy my enemy. That is a fact. And that enemy is all–"

"All around, yes, I know," Lana said, exasperated.

Xerus gazed at her, his eyes darkening. "In time you will know and you will understand."

Lana made a noise and put her hands up in defeat. She turned from the window and went back to her ISpad. "Forget it." She went to turn back on the recorder.

"Some of your theories were correct..."

Lana paused and glanced back at him.

"...And some of them weren't." Xerus said.

Lana carefully set her ISpad back on the table. She crept back to the window, listening.

"We do like dark, warm places. The hotter the better. We have a high tolerance for heat. We use shooters only if we can't get close. Otherwise, we use *scyths,* weapons made from the spikes and tails of our dead. Given freely..."

Lana knew she should be writing this down but she was too transfixed to move.

"We use our claws and tails as well. The so-called pores along my neck are to absorb oxygen when there is very little, allowing us to move through airless environments or within the water." Xerus straightened and took a step back. "And we do not come from planet 421."

Speechless, Lana opened her mouth but before she could make a sound, her ISpad beeped and Cole's voice filled the room.

"That's five minutes, Lana."

Lana didn't move right away. She looked to Xerus for a long moment and he stared back at her. Eventually, she tore her gaze away and sat down in the chair. She picked up her ISpad and turned the recorder back on. She sat for a moment in silence and Xerus waited.

He just gave her several weeks-worth of information. And with all the answers came a hundred different questions. But what really brought her around was that he was trusting her.

Lana clutched her tablet tightly and dared to let her eyes wander over him, taking in the alien before her. She never thought much to really *look* at him, her gaze only ever falling on his form for brief moments unless they locked eyes. Maybe because she had always been afraid of his menacing physique. But now she really looked at him, saw him.

"I'm turning on the lights," Lana finally said.

Xerus' nostrils flared and he tilted his head slightly. Before she would think to stop herself, Lana brought up the controls for the lights and changed them from the dull orange they had been to the bright white.

Xerus winced and his outer and inner lids blinked several times. He shook his head and kept his eyes narrowed. When the light washed over him completely, Lana had to stifle a gasp.

My god, he was...beautiful. No, enthralling. That was the first thought that popped into her head. The dark red and orange light had shown the demonic shades of him, but the brilliant white light showed his true colors. He was still a deep red, but with shades of purple and violet shimmering along his scales. He was still terrifying, there was no doubt about that, and in the light, she could really see the sharp edges of him. But the way the light caught his scales, how the colors melded, and the way his eyes glowed, was like looking at a creature made from a fiery nebula.

Lana was speechless once again. She nearly dropped her tablet on the ground.

"Still just as horrifying no doubt." Xerus' mouth twitched. He raised a hand over his eyes to block out some of the light.

Lana laughed softly. "Yes, a little." She shook her head, letting her eyes drink him in. "But...no. Xerus, you are bea–"

The ISpad beeped. "Lana, the lights are supposed to be off as per protocol. Please turn them back." Cole's demeaning voice snapped.

Heat rose in her neck and face and Lana pursed her lips. She didn't want to turn them back, she wanted to spend the whole time just watching Xerus, watch his lithe body move, watch the light catching in his skin.

The heat rose higher and Lana forced herself to look away from him. She cleared her throat and reluctantly turned the lights back to their dull orange.

Xerus observed her and Lana found she couldn't meet his eyes yet again. She smiled at him and brushed a lock of brown hair from her face.

"I want to thank you for...what you've given me today," Lana said.

Xerus seemed to understand. He bowed his head. "So you no longer want to strike my hide?"

Lana arched a brow. "What?"

"A saying from my kind." His mouth widened, showing the tips of his fangs. "You aren't upset?"

Lana let out a short laugh. "No. You are forgiven."

CHAPTER TEN

It was the first time Lana lied in her report and she was happy to feel no sense of guilt. She valued Xerus' trust now more than she did giving away his secrets to those who would see him imprisoned forever or dead.

She was still weary about his need to fulfill his mission and the chances of him hurting others. But Lana was adamant that they were not his enemy. Something or someone was, but not the human race as a whole. At least that's what she forced herself to believe. She'd come to accept that his chances of integrating into human society were slim, but she still believed he could be persuaded to leave peacefully upon release. It was all she could hope for now and, though it wasn't her original goal, she wanted to help Xerus be free either way.

After the incident with the Scibot, Lana knew she was going to have to do some serious damage control. She called Jacob on video chat as soon as she was able and begged him to allow her to still have a chance to show Xerus could be trusted.

"I'll give him this one shot, Lana. But it's going to take some serious convincing," Jacob had said. "Because you are my friend and I trust your judgment. But this is his last chance."

Lana felt confident enough that in a month's time she could get Xerus to cooperate. As she walked back into the facility, she walked in with a new, hardened determination. Not even Cole's critical gaze or Officer Galger's wolfish smile and off-putting stare could phase her.

"I'm ready to enter the unit," Lana said to Officer Torrence without even looking at him.

When Torrence said nothing, Lana side-eyed him and shivered. His mouth was tilted up in a smug sort of smile.

"What is it?" she asked, not too friendly.

"Got the announcement from General Hartin. He told us about your little ploy to convince him and the other generals of letting that thing out."

Lana tensed. "Yes. That's correct. That is after all why I've been here this whole time, Officer Torrence, not that I expect you to still comprehend that."

Officer Torrence's smile widened but his eyes read murder. "It just seems a little hopeless to even attempt. Not that I don't expect you won't try anyway. But there's something you might want to see first." Torrence shifted in his seat. Turning toward his computer, he pulled up what looked to be video feed of the edge of a dark forest. Lana moved closer as he pressed play and saw that it was footage from a soldier's helmet-cam.

The sound was low enough so only they could hear. There was a rustling as the soldier moved through the grass. Around him was a military set-up, a base camp with movable units, and standardized armored vehicles. When the soldier turned his head, she could see lab testing equipment in the distance along with a few warehouse bots lumbering about, carrying metal crates. The soldier seemed to be a lookout, guarding the camp for the night. There was a giant, orange moon in the sky with a small yellow one beside it. It was too dark to make out the trees but, in the grass, Lana noticed little blue and green mushrooms glowing softly. The soldier was talking with one of his teammates, sitting by a post, when a low rumble was heard in the distance.

"What was that?" the soldier said, twisting his head around.

The rumble came again and the soldier clicked on the flashlight atop his gun and directed it toward the forest. He skimmed the area then swerved his light to the left in response to the snapping of branches.

"What the hell?" he whispered.

There was silence for a moment. Then a huge shadow flashed between the trees. The soldier jumped up and yelled and his teammate drew up his gun and began shooting. They shot toward the forest, into the darkness. The soldier turned on his communicator.

"We have a situation in the forest, something is moving within, requesting backup, over."

A second later someone responded, "We don't see anything on our scans, private, are you sure it isn't just—"

The forest turned white and the sky lit up. There was a brilliant blast after and a cloud of flames erupted down by the camp.

Another blast then another and the soldiers hurtle themselves to the ground.

There was a lot of screaming and roaring and gunshots. The feed was a dizzying image of foliage, the night sky, and fire.

The soldier weaved through the camp as contents flew around him, his gun going off in different directions. When he made it to the center of the camp, his light caught the end of a spiked tail as it slipped past an armored vehicle.

"Camp to base," the soldier yelled into his communicator. "We are under attack, need back up immediately!"

Another explosion and the soldier twisted around to see a menacing-looking silhouette against the flames. The silhouette turned and ripped open one of the gas tanks with its tail. Then it leaped into the air and landed on one of the testing units. It tore the roof open and dropped inside.

Breathless, the soldier sprinted away, avoiding the fires and the rush of bullets. He ran for the air pads where the ships were stationed. One ship was already starting to take off but as it began to ascend, a flash of blue hit its right wing and it burst into flames. The ship swerved and began to fall.

The soldier stumbled back and retreated to hunker down behind a metal crate. For a moment there was only darkness, then the soldier looked around and, from the side of the air pad, a creature stalked passed.

Lana's stomach dropped and her heart leaped as she watched Xerus on the feed. His eyes glowed red in the darkness, reflecting the fire's light. He looked lethal. Feral. He stopped beside one of the lab containment pods and sliced it open, letting whatever contents inside spill out.

A scraping of metal sounded nearby and out from one of the units, a man in a lab coat stumbled into the clearing, toward Xerus. The way he walked seemed to indicate he was injured. His limbs shook and black blood trickled down his nose and mouth.

He stopped in front of Xerus and started to speak at him, but the soldier was too far away to hear.

Xerus stood towering over the man, his nostrils flaring, his eyes narrowed into slits. His mouth grew wide with fangs bared. He looked enraged. Maddened by hate. A beast with no other purpose. He hissed and growled and bent low and Lana almost had to look away because she knew what was coming.

As quick as a spider, Xerus lunged at the man and bit into his neck. Dark blood gushed and sprayed them both but Xerus didn't let go.

"Oh fuck, oh christ!" whimpered the soldier.

The blood covered the alien's face and neck and chest. Xerus twisted his head like a wild dog until he ripped the man's head off with his teeth.

Lana clamped a hand to her mouth to stifle her cry.

The soldier screamed and stumbled up and ran in the opposite direction. He ran through the camp and into the night.

Torrence stopped the video and stared up at her with his black eyes. "Really extraordinary huh?" Torrence leaned in towards her and grabbed a container by the computer, "Sorry it had to come to this but I think you needed a little dose of reality." He popped open the lid and dropped a piece of gum in his mouth, chewing slowly.

Lana dropped her hand from her mouth. "Where...where did you get this video?" she asked. There was no way he had the authorization to access the files from the night of Xerus' capture. Only top security officials should have that data.

Torrence shrugged. "I have friends in high places."

She shook her head, trying to keep her composure. "I don't..."

Torrence tried to take her hand and Lana flinched back. Torrence put up his hands. "Hey, listen, no need to get all hysterical. I'm just trying to save you the time and effort. This way it's easier. Just leave the demon to us. I can convince Cole that it isn't working out and you can be on your way before–"

"No." Lana took a step back. "I want into unit three."

Torrence looked at her like she was crazy. "You aren't serious. After what you just saw you still want to do this?"

Lana looked at him squarely. "Yes."

Torrence clicked his tongue. "You're an idiot then."

Lana bit her tongue to keep her response to herself, colorful as it was. No, she must remain professional.

"Think what you like," she whispered. "I still want into unit three."

Torrence's lips thinned. "Fine, do what you like. But you should know something. If you fail on this, I've been given permission to take out the asset."

Lana's body went cold. "What?"

"Yea, it was a hard decision for some. They really were hoping to gain something from the beast. We're willing to be patient. But that patience slipped after the incident with the Scibot. I'm afraid it's looking pretty grim. So if you can't convince those generals when they come, Asset X will have to be put down. I've volunteered to do it.

They are even going to let me keep one of its horns as a souvenir."
Torrence sat back in his chair. "I wanted the tail but they said they
wanted to keep the rest of him to study."

Her body went from cold to boiling. "I won't let you near him."
She shook.

Torrence raised his eyebrows. "Don't think you've got a choice,
Ms. Hart. But, hey, just think, if you are somehow successful, he gets
to stick around a little longer, eh?" Torrence turned back to his
computer and put in the code for unit three. The door began to slide
open. He looked back at her and gave her that nasty smile. "Good
luck, Hart. No pressure or anything."

* * *

Lana sat in her chair, staring at the milky orange cloud before her.
Her thoughts wavered in and out of dark places as she contemplated
whether to lift the screen.

'How could he do it?' one part of her subconscious cried.

'He is a killer,' another part said. *You knew this.*

That one stung. But she came back over and over to remind
herself of what she also knew. That Xerus had given her trust, and
through that little kindness, there was hope. She knew he wasn't a
complete savage. Wasn't just some baseless animal whose only
purpose was to hunt and kill. She had said it before and she'd remind
herself once again that, even though he had been put on a mission, he
could still make his own choices. He could choose to stop. There had
to be other ways to win his war.

Lana lifted the screen and found Xerus sitting before her as if he
had been waiting.

"You take your sweet time changing the glass. Don't tell me you're
turning shy," he teased.

Lana couldn't help smiling. "Just needed a minute."

Xerus looked at her curiously, his tail swaying lazily beside him.
"Something bothers you."

Her eyes fell to her lap. "Yes."

"Is it something I did again?"

Lana laughed. "Isn't it always?"

Xerus tilted his head in a shrug.

Lana's smile disappeared. "No, It's just..." Lana couldn't bring herself to tell him about what they planned to do to him if she failed. Not yet. She would rather see to it that it wasn't something to even worry about. Because she was going to get through to him.

And even if she did tell him the truth, she knew what his response would probably be. He didn't fear death.

Lana raised her eyes to meet him. "I wanted to tell you. When I was barred from seeing you after the...incident. I started to study your language on my own. I'm not very far and I'm afraid even using the data from the QS translator isn't the most effective but...even with my best efforts I really need someone who can teach me..."

Xerus' pupils dilated and he blinked. He rose from his sitting position and walked the length of the window as if thinking. He paced for a moment then he stopped to look back at her. "Yes." He bowed his head. "I will teach you."

CHAPTER ELEVEN

It took some time to find a way to properly program the translator so that when Xerus spoke he wouldn't just repeat his words in English when trying to teach her various meanings and phrases. She went to Ben for assistance who knew the QS translator's coding and system. The best they could think was to utilize Xerus' useful talent at changing the pitch and tone of his voice. When he spoke a specific way (his voice a little higher and more clipped than usual), the translator would stop for a brief time until he changed his voice back. This allowed him to still speak both in his native tongue and in hers.

When she informed Cole of her plans, she was relieved to find he was supportive for once. After all, if they had someone who could understand his language without the translator it could be helpful in learning more useful information about the subject. Or if at some point they needed a translator when encountering more of Xerus' kind.

When they finally got the updated QS translator running, Xerus was adamant about starting right away. They linked the translator's data to Lana's tablet so when they used the window like a dry erase board, whenever Xerus wrote a word out on the glass in the slashes and dashes of his language, the English equivalent would pop up next to it along with an image if it were an object.

Xerus was a demanding yet patient teacher. Every session was dedicated to her learning and nothing else. He was always prepared with some new subject when she arrived and when she left, she was given a night's worth of homework. Lana didn't mind. When she didn't understand a phrase fully and it took her longer to get the *esses* and *arrs* right, Xerus was happy to repeat a lesson until she understood fully.

Thankfully, his language wasn't too complicated. He sighted this reason being that it was ancient and rarely changed from its original form. This was because *Rikasha* and *Veradis* willed it so. To remain as pure as possible from their first making of the words.

"Are they your gods?" Lana dared ask after taking a break from their lesson. She had theorized for some time that they were.

Xerus shook his head. "No. But they were the first of us. And thus are treated as such."

"So they created your language together? Just the two of them? That's really impressive."

"It was said *Rikasha* had more of a hand in it then *Veradis* but, yes, he did aid her. She had more of a say on the final language."

"Why was that?" Lana asked.

"She was a queen," Xerus said.

Lana's eyes widened. "Oh." She paced the window, stretching her legs. Her brows tightened in confusion. "But wouldn't the king be more inclined to have a say? Or does the queen hold more authority?"

Xerus huffed. "*Veradis* was not a king."

" Oh, I'm sorry, I assumed since they were the first that...you know...they were together. And therefore he would be her..."

Xerus' mouth twitched. "They were mated yes. But we do not have kings, only queens."

Lana made a silent oh and nodded her head. "So what was he then? Just her mate?"

When Xerus didn't speak, Lana looked over at him and saw him standing straight with his hands behind his back, like some military official.

Lana pursed her lips. "Sorry, too many, questions." She turned away.

"He was her *Predomis*."

Lana froze and frowned, remembering that word. She looked back at him. "What does that mean?"

"It is the guardian of the queen."

Lana turned her gaze away and cleared her throat. "So do all *Predomis*...do they all mate with a queen."

"Yes."

For some reason Lana felt a jab in her chest; like someone had poked her with a long, sharp nail. She twisted around to face him and smiled. "Wow. So that's what you are to become. That's amazing."

Xerus watched her response carefully. He showed little expression of his own. She had no way to gauge if he was happy or not with the prospect or if it was just a matter of duty.

His eyes never left hers as he said, "It is an honor to be chosen and I will serve my queen well."

Lana went to say more when Xerus held up his hand to stop her.

"No more questions." He tapped on the window. "Only words."

* * *

"I've spoken with General Hartin about Asset X's evaluation," Cole said to Lana as she worked at her desk in the central lab, filing another report for the evening. She nodded her head but didn't look up at him. She could only guess he had agreed to the orders to have Xerus killed if this so-called evaluation failed. So much for the preservation of the species.

Cole shifted beside her. "And you should know that for Xerus to pass he will have to perform a test of our choosing."

Lana took a deep breath and held it. "What sort of test?"

"That will be determined on the day of."

In other words, she wasn't going to be told about it. Lana exhaled. "Fine."

"It will be simple enough," Cole said. "If Asset X is cooperative, it should be a fairly easy test. If not..."

"I know." Lana frowned.

At the corner of her eye, she saw Cole place his hands in his pockets. "I'm sorry it had to come down to this, Lana. But ever since the destruction of the bot...Asset X may be too much of a threat to be helped."

And that was utter bullshit if he knew everything that she knew. But it didn't matter. They would only see him for what they believed he was. A cold-blooded monster.

Lana turned her gaze up to him to speak her mind but instead fell silent, her eyes widening. "You're bleeding," she said.

Blood dripped onto Cole's uniform, spilling from his nose. Cole drew his hand from his pocket and wiped the blood away with his sleeve.

"Damn nose bleeds." He chuckled. Something was up with his eyes too, Lana noticed. They were bloodshot.

Lana turned in her chair. "Maybe you should visit the medical bay."

Cole waved his hand. "It'll be fine. Nothing to worry about. We will talk tomorrow." He moved away and Lana watched him as he left the lab. When he was out of sight, Lana brought up her email on her computer and began a message to Nicole. When she finished the message and sent it, she logged off her computer and went over to a large walk-in refrigerator tucked to one side of the lab. Since the Scibot was gone, it was up to Lana now to prepare Xerus' food. The food was already prepared; it just needed to be heated. Lana took out his specialty cut meats, making sure there were no bones, then cut up a mango into slices and disposed of the seed. She placed the meat in a special oven and waited.

"So you are in love with that thing?"

Taken back, Lana twisted around and saw Officer Galger leaning forward on a table, watching her.

"Excuse me?" Lana said.

Galger shrugged, giving her a wide grin. "You smile when you go through that door," he pointed at unit three with his thumb, "and are smiling when you come out. Like a little girl returning from a candy store. It's cute."

When Lana didn't say anything Galger laughed, pushing himself from the table. "Aye, a joke, eh? That's all." He got closer and Lana stiffened.

"Just weird to see a lady like yourself so excited to be working with something so nasty, ya know?" Lana took a step back as Galger got close enough she could smell his alcohol-laced breath. He leaned against the table with Xerus' food and stared at her, his eyes dropping to her chest and then back to her face. "What's it take, eh? Do I just need to sprout some horns?"

Lana clenched her jaw and fixed her eyes with his. "No, you just have to be intelligent."

Galger's brows raised and his smile widened. "Ouch, and she shows her fangs. It's ok though I like 'em feisty."

The oven beeped and Lana took out the meat, setting it on the tray with the mango, making sure to avoid Galger's gaze.

"I'm just playing with ya, sweetheart, no hard feelings, eh?" Galger moved behind her and Lana gasped and nearly dropped the tray as he gripped her shoulders, pulling her to him so she felt his chest against her back. "Ya just need to relax."

"Please take your hands off me," Lana said, gripping the tray.

Galger let his hands fall from her shoulders to her arms, then he dropped them and shifted away from her. When Lana turned around, she had to squeeze passed him with the tray.

"No need to be so uptight, sweetheart. Men don't find that shit attractive." He laughed. "Just some advice. But it's cool, I still like ya."

Lana didn't stop as she walked across the lab toward unit three. She realized she was the only one left before the night shift arrived.

She glanced at Torrence as she went by and he gave her a cold stare before opening the door.

Once inside Xerus' unit, Lana went over to the transfer box and opened it.

"Not even a hello? I am a little hurt."

Lana paused, then set the food inside and closed the box. She put the tray on the table and went over to the wall controls and lifted the screen from the window. Xerus looked down at her curiously, his arm raised to the glass as he leaned against it.

"Sorry I, um, I'm just tired, is all, and..."

Xerus stiffened. He lowered his arm and his nostrils flared. "You have a mate."

Lana was dumbstruck. "I'm sorry...what?"

Xerus turned from her and moved from the window. "I can smell the male on you. Are you newly mated?" His tail curled behind him and Lana thought she caught the black shine of his fangs. His voice was clipped, almost cold.

Lana almost laughed. "No, no, you are wrong. Dead wrong."

Xerus glanced back at her, confused. "Dead wrong?"

"Yes. Really wrong."

Xerus turned back to her. "Then why do you smell like one of those males? His scent is all over you so he must have touched you."

Lana couldn't believe what she was hearing. She made a noise of frustration and picked up the tray. "Yes, he did touch me." Lana's stomach twisted remembering the feel of Galger's heavy hand on her.

If Xerus had fur Lana suspected his hackles would be up. Then he seemed to calm. "Forgive me, I am not used to human customs. It confuses me. Do you not take mates?"

"We do and that's not something we need to discuss at this moment."

Xerus titled his head down and his eyes darkened. He looked like he was about to say something but thought against it.

"Now, I really am tired." Lana moved to the wall controls. She gave Xerus one quick glance, meeting his intense stare, before putting back the screen.

* * *

Lana gasped as she sprung upward from her bed. She stared wide-eyed into the darkness and blinked several times, knowing now she was awake. She untangled her legs from the sheets and dragged her feet over the side, sitting with her back bent forward and her head down. She took long, deep breaths and wiped away the damp hair clinging to her brow. She looked down confused and touched herself between her thighs to find her pajama shorts soaked. Cursing she flung them off along with her drenched tank and padded over to the bathroom.

These...nightmares were getting out of hand.

She turned on the shower and set it to cool then forced herself inside, wincing as the water rushed along her back. She tried not to think of the dream as she cleaned herself up but her mind was too wired and her control was slipping. Images of Xerus stepping out of the cell, coming toward her, had been a regular routine in her sleep. But the moments after were new. And disturbing.

Lana cursed again and shut her eyes, letting the water pour down her head. Images continued to assault her: Xerus inches from her, his tail sliding up her leg, his devilish hands on her hips, nails digging into her skin, pulling her closer. His tongue slipping out between black fangs and...

Lana shut the water off and stepped out. Shivering, she turned on the heater and a blast of hot air blew around her. When she was dry enough, she shut the heater off and put on a robe, wrapping it tightly around her. She walked back out into her room and went for the computer.

As soon as she logged on she saw a message from Nicole in response to her email. Lana read it carefully, her expression growing more concerned as she skimmed through the message.

. . .

Lana,

Thank you for your concern for Dr. Kingsley. I assure you he is under the best of care and his condition is nothing to be worried about. But I thank you dearly for making me aware of the situation, regardless. If you happen to notice any other odd occurrences down in twelve, please do not hesitate to contact me. Thank you!

Nicole Kingsley

If it wasn't something to be worried about then why did she want to know about any other *odd* occurrences on twelve? Something seemed off about the message but Lana couldn't figure what. She closed out the email but didn't move from her desk. Just sat for a long time, staring at nothing.

When the clock read 6:30 and the lights in her room began to slowly turn on, Lana decided it was time she got ready for the day. As she went about her morning routine, making coffee and warming a bagel then setting out her uniform, she heard the ding on her computer of another message coming through. Lana opened her email and saw it was from Jacob.

Lana,

Just wanted to give you a heads-up about the Gala next week. You'll be sitting at my table. I will send you a link with more details. Bring a plus one if you like.

. . .

Jacob Hartin

Lana logged off her computer and sighed. She'd completely forgotten about the event. The forty-second anniversary of humanity's colonization of space and deep system exploration. The generals were to arrive a few days before. She was so swamped with... everything else she didn't care to remind herself about the gala.

Quickly she dressed and picked up her ISpad and slipped out the door.

Once inside the lab, Lana went over to her work desk and logged on to her work computer. She set to her daily tasks, organizing notes and reports, studying up on some more of Xerus' language, readying herself for their next lesson. The lights flashed and a bell rang as one of the doors was opening but Lana was so used to it by now she barely noticed. A moment later the door shut and someone walked passed. She figured it had to be one of the other biologists. Trying to still keep an air of professionalism and politeness, she glanced up to greet them with a smile when she froze, her smile dropping straight into a frown.

Standing a few feet away was a man she had seen only a few times before. He was a lean, gangly sort of man with sad droopy eyes. If Lana recalled rightly, his name was Jeff and he was one of the few people she had seen going in and out of the unnumbered unit. The one leading to the disease and virus lab.

What made her freeze was that something was very off about him. For one, he was still wearing his hazmat suit. A big safety no-no. Secondly, he was bent forward, dragging his feet as he walked, and his mouth was moving as if he were mumbling to himself but what he was saying she couldn't hear. And thirdly, blood was dripping from his nose.

Lana watched as Jeff lumbered passed. Watched as he went over to one of the computers and attempted to log in to each of the unit's controls and override the security codes.

Lana stood up. "Ah, sir, I don't think you are supposed to be going in there."

The man completely ignored her like he hadn't heard a word she said. He gibbered on and continued pressing buttons.

Dahlia was working close by and saw him as well. She stood up from her desk and looked over at Lana with just as much confusion. Then she turned and quickly made her way toward the security desk.

Lana looked back at Jeff and licked her lips. "Sir?" She stepped away from her desk and moved closer. With Jeff's back toward her, Lana lifted her hand to touch his shoulder. When she made contact, Jeff twisted around so quick Lana had to stumble back.

His face was pale and he blinked several times. He moved his mouth and clicked his tongue but Lana could understand his words. He stepped toward her and Lana backed away.

As he looked just about ready to lunge at her, Torrence, Galger, and five other guards swarmed around them, guns drawn.

"That's far enough," Torrence said. Raising his gun to aim at Jeff's head.

Jeff swayed. He murmured something then turned back to the computer.

"You aren't authorized to access that computer. Back away," Torrence said. Jeff didn't listen. As he began typing madly. Torrence gestured to the others. "Take him."

Two guards lowered their weapons and went for the man. They grabbed his arms and pulled him back. Jeff struggled against them and fell to the ground where the two men pinned him in place. One took out a pair of cuffs and locked Jeff's hands behind his back.

"Take him to the medical bay first. Then to level five," Torrence ordered.

Lana felt a heavy hand on her shoulder and jumped. "You good?" Officer Galger asked, his other hand with the gun still aiming at the man.

Lana nodded, stepping back.

Galger looked her over then dropped his gun. "Let's go," he said to the others. He nodded once to Torrence then led the way as they took Jeff—or rather dragged him—out of the facility.

Dahlia came back to stand beside Lana as they both watched them go.

"Jesus," Dahlia whispered. "The things that happen in this place."

CHAPTER TWELVE

Lana stood in front of her bathroom mirror fixing her hair for the third time and readjusting her dress. She turned one way and then the other, checking out her bare back and frowning. The dress was nice but a little too revealing for her taste. With straps smaller than her pinky barely hanging on to her shoulders and the front exposing the tops of her breasts in a v-neck pattern, Lana thought she might need to wear a shawl just to feel better covered up. Or maybe should have worn her hair down instead. Thankfully the red chiffon went past her ankles so she didn't have to worry about her legs.

It wasn't her dress after all. She hadn't even thought to bring one with her when she first came to Lazris. No, it was Nicole who had been kind enough to let her borrow the lovely piece.

She had only a few simple pieces of jewelry that were her mothers, twin pearl earrings, a gold necklace, and a thin diamond bracelet. They didn't go completely but they would do. She didn't wear makeup too often but decided the occasion probably called for it. She rechecked her lipstick in the mirror when the buzzer at her door went off.

Stepping over to the pad near the door, she looked at the camera feed and when she saw who it was she opened the door.

"Lana, hi! Oh, you look wonderful!" Nicole smiled brightly. She wore a gold dress that hugged her legs and sparkled. Her hair, up just like Lana's, had a sparkly diamond clip in the shape of a star. "I knew that dress would work perfectly for you."

Lana smiled timidly. "It is lovely. But do you think I should bring a shawl?"

Nicole waved her hand and shook her head. "Oh, I wouldn't, it won't be cold there in the least and I think you look so elegant without one."

"Alright, thanks again, Nicole." Lana picked up her small purse from the bedside then followed Nicole into the hall. "You look absolutely stunning as well, by the way, the gold suits you."

"You think? I've never worn gold before. I'll probably blind people." Nicole laughed.

"Only because of how brilliant you look," Lana said.

Nicole thanked her as they made it to the elevators. As they stepped inside and pressed the button for level one, Lana clutched her purse tight and chewed on her lip.

"Nervous?" Nicole asked.

"Very." Lana looked over at her. "If I say anything stupid in front of the generals, promise to kick me."

Nicole laughed. "I don't think you have to worry."

Lana sighed. "I'm afraid of what the others are going to say too. You know they are going to talk about..."

Nicole put a hand on her shoulder. "I know. Don't let it get to you, Lana. Remember, no matter what, they promised you they would give Asset X a chance. Just try to enjoy yourself tonight and not think too much about it. I know you're stressing yourself over it."

Lana closed her eyes and nodded. Of course she was stressing out. They had one more week left. Nicole squeezed her shoulder before releasing her hand as the elevator came to a stop and the doors opened.

The gala was being held in the very foyer of the city sector. The skylight above had been dimmed down to look like a starry night and the fountain–the center point–glowed with blue lights. Lanterns had been set up all along the walkways and the banners displayed a solid silver color with the Lazris star in the middle.

As her eyes searched around, Lana noticed the drones were gone. The buzzing and whirring and red lights would probably lessen the effect of the party.

Nicole took Lana by the hand to not lose her in the throngs of people. Men wore black and white suits and the women wore all variants of colors and styles. It was one of the few times on any given base that military men were allowed to wear something besides their uniform.

As they passed the fountain, up ahead was a roped-off area of tables reserved for the generals, head officers, and those chosen to sit with them. Ahead of that, at the very end of the massive foyer, was a stage.

Already people were beginning to take their seats and Lana saw Jacob standing by their table, talking with a red-headed beauty.

When he turned his head and saw them, he grinned and held up his champagne glass. "Lana!"

Lana and Nicole approached and he hugged them both then looked them over. "You both look gorgeous. Take a seat we are going to begin soon." Jacob put his hand on the redhead's back and whispered something in her ear and she sauntered back to her table.

Not long after, several men and a few women joined them. Jacob introduced each of the generals all of which wore badges on their suits. There were four in total including Jacob. Two were older gentlemen in their mid-fifties. The third looked like he was in his early forties. Jacob looked the youngest out of all of them. The older ones looked a bit stoney-eyed and tight-lipped but the forty year old–General Holk if she heard correctly–had a friendly smile and demeanor, similar to Jacob's.

As they settled, Lana tensed as Officer Galger appeared and took a seat at a table opposite her and Nicole, behind General Vearez. A dark-complected woman joining him. His eyes met hers and he winked before shaking hands with the others.

If she had been a fool, it would have been Lana sitting next to him instead of the woman. But thankfully she turned Galger's offer down a few days ago when she already planned on having Nicole as her plus one.

"Where is Cole?" Lana asked as she saw the seat that was meant to be his at a table nearby empty. Nicole shifted around and Lana saw her mouth turn down.

"He's...probably still in the lab. Or running late knowing him."

Lana noticed Torrence wasn't around either but that one didn't surprise her. He was rarely ever off duty.

As everyone finally settled, several people took the stage at the front. Lana leaned back but barely listened as they droned on about history she already knew and events she had already seen. They gave out a few congratulatory awards and had a few toasts before dinner was finally served.

"So, Dr. Hart, Jacob has told us a lot about your work. Impressive," said General Holk as he bit into his salad. "You've been working with this specimen for almost two months and have made considerably more progress than the previous doctors so far I've heard."

Lana took a sip of water and cleared her throat. "Yes, it's been challenging but I feel I've made good progress."

"So tell us, Ms. Hart," General Williams asked, leaning forward, "Is it friendly toward you?"

Lana straightened. "Yes, I would say so."

"And you trust it?" he asked.

"Yes," Lana said without hesitation.

The generals nodded as they ate and sipped their champagne.

"Well, that's a good sign then," said General Williams as he cut into his steak. "I trust then you believe that the incident with the bot was just a bad misunderstanding?"

She chewed on a sliced golden potato and swallowed before saying, "It was. I assure you such an incident won't happen again."

General Williams raised his brows and nodded again but said no more.

"I heard it looks like a cross between a lizard and an insect, that true?" asked General Vearez.

Lana pursed her lips. "I don't know about insect, but the lizard part...yes."

The older generals frowned as if they were a bit put off, General Holk seemed fascinated.

"I read through some of your reports. Is it really as intelligent as you say?" Holk asked.

"Even more so, General, I believe even more than an average human."

Somehow the generals seemed even more put off by this.

"More intelligent than a human?" General Vearez laughed. "Hard to believe if it got itself caught, eh?" he said more to the others than to her.

Heat rippled in her chest and filled up her neck and face as the others laughed. A memory of her first encounter with Xerus flashed in her head.

"Didn't you say, General Hartin, that the day it was caught it practically led itself into the trap?" General Vearez asked. "What creature could be that intelligent if it just let itself get taken like that?"

Wide-eyed, Lana looked to Jacob, who merely shrugged and smiled. "Maybe it just got confused. Even smart-asses like yourself get confused every so often, especially when you're down a few gin and tonics."

The generals laughed and, as if on cue, took long swings of their drinks. Lana blinked as if she was confused herself. Jacob had never mentioned before about Xerus' capture. Never mentioned that the alien had given itself up.

Why? Why would Xerus do such a thing?

She felt a hand on her knee and when she looked over, Nicole smiled at her assuredly. Lana gave her a quick smile back, but deep inside she wanted to scream.

As dinner ended and dessert and coffee were being distributed, another spokesperson went to the stage.

"As a thank you to all of you for your dedication and service to the base, we present to you these special gifts sent here from earth. We know how many of you have been away for a long time and hope this will serve as a reminder of your home and how far we have come. Thank you."

The gifts were sent round by servers, small blue boxes with the Lazris star engraved on top. When Lana opened hers she found a silver bracelet with two charms dangling from its ends. One of the Lazris stars in onyx and one of earth cut from emerald.

"Ooh, so pretty!" Nicole exclaimed. "The green almost matches your eyes, Lana."

That seemed a bit of an overstatement, but Lana took the compliment.

"And looks like the men got watches. How nice." Nicole said. Lana looked over and saw them oohing and ahhing.

"Here let me help you put it on," Lana said as she saw Nicole struggling to link the chain around her wrist. Nicole gladly gave her hand up so that Lana could put the bracelet on her.

"Here let me help with yours," Nicole said as she let her bracelet slide down her arm.

Lana wasn't much of a jewelry person but she allowed Nicole to put it on her. She turned her wrist both ways and pretended to admire it.

As dessert ended, the music, which had been a soft melody in the background, grew louder, indicating the dance floor was opening just below the stage area. Couples made their way over, hand in hand while others got up to mingle. Nicole found a few of her other friends and introduced them to Lana. They talked for a while until Lana had to excuse herself for the bathroom. When she came out and looked around the vast foyer she couldn't help wondering what Xerus would think of all of it.

She started to laugh softly to herself as she imagined what it be like to see him in a suit tailored for him (if even possible) walking around, trying not to smack his tail against people's back-sides, complaining it was too packed as he towered over everyone, grumbling as he went. He wouldn't dance even if she begged him. But he would watch her. He'd try one of the wines per her request and end up accidentally shattering the glass in his tight grip. She would have to take him to the bathroom to get cleaned.

It was an odd fantasy but for whatever reason she let it play out in her head. She looked down at the bracelet on her wrist and fingered the charms, smiling.

"I tell ya, if I had been on that mission, there's no way that thing would still be around. Sure they were happy to get it alive but, come on, what couldn't you find out just by dissecting it?"

Lana heard this to her right and spotted Galger and General Vearez talking by a pillar. Quickly she stepped behind it so they wouldn't catch her watching them.

"I mean, okay sure, they could learn where the fuck the rest of em are and that be good for us, ya know, so if shit hit the fan we could be ready for any kind of war. Blow them out of the water before they got to us or something. But ya, the damage that thing did on 421...shit. Straight terrorist tactics. We've seen it all, sir, let me tell ya."

"It is disappointing that after months we still have no good intel on the subject," General Vearez said. "No clue of its home whereabouts. We did have a team scan every bit of that hell planet and didn't find a trace."

"All I'm saying is I've talked to Officer Torrence, the head of security. He wants that thing dead too. But I've been thinking lately that we should maybe wait on that, ya know?"

General Vearez got closer to the officer and Lana had to focus hard to hear them.

"What are you thinking?" Vearez said.

"I'm thinking we don't blow it's head off just yet. They've been trying this whole time to play good cop with it but I think it's time to switch gears. And I think I can be the one to get it to talk."

Lana didn't hear anything after that as they began to speak too low but she could guess what they were planning. Like a sleepwalker, she moved back to the table and picked up her purse.

"Lana, hey where have you been?" Nicole waved at her as she stood by a group of friends. Her expression grew concerned and she moved toward her. "Hey, is everything okay?"

Lana swallowed hard. "I...um...I'm so sorry about this but I think I'm going to head off."

"Okay. Will you tell me what's wrong?"

"I'm just...not feeling well."

Nicole's expression went from concern to nearly horrified, her tone turning gravely serious. "What symptoms are you feeling? Do you feel dizzy? Confused?"

Lana looked at her strangely but just shook her head. "No, no, nothing like that. I just...I just need to be alone. I'm sorry."

The relief on Nicole's face wasn't hard to miss. "No problem, Lana, of course. I will be just fine here. You take care, okay?"

"Thanks, Nicole."

Lana didn't miss a beat taking her leave. She would have searched for Jacob but when she couldn't find him right away, she decided to just speak with him later. She made for the elevators at breakneck speed, making sure to avoid Galger or any of the generals.

As Lana came to her door, she paused before opening it. As much as she wanted to leave the gala, she also came to realize she didn't want to be alone in this moment. Afraid the frustration and anxiety might consume her as soon as she walked into her lonely little unit, she feared to walk inside and be taken unwillingly into that black abyss.

Leaning against the door, she took a few deep breaths, then let out a cry and hit the metal siding with her fist. She turned over, leaning against the wall. She could feel tears welling up but she refused to let them fall. She blinked several times to dry her eyes then bowed her head. When she caught the gleam of her new bracelet, she rose her hand up and rubbed the charms between her fingers. For a long moment, she just stared at it, thinking of everything and nothing.

She really didn't care for jewelry. She'd likely never wear the thing again. It would just collect dust in some corner of her room.

She thought again for a long moment then a smile slowly pulled at her lips. He might be annoyed but Xerus never refused any of her gifts before.

Without even going to her room to change, Lana went back to the elevators and this time pushed the button for twelve.

When she got to the security desk she pulled out her security badge from her little purse and, though David gave her a weird look, he let her through. She went across the central lab, straight for Torrence's desk.

"What the hell are you doing here?" He said in greeting.

"I'd like into unit three, please."

Torrence looked her over, a lot longer than usual. When he was still sure he was unsatisfied by her in some way, he leaned back in his chair. "You're off the clock."

"But I still have authorization to see my client at any hour."

Torrence didn't say anything nor did he move.

"Alright, I guess I'll contact Cole then and let him–"

"He's not contactable right now." Torrence grimaced.

Lana raised a brow. "Well I have his number, I'll just message–"

Torrence made an angry grunting sound and put in the security code for unit three. "Make it quick."

Smiling, Lana turned and headed for the opening. As she waited for the door to close behind her and for the sliding door to open into the room, she unclasped the bracelet from her wrist and hid it in her hand. When the sliding door opened, she went straight for the wall controls.

"This is a surprise," she heard Xerus say. "What brings the good doctor here at such a..."

When the screen lifted and Xerus got a good look at her, he froze. Even his tail stopped moving.

Lana felt a blush coming on and realized it was because of the way he looked at her. She hadn't expected to get such a reaction from him despite her fancy get up.

"I...um...I have a present for you," Lana said sheepishly.

Xerus lowered his tail slowly to the ground and dipped his head. "Oh?...and what might that be?" He said in a strangely low, husky voice.

Like a little girl, Lana skipped over to the transfer box and carefully slid the bracelet in. She stepped back to the glass to gauge his reaction. Xerus didn't move right away. He watched her instead and Lana had to coax him to open the box.

Eventually, he did. When he entwined the bracelet in his fingers, he looked at it curiously, letting the light hit the gems, making them sparkle. He looked at her, confused.

"What is it?"

Lana giggled. "It's a bracelet. It goes around your wrist. Like this." Lana held up her other hand that had the slim diamond bracelet.

Xerus looked it over again then glanced back at her. "But...why?"

She wasn't sure if he was asking why it went around your wrist or why she was giving it to him. She chose to believe it was the former.

"It's just meant to be like an...ornament. Something nice to wear."

Xerus held it up higher to the light so that he could make out the charms.

"Ah, the star...well you already know that symbol." Lana pointed out. "But the other one is of my homeworld. Earth."

He tilted his head and grunted. Carefully taking it in his claws he tried to lay it out on his wrist and to both of their dismay, the bracelet was much too small. It looked like something a child wore compared to his size.

"Oh, well...I hadn't really thought about it fitting you," Lana said. "It was just last minute and I understand if you–"

"Thank you."

Lana's eyes widened. She watched as Xerus went over to the bed he rarely used and placed it on top. Right next to the lock of hair she had given him over a game of chess. She stared at them, and at Xerus, then moved closer to the glass.

As if in sync, Xerus too came up beside the window and, when Lana placed her hand on the glass, he placed his against hers.

Lana swallowed as her throat tightened. "Xerus...there's something I have to tell you. Something I should have told you before and I'm sorry...I'm sorry I didn't." She licked her lips. "You should know, you need to know, that in a week's time they are going to test you. To prove that you can be trusted."

Xerus' expression darkened. "Tested how?"

Lana shook her head. "I don't know, they wouldn't say but if you succeeded, they promised me you would be given more lax holdings, you might even be allowed out from time to time."

Xerus lowered his hand from the glass. "And if I fail?"

Lana looked away and in that Xerus knew.

"They won't just kill you though, Xerus, they plan to torture you."

Xerus turned from her and Lana dropped her hand. "Please...please," she said. "If you do this. If you work with me I promise you, I will do everything in my power to help you. To help even with your mission."

Xerus turned back to her. "Even if that mission meant killing humans?"

Lana opened her mouth then closed it.

"I didn't think so."

"You know I can't. And I don't believe you would do that."

"You don't know," he said in a hushed tone.

"Then tell me. Help me understand."

Xerus shook his head and it was the first she'd seen him use the human gesture. He averted his eyes from her and fixed his gaze on the bracelet. He stared at it for a long time before he looked back at her.

"You are an enigma, you know. Just you," he said.

Lana frowned in confusion and Xerus blew out a hard breath through his snout. His eyes fell over her once again. "Turn for me."

Lana hesitated then did as he asked, letting him see her bare back and the twirl of her dress.

Xerus grunted low. He said something in a whisper that Lana didn't catch.

"You make everything more difficult," Xerus said, rubbing his face and exposing his fangs. He tugged on one horn and turned from her. "If things were different, maybe..."

Yes, if things could be different. If he would only trust her more.

"If you don't comply with the test, you will automatically fail. Try for me, Xerus. You can't win your mission if you are dead."

Xerus bowed his head as if in defeat. Lana waited for a response but he was silent. Even though he said nothing he must know that she was right.

"Xerus..."

He eyed her over his shoulder and the look he gave her was crushing. He gave her a single nod. "I will...try."

Lana closed her eyes and sighed, relieved.

"Stay with me tonight."

When she opened her eyes, she saw him back at the glass, his hand up against it. She smiled and placed her palm to his. "Okay."

* * *

Lana woke up to the sound of someone calling her name.

"Ms. Hart, get up."

Her eyes fluttered open and she lifted her head with a groan. The first image she saw was of Xerus laying beside her against the glass. She sat up slowly and saw he was awake, watching her.

The intercom went off. "Ms. Hart, please return to the lab."

Lana rubbed her temples and grimaced as her arm tingled and her neck ached. The floor was not a comfortable way to sleep. Xerus rose before her and stepped back from the window.

"You should go," he said.

Lana looked over to the digital clock on the wall and saw it was four in the morning. Carefully standing up, she sluggishly went over to the wall controls. Before she put the screen back, she smiled at Xerus and nodded. "See you tomorrow."

As she left the room and headed for the lab, she felt weightless. Dare she say even a little content for the first time she'd stepped foot in Lazris.

Even Torrence's seething glare couldn't phase her.

"You fell asleep in there and left the screen down, that's against protocol and I'll have to write you up."

Lana smiled at him. "Have a good night, Torrence."

He mumbled something as she walked past his desk but Lana couldn't care less. As she left the facility and took the elevator up to her room, she thought about tonight. And she had hope.

CHAPTER THIRTEEN

The week started well. Besides the usual annoyances (Galger making inappropriate comments, Torrence's daily attitude, and Cole being more distant than ever) Lana was feeling good about the coming test. She continued to learn Xerus' language and work with him as normal and felt she was making good progress. Having studied linguistics at university helped make her a quick learner. Some days she even attempted to speak in just Xerian (as she called it) though she could only manage a few simple sentences. She was better understanding it so far than speaking it.

She focused all her time on Xerus. So much so that she hadn't really thought much about the fact that she didn't notice Cole's absence the past couple of days until one of the others mentioned it, or that everyone seemed on edge.

"I need a vacation," a lab tech named Vigo said. "Those damn raptors have been screeching for days. And Asset T is moving around a lot more than usual. Thing gives me the damn creeps."

"Has anyone heard about Jeff, by the way?" Samantha, another lab tech, asked. "Wonder if he's still feeling unwell."

"Heard he was put on leave, but that's it," said another.

The rest were silent, working on autopilot as they went about their daily tasks. Lana didn't think much of it, only that she noticed the lab was more quiet than usual. She caught Dahlia and Dr. Yanlin whispering to each other a few times, their faces tight with concern. She saw them looking in her direction once or twice but she thought nothing of it. She had other things on her mind than base drama.

When there were only two days left until the test, that was when Lana began to feel the tug of anxiety. She couldn't help feeling as if she were being left out of some secret plan as everyone spoke in whispers around her and Torrence and Galger seemed to have more private conversations than usual. Already they had begun to plan their set up, with several guards to accompany the generals into the unit and stay by the doors. Torrence would be monitoring from his desk while Galger stayed in the room giving any necessary orders.

Lana only knew this from the other guards talking not from anyone bothering to inform her. She also learned that the generals would come down to twelve as early as six in the morning to assess the rest of the facility and the test would be done last. This Dahlia told her.

"If all goes well, we can take off early for the day, though some will still have to take their night shifts," Dahlia said.

"Did you speak to Cole about this?" Lana asked.

Dahlia shook her head. "Just got the info from Dr. Yanlin. He said Cole has other matters he's been attending to."

Lana frowned. 'What other matters could be possibly more important than this?' she thought.

Sick of being left in the dark, she had half a mind to call him herself. When she got the courage to actually do it, she was left with his voicemail. She tried calling Nicole after, but she didn't pick up either. Her anxiety growing and her frustrations returning, Lana emailed Nicole on her work computer but didn't expect a callback.

"I'm going to make dinner and come back after," Lana told Dahlia.

"I'll be gone by then. See you tomorrow."

Lana nodded and turned off her work computer and left. She

went back up to her room and had a quick meal and shower before going back down to twelve to prepare Xerus' meals. She decided to leave him alone the day before the test, giving him time to rest and be prepared, even if he argued that he didn't need it. Wanting to give him as much time as possible, she planned to make him an extra meal so he had something for tomorrow despite him arguing he didn't need that either.

Once she got back to the lab, she went straight for the food prep area and made the usual meat and mango combo. As she picked up the trays and headed for the unit she glanced up and happened to notice Xerus' video feed was stopped, the monitor black. Frowning, she went over to Torrence's desk and saw he was watching his computer screen with intense interest. As she crept closer, she saw on his monitor the live feed of Xerus' room. Someone was talking to him at the window.

"What's going on?" she asked.

Torrence immediately minimized the screen and twisted around to give her a dirty look. "I don't appreciate the eavesdropping, Ms. Hart."

"I wasn't trying to...forget it. I need to give Xerus his meals so can you please open up–"

"Now isn't a good time. Come back later."

Lana pursed her lips then set the trays down on another desk nearby. "Who was that in the room?"

When Torrence didn't say anything, Lana made for her computer where she could gain access to the room's feed if she liked.

"Dr. Kingsley is inside just checking on the thing, alright," he called out to her.

"I want to know what he is saying to him." Lana turned on her computer and logged in. As she went to pull up the unit's feed she heard Torrence curse. As the video popped up, she saw Cole close to the glass but she couldn't hear his words. Xerus stood before him and he looked–

The feed froze and she was kicked out of the program with a pop-up saying she didn't have permission to access the feed. Lana's hands curled into fists.

"You don't have the right to keep me from seeing," she snapped at Torrence who was at his desk editing permissions. She got up from her desk and was about to stalk over and do–she wasn't sure what– when Cole's voice picked up on the intercom at Torrence's desk telling him to open the doors. Torrence put in the code and the door began to slide up. Lana took the moment to pick up her trays and go for the door, hearing Torrence's belligerent protests behind her. As she marched down the hall, the sliding door at the end opened. She froze as she saw Cole step out.

"Lana." He smiled at her. But the smile seemed different. Colder. "Sorry, did I keep you from your task? I just needed a moment with the asset."

His voice was off too but she couldn't place what it was.

"I was just bringing his meals," she said quietly.

"Well...don't let me keep you." He walked past her and Lana caught a whiff of something that smelled like copper. Frowning she looked back at him and, as if noticing her stare, he turned to look at her.

"Asset X isn't feeling well though. Might be one of his moods again. I would be careful," he said.

'Why would he be in a mood? What did you say?' she wanted to yell at him. Instead, she kept her lips tightly shut and only nodded, turning from him. She waited for Cole to pass the door and let it shut behind him. Then she bolted into the room.

"Xerus?"

There was no response. Lana placed the trays on the table and went for the controls. As she was about to turn off the screen she heard a low, sharp growl.

"Don't."

Lana paused. She lowered her hand and peeled her eyes over to the film of the window where she could see Xerus' silhouette.

"Xerus, what happened? What did he say to you?"

More silence then, "I need you to go."

"But I–"

He hissed. "Dammit, do as I say."

That sharp needle of pain hit her chest. Not wanting to anger him further, she did as told, quickly placing the trays in the transfer box and forcing herself back to the door. She looked back and opened her mouth to say something but thought against it. Without another word she left. As she walked the hall back to the lab, she felt pressure in her head and in her chest, her body hot and shaking.

As the door opened, she walked out but saw Cole was already gone.

"Where is he?" she asked.

Torrence leaned back in his seat and shrugged indifferently. "He left. Probably for the night. It's not your business what–"

"I want to see the recording." Lana stepped closer to his desk. "I want to see it."

"Afraid not, Ms. Hart."

"Why?" she nearly yelled.

Torrence put up his hands. "Classified. And you need to calm down. Or does someone need to escort you to your rooms again?"

Lana made a frustrated noise. "No thanks." She stalked past his desk and left the lab. As she went to the elevators and thought to go up to Cole's room and demand he tell her what he said, she stopped herself and a wave of cold hit her.

If she harassed him, he could boot her instantly. And she feared she was already on thin ice. As she pressed the button for her floor instead and headed back to her room, she knew whatever had happened was beyond her to fix now.

CHAPTER FOURTEEN

Lana barely slept the night before the test. As the lights in her room brightened and the soft ding of the alarm went off, she groggily rose from her bed and made for the shower. Anxiety already began to claw its way up her chest and into her throat as she washed quickly and put on her uniform. Nicole still hadn't gotten back to her about Cole as she ate breakfast while checking her messages.

It didn't matter, anyway. She would see Cole later today and would be sure to give him her exact thoughts. For now, her main focus was on Xerus.

When she finally made it down to the lab, the generals were already there looking over some of the less problematic specimens and general experimentations being done throughout the facility. Her eyes instinctively flew up towards the monitors where she saw Xerus standing with his back turned away from the camera. He didn't move. Even his tail lay still on the ground.

"Good luck today, Dr. Hart."

Lana looked down and saw one of the lab tech's, Sara, smiling at her. Lana reluctantly smiled back, giving her a slight nod. As the girl passed her, Lana saw Galger nearby with Torrence and his group of men, readying themselves for when the generals assessed the higher risk assets. Galger's eyes met hers and he gave her a wink. Lana looked away and immediately went to her work desk and slunk down in her chair.

She pretended to work on her reports but, in truth, she was too distracted–too on edge–to concentrate. Her eyes kept flipping up to Xerus who still hadn't moved from his spot. Rubbing her temples, she went back to the work on her computer, trying to ignore the eyes of the guards.

The day dragged as she watched the generals pass by a few times. Jacob smiled at her once, then turned away to focus on the massive tank of coral specimens before him as one of the biologists talked through their examinations. At one point Lana had to leave to take a walk and calm her nerves. Cole was nowhere to be seen and that worried her a lot. When she returned, he was still not there and she was very close to contacting Nicole again to figure out what was happening.

"I don't know anything," Dr. Yanlin said when she tried to ask him. "I'm too busy now to worry about it. Why don't you call him."

"I've tried," Lana said. "Don't you think it's a little crazy though that he wouldn't be here for this?"

Dr. Yanlin turned his nose up at her. "He likely isn't feeling well and had to call off. Shouldn't you be worrying about other things, Dr. Hart?"

"Then shouldn't we know about it?" Lana said, ignoring his comment.

Dr. Yanlin shrugged and stepped around her, going back to his task. Lana put her arms up in defeat. The generals were assessing the last unit before the test and were almost done. Lana made her rounds, checking on Xerus yet again. He still was motionless. She frowned as she watched him, but tried to think nothing of it. He was likely meditating, that was all.

When the door to unit four finally opened and the generals, along with Galger and his team, stepped out, Lana could see the tight grimaces of General Vearez and General Williams, the look of excited curiosity in General Holk, and the solemn look of General Hartin as they re-entered the lab. They just had their first—and likely last—encounter with Asset T.

"Thank you, gentlemen, for your time," Dahlia said as she followed close behind them, the door beginning to slide shut behind her. "I will send you all the records and data on Asset T as soon as possible just as you asked, General Holk."

"Yes, thank you, Dr. Gray. Fascinating, seriously fascinating," General Holk replied, shaking her hand.

"Sure. If you have a hard-on for giant spiders," General Vearez said. The generals laughed as did Galger and his men.

"And I'd like a sample of that venom you've acquired as well, Doctor," General Williams said. "Grotesque as it is, at least it might contain something useful in that."

Dahlia bowed her head. "Will do, sir."

"Good job in there." He shook her hand as well and the others followed suit, congratulating her on her work. Dahlia grinned, her eyes bright and proud.

As they took a small break to ready themselves for the final assessment, Lana gathered her ISpad and waited as patiently as she could, watching Galger and his team prepare to enter the unit. Their guns locked and loaded. Torrence gave Galger permission to use the window's electro-defense system in case of an emergency as he would be observing from the lab.

A hand fell on her shoulder and Lana jumped.

"You look tense." Jacob gave Lana a smirk.

Lana let out a deep breath. "Yes."

Jacob placed his hands behind his back, taking a military stance. "You got this, Lana. Just relax."

God, she wished she could. She gave him a tight smile and he patted her on the back. "Let's do this."

Once the generals and Galger's team were ready, Torrence

opened the door to unit three. Clutching her workpad tight, Lana followed close behind as they made their way inside.

The room was dark as usual and someone had turned the cell's lights back to red. The milky screen rippled as sparks of electricity jumped across the glass.

"Did someone spill burnt coffee in here or what?" General Williams asked.

"That's just the asset's pheromones, General," said Lana behind them.

They looked at her curiously. General William's and Vearez's lips tightened and brows furrowed. "It smells awful," General Vereaz said, crinkling his nose. "It stings my nose." He took out a Kleenex from his pocket and wiped his forehead and his neck. The others seemed to be sweating as well, their faces glistening. And it wasn't because the room was hot. Far from it. All of the men shifted uncomfortably on their feet and cleared their throats. Galger and his team looked on edge, their fingers trigger ready.

Lana, on the other hand, felt perfectly calm. In fact, the scent smelled lovely to her, like freshly brewed coffee. She eventually learned that the scent was coming from Xerus when she concluded that no one had been going into his unit to make or drink coffee. He hadn't really given her a reason as to why he was secreting the pheromones, only that it had varying purposes.

And right now it was clear he was using it to tell the men that they should be running for their lives.

"Let's just get this over with," General Williams said, wiping his face with a shaky hand.

The door behind them opened and Cole entered the room.

"Sorry I am late, gentlemen." He didn't so much as glance at Lana as he passed her and Lana could see there was still something off about him even in the red light. Following behind him were two other lab techs whose names Lana couldn't remember. The boy and girl duo looked over at her with blank expressions though the boy had more fear in his eyes than the girl.

Cole nodded to the boy who went over to the wall controls and lifted the screen. He backed away quickly as it disappeared, revealing Xerus standing before them.

"Holy fuck," Lana heard someone whisper close by. A few others cursed and subconsciously took a step back.

"No need to be afraid, gentlemen," Cole tried to assure them. "It can't harm you." He knocked on the glass and a little smirk tugged on his lips as he glanced at Xerus. "The window and room itself have electrical defenses and are thicker than your fists."

"Damn thing assaults me just looking at it," said General Vearez in a low voice.

Slack-jawed and wide-eyed, General Holk took a cautious step towards the glass. "My god...it looks..."

"Like a damn demon," General Vearez said.

"I would be careful what you say, General," Lana piped up, moving closer to the glass. "He *can* understand you."

The generals frowned, shifting uncomfortably. Lana turned to face Xerus who stared back at the generals with narrowed, hellfire eyes. His eyes shifted around the room to each of the men, his eyes falling last to Cole. His mouth tightened, revealing the tips of his fangs and his eyes darkened. Lana had an odd feeling she'd seen that look on him somewhere before but couldn't place where. It made her heart race.

Cole didn't seem too concerned by the look Xerus was giving him. He turned his back and gave the generals a brief understanding of how the QS translator worked.

"Xerus," Lana whispered, wanting him to look at her. To say something. When his eyes peeled away from the doctor to finally look down at her, Lana felt an icy cold drip down her spine. For the first time in weeks, she felt fear.

He didn't see her. It was like looking at a stranger.

"Now that you have some understanding, why don't we say hello," Cole said in his calm manner. "Hello Asset X. How are you today?"

Xerus' eyes flicked back to Dr. Kingsley. His tail curled but he remained silent.

"Oh, come now, Asset X, I know you aren't shy," Cole said. A few laughed nervously. "Come on, introduce yourself."

Xerus didn't move or speak. His eyes only focused on the doctor.

"I–I think he's just a little overwhelmed right now. He's not used to so many people," Lana said, hoping the excuse was enough.

"Well, we have plenty of recordings of the asset speaking that I will gladly have sent to you each," Cole said with disappointment. "For now let's begin the test." He nodded to the girl who brought up her own ISpad and began tapping and sliding her finger. " Yevonne here has been running tests on various animals also housed in the facility and using them to gauge responsiveness to extraterrestrial stimuli. We thought this might make the perfect opportunity to engage both sides."

As Yevonne worked the controls on her workpad, a small hole—not large enough for Xerus to fit through in the slightest–opened up from the ceiling above his cell and a glass container dropped down slowly. Inside was a chimpanzee.

The container opened and the chimp, likely through training, exited the container and shut its lid. Yevonne acknowledged the chimp as Max. Gesturing in sign language for him to do as she said.

When the chimp entered the cell, Xerus' head shot over to it and his nostrils flared. His pupils narrowed and he shifted his body towards it.

Lana watched with growing fear. Anxiety twisting her insides.

"Let us see how well Asset X interacts with Max," Cole said. "Though Max isn't human, he is our closest choice in order to gather information in the safest way possible."

The chimp reluctantly moved closer to Xerus per Yevonne's orders. Xerus, however, did not move a step to approach it, only looked at it with intense curiosity.

"Xerus, it's okay," Lana said quietly, placing her hand on the glass.

As the chimp got only a few feet away, it stopped abruptly,

looking to Yevonne for reassurance. It didn't move despite Yevonne signing at it to move closer. Xerus this time stepped closer, his head raised, his eyes rolling back and shutting as he sniffed the air. He remained that way for some time as if he were searching for something, some scent they couldn't detect. When he lowered his head and opened his eyes, he shot his gaze towards Cole and there was such hatred there in his expression Lana felt the heat.

Before she could shout for them to get the chimp out, Xerus bared his fangs in a snarl and narrowed his eyes into red slits. His mouth widened and a low, feral growl ripped from his throat. Lana knew where she'd seen the expression before. From the video feed that Torrence had shown her from the night of Xerus' capture.

"Get Max out," Lana said to Yevonne. The girl's face went pale and she frantically signaled for the chimp to get back into the container.

The chimp yelped and screeched, backing away, as Xerus crouched into a predatory stance.

"No, Xerus don't!" Lana shouted. He seemed to pause for only a moment at her words. His eyes, wicked and murderous, looked back at her. And she saw, for only a second, something mournful in his gaze. His face twisted and he straightened.

"Xi xilera ni kissala."

He said it to her. And Lana froze, uncertain if she had heard him correctly. As she tried to register his words, Xerus lifted his tail and swung.

With whip-like reflexes, his tail cut through the air and hit the chimp square in the chest, slicing it in half. Blood spurted against the wall and on the glass. Yevonne screamed.

"Christ!" General Vearez shouted.

"You two get them all out of here," Galger commanded his men. The others took up their guns and moved to the window. Galger brought up the controls for the glass and hit the charge. Volts of electricity slashed through the room.

"No!" Lana cried. "No!" She could feel hands encompassing her arms but she fought them.

"Gentlemen, I am so sorry," she heard Cole say. "Yevonne, Derrick, come."

Yevonne, with tears streaming down her face and her mouth covered, trying to keep from being sick, turned and followed Cole. She gave Lana a hateful look before exiting.

"Calm down, Dr. Hart, let's go, you have to go," said the soldier, tugging her away. Lana watched helplessly as Xerus was once again shocked into submission. His eyes found hers and he roared as the lights flashed and the soldiers shouted.

"Get her the fuck out of here," Galger shouted. Lana was lifted from the ground and forced from the room.

CHAPTER FIFTEEN

"I'm not leaving this lab until I get to see him," Lana snapped. Five guards made a human wall around her, preventing her from getting closer to the unit doors.

"That isn't your call, Ms. Hart," Torrence said from his desk.

"It's been eight hours. Asset X is mobile and I want to talk to him before..."

Torrence swung around in his seat to look square at her. He took out a wrapper and popped the gum in his mouth. He chewed slowly before saying, "Your work is finished here. The asset will remain in complete lockdown before we move to the next phase. I suggest you start gathering your things."

"*That* isn't your call," Lana said. "Cole still–"

"Dr. Kingsley has given me the permissions necessary to move forward, including what shall be done with staff. For security purposes, you will be removed from the facility and unauthorized to return. They shouldn't have let you in even now."

"I will speak with Dr. Kingsley myself then," Lana said through gritted teeth. She stepped back and turned from them, heading for her desk.

"I wouldn't advise it, Ms. Hart," Torrence called to her.

Lana ignored him as she took out her phone. Instead of calling Cole, however, she pressed the number for Nicole.

Lana cursed as the voicemail went off yet again.

As soon as she had been booted from Xerus' unit they had taken her straight out of the place and forced her back to her room. She hadn't had a single chance to speak to anyone. She had tried several emails to both Cole and Nicole but neither responded. She hadn't slept since the test and could only make it a single shift cycle before she left her room and went back to level twelve in hopes of talking them into letting her see Xerus.

It should have been no surprise that Cole was missing yet again and the security team was taking control.

Desperation took hold of her and Lana did the last thing she knew she should. She called Jacob.

Several long beeps went through before she heard a soft click.

"Lana..." Jacob's voice was low.

"Jacob," Lana said softly. "Please I need your help."

When he said nothing, Lana continued. "I...I know there's no hope now for...for Asset X." She paused trying to keep her voice from cracking. "But please, I need one last session with him. I can't get a hold of Cole and the guards won't let me in."

"Lana, I'm sorry, I really don't think–"

"Please, Jacob, I know it's not fair to ask this of you, but I need this as a friend. I don't expect...I know I can't save him now, but I need to at least speak with him one last time."

There was a long pause before he blew out a breath. "Give me an hour and I will be down."

Lana closed her eyes and pursed her lips. "Thank you. Thank you, Jacob."

When she hung up, she made sure to take her sweet time at her computer, pretending to work on any final reports, watching the guards carefully for any signs of change.

When the doors to the facility opened and Jacob stepped

through, the guards paused in their affairs and saluted. Torrence stood up from his desk with a frown.

"General Hartin," Torrence just barely remembered to salute before saying, "what are you doing here, sir?"

When Jacob's eyes looked over to Lana, Torrence's expression went from surprise to red-hot anger.

"Sir, I'm sorry, but she isn't authorized–"

Jacob put up his hand. "One moment, Officer Torrence, please." He approached Lana who met him halfway.

"Thank you, Jacob, for coming. I didn't know what else to do and..." Lana shook her head and closed her eyes, taking deep breaths. "I'm sorry I failed you. But I need this last favor."

Jacob went to place a hand on her shoulder, but when he saw Torrence eyeing them, he thought against it and dropped his hand. "I'm sorry this happened. And the failure wasn't yours. Not by a long shot. You did everything you could do, Lana. And despite what the others think, you did better than the rest... but getting through to Asset X was clearly impossible."

Lana lowered her eyes, not wanting him to see. She wouldn't dare let him see what she was feeling.

She was so sure. She had been so sure she and Xerus were...But somehow she had been wrong. That was why she needed to speak with him. She needed to know why.

"Give me this last moment with him. For everything I did, I would at least say goodbye."

Jacob bowed his head. "Alright. But after that, Lana, I can do no more. I will give you permission to enter the unit this last time and grant you twenty-fours hours to gather your things within the facility. After that, we will...discuss."

Lana wanted to hug him but Torrence was still watching. Instead, she let out a relieved breath and gave him a little smile. "Thank you, Jacob, thank you."

Jacob nodded and turned from her, stepping back over to Torrence. "Officer Torrence you will grant Dr. Hart admittance into unit three one last time." Torrence opened his mouth to protest and Jacob gestured to the door. "That is an order. And she will be granted time to gather her things from the facility before her keycard is deactivated is that clear?"

Torrence went tight-lipped and silent. He chewed slowly on his gum and nodded his head.

"Good. Dr. Hart?" Jacob waved her over. Lana came to him and followed him towards the facility door. "If they give you issues, don't hesitate to contact me."

Lana nodded and thanked him once more before he left. She looked to Torrence whose glare was black and cold.

"Open the door to unit three, please," Lana said as she walked back over.

Torrence turned back to his computer and punched in the code for unit three. As the door opened and she began straight for it, she gasped as a hand caught her arm and gripped it tight enough to hurt.

"You can shove a general's cock in your mouth to get your way for now but that won't work in the long run. Asset X is done for and anything you say won't change that." Torrence let go of her with a shove, making her stumble. "Make it quick. You got fifteen minutes."

Lana twisted around to shout at him that he couldn't treat her like that but saw the other guards watching, none moving to intervene. Hands curling into fists, she told herself it wasn't worth it and to focus on the time she had left. She turned back without a word and rushed down the way toward Xerus' cell.

* * *

When the sliding door opened to her and she stepped into the room, the first thing Lana noticed was that the screen was down. The second thing she noticed was Xerus' back facing the window, still as a statue. The third thing she noticed was Galger sitting back in her chair, his gun laid out on the table.

"What are you doing here?" Lana asked.

As Galger twisted his head around to look at her, Xerus also raised his head slightly.

"Ah, Hart, come to join the fun? Me and the big guy here were just having a little chat. Just giving him a little run down of what's to come."

"Get out," Lana said, stepping away from the door.

"Now that's not very polite." Galger stood up and stretched then took up his gun. "But I'll give ya a pass since you're clearly having a bad day. Or two or three." Galger laughed. He turned and walked toward her, taking his time. "But, hey, don't go getting yourself worked up, eh?" He raised his hand to her but Lana skirted around it before he could touch her. "Alright, sweetheart, alright. No need for the attitude. I'm gone." He smiled. "Just be careful. Spiney here isn't very happy." He sauntered out of the room.

As the sliding door closed behind him, the silence took over. Lana stood in place for a moment just watching Xerus in his cell, trying to find the words. The glass was still stained of the chimp's blood, now black in color against the red light.

Lana made her way to the glass. "Xerus," she said in a near whisper.

Xerus didn't turn to look at her nor did he respond.

"Xerus, please talk to me."

When he still didn't speak, Lana placed her hands on the window, her face almost touching the glass. "Fine...fine. If you won't speak then I will." Her voice grew louder. "I just wanted to say that you are an idiot."

Xerus bowed his head.

"You had a chance. You had a chance to be rid of this cage and you chose death. And all for what?" Lana's voice cracked. "All for what? Your mission won't be completed. They will take you from here and torture you and you...you don't care." Lana pounded her fist lightly on the glass. "Damnit, Xerus, just tell me why. Why did you do it?" She could feel her vision begin to blur. "I thought we had something. I thought you and I were...I thought I could honestly say I was your...your friend."

A low sound emanated from Xerus and it took Lana a moment to realize what it was.

He was laughing.

"You really thought that...?" He said in a venomous tone. "How stupid of you. How sad really. You humans are just as weak in mind as you are in body."

Lana stiffened, pulling her hands from the glass. "I don't understand."

When Xerus twisted around to look at her, Lana let out a sharp gasp. She backed away and felt her heart sink.

Xerus' eyes were bright with fury and hatred, his lips pulled back in a snarl, showing off his razor teeth, giving him an ominous sort of smile.

"Look at you. So small. Pathetic. Playing with you was amusing at first I admit, but I'm sick of the whole human interaction now. I'm sick of you."

Lana shook her head and felt silent tears wet her face. "I don't believe you mean that. I don't believe you."

Xerus slammed his fist so hard against the glass Lana let out a little shriek in surprise. Little sparks of electricity rippled across the window. Lana froze in place, her arms crossing over her chest. Xerus' breath fogged the glass.

"Believe it," he hissed. "And if you knew what was good for you, you would leave this place entirely. Leave and never come back. Because when I get out of here I will slaughter every single human I see and I will hunt you down personally. You are nothing to me. Just weak, annoying prey."

Prey.

That word was an unexpected trigger and an image, dark and twisted, flashed in her brain.

You will be perfect. My prey.

And with no warning at all, Lana became absolutely terrified.

Tears streamed down her face and her breath came in gasps; her heart pounded like she had been running for miles.

She couldn't seem to form words though she tried; her head shook back and forth in a continuous movement as if she couldn't stop.

"No...no," she finally blurted. "You won't get out. You won't do that."

"I will. Mark me, human. Do you honestly think I can't?" He laughed again. "You honestly think your species could have ever captured me on my own? Just as I said, you think too highly of yourselves. The sphere is thinning and the darkness has arrived. And you're too late to stop it."

Lana covered her mouth and subconsciously lengthened the distance between them, ready to bolt.

"I needed to be here. I had to bide my time. But that time is done." Xerus raised his head, his eyes flashing, searing through her. "And so are you."

Xerus placed both hands on the window and lowered his head, his horns resting against the glass.

"Run."

And Lana did. She flew for the door and let out a cry of relief when it actually opened for her. She sprinted down the hall and nearly pounded on the door to be let out. When the door slid open and there was a large enough gap to slip through, she did so, falling to her knees on the ground just outside the entrance.

"Close it! Close it now!" she cried.

For once Torrence complied immediately. The door closed and Lana crawled away, fumbling to her feet.

"Jesus, what happened? You alright, sweetheart?"

Galger held her arm to balance her and Lana didn't care that he touched her. She didn't care about anything. She wept in front of them, covering her face with her hands.

"She's having a panic attack," she heard Torrence say. "Take her up to level six."

Lana allowed herself to be led out of the facility. Through teary eyes, she saw everyone frozen in shock as they stared at her. But she didn't care.

CHAPTER SIXTEEN

Lana sat on the medical bed, staring down at her feet, thinking of everything and nothing. Her phone rested on the table nearby and her eyes flashed over to it but it lay silent. Her eyes dropped back to the ground and she clasped her hands together.

It had been ten hours now since she'd been taken up to the medical bay and she had slept for three. And only because of the medication they had given her. When she had woken up in a near panic, she had immediately gone to her phone and called to twelve. Asking for Torrence.

"We are watching him carefully, Ms. Hart. I assure you there's no way he can get out."

"He said he could," Lana protested. "He said he was going to..."

"I reviewed the footage, I heard what he said. He just wanted to scare you, Ms. Hart. And he did a good job."

Lana chewed on her lip and shut her eyes, rubbing her temples. Her throat was still dry and scratched from the sobbing and her nose was still stuffed; her eyes were still a little puffy and dark from tears and lack of sleep.

"He will be taken care of as soon as we get the go-ahead from the generals," Torrence stated. " Until then I have everything under control. Now worry about yourself."

"I know Galger plans to torture him. You can't let him do it," Lana said, her hand shaking. "No one should go near him."

"Ms. Hart–"

"You said you heard him. He had planned to get captured all along, doesn't that concern you?" Lana nearly yelled.

"Ms. Hart. He probably said that to, I don't know, spare his ego or something. But as I said he is going to be taken care of soon, regardless. Now I have work to do so, goodbye." The phone went dead and Lana wanted to fling it at the wall. Instead, she dialed for Jacob.

When he didn't pick up, she left a voicemail and waited.

It had been an hour now and still he hadn't called her back. Rising from her bed she began to pace.

Her thoughts began to shift back to her and Xerus' final conversation but she forced them away. There was no point dwelling on his words now, save for those that put everyone in danger. She felt the stabbing pain in her chest again but she ignored it as best she could. What was done was done. Maybe she had been a fool all along for trusting him.

The door to her room opened and Lana stopped to stare at the one who entered.

"You finally came."

Nicole barely smiled at her as she closed the door behind her. "I'm so sorry, Lana. Are you–"

"Please." Lana sat back down on the bed. "Don't finish that sentence."

Nicole came up to stand before her. "I'm sorry I missed your messages. I really am. I wish..." She shook her head. " A lot has happened in the last few days."

Lana let out a little laugh. "You're telling me."

Nicole had Lana slide over so that she could sit next to her.

"Lana, I'm sorry to hear what happened with Xerus. Some things came up and I couldn't get away. But I wanted to help you."

"Did these things have to do with your uncle?" Lana dare asked.

Nicole's lips tightened.

"You can't tell me."

"It's confidential, Lana, I'm sorry–"

Lana leaped from the bed. "Stop saying you're sorry."

"But I am. Trust me, Lana, if I could tell you everything I would. But this is military protocol. And what's going on right now with my uncle is complicated."

"He has been failing at his job, is what it is. And don't speak to me of military protocol. Everything here has been against protocol. Torrence has taken over level twelve per your uncle's orders which is insane, you know?" Lana waved her hand. "You told me not to worry before but something is honestly wrong with Cole and I know it."

Nicole shook her head. "Lana, I think... I think it's best if you leave Lazris as soon as possible."

"Is that your professional opinion or are you asking me as a friend?"

Nicole looked up at her and Lana could see she was gravely serious. "Both."

Lana turned away and rubbed her eyes. "Everyone keeps telling me to go. But something isn't right. And I fear Asset X..." Lana laughed. "I just fear him now. But I feel like I can't leave. Not yet." she opened her eyes and looked back at Nicole. "I think he is going to escape somehow."

Nicole shook her head, her face paling. "That's not possible."

"I know and I don't know how but... something is missing in all this. He said he let himself come here, Nicole. Why would he do that?"

Nicole's face went from pale to ashen. "You think because of his mission?"

"It must be."

"But he is set to be terminated in a few days," Nicole said. "And if he claims he can escape why hasn't he tried before?"

Lana crossed her arms, her throat tightening. "I don't know. But he said he was biding his time. Something must have finally triggered him."

Nicole hid her eyes from Lana as she rose from the bed. "I am glad you are okay. I'm afraid I can't stay." Nicole went to the door and paused. "If I could change what happened I would," she said softly. She glanced back at Lana. "Be safe, Lana."

When Lana was alone again, she slumped back down on the bed.

She should go. What did it matter if she didn't find out what Xerus' mission was really about? Or what was wrong with Cole. Or what secrets were being kept. Her main reason for coming to Lazris had failed. Xerus was beyond her help now. And that hurt more than anything.

When she was finally able to get a nurse, she asked to be let go from the medical bay. Thankfully, Nicole had given them orders to let her leave when she was ready. Lana picked up her phone and followed the nurse out of the room and out of the facility, where she left her at the elevators.

As Lana made her way back down to her room, she couldn't help thinking about Xerus again. Despite everything he had said to her, she still hated the fact that, assuming he really couldn't get out, he was going to be tortured and killed. For a second she had the insane idea to ask for a private meeting with the generals to try to convince them to keep him alive a little longer, albeit inside a more secure holding, when the elevator doors opened and her phone went off.

Thinking it must be Jacob, she picked up immediately. "Jacob I–"

"Lana, it's Dahlia."

Lana paused then stepped out of the elevators towards her room. "Hi, Dahlia, is everything okay?"

There was a long pause then, "I thought it best to tell you right away before you found out some other way. I didn't expect Officer Torrence to tell you or Dr. Kingsley for that matter..."

Lana stopped at her door, fumbling for her key card. "What is it?"

"He's dead."

Lana froze. "I-I'm sorry."

"Asset X. He's gone."

CHAPTER SEVENTEEN

Lana walked into level twelve uncertain if she was awake or dreaming. She didn't take Dahlia for a liar but still, she had to see for herself. Galger, Torrence, and their team of men all congregated around unit three's door which was now wide open. Speaking in hurried voices, they seemed to be waiting outside the entrance, Galger's face red, while Torrence's was bright with anticipation.

Lana looked up at the monitors and saw several workers inside Xerus' unit, stepping in and out of his cell which now lay empty. As soon as she made it into the lab, Dr. Yaulin and several lab techs walked out of unit three pushing a large roller table. As the guards backed away, Lana could see a huge shape on the steel slab covered by a sheet. A spiny tail was held up carefully with a metal pole by one of the techs.

As the guards watched, some of them instinctively held up their guns. They encircled around the lab as the table was pushed into the center, placing it next to a shelf of medical equipment.

Lana felt her feet move toward the table as if she couldn't control her body. Only when a gentle hand gripped her shoulder did she stop moving.

When she gazed around, she saw Dahlia standing beside her. The woman's mouth turned up in a sad smile.

Lana licked her lips, her throat dry. "How?" she croaked.

"They aren't sure," Dahlia replied. "Torrence noticed on the feed the asset going to lie down as if to sleep. His vitals were all fine, he just looked like he was sleeping. He had been like that for several hours. Then suddenly his vitals flatlined. We thought at first there was a glitch in the system. Took a couple more hours to convince Torrence and the others that he wasn't breathing. I called you when they went in to retrieve the body. I'm sorry, Dr. Hart."

All Lana could seem to do was nod her head. Dahlia patted her on the shoulder and left her alone. Lana watched as Dr. Yanlin and the techs situated the alien's body then went their separate ways, logging on to computers to begin their reports. As Lana took a step toward the table, she could see the guards closing in.

"I wouldn't if I were you, Dr. Hart," Torrence said nearby. "Thing might be dangerous to touch. And you're only supposed to be here to pack your things."

"Officer Torrence, perhaps allowing her to see the asset wouldn't be so wrong," Dahlia said.

"It's okay, Dahlia," Lana heard herself say. "I'll just...start getting my things." Lana forced herself away and went for her office desk. Torrence watched her carefully as she began to close out her computer, transferring all necessary files and credentials. When his gaze finally left hers, she turned to watch him instead.

She pretended to gather her things for nearly an hour before a tech requested Torrence's assistance in dealing with one of the specimens in unit two. And by assistance, they meant 'shock therapy' as one of the assets likely wasn't complying. When Torrence and his men were out of sight, as were most of the other staff, Lana rose from her chair and slipped around her desk. She made her way over to the table until she was standing beside it.

For a moment all she could do was stand there. It still seemed so unreal. Still so hard to believe. When only hours ago she feared he would escape. Now, here Xerus was.

'He had escaped in a way', Lana thought. But something seemed wrong. Very wrong. Her eyes flickered up toward Torrence's desk and she couldn't help wondering if he had cut Xerus' life short. Perhaps gassed his cell or drained it of oxygen. If she could just access the video feed on her computer she could see Xerus' last moments. But that just wasn't going to happen.

Instead, Lana lifted her hand and carefully peeled away the sheet covering him.

Seeing him so close, and with no glass between them, was surreal. In the bright, albeit yellowish, light of the lab, she got a good look at his glistening, deep red scales and his dark purple horns. She let the cover slip from her hands to rest on Xerus' chest. Glancing around, and seeing no one watching her, Lana gently placed her hand on Xerus' chest. Her heart leaped at the first raw contact. His body was still warm, though not by much. His skin was hard yet smooth. She waited a moment, then lowered her head toward his face. She remained in that position for some time until she was truly convinced she felt no rise or fall of his chest or the slightest whisper of breath. She took her hand from his chest and encircled her own throat. She stared at him, wondering if she stared long enough would his eyes open. And if they did, would she be relieved or horrified.

With shaky fingers, she touched the side of Xerus' face and tears once again started to fall.

"Why, Xerus, oh god," she whispered. Her hands cupped his jaw and her fingers traced his mouth. "This didn't have to happen. Why couldn't you trust me?" Her tears hit his face as she lowered her head to his. Her vision swam. She clutched his face tighter and, before anyone could see, she dared kiss him. Likely dangerous as it was, Lana didn't think much of it nor care. This was her goodbye. She lifted her head and released her hands from him. As she straightened, she quickly placed the cover back over his face.

Wiping away the tears, she went to turn away when a glint caught her eye. Beside the table, on a small desk, was the bracelet she had given Xerus and the lock of her hair. She thought about taking them but decided against it. Walking back to her desk, Lana shut down her computer and gathered her things then left the facility, this time she assumed for good.

* * *

Back in her room, Lana began to pack her things. There was a ship leaving the base tomorrow morning and she figured she should be on it. There was nothing left here to do so there was no longer a reason to stay.

Except the problem was she couldn't seem to get herself moving fast enough. Half the time she was folding and refolding clothes and the other half she was staring into space. She checked her email several times but all she found were daily announcements, dates for a sporting event, and some unimportant news about the oil strikes off of TL40. She thought about taking a trip up to the city sector and just walking around for a few hours to get her mind off of everything, but she couldn't bring herself to go outside either.

It had been so long since she'd felt like this. So completely lost and uncertain. She thought about her father and what he used to say while they sailed on his boat.

The sea may be vast and frightening but there's always a way back to land somehow. You just have to choose a direction and just go, Lana.

And here she was lost at sea. And her father wasn't here to guide her. She had started one direction but now was hesitant to continue. She could leave Lazris and stay with her aunt on one of the civilian worlds until she got back on her feet or maybe even return to her original base. But none of those felt right.

One ill logic her father forgot to mention was that the land you found might not be the one you wanted to end up on.

So Lana continued to pack but with no real purpose. She thought about what would have happened if everything had gone right instead of wrong. If Xerus had passed the test. If he hadn't betrayed her. It would have taken a lot more time probably but she was willing to bet she would have gotten the chance to go in the cell and interact with him. He would have demanded she complete the favors she had promised and she would have done what she could even if it drove her crazy.

A soft ping signaled a message on her computer. When Lana went to check it she saw it was from Jacob.

Lana,

Thank you again for all you have done. I'm sorry it had to end like this. Know that I will give you any referral you need in the future. Despite all your efforts, you did a great job and I have no regrets in bringing you in. I will be off base for a week or two but as I said before do not hesitate to contact me.

As you might already know, the heads of level twelve are planning to do an autopsy on Asset X. I give you permission to view the autopsy if you so desire and be given any recorded data on the procedure and their findings.

Good luck to you and see you soon.

Officer Jacob Hartin

Lana signed off and sat back in her chair. She wanted to cry again but she fought back the tears. Xerus had been right all along. They would dissect him and likely cut him to pieces to study his body and internal organs. The thought of it made her sick for some reason even though she had seen autopsies many times before. She looked back at all her efforts to pack and sighed.

If you knew what was good for you, you would leave this place entirely. Leave and never come back.

Xerus' voice echoed in her head, dull and distant. It was like he wanted her to leave. But the funny thing was the biggest threat that she knew of was gone.

* * *

Lana decided not to take the ship that morning. Though something in her screamed she should go, another part of her fought to stay. As much as it might pain her, she wanted to be there for the autopsy which was said to take place tomorrow afternoon. After that, she told herself she would leave for good. She had most of her things packed up and ready to go and would leave on the next available ship, which departed usually every couple of days. She had called her aunt and was told she was more than welcome to stay for as long as she liked. The best plan Lana could think of was to stay at her aunt's place while looking into other possible research bases across the known map. There was said to be a base way off on the outer regions of the governed territory that was researching deep-sea creatures said to be intelligent enough to communicate. Since she had so much knowledge already on water-based creatures, she figured it was a solid chance. She also planned to take another trip back to the Gyda's territory, to see how things had progressed there.

Because in the back of her mind she thought that maybe, just maybe, she could find out more about Xerus' people. The Gyda never mentioned other races they knew of but maybe they would know of something if she dug far enough. And if they didn't know then maybe the deep-sea creatures of T19 would.

Now there wasn't much more to do but wait. Lana forced herself from her room and went up to the city sector. She thought about calling Nicole to join her one last time at one of the restaurants but quickly chose against it, figuring she was likely too busy with matters Lana couldn't know about. She didn't bother to try to get a hold of

Cole again either. Even to say goodbye. She walked around the sector and hung around, even had a drink at one of the bars, and bought a small trinket at one of the shops for her aunt.

When the digital sky above began to darken, Lana figured it was time she returned to her room and readied herself for tomorrow, even if the thought of it made her stomach twist.

Back in her room she dropped her aunt's gift on the bed and headed straight for the shower. As soon as the water was heated perfectly, she unclothed and stepped inside. She took a lot longer to wash up than usual, just letting the hot water pour down her back.

After about forty minutes, Lana went to press the button to turn off the water when the lights flickered and went from the usual bluish-white to a dull orange. With a confused frown, she turned off the water and, as the noise of the stream was cut off, a muffled beep could be heard outside the bathroom.

Lana stepped out and, as she dried off and wrapped a towel around her, she listened as the low beep continued, followed by the sound of someone speaking over an intercom. The sounds were coming from outside her unit.

As she moved back into her main room, she saw a flashing white light flickering from her computer. She turned it on and the screen flashed to a bright red. As Lana read the message on the screen her eyes widened and her heart dropped. Flinging off her towel, she dashed for her bag of clothes and put on the first set she found: a pair of panties and a sports bra followed by gray coveralls with the Lazris star on the left breast. She slipped them on and fumbled with the buttons then snatched her phone off the computer desk and shoved it into one of the side pockets along with her keycard. As she went to the door, she paused for a mere second, hoping to god that it was all just a mistake, or maybe just a drill. She opened her door and the noise which had been muffled before now blasted out at her, making her ears ring. The low beep was now a siren that whooped down the hall which was now a dim tunnel bathed in an orangish glow from the emergency lights overhead.

The siren quieted momentarily and a calm inhuman female voice rang out over it.

"Base lockdown procedures in place. All personnel must return to their units or make their way to the nearest secure saferooms on designated levels... The base is in full lockdown, all civilian and military personnel must go to units or saferooms. Security to take the planned protocol measures."

The siren started again. Lana took one step out into the hall and a large blast shook the base.

CHAPTER EIGHTEEN

Lana nearly fell to the ground as the earth trembled under her. She shot her hands out to catch the wall and keep her balance. The lights flickered and another set of bells rang as the security system went down. The door locks to each room went from blue to red indicating they were no longer in working order. So much for staying in her room.

A few others came tumbling out of their rooms, some in uniform others in sleepwear.

"What the hell?" one shouted. They all looked around in terror. A mirror image of what Lana was also feeling.

One man, still in uniform, calmly went to the door lock and examined it. "We aren't secure here, we have to go."

The others shouted and argued while Lana backed herself to the wall looking down each direction of the passageway. The elevators were still running from what she could tell, which was a good sign, but the blast which had happened from below could happen again and stop them altogether.

Lana's mind raced as she came to one bad assumption after another. The one that hit her the hardest was that she was absolutely certain whatever had caused the lockdown and the blast had something to do with level twelve.

"Come on everyone we have to go," said the man.

"Where?" asked another.

"Down to level ten," said the man.

"Are you nuts? We aren't going down! Did you not feel that?"

"We don't have a choice. That's the closest saferoom. And per protocol, this level is designated to that room."

Lana listened to them but didn't respond though she knew the uniformed man was right. Even if going down meant getting closer to the blast site.

Reluctantly they followed the man to the elevators, Lana looked behind her at the end of the hall before stepping into the elevator as if she feared to see something crawling around the corner and come racing down the hall.

But no, it couldn't be possible. There was no way any of the specimens could get out.

They rode in silence down and when the elevator doors opened to level ten they were met with a large hallway filled with people and chaos.

There were dozens if not hundreds of people packed inside, all forming at the door to the saferoom. Shouts and screams could be heard over the sirens and the repeated announcement from the female voice. Guards with guns order people back as they brought equipment in from another room and stored it into the saferoom first. People huddled together then broke in a wave as the officer allowed them to enter the saferoom a few groups at a time. The floor trembled again and a few people shrieked, officers pushed back a few to wait their turn.

"This is fucking crazy," someone said behind her. Lana couldn't agree more, but she was too speechless to react. She was pushed gently toward the saferoom until she squeezed through the door and found herself in a large concrete-floored and steel-walled room the size of a small gymnasium. There was a medical box in each corner along with several food crates and bed mats. The military equipment was set to the front side of the room while, to one corner, guards directed people away to make space as a set of men entered the room with a small group and brought them over to the sit by the medical box. The group was clearly injured in some way as one was being carried and a few others had bandages on their faces and arms. As Lana moved a little closer to see the group she recognized a few of them.

"Those are my colleagues," she said aloud. She pushed through the throng of people until she was standing before the injured group. Ben was resting Dahlia against the wall while Sarah, the lab tech, was huddled beside them in tears, another tech trying to comfort her.

As Lana stepped forward, a guard got in her way. "Maam, please step back–"

"Those are my colleagues," Lana repeated. "I work with them on twelve."

The guard glanced over at an officer who nodded his head. He stepped aside. "Alright, but keep out of the medical staff's way."

Lana nodded, noticing a few from level six opening up the medical box and gathering supplies. She hurried over to where Ben was searching through a bag he had placed on the ground while keeping Dahlia company.

"Ben, is everyone okay?"

As Ben swerved around to look at her, Lana nearly jumped at the sight of him. He was pale as a ghost, his eyes wide and his mouth slack-jawed. His fingers and legs trembled as he shifted over to sit beside Dahlia. "Lana...Jesus." He wiped his face with the back of his hand. "How did you...I thought you left."

Lana knelt beside him. She glanced at Dahlia who had her eyes shut, a bandage wrapped around her head, covering her left eye. "No, I was going to stay for...nevermind. What happened?"

Ben wiped at his face again then took out the e-cigarette from his pocket. With shaky hands, he put it in his mouth.

"Sir, no smoking in here," the officer said. Ben grimaced and cursed and shoved the cigarette back in his pocket.

"Fuck," he whispered combing a hand through his hair. "It's bad, it's so fucking bad."

Lana frowned and leaned forward, examining Dahlia a little closer, giving Ben time to calm down and explain.

"She'll be cool I think. The medical staff says the glass missed her eye," Ben said.

"I heard the blast."

Ben nodded. "Yeah. Those fucking asshole marines didn't even give anyone a chance to take cover."

Lana's brow wrinkled. "Marines?"

Ben shook his head. "Sorry. Galger, and his team." He rested his head against the wall and shut his eyes, taking deep breaths. "Those bastards shot up the whole place. Didn't even wait to get the others out first. I was coming back from a cig break when it all went down and saw everyone running out and heard the shots. We only just made it through to the elevators before they let off the bomb. And much good it fucking did."

Lana shivered. "I don't understand. Why would they..."

Ben's eyes shot open and he bent forward from the wall. "Can you assholes please shut that door already!" He yelled at the guards in front of the door who were still bringing in more equipment while waiting for the possibility for others to arrive seeking shelter. "Tell them they need to close the doors now!" Ben shouted at the officer standing near them.

"Sir, we have to wait for others."

"There are things–" Ben began to shout again then stopped himself. "Just keep the guards watching the halls will ya."

"They are patrolling, just calm down."

Ben dropped back to the wall with a *thunk* and mumbled something Lana didn't catch.

"Ben," Lana tried to get his attention. "Why would they do that?"

Ben finally looked her in the eye. "They got out," he said softly. "They all got out."

Lana went cold. "The specimens?"

Ben shut his eyes and nodded.

"How?"

"It was him," came a shrill voice next to her. Lana looked over and saw Sarah's tear-stained face twisted with fear. "It was him, I saw it."

"You don't know what you're talking about," Ben said with a detached voice.

"Like hell I don't," Sarah cried. "Just look at the feed for yourself." Sarah tugged away from the other tech who was trying to comfort her. She slid closer to Lana, her mouth trembling. "I saw Dr. Kingsley go into the computer. I watched him deactivate the security system. I–I would have said something b-but..."

"It wasn't him, it's not possible," Ben said.

Sarah slammed her fist on the ground. "How else could the units have been unlocked?" she shrieked at him through clenched teeth. "No one else has authorization to do that! And you know no one can hack the system!"

Ben shook his head again, refusing to believe. "Officer Torrence has access as well."

"Officer Torrence was the one who tried to stop him!" she nearly screamed.

"Miss, calm down," the standing officer ordered.

Sarah clamped her mouth shut and hot tears spilled down her face. She looked to Lana with tight desperation, grabbing her sleeve. "You have to believe me. I know it seems impossible that he would do such a thing, but I know what I saw. He let them out...he let them out!"

Calmly, Lana grasped the girl's hand, releasing it from her arm then holding it gently. As hard as it might be for others to believe, Lana knew the girl might be telling the truth. There had been something wrong with Cole for a while.

"Did you see his face?" Lana asked.

Sarah nodded her head.

"Was he bleeding? Like from his nose?"

Sarah nodded again. "And from his mouth. His eyes were messed up too. He looked..."

"Sick?"

Sarah bowed her head and let her hand slip from Lana's. Lana gazed back at Ben. "It was like what happened to Jeff, you remember?"

"That gangly guy who worked in the bacteria lab? Jesus, yea. But what does it mean?"

Lana shook her head. " I don't know. But whatever it is, it's compromised the facility."

Dahlia stirred and moaned and Lana placed a hand on her arm. When she opened her eye, she looked around and frowned. "What happened?"

Ben explained everything while Lana watched as the officers finally ordered the guards to shut the door to the saferoom for good.

"Did they at least hit any of them?" Dahlia asked as Ben told her Galger and his men had bombed the facility.

"Everything happened too quickly..." Sarah replied. " I think the giant ones didn't make it for sure but the others," she tried to wipe her tears away but it was futile, "they got out through the vents."

Dahlia closed her eyes.

"But it's okay, we are safe," Ben said. "We are in the saferoom now and they just closed the doors."

"You really think so?" Dahlia asked.

"What?"

"That we are safe?"

Ben glanced at Lana as if looking for reassurance. Lana tried to give them a hopeful smile despite the panic beginning to fester inside. "I'm sure we are."

As everyone began to settle in and blankets and food were distributed. Lana made a place for herself beside her coworkers on the wall. As Ben tended to Dahlia and Sarah lay sleeping in a curled position nearby, Lana watched in silence, trying to choke back the terror that was building in her.

With the specimens out of their cells, there was no telling how long they might be stuck inside the room. Along with the fear of one of them somehow getting in disturbing her thoughts, her mind also turned to even more depressing matters. With the facility bombed it meant everything would have been destroyed. Even what was left of Xerus' body. It shouldn't have bothered her, but it did.

Hours seemed to pass. The officers and guards had grouped together and had been talking for some time. They had managed to bring in a Scibot into the saferoom with them and so were able to use its computer interface to gain access to each level's status. They brought over an engineer from level five to deactivate certain security parameters in hopes that they could also gain access to live video feed. Something he had been working on for a couple of hours now.

With no clocks in the room, most relied on their watches and phones. Around 1 AM the officers dimmed the lights just enough so that some could hopefully sleep while still being able to see everything. Many laid out on the sleeping mats on the floor while those who knew they would get no kind of sleep stuck to the wall.

Lana was one of these and so she watched the others around her instead. Her eyes fell several times on the men at the door and those working on the Scibot then around to the ceiling and the walls. She noticed one vent by the wall. Though blocked by one of the crates, it still gave her anxiety.

When her gaze happened to shift over to check on Dahlia, she noticed Ben staring at her. He looked pale still and had been oddly silent for the past couple hours. She tried to smile at him and he looked away. She thought nothing of it until a few moments later she caught him eyeing her again.

"Everything okay?" she asked in a low voice.

Ben frowned, shifting uncomfortably. "There's something...I don't know."

"What?"

Ben let out a deep, shaky, breath and combed fingers through his hair. "There's something I need to show you. I didn't say anything at first because I didn't want you to freak out. Or any of the others for that matter. But especially you."

Lana's brows furrowed. "What is it?"

Ben rubbed his forehead as if thinking. "Fuck it," he whispered, and from a bag next to him, he took out a small pocket laptop and turned it on. "Officer Torrence wanted to keep this under wraps but there doesn't seem much point now." He tapped his fingers along the keyboard, bringing up a single file.

"Before everything basically hit the shitter I was just about to get off shift when...this happened." Ben brought up a video recording of the lab. Before he hit the play button he looked at her seriously. "Please try not to scream."

He hit the button and Lana watched closely. There was no sound, just an image of the lab from above. Torrence wasn't at his desk and only a few guards were at the door. Dr. Yanlin and two other techs were working in the lab along with Ben as the lone engineer who she could see working on his computer in the far right corner. This was no surprise as the night shift was usually pretty scarce of people, and even the great Officer Torrence had to sleep sometime.

Dr. Yanlin moved away from his desk and gestured for the techs to follow him. They moved over to the station of medical equipment where Xerus' body was still resting on the table. They had removed the sheet and, with gloved hands, they carefully prodded him and moved his head. One of the techs picked up a metal rod and placed it under Xerus' tail. Dr. Yanlin and the third tech moved to each side of the table getting ready to move it.

Lana knew what they were doing. They were getting ready to place his body in a cleansing chamber, to wash down his body before the autopsy. Then, if she remembered correctly, he would have then been placed in an isolation pod to keep him staying fresh until the surgery. She stared down at Xerus' lifeless body and a hard lump grew in her throat. She wished it wasn't so hard to look at him.

The team moved the rolling table around and started to make their way to the cleansing chamber. Nothing seemed out of the ordinary until they stopped in front of the chamber and were about to drop him in.

They seemed to hesitate dropping him in. As Dr. Yanlin bent forward to examine his body again they all simultaneously leaped back as if struck by a bolt of lightning. One tech slammed into a cart of equipment knocking it over and the other fell to the ground and crawled away. Dr. Yanlin was waving his arms frantically for the guards.

Their panic was justified. Because Xerus had moved.

Lana grew as still as a shadow as she watched Xerus rise from the table. His movements were slow at first as if he were just waking up, but as soon as the guards had their guns drawn and pointed at him, he leaped from the table and bolted away. Brilliant white light burst over the screen as shots fired in his direction. But, from what could be seen, it was already too late. Xerus had slipped into the ventilation system.

Ben started to say something but Lana didn't hear it. She didn't scream. Just like he asked. Instead, she felt herself falling forward and her vision going black.

CHAPTER NINETEEN

"Stand back and let me see her," came a muffled voice in the darkness. A hand cupped Lana's jaw, tilting her head back. She groaned as something was pressed into her left nostril and a puff of air followed by a strong bitter scent stung her nose. Lana opened her eyes and the fuzzy, black vision began to clear. She felt hands on her shoulders as she was laid out on her side with her knees to her chest. "She'll be fine, just a little faint. Keep watch and give her some water." Lana saw the nurse step around her and leave to check on others. She blinked several times and swallowed, her throat dry. A heavier hand gently landed on her arm and her eyes rolled upward to see Ben looking down at her.

"Lana, fuck, I'm sorry, I honestly didn't realize it would mess you up that bad."

Lana licked her lips and tried to lift her head. There was a brief instance of lightheadedness but nothing more severe. Slowly she lifted the rest of her body until she was sitting hunched over. A water bottle came into her field of vision and she took it gladly, taking large gulps until the bottle was half empty. She exhaled and gave the bottle back to Ben who placed it on the ground. "Thank you," she mumbled.

"Hey, no problem. You okay?"

Lana closed her eyes and forced a nod even though she was far from okay. As soon as the fog cleared and her mind was back up to speed she had to fight down the panic that was dangerously close to spilling over and making her lose control. She took a few deep breaths, trying to keep from being sick.

"Where, um...where did you get the footage at?" It really didn't matter but Lana needed something to focus while trying to calm her nerves.

Ben shifted beside her. "I transferred the video files from the recording program. I had the password to access it in case something needed a fix. Figured in case I get called in for questioning I'd have something to bargain with."

"And you said...that Torrence wanted it kept secret?"

"Yea. It was fucked up but he forced us to keep quiet. Officer Galger and his team went out in secret looking for it. Asset X I mean. They were so focused on that for those several hours they didn't think about anything else. Which was probably why this all happened. I don't know if I can still believe it was Dr. Kingsley who did it though. Just seems too crazy to believe, but, shit, I don't know." He coughed a little and cleared his throat. "I saw the team briefly when I went to leave and they came back empty-handed so it's probably good to assume that, you know, the alien is still..."

Lana opened her eyes and her gaze immediately fell on the vent behind the crate at the back wall. Why did all the vents have to be so large?

Her body began to tremble. "I have to get out of here," she whispered.

"Why?" Ben asked.

Because if they all knew what she knew they would be trying to escape the base, not sitting locked up in a room that would barely keep them secure. Lana looked over at him. "We aren't safe."

Before he could say anything, Lana got to her feet and began heading toward the officers and guards stationed near the door. They were all huddled together, nine in total–four officers and five guards, still conversing softly as she stumbled past mats of sleeping people.

One of the officers, a tall, dark-complected man, saw her and signaled for the others to be quiet. "Maam, is there an issue?"

"We have to get out," she said.

They all went still and gave her an odd look.

"No, ma'am, I think you are confused–"

"I'm not confused. We are in danger here." Lana said loud enough for others to catch notice. A few turned their heads in her direction while some sat up on their mats. "We need to get off base. The elevators must still be working, if we are quick we can make it to the ships and–"

"Maam, we are under strict orders not to leave this room."

"Do you even know what's happening?" Lana snapped.

The guards shifted and looked away. The officer held her gaze. "We are acquiring information and will have a report soon."

"It's unnecessary because I can already tell you. We are in serious danger," Lana said.

"What sort of danger?" Lana looked around and saw a warehouse employee and a few technicians sitting up, listening with interest. The one who spoke looked young and was clearly a new recruit with a shaved head and slightly unkempt uniform.

"Everything is fine, please go back to sleep," the officer said to them then looked back at her. "I think you need to go back over to the wall now."

Lana clenched her jaw then turned fully around to the dozen or so pairs of eyes watching. "Please, listen. I come from level twelve. There has been an accident and there are specimens that have escaped and some are very smart and they will find a way in."

The officer gestured to the guards to grab her. "Maam, do not spout false accusations."

"They aren't false!" she tore her arm from one of the guards trying to take hold of her.

"What sort of specimens?" one of the technicians asked.

"Like animals?" asked another.

More and more people were beginning to stir and listen in. Lana saw Ben standing up by the wall and Sarah watching with wild eyes.

"They aren't human but they are more advanced than the animals you know. And some are...hunters. They see us as prey and will come looking for us."

The crowd murmured and a few shook their heads. Some looked confused. Others, frightened.

"Enough. Restrain her," the officer commanded.

Lana felt herself being grabbed from behind. She looked again at her colleagues. "Ben, tell them. Show them the footage."

Ben stood there, pale and dumbfounded. He opened his mouth as if to form words as heads turned in his direction. "I, uh, I don't know..."

The officer stepped in front of her. "Sir." He gestured for Ben to come forward. Reluctantly Ben made his way through the groups of people. "If you have information that concerns this situation," the officer said to him in a low voice, "we need to look it over."

Ben glanced at Lana then turned back to the officer. "Yea, alright." He went back to his bag and brought it over.

The guards released Lana momentarily as Ben showed the officers the footage. The officers' expressions varied but they did well to keep their emotions hidden from the others.

"I think we should call the heads," one of them whispered.

"We are supposed to wait for their response on what to do next," hissed another.

"The others need to know."

They each glanced back at Ben and Lana. The tall officer spoke to Ben, "Can you send this file to us?"

Ben nodded and began working on his laptop.

"So do you understand now?" Lana said.

The tall officer glared back at her. "We aren't leaving this room. Not until we have confirmation that it is safe to move."

Lana shook her head in angry disbelief. "Then we are just waiting for the slaughter. You see those vents over there?" Lana pointed. "They can get through those."

The officers looked at each other and the tall one nodded. "Everyone please go back to sleep, everything is fine," the tall officer announced to those listening.

"You can't be serious," Lana seethed.

"Maam, we don't need panic. Go back to the wall," he said to her. The officer commanded the guards to take up heavy equipment and stash it over to the other side of the room to hide the vent.

A few grumbled but didn't argue as they were forced to move. Some looked at her with curiosity but remained silent. They did as the officers ordered and no one asked any more questions.

"Come on, Lana, just give them time. Some are still in shock, you know?" Ben said trying to gently coax her back over to their sitting spot by the wall. "And the officer is right, we really don't need panic right now."

Lana allowed him to lead her back to the wall, but she still wasn't happy. Far from it. With the revelation that Xerus was somehow alive, the words he spoke in their final moments together rang out like a death toll. He would come for her. She knew. And he would decimate anything and everything in his way. Forget the other specimens lurking around. If Xerus found out where she was, the others were goners. And even then it might not matter. He had said himself he would kill every human. She didn't want to believe it then and she didn't want to now.

But if she got away from everyone and they could make their way to the loading docks, they might have a chance.

Lana slumped down next to Dahlia who opened her eyes and gazed at her.

"What's going on?" she asked.

Lana fixed her eyes up at Ben who met her stare. She looked down at Dahlia. "I tried to warn people about what happened on twelve but the officers won't move us."

Dahlia groaned as she shifted herself into a seating position. "Why do we need to move? Aren't we safe here?"

"Not anymore."

"Lana—"

"They need to know, Ben," Lana snapped. Then said more softly, "I'm sorry but we can't afford any more secrets. People's lives are at stake."

Ben cursed softly. He took a seat nearby, putting his back to them and eyeing the officers while sneaking a hit from his e-cigarette. Lana turned back to Dahlia.

"Asset X is alive," she said in a low voice.

Dahlia's eyes widened. "That's not possible," she whispered.

"I know."

"He had no vitals, he wasn't breathing, how could he...?"

Lana shook her head. "I don't know, I don't..." she frowned and a thought came to her. A memory of her and Xerus' sessions. Of them talking about his physical traits.

And then she knew.

"His pores. Oh god, he had told me straight to my face and I didn't even think..." Lana breathed. Dahlia gave her a confused look. "He has this way of absorbing oxygen into his skin. He must have absorbed enough to slow his heart rate so low our machines couldn't detect it. And he didn't need his lungs for breath with the oxygen already stored in his body."

"He could do that?"

"He said his kind used it to traverse through water and low oxygen environments." Lana rubbed her temples. "I would have never believed though that he could use the trait to such extreme measures."

"Well," Dahlia said. "We know now. Too bad we hadn't figured it out in time. Not that it would have mattered. He would have just been let out like the others. But guess one thing he can't do is predict the future."

Lana couldn't help laughing. "Yea. One thing."

"Do you think he can somehow get in here?"

"I don't think. I know. He will find a way. We need to get out of the base entirely if we want to avoid any encounters and remain unscathed."

"But they aren't letting anyone leave, correct?"

Lana shook her head. "No.

"Even though you've told them about what happened?"

"Pretty much."

Dahlia closed her eyes and sighed. "It's no surprise. They have to stick to the mandatory procedures. Emergency or no." She slid back down and curled up on the mat given to her. "All we can do is wait."

Lana pursed her lips but decidedly said nothing, letting Dahlia fall back to sleep. But inside she was on the edge of erupting. She was done with waiting.

* * *

Everything was quiet for some time after and somehow Lana was able to gain an hour of sleep, albeit not deep by any means. When she opened her eyes, she noticed the officers grouped tightly around the Scibot, watching its screen. They must have finally accessed the live video feeds.

Quietly, Lana unlatched from the wall and crept over, pretending to grab water at one of the food supply crates. From her vantage point, she could see they were flipping through different screens showing different hallways, corridors, and rooms. Most were completely vacant. Some of the rooms had been destroyed, with debris scattered all over the floor but no one was in sight. She couldn't quite follow which levels they were observing until they switched the feed to that of an entrance hall and she recognized it immediately.

"The warning call was from here I think," said one of the officers. "Shit. Looks like we aren't taking any of the injured to medical..."

Lana watched with horror as several of the blue raptors from unit five traversed the main foyer and halls of level six. The sliding door was ripped open and hanging off the door frame behind them. The officers flipped through other sections of the facility to discover some parts destroyed and others still intact but with raptors slipping in and out of view. Broken lights flickered and a few pipes, torn from the walls, belted out steam. They flipped to another view and Lana saw the door to Nicole's study wrenched open, showing darkness within.

Lana pressed a hand to her mouth so as not to make a sound.

Nicole. Oh, god had she been in there when the raptors came? Lana hadn't even had a moment to think about her friend in all the chaos until now. Silently, she slipped back over to one corner with few people and took out her phone. She selected Nicole's number and held the phone to her ear, praying that Nicole hadn't been in the medical bay at the time. That she had been off work and in her room.

A low ring sounded for several moments, far longer than usual. Lana was about to hang up when she heard a sharp click on the other end.

"L-Lana," came a soft, hushed voice laced with panic.

Lana clutched her phone tightly and turned her head toward the wall. "Nicole?" she said in a low voice. "Nicole, where are you?"

There was a low moan, then the rough grating of metal. "I-I'm in one of the operating rooms on six."

Lana closed her eyes. "Okay. Are you secure in one of the rooms?"

"The door is shut now...I don't think they can get in but..." There was another low moan.

Lana opened her eyes. "Are you hurt?"

"I-I think so. I was running and was able to get inside before one of those things got in but..."

"Can you move?"

"I don't know." There was a sound of shifting and a grunt then Nicole's breathless voice. "I don't think I can. I think my leg is broken. One of the machines fell and pinned me."

"Okay...okay. Nicole, we will come to get you, don't worry. I'm in one of the saferooms and will tell the officers to send help."

"I-I can hear them," Nicole whimpered. "They are outside the door. Lana, oh, god, I'm sorry, this is my fault," she cried.

"It's not. How could it be?" Lana said.

"I knew. I knew something wasn't right with him. I should have stopped him."

Lana frowned, biting her lip. "With your uncle?"

"Yes. The base is compromised."

"I know, with the specimens. I'm trying to convince them of that but they won't listen."

"Not with just the specimens." Nicole's voice shook. "I should have told you but he forced my silence. There's something else. Something–"

There was a loud bang on the other end and a shrill shriek.

"Nicole? Nicole!"

A sharp click and the line went dead. Lana cursed. She tried to call back but there was no response.

"Dammit!"

"Hey keep it down," someone grumbled nearby.

Lana jammed her phone back into her pocket and made for the group of officers.

"We need to get help to level six. They are in trouble," she said as she entered their circle.

The tall, dark, officer looked over at her, exasperated. "How did you know...nevermind. Maam, you need to let us do our job."

"And that is what? To wait here for orders?"

"There is a team outside who is handling the situation," he said.

Lana could guess which team. But Galger and his men weren't looking to help people. They were out to hunt down every non-human target they could find.

"There has to be someone else. Another team that can help six. Can't you call someone and–"

The officer swerved on her, getting up in her face. "Get back to the wall now, or I will have you escorted there."

At the corner of her eye, Lana saw the guards stepping closer, ready to manhandle her back to her spot. Lana clenched her jaw and stared the officer down before turning away.

Damn them. But what could she do?

She slunk back over to the corner and attempted to call Jacob. It was no surprise when he didn't pick up. Lana slid to the ground and crunched into a ball, placing her head between her knees. Nicole was running out of time. She was either about to be raptor food or already was.

Lana sat for a long moment desperately trying to think of a plan when a loud knocking started at the saferoom door.

CHAPTER TWENTY

The guards immediately had their guns drawn and pointed at the door. The officers held their hands up, ordering them to wait. The knocking came again with a loud, heavy thud, waking most of the people near the door.

Lana's head shot up as she stared wide-eyed at the entrance. She rose and peeled from the wall to move closer to the entrance.

"Who's there?" called one officer.

There was silence and the officers looked at each other and the guards moved to each side of the door.

"Identify yourself!"

A pause and then, "This is General Vearez. I order you to open this door."

The men went still as did Lana. What was the general doing on level ten of all places? This couldn't be right. Lana hadn't been too sure but she could have sworn he was supposed to leave the base.

The officers looked to one another again in shock and likely wondering the same but they didn't hesitate for long. One officer started for the door latch while the others stepped back. "Right away, sir," the tall officer called, waving the guards away from the door.

Just as they were about to unlock the door, the overpowering scent of coffee hit Lana like a smack in the face. Her heart leaped in her throat and a shriek escaped her lips.

"Don't!" she shouted, throwing out her arms. "Don't open the door! It's not him!"

The officer about to press the button to unlatch the door froze. His eyes leaped to her then peered at the others with uncertainty.

"What are you doing, open the door!" snapped the tall officer.

Lana reached them and tried to block the door when two guards restrained her. "Don't do it. It's not him!" she repeated.

"I've had enough of her. Tie her up and put her by the equipment."

Lana cried and fought as the guards attempted to put her on the ground. By now the whole room was awake and watching but none moved to defend her.

"Please you have to believe me! He can mimic other's voices!"

"She's crazy. Officer Marks open that door for the general now!" ordered the tall one.

Officer Marks, who was at the door latch, paused for only a second before slamming his palm on the button. There was the sound of grinding and a dull click and the door began to slowly slide open.

The door stood wide open and, beyond it, there was no one. The large hall lay empty. Lana held her breath as the guards stepped out and looked around.

"There's no one," said one guard, standing just outside the doorway. He turned to look at them. "Sir, there's no one her—"

A spiny tail whipped out from above and hit the guard square in the chest causing him to go flying.

The others shouted and turned up their guns and started blasting.

The gym filled with the sounds of bullets and screams. People jumped up and began scrambling away, like a huge wave breaking out from the center. The guards who had Lana let her go in order to help the others. They drew their weapons and started firing.

Lana crawled away then fumbled to her feet. As she straightened, she caught Ben struggling to help Dahlia to her feet while Sarah lay in a ball on the floor as the other lab tech left her behind. Lana flew over to them and took Dahlia's other arm to support her.

"Take the elevators up to the city sector and get to the docks," Lana yelled over the gunfire.

"We need to get to the medical bay," Ben shouted.

"It's compromised." Lana glanced at the door and saw the guards were out of the room, firing down the hall and people were fleeing. "Let's go! Come on, Sarah, get up!"

As Sarah got up to follow, they rushed for the door and snuck around the corner, heading toward the elevators. To Lana's annoyance, everyone had jammed themselves at the entrance, waiting to get in a car. She looked back behind her and saw the soldiers firing aimlessly into the dark hall and people still rushing away but she saw no glimpse of Xerus though she knew he was there in the fray. Desperate, she searched around until she glimpsed through an open doorway across a warehouse in the cargo elevator.

"Come with me, come on." Lana tugged Dahlia's arm, imploring the group to follow her.

"Where are we going?" Ben asked.

Lana pointed to the cargo elevator. "That should take you straight to the docks."

Ben didn't fight her as they made their way over. Sarah, though sobbing, followed closely behind. They hurried into the dark warehouse full of tank-sized crates and motionless robots until they reached the hulking elevator at the back. Lana let go of Dahlia for a moment so she could pull the latch and press the button for the elevator. They could hear the elevator moving down as they waited. The shouts of the guards grew closer and when Lana shot her eyes around, she saw one of them go flying to land in the hall. When their elevator car came to a stop, the door slid open along with a metal slide and Lana allowed the others to step in before her. Gunfire grew louder but less frequent though the shouts never ceased. Lana could see some of the guards from the warehouse door as they backed away, some fleeing with the others into the main elevators.

Heart pounding, Lana hit the button to close the elevator door. As it began to slide close, Xerus came into view, taking up the door-frame to the warehouse. He towered over the others even with legs bent. His head was turned to search the crowd of screaming people until he twisted around and saw her. And their eyes locked. She stared, body draining of heat, as he bent his head and his eyes tore into her, full of fire and something else she couldn't guess. He didn't bother to rush for her as the door shut completely but Lana backed away regardless, fear twisting her stomach.

"Fuck," Ben whispered. They were all shaking. Lana took a few deep breaths then went over to the level pad and pressed two buttons. She then went back over to the others and carefully supported Dahlia once more with her body. The cargo elevator moved way slower than the rest as it was huge and heavy. It trembled underneath their feet and made a low humming sound as it rose upward. It felt like years before the elevator finally began to slow and come to a stop.

"Why are we stopping here?" Ben asked. "I thought you said six wasn't safe."

Lana gently grasped Dahlia's arm then gestured for Sarah to take her. They swapped positions, with Sarah holding the woman up. They all looked to Lana as she stepped to the door. "I will meet you at the docks. But I need to help a friend first."

"You're going in alone?" Ben asked.

Lana nodded. "I shouldn't be long. Take the elevators up to the top and don't stop."

The elevator opened to darkness and slow flashing yellow lights. The medical bay warehouse was empty save for a few pieces of equipment. Lana stepped out and peered around but saw no move-ment. She turned back to them and forced a smile. "It's okay. See you guys."

They said nothing, only looked at her gravely, as if they didn't expect to see her soon. Lana turned from them and started to walk away.

"Lana, wait."

Lana looked back and saw Dahlia straighten. "If you are unfortunate to see Asset T...use fire."

Lana gave her a single nod. The doors to the elevator began to slide close.

"And whatever you do, don't get caught."

The door shut and Lana stood silent and still in the dark. She heard the elevator moving upward, its humming noise slipping away. She turned from there and made for the warehouse exit.

Beyond the room, Lana saw the flickering of lights down each hall, debris and equipment scattered over the floors forcing her to weave. There was no sound save for the soft beeps of machines in some of the rooms. Lana tried to keep to the wall for balance, letting her hand slide across, trying her best not to make noise as she felt glass crunch against her feet and metal scrape along the floor. She found a pair of medical scissors on the ground. Grasping it firmly in her free hand, she crept down one hall and carefully peered around the corner.

There was no one in sight, not even security. Lana quickly made her way down another hall and turned once, looking up at the cameras every so often to gauge their angle. When she made it to one end and went to turn another corner, she quickly jumped back, pressing herself against the wall as a blue raptor whisked by at the other end. Heart pounding in her ears, Lana checked the hall again and saw the raptor had disappeared down another way.

"You can do this, Lana," she whispered to herself and with a deep breath, pushed herself from the wall and scurried down the hallway.

That's when she saw her first set of dead bodies. Limbs bent the wrong way, slumped against the wall and curled on the floor, blood soaking the ground. The scent of blood made her gag and Lana clamped a hand tightly over her mouth as she stepped carefully over the corpses. Some partially devoured. She dared not investigate but continued on. Hoping she didn't find Nicole in the same awful state next.

As she came to a larger waiting area, she spied a sign pointing her to surgery. A few Scibots lumbered about aimlessly as she passed and she could see into various rooms through wide windows. She crouched low as she went by one in particular where a few blue raptors were feasting on remains of a medical tech.

The door to surgery slid open and Lana stepped though, recognizing the space immediately from the video feed. She went over to the door to the operation room and saw it had deep gashes down its metal front but the door remained intact. Relieved, Lana pressed on the door latch and the door shuddered open only to stop midway. Lana squeezed herself through and stepped into the dark room, it's only light a blue glow from a prep room in the back.

"Nicole," Lana whispered. "Nicole, are you here?"

There was no response and Lana tried her best to step lightly, her arms outstretched. When her eyes began to adjust to the room around her, she could see the operating table at the center and the medical equipment surrounding it.

There was the sound of grating metal against the floor and Lana swerved around, scissors raised.

"L-Lana?" Nicole cried softly.

Lana dropped the scissors on the ground and rushed to her friend who, by what she could tell in the dim light, was pinned under some kind of large robotic machine. She crouched down beside her and took her hand as Nicole reached for her.

"Oh, god, you're really here," Nicole breathed.

"I came to get you," Lana said.

"You shouldn't be here. Those creatures are still outside. And the base is—"

"I know. But I wasn't going to leave you here." Lana gently tugged her hand away and bent down so she could examine the machine pinned against Nicole's leg.

"I'm going to try to lift this," she said. "It might hurt. Be careful not to make too much noise."

Nicole nodded and seemed to brace herself as Lana grasped the bottom of the machine firmly and, with all her strength, began to pull it upward.

The machine was extremely heavy and Lana could only move it enough to give Nicole an inch of leeway in order to slide herself out. When she was free, Lana tried her best to set the machine down as carefully as possible, only making a dull thud. She could see Nicole's face twisted with pain. When Lana gazed down at her leg she could see her foot was bent the wrong way.

"Think it's safe to say it's definitely broken," Lana said.

Nicole laughed softly then winced in pain.

"I'll try to carry you to the cargo elevator and we can take it up to–"

"No," Nicole shook her head. "No, Lana, you don't understand, it's too late now. We can't leave."

Lana frowned at her in confusion. "Why?"

Nicole shifted, trying to get up and Lana grabbed her arm and wrapped a hand around her waist, pulling her off the floor.

"I'll explain once you get me to my office," Nicole said breathing heavily, beads of sweat forming on her face.

"Nicole, you can't be serious."

"I am."

"There are others waiting to get to the docks," Lana protested.

Nicole shook her head weakly. "They will have the ships shut down. By now they know what's happening and they won't allow anyone to go."

Lana stared at Nicole's face and could see she was completely serious.

"So then where can people go?" Lana asked.

Nicole moaned, bending forward and Lana struggled to keep her upright as Nicole balanced on one foot. "They can stay in the safer-ooms but they might not be secure for long. Otherwise...I don't know."

Lana frowned. She thought of Dahlia and the others and what they would do, but she could do nothing for them now. "Is your office safe?" she asked.

Nicole nodded. "Yes. I have security measures in place. We should hurry."

Lana agreed. She could hear in the distance gunfire, likely coming from the level below them. And the shrill calls of the raptors close by. She tightened her hold around Nicole and slowly walked her out of the operation room. Nicole hobbled along at an excruciating pace and Lana thought to carry her but worried she wouldn't have the strength and might hurt Nicole more. So she continued to walk along with her as they slunk down the hall, Nicole pointing her in the right direction.

By some miracle, they got to her office without a single encounter. Lana brought Nicole over to the keypad so she could open the door. As soon as the door slid open, Lana rushed inside and Nicole quickly let the door close and lock behind them.

"Over...to...my desk," Nicole gestured. Lana did as she asked and carefully sat Nicole down in her chair. Wiping sweat from her brow, Nicole turned on her computer and logged into the database.

"We need to find a way to wrap your leg," Lana said, looking down at the mangled ankle with worry. "Do you have any gauze?"

Nicole pointed at a small medical box on the wall. Lana went over and took out some wrappings. As Nicole accessed files on her computer, Lana went to binding her foot as best she could.

"Sorry, I didn't do the best job."

"Don't worry about it, thank you," Nicole said.

Lana took a seat by the desk. "So the lockdown means no one can leave. I get that. But something tells me there's another reason isn't there?"

Nicole shifted in her seat, wincing as she moved her leg. "Yes."

"You said the base was compromised but not just by the specimens."

Nicole closed her eyes and frowned. "Yes. There is another threat. Something me and my uncle had been keeping under wraps."

"It's some sort of sickness?"

Nicole opened her eyes and looked at Lana sadly. "In a way, yes. It is a parasite. Found on planet 421. We were studying it there, taking samples. it was being transported here when...When Asset X attacked the camp. The day we brought it into the base was the day Xerus was captured and brought as well."

Lana grew still, her hands tightening on her lap. "His enemy...is all around," she whispered.

Nicole nodded. "I was assigned to help my uncle study it here. To test it. To experiment how it infected and grew. We called it Asset S or Spectre. Once it gets into a living being it slowly takes over mind and body." Nicole clicked open a file, bringing up a video. It was of Dr. Grimmer sitting in a small room. She started the video and Lana leaned forward, watching carefully.

"Is this Dr. Grimmer I'm still speaking to?" Cole's voice came through the feed in a clipped tone.

Dr. Grimmer smiled, his fists clenching and unclenching. He looked on the verge of death, his body was skeletal, his skin pale. There was crusted blood under his nose and his pupils were black. "No," he croaked.

There was a pause. "Is this Spectre?" Cole asked.

Dr.Grimmer bowed his head. "This body...won't last. So weak. We need better."

"Dr. Grimmer was already a sick man. Though he didn't know it yet."

Dr. Grimmer scowled. "Let us out."

Before Cole could respond Dr. Grimmer bent forward and threw up blood all over himself, Black blood like oil. The video stopped there and Lana felt sick.

"He had been here all this time," Lana said in shock. "He was sick. And Xerus had known." She caught Nicole's eyes. "And so did you."

Nicole looked on the verge of tears. "I did. I did but I couldn't tell you or anyone. It was mine and Cole's project and only a few chosen others assisted us."

"Like that lab tech, Jeff. He had it." Lana's expression darkened. "Is he dead too?"

Nicole nodded. "Some die. Others...become its puppet. It takes over until there is nothing left of who the person once was. We only discovered it on planet 421 because a soldier had been the first to be infected by it. Cole wanted to know more so he signed to have it studied and brought here. It was a mistake. A horrible mistake," Nicole cried softly. She took a deep breath and Lana waited for her to continue. "W-when he started to display signs...I tried to tell him he needed to get examined. I really did. But I couldn't get him to budge. I was able to convince him to keep away from others, to stick to his room or the virus lab, but he refused to stop his work. And now...oh, god now he must be under Spectre's full control. He let the specimen's out because he knew that if such a catastrophic situation took place the base would be forced into lockdown. That way the parasite can attempt to get to other hosts easier."

Lana couldn't believe what she was hearing and yet she wanted to smack herself for not realizing what was going on sooner. There had been so many signs, but she had been so focused on helping Xerus she hadn't tried harder to contemplate what was happening around her save for the changes in Cole.

"So the base is essentially a ticking time-bomb," Lana said. "And when it infects everyone, then what?"

Nicole inclined her head, biting her lip. "My guess? It will take the ships. And spread farther."

Lana looked back at the computer screen, at the distorted image of Dr. Grimmer and his trail of blood. "Is there any way to tell if someone has it?"

"Besides the obvious symptoms?" Nicole shook her head. "We had machines that could test early signs but they are all down at twelve which I gather is an impossible mess at this point and too dangerous to enter."

"And how long after signs is the person completely gone?"

Nicole shrugged. "It's hard to say. Everyone is different. Cole was able to keep control of himself for an impressively long time. Dr. Grimmer not as long. And Jeff was nearly instantaneous. We hadn't gathered enough data yet as to know why some cave quicker than others."

Lana looked down at her hands, feeling angry heat rise in her neck and face. A part of her wanted to scream at Nicole. To shake her till her eyes popped out. Despite her best qualities, she had allowed this deadly parasite into the base. Had kept it secret when things were starting to get out of hand instead of taking action. Like going against her uncle. She was either too subservient or too proud, or both.

"Well if we can't leave base then I guess our best option is to hide and stay away from as many people as possible," Lana said in a low voice, refusing to meet her friend's eyes. "Do you know how it spreads at least?"

"Usually through blood or saliva. It's not airborne thank god, and if my knowledge so far is correct only once someone displays symptoms are they susceptible to transfer the parasite."

"And there's no way to flush it from someone's system? No way to get rid of it?" Lana said, her gaze darting back up to Nicole.

Nicole wiped away a few tears and looked at the computer screen. "No. Only through death."

A sharp, ear-splitting screech cut through the silence of the room. Lana jumped up and Nicole yelped as their eyes shot to the door.

"We have to go. We can't stay here," Lana said.

"They can't get in." Nicole's voice cracked.

"Those raptors are smarter than they look. Together they might find a way given enough time. We need to get out of level six."

"Where can we go?" Nicole asked, her voice rising in panic.

"I think we should still try to make for the docks. Or at least get to the city sector and find a way to hide there. That way we are closer to the surface, closer when help arrives. Someone by now has surely contacted another base close by."

Nicole grasped Lana's sleeve as she went to help her up. "We can't let Spectre spread. We need to let others know. So when help arrives they won't let everyone out."

Lana frowned then wrapped an arm around Nicole's waist to help her stand. "We will figure something out. For now, let's just go."

Nicole didn't argue as she rested her arm around Lana's neck and used her body for support as they hobbled toward the door.

"We will have to take the main elevators since they are closer," Lana said as they paused to ready themselves.

"Wait, I have a pocket knife in my desk drawer," said Nicole. "Take it in case..."

Lana nodded and, letting Nicole use the wall momentarily for support, she hurried over to the desk and rummaged through the drawers until she found a small red pocket knife. Flipping open the blade, she went back over to Nicole and supported her once more. With deep breaths, Nicole unlocked the door and it slid open. They paused to peer out, making sure there was nothing about to jump out at them.

"There's something I forgot to mention," Lana said before allowing Nicole to step out. "Xerus is alive. And he's...hunting me."

Nicole stared at Lana with her mouth agape. "Oh, god...how?"

"He had tricked us. But it doesn't matter now. I just needed you to know that." Lana couldn't stop the trembling in her limbs. "So one more thing to worry about I guess." She laughed nervously.

There was a small tremor and Lana had to quickly keep her balance to not have them both fall over. The lights flickered and a low beep echoed down the hall. Lana tightened her grip around Nicole and staggered out into the passage. They took a sharp left and did their best to step over and weave around equipment, a couple of times Lana having to use all her strength to lift Nicole over fallen debris. When they rounded a corner and saw the foyer with the elevators in sight, Lana didn't hesitate but made straight for them.

Lana punched the elevator button with her knife-holding hand then swerved around with Nicole so the elevators were behind them. Her knife at the ready, she waited for either the elevator to come or for one of the blue raptors to make an appearance. She could hear their calls getting closer.

"Lana..." Nicole said nervously.

"It's coming," Lana replied. She could hear the hum of the elevator car now.

When she heard a ding and felt a puff of air at her back from the elevator doors opening, Lana shuffled inside. She pressed the button to close the doors. As they began to slide close, a raptor leaped out from one hallway and came charging at them.

Lana cursed and Nicole shouted in surprise as the raptor closed the distance and shot its hand through the small opening to grab at them. Lana kicked at it as it tried to jam its head through, forcing the elevator doors to open. Lana cried out and blindly struck at the creature with her knife. It slashed its razor talons out and caught Lana's leg. Lana screamed at the searing pain as its talon hooked her pant leg and sliced downward. As the raptor tried to drag her out, Lana attacked its arm and sliced its snout. The raptor hissed and backed away as blood gushed from its nose, it barked in annoyance as it shook its head.

With pure adrenaline, Lana forced herself up on her knees and slammed her hand on the elevator buttons, uncaring what floor got picked as long as the doors shut. The raptor came back again, but this time Lana was ready. She swept her arm outward and focused toward its face. Somehow she managed to cut close to its eye. Though not before it sliced her arm. The raptor yelped and swerved back and the elevator doors began to close again. Just before the doors shut completely, two more raptors appeared. They surged forward but didn't catch the doors in time. Lana dropped backward to lay on the ground by Nicole's feet as the elevator shook from the raptors pounding against the metal.

Lana felt Nicole grasp her shoulder and Lana tried to sit up as the elevator began to move, going down instead of up. The shrill cries of the raptors died out until only Lana and Nicole's harsh breaths filled the quiet.

"Your bleeding, let me see," Nicole said with a pained expression as she carefully moved her bad leg away. Lana shifted to her side so they could both look. Both her arm and leg were bleeding pretty bad, her leg worse than her arm. The warm liquid trickled down her foot and hand, dripping onto the floor.

Before Nicole could examine her better, the elevator came to a stop on floor eight. The doors opened to reveal a dark wide passage leading to a large warehouse beyond. Level eight was where they stored and fixed bots from Scibots to storage bots.

The level was deathly quiet. Lana went to reach for the elevator buttons again when Nicole stopped her.

"Hold on, there's got to be a medkit nearby. We need to get you bandaged up."

Lana protested but Nicole was already pushing herself up and exiting the car, jumping on one foot.

"Nicole, wait, I don't like this," Lana said, shifting around. As the elevator doors began to close, Lana cursed and pulled herself out before they shut completely. She watched as Nicole jumped then went back to her hands and knees to crawl over to the warehouse entrance.

"Here! I see one!" Nicole hoisted herself up on a nearby table and went to a box on the side of the wall entrance that Lana couldn't see.

Lana carefully stood up. "Wait there, I'll come to you." She staggered over then leaned against the table where Nicole also now sat. Taking out a cloth and disinfectant, Nicole did her best to clean Lana's arm first. "It doesn't look like you will need anything done on your arm thankfully, but the wound might leave scarring," Nicole said as she wrapped her arm. "Your leg I'm afraid will need to be closed up immediately. There's a Meldpen here so it shouldn't take long, but it's going to hurt." She did the same routine with Lana's leg, which Lana held propped up on the table, cleaning it before turning on the Meldpen which heated up quickly.

It took several minutes to seal the wound on her leg with the Meldpen, with Nicole having to pause to clean as she went. Lana had to bite down on her arm to try not to scream from the burning pain, tears stinging her eyes. When she finished, Lana carefully set her leg down and tried to catch her breath, wiping sweat from her face. When she could muster the strength, she placed her weight on her foot and slowly stood. Nicole, too, carefully lifted herself off the table.

"Alright let's go," Lana said. As she took Nicole's arm and wrapped it around her neck a rattling noise sounded behind them.

"May I be of assistance?"

Lana swerved around, almost dropping Nicole. In front of them was a Scibot, appearing out from somewhere in the warehouse. Both she and Nicole let out a shaky breath of relief.

"You think you can help carry us," Lana asked, joking. The Scibots weren't known for assisting in such physical matters.

The Scibot paused as if calculating its answer. "I'm afraid I don't understand the–"

In an instant, it was ripped away into the darkness and in its place was a large slithering creature, looking down at them with four eyes. It roared.

Lana fell with Nicole, hitting the hard ground with a painful crash. Nicole screamed as the creature reared its head up like a snake, ready to strike, it bared fangs and opened its wide jaws. It lunged forward and Lana brought her hands up as if she could somehow defend herself.

There were shouts from somewhere close and gunfire lit the room, bullets hitting the creature in the face, making it rear back. It screeched with rage until a bullet bomb hit it square between the eyes, tearing its face wide open. It hit the ground with a loud thud and went limp, its green blood flowing out like a loose pipe.

Lana tried to take hold of Nicole while attempting to scramble to her feet when a heavy hand grabbed her and pulled her up. She twisted around and came face to face with Galger.

"Well, you're tougher than you look, sweetheart." He grinned.

CHAPTER TWENTY-ONE

Despite Lana's protests, Galger insisted on carrying her. She shifted uncomfortably in his sweaty arms and thought several times about squirming out of them but at the moment they were rushing for the elevators and she wanted to get away as quick as possible and they could run much faster. Nicole was silent and looked more grateful to the man carrying her, another team member named Jerard. As they got into the elevators, Lana saw one of the men press the button for level five.

"Why are we going to the security sector?" Lana asked.

"Because it's secure," Galger said as if it were obvious.

Lana tried not to roll her eyes. "Is there a saferoom?"

"For us, yeah," he said.

Lana didn't exactly understand until the doors opened to level five and the team rushed out taking them through several passageways until they came to a rather large door, leading to level five's storage room. When they opened the door Lana found the room had been taken over by Galger's team and turned into a makeshift saferoom. Doors were locked and under watch, crates were pushed to the walls so that at the center, where Galger placed her and Nicole, was piled with military gear, tools and, of course, weapons of all shapes and sizes. Other members sat on smaller crates around the center, unloading guns and counting bullets, checking inventory. One man was seen working on a Scibot which, like the one in the saferoom she had first been in, was hacked to show security footage throughout the base.

Many men stopped to look at them, some giving curious looks. Others, hungry. Lana quickly made to huddle close to Nicole on a mat as if to protect her.

"Where the hell did you get those two?" came a familiar voice. When Lana turned her head, she caught the cold black stare of Officer Torrence's eyes.

"Can you believe they were just wandering around on eight? A little beat up but somehow intact," Galger said with his wolfish grin.

Torrence said nothing, only glared down at her, and Lana held his stare, jaw clenched. He chewed slowly on his gum, checking the gun on his waist. "They can't stay here."

Galger raised his eyebrows. "Oh, come off it Torrence, we have enough food and shit. And they can keep the others company."

Lana's stomach twisted and her face burned. She didn't even want to know what he meant by keeping the others company. And the way they talked like she and Nicole weren't even there was infuriating.

"If I may be so bold as to say we don't want to be here either," she said, grasping Nicole's shaky hand. "Just take us to the nearest saferoom and be done with it."

"Now, now," said Galger. "Let's talk this through, eh?" He said crouching beside them. "How about we get you fixed up, have a nice meal and will figure things out. Sound okay, Torrence?"

Torrence just chewed his gum. "Did you at least hit anything out there?" he asked Galger.

"Yea, got the giant worm. Should see the look on its face. Or lack of." Galger laughed.

"Good. I'm readying the others for the next trip. Dillon says he saw the spider. It made its nest nearby. Want to get to it before it disappears into the vents again. Otherwise, we can smoke it out."

Lana clenched her hands into fists. The hunt was more than just a job to them, it was a game. She knew she had to warn them about the parasite but feared they'd turn mowing down individuals as a game also.

But what choice did she have? If any got exposed it could mean the death of them all.

Lana rubbed her temples. "There's something you two need to know before you go back out there. About another threat."

"Oh, yea, we know about Asset X," Galger said. "Don't worry he is top on our list. Tricky fucker has to show up sometime...ah, sorry, maybe you didn't know he was back up and kickin..."

Lana looked up at him wide-eyed. Oh, god. Of course, they were going after him too.

"Yes, I know he's alive," Lana said.

"Of course you do," Torrence mumbled.

Lana gave him a nasty look. "But no, it's not about him."

Galger arched a brow. "Oh?"

Lana looked to Nicole. "Tell them."

Nicole gazed up at them nervously, her voice soft at first then growing bolder. She told them of Spectre and Dr. Kingsley and the others being exposed. Lana watched their expression carefully as she explained. Galger's face twisted with annoyance while Torrence looked strangely calm.

"Fuck me," Galger said. "So that's what happened?" He eyed Torrence. "Looks like we have a change of plans."

"I wouldn't credit this story right away," Torrence said.

"Nicole was working with Cole to study the parasite, Torrence," Lana said through gritted teeth. "She knew better than anyone. Or would you rather go looking for Dr. Kingsley yourself and ask him? Except you know he was the one who let the specimens out. And Dr. Kinglsey wouldn't do that, not unless he wasn't right in the head."

"Enough," Torrence snapped. "We will discuss it then. Right now we have an important job to do." He looked to Galger who rose to stand beside him. "They can stay for now until we figure out what to do with them. But they need to go, eventually. If this parasite is really a thing, they may even be a risk."

Lana leaped to her feet and Galger put up his hand to stop her. "Alright, Alright. Let's settle down then. You two clean yourselves up, have a nice meal, and rest and we should be back in no time."

"Galger, you put your men at risk by going out there," Lana said.

Galger patted the large gun strapped to his shoulder. "I think we are just fine." He winked. "Oh, and if we see Asset X, we will be sure to tell him you said hello. Before we blow him to bits." He laughed.

Lana shook her head, paling. "You don't know what he is capable of," she whispered. Her heart surged at the thought of the two meeting and the aftereffects.

Galger only smirked at her then turned away. Torrence gave her one last cold look before following him.

* * *

Lana was just settling down with Nicole after eating a few hard protein bars washed down with cold water when Galger, Torrence, and several of their team were heading out for their hunt. Only four others volunteered to stay behind. Lana watched them wearily as they sat in a group nearby, unloading and reloading guns. They whispered to each other, a few glancing in their direction.

She was exhausted. But fear of the monsters outside (and maybe the few inside) kept her from getting much sleep. Nicole shifted beside her, moaning. Lana wrapped an arm around her and closed her eyes.

She must have somehow fallen asleep after all because she woke up to the sound of footsteps and low voices. When she opened her eyes to the blurry scene, she saw men taking positions at the entrance she and Nicole had come from.

"What's happening?" Lana asked as she sat up slowly. Nicole

didn't stir.

"Something is outside," one of them said. A man with dark green eyes and military cut hair like the others. They drew up their guns while the green-eyed man moved to the Scibot and brought up the feed. "Not seeing anything from the outside cameras yet," he said.

The others waited, barely moving. Lana gazed up at the ceiling, at the large pipes cutting across the roof. There was the usual quiet, then she heard it, a dull scuttering up in the walls. She leaped up, doing a three-sixty, her heart hammering.

Was it Xerus? Had he found her again?

The men pointed their guns toward the noise as the shifting sound cut across one wall to the other. Something was in the walls.

Lana checked the vents and saw they had been plugged up by the men save for a small hole cut to let some air through. She stared at them, her body tensing, ready to run.

The noise went off a few more times then quieted. They waited for what felt like forever before the men dropped their guns and Lana relaxed. She went over and checked on Nicole. Her eyes were wide open as she stared at nothing.

"You okay?" Lana asked.

Nicole's eyes swiveled toward her but didn't seem to see her. "Tired," she whispered.

Lana laid back down beside her. "Me too."

She felt Nicole tremble. When Lana put a hand on her arm, her skin was ice cold. Lana frowned then got up to get a blanket, covering it over her.

"Team says they will be out longer. Got a few of the raptors that somehow slipped out of six so went to try to take out the rest," Lana heard the green-eyed man say. "I'll warn them something is lurking around here."

Lana stared back up at the ceiling and her body shook. As Nicole went back to sleep and the men went back to talking and cleaning guns, she sat alone, letting her thoughts wander into dark territory. Thinking of Xerus.

She imagined him lurking in the dark somewhere. His red, serpentine-eyes glowing in the pitch-black. She could hear his low growl, feel his warm breath on her neck, see his shiny black fangs about to pierce her skin. She wanted to cry.

If only there was some way even now she could get through to him. But what little hope she had was lost in the terror of him reaching her. And what he would do to her if he did.

Closing her eyes, she forced herself to lay back down and try not to think about him anymore.

* * *

"Hey, what are you doing!"

Lana's eyes shot open and she bolted up. The space beside her was empty and when she looked around, she caught Nicole at the door with her back turned, somehow standing with her bad leg. The men were scrambling up from where they had been sitting to stop her. But it was too late. Nicole unlocked the door and it slid open.

As Nicole turned to face them, Lana froze and her heart dropped. Nicole was ashen. Her eyes black.

"Death is the only way," she said in an emotionless voice. She wiped a shaky hand across her nose, smearing blood over her knuckles. Lana stood there too shocked to move as the men went for the door to try to close it. She couldn't even scream as a large shadow appeared behind Nicole and surged across the entrance forcing the men back.

Asset T struck fast, plunging its fangs into Nicole's neck. Blood splashed across the ground and on the wall. It flung Nicole away then crawled up the wall with such speed, Lana could barely follow it. The men rushed back and fumbled for their guns but the spider-like creature was already upon them. It ripped open one of the men then went for another before they were finally able to draw their guns and start shooting.

As bullets flew, Lana dropped to the ground and crawled

behind one of the crates, crushing herself against the metal, hands pressed to her ears. She heard screams above the firestorm and when she looked around, she saw an armless body go flying. Lana cried out as the last man, the green-eyed one, tried to fend the creature off. He didn't pay attention to where his bullets flew only that he was trying to hit the spider. One went past Lana's head and another hit a small gas generator at one end of the room. A fire erupted and Asset T screeched, swerving away. It flew back up the ceiling then dropped down on the man, whose screams turned to gurgles.

He went silent and his gun dropped, letting off a few more bullets before it hit the ground. Asset T hovered over the man as Lana peered around, her hand covering her mouth to stifle her cries. Everyone was gone. She gazed over by the door and saw Nicole's lifeless body, eyes unseeing as blood trickled down her nose and from her neck.

Asset T let out a sharp hiss and Lana hid back behind the crate. She could feel the heat of the flames from the gas fire and see the orange glow on the wall. Frantic, she looked around her but saw no weapons close enough. She snuck a peek back over the crate. A few feet away, by some of the equipment, was a duffle bag filled with flares.

She went back against the crate and closed her eyes, taking a few deep breaths. She could try to stay hidden but the smoke from the fire would eventually draw her out. And Asset T would be waiting. She had to go now.

Taking one last deep breath, Lana flung herself away from behind the crate and made for the duffle bag. Just as she got her hand on a flare, she saw Asset T move at the corner of her eye. Screaming, she fell to the ground as the spider leaped on her. She set off the flare and struck at the spider's face. It shrieked with rage and brought its appendage down on her, causing the flare to slip from her hand and drop on her stomach. The flames from the flare burned the side of her thigh as it rolled out, singeing her pant leg and searing her skin. Lana let out a painful cry as the spider swatted the flare away with a leg and raised its body up.

Lana tried to kick at it and swing her arms, but couldn't connect. It raised its head, ready to strike, and Lana blocked her face with her arms, waiting for the excruciating pain from Asset T's fangs to stab into her.

The pain never came. Instead, an ear-shattering cry escaped the creature's mouth and, when Lana turned to look, she saw blood spraying from the spider's back. Asset T unlatched itself from on top of her and swerved around, coming face to face with a devil.

Xerus bared his fangs, a low growl ripping from his throat.

"Isha xi ess," he hissed. Lana understood the words.

She's mine.

Asset T shrieked and lunged at Xerus who leaped back just as swiftly, his speed matching the spider's. Lana watched helplessly as Xerus darted and struck, whipping his tail out and slashing at the spider's limbs. Asset T growled and backed away but wasn't looking to run. It attempted to strike out as well, protruding its long, curved fangs. Lana dragged herself back until she hit the side of a crate, desperate to get away while the two were occupied. She glanced around and saw another door leading out to the back and began to slide her way over to it.

The gas fire grew and let off little bursts of explosive flames. Debris pelted the ground and the floor shook causing several stacked crates to capsize. A small piece of metal flew across the room and hit Lana on the side of her face and shoulder. Her vision blurred for a moment as tears stung her eyes from the smoke and the pain. She could just barely make out the figures of the two aliens still fighting despite the surrounding chaos, dodging flames and equipment as they attacked, not aware of the danger around them.

Xerus flung his tail out and sliced one of Asset T's legs. The creature hissed and limped to the side, it's back against a wall of flames. As if in a last desperate measure, the spider flung itself at Xerus, attempting to pierce its fangs into his chest. Xerus swerved away, then swung out his massive claw, slicing the spider's side. He hooked his hand into the spider's back and slammed his other hand down on the beast's head, forcing it down on the ground. He jumped on its back and Asset T struggled and squirmed under him, yowling with rage. With one swift motion, Xerus tightened his hold, grasping the spider's slashed leg and ripping it from the creature's body. He released himself and jumped off as the spider bucked. When Asset T turned to face him, Xerus shot his tail out and sliced the spider's neck in one deep, clean cut. Asset T went motionless, then its head slipped from its body, rolling to the ground. The body went limp and dropped soon after.

Xerus looked over the body, pushing it aside with his long leg. Shaking, Lana crawled for the door, stretching her arm up to unlock it. She tried to stand, but the dizziness made her fall back down. Whimpering, she made a feeble attempt to drag herself from the room.

Xerus turned away from the corpse and began to approach her, moving with languid, unhurried steps in her direction. She continued to make the effort to get away from him, but once he was on top of her, she knew it was no use. She wouldn't fight him. Because there was no point. She went still, looking up at him as tears slid down her face. He was just a blurry, menacing shape above her. A nightmare come to life.

With trembling lips, Lana tried to speak, but the words wouldn't come. Not even a scream. Her heart felt like it might burst when he bent down and reached for her. Lana let out a pitiful sob and curled into a ball like a terrified child as she felt his smooth hands touch her, grabbing her and lifting her up. Lana tensed, didn't dare squirm away as he wrapped his arms under her and cradled her against him.

He said nothing as he carried her away from the room, into the dark passage beyond. Lana heard the shouts of men behind them and knew it must be Galger's men finally returning, only all too late. The door slid closed behind, slipping her into nothing but darkness and the glow of red eyes.

CHAPTER TWENTY-TWO

She lay limp against him, her cheek on his shoulder, his arms holding her so firmly she could barely feel his movements, only the slightest bobbing and swaying as he slipped silently through the dark corridors.

She couldn't make out where he was taking her only that he was in no real hurry to get here. He paused at certain intervals as if to assess the area. Listening for any danger ahead. Then he would move again, with long, graceful strides. He was so quiet she couldn't even hear him breathing, as if carrying her was no exertion to him at all. Even when he crept up a set of emergency stairs, she could barely feel the rise and fall of his chest.

As he made his way through the dark, her body began to tremble uncontrollably. Her teeth chattering in her mouth. Not from cold, as Xerus' body heat kept her warm, but from the endless terror of what was in store for her.

Where was he taking her? And why? Why not end her now or back at the room? He'd found her as he promised but why wasn't she dead?

These morbid questions had equally upsetting answers. Maybe

he was going to take his time with her. Maybe he was taking her back to some nest and was going to work her slowly, destroying every little bit of her until there was nothing left. More tears spilled from her eyes at the thought. She wept silently in his arms but he didn't stop to check her, his eyes barely looked at her. Her chest felt heavy like her heart had turned to stone and was sinking into her stomach.

She felt too tired to fight, her body so heavy. She just wanted to sleep. To just get it over with. She closed her eyes and let her head fall back, surrendering to her fate as Xerus weaved through the dark.

Eventually, he stopped and shifted her to one arm. Lana raised her head slightly and opened one eye to see his fingers working at a door pad. Frowning, she glanced over at the metal door before them and saw the Lazris star in the very center, painted in gold.

Confused, Lana watched as Xerus successfully entered the code and unlocked the door, entering the small foyer beyond. He did the same for the second door at the end until it too opened. He swept inside and Lana caught a few choice glimpses at the room—or rooms rather—that they had entered. It was similar to Jacob's unit only bigger. Much bigger. And like they had just stepped into an exotic resort suite, with a large entrance room that connected several other rooms and a balcony at the back displaying fake scenery. Lana didn't have a chance to register it all as Xerus took her through a doorway to the right, passing through to a large bedroom with a wide, fake window displaying some kind of beach scene. He set her on the bed then promptly left her before she could get a word in.

What the *hell*.

Lana wiped at her wet face, wincing as her face still stung from the blow, and tried to sit up when she felt the searing pain in her thigh and waist. She looked down and saw her suit was burned on one side from where the flare had caught it. Hissing in pain, she could feel that it was sticking to her skin.

She peered around the room and saw an opening to her left, showing a large bathroom with a marble tub. Everything was white and pristine and rich looking like some kind of modern summer house that her aunt used to live in. There was a large TV screen on the wall opposite her and a few choice pieces of furniture more decorative than useful. As she studied the room, Lana began to realize where she was.

This was the commander's suite.

She sat there in confused shock, staring at everything when the pain of her leg brought her back. The horrible stinging throb in her thigh made her groan and hunch over, tears still stinging her eyes. She didn't know where Xerus went but she wasn't going to wait for him to come back and do...whatever it was he planned to do with her. Carefully she got up from the bed and tried to stand. When she took a step, she fell over from a spasm of dizziness and pain. She swallowed a few breaths as she crouched on the floor. She went back to crawling and made her way over to the open door of the room. She slid her way back through the hall until she was inside the main entrance room. Xerus was nowhere in sight. Groaning from the movement, she slid passed a bar situated by the wall next to the door and was surprised to see a Scibot sitting beside it, bent back on a high seat, with wires hanging from its body and its computer displaying a loading screen. Frowning, Lana paused to wonder what Xerus was doing with it then decided not to stick around to find out. She crawled passed and went for the door.

Rising on her knees, she clawed at the door lock, getting the door to open, when she was abruptly pulled back. Lana let out a weak little scream as Xerus, appearing from seemingly nowhere, lifted her up over his shoulder with one arm and carried her back to the bedroom. She cried and kicked at him but it did absolutely nothing. Xerus dropped her back on the bed where she tried to squirm away from him.

"No, don't!" she cried as he reached for her. Panic and adrenaline from the pain brought back a new resolve, making her want to fight after all, even if it was still likely pointless. She kicked at him as he grabbed her leg and pulled her closer to the edge of the bed.

Lana looked up at his face and could read little of his expression. He was surprisingly calm. Too calm. And that somehow scared her more.

His eyes wouldn't meet hers. Instead, they focused on her body. He dropped a case beside the bed that she hadn't noticed he'd been carrying and brought his other hand down to take hold of the opening to her coveralls. When his talon-like fingers ripped her clothing partially down to display her bra, Lana turned wild.

'Oh my god, he's going to eat me,' was the first crazy thought that jumped in her head. Like a small, terrified animal, Lana screamed and thrashed frantically as Xerus' face bent down towards her.

He caught her arms and pinned her down. *"Eris sifa na enexi, kissala,"* he growled.

Lana didn't bother to try to understand. She writhed and squirmed in his grasp. He continued to say something to her but she didn't want to listen.

"Lina..."

Lana struggled against him for a moment longer until she realized what he said and grew still. She blinked away tears, her breath coming in short bursts, but she let herself be still.

"What...What did you just say?" she choked.

"Lina. Na enex." He said in a low, soft tone.

Her name. He was saying her name though it came out a little off with his accent.

Lana, be calm.

Lana blinked several times and remained frozen though she still trembled under him. A tiny whimper still vibrating in her throat.

"I-I don't understand," she said softly.

His eyes met hers and, in them, she could see a calming blaze, not a raging inferno. There was no hatred there. Not for her.

Gently this time, he placed his giant hand on her chest, near her heart. He closed his eyes as if listening then bent his head back down toward her and inhaled through his nose, the slits of his nostrils expanding. Lana dared not move. She waited, watching him intensely for any sign of change to his oddly calm demeanor. When he finally opened his eyes, he sat back and exhaled.

"Clean..." he said in English. Though the word came out a bit off, Lana was surprised by the clarity.

"Clean?" Lana repeated as a question. What did that mean? She looked far from clean. Her clothes were stained and full of soot and blood, her skin not much better.

His hand slipped to her stomach and then down to her waist and thigh where her clothes were burned. Lana winced as he touched at the wound. His eyes slipped back up to her chest and he gestured to her collar. "Off," he growled. He moved to grip her coveralls again, but Lana flinched away.

"Okay...alright," she said, still trying to keep calm. With shaky fingers, she unbuttoned the top and let it slip to her waist. Heat burned in her face at his gaze. Her heart still pounded with fear, but her breath was beginning to slow. As he reached for her yet again, she curled away.

"What are you going to do?" She had to know. She was still reminded of their last encounter together before his fake death. About his threats and promises.

Xerus seemed to understand. Carefully he sat beside her on the bed. *"Yinas vir iz rok."*

Lana stared at him. "Iz rok?"

Xerus bowed his head.

You were supposed to go.

Lana shook her head. Her face twisted, thinking she might shout at him or cry again. "Are you telling me," she said, her voice shaking, "that you were lying then? That you said all those hurtful things to get me to leave the base?"

When he nodded his head once, Lana felt a surge of anger and relief. A few tears slipped down her cheeks and she angrily brushed them away. "I was beyond terrified. For me and others because of you! And how could I not be? You murdered those..." Lana brought a hand to her mouth, her stomach twisting. "I trusted you. And you couldn't trust me with the truth." She dropped her hand, her fingers curling into fists.

Xerus didn't respond, only gazed at her.

"And then you...I thought that you had...died," Lana bit her lip as it trembled. "And I couldn't bring myself to go. I was so..." she covered her face in her hands unable to say more. She choked down her tears, sick of crying.

When she felt a brush against her leg, she jumped and looked over to see Xerus had moved closer, his tail grazing across the bed. A tail stained with blood.

Lana wiped at her face and sniffed. "I want to take a shower." She met his eyes. "I want to get clean."

Xerus moved to carry her again. She tried to refuse him but he wouldn't budge. He picked her up and brought her into the bathroom, taking her over to the bath instead of the shower. Lana didn't argue. A bath sounded just as good if not better. He sat her on the edge and she watched as he examined the tub then twisted the knobs, water gushing out.

As the bath filled, Xerus came around and knelt before her. He tugged at her clothing and Lana got the message.

"I can do it myself. You can leave now." She was still upset. With him and with everything. She still had so many questions and few answers. She had just lost her friend and saw the slaughter of several people. And she was still coming out of the terror she felt from believing Xerus had planned to harm her. She still felt an edge of fear even now. With him so close. No more barriers between them. "Please just go. I want to be alone."

Angry heat filled her when she saw his mouth twitch into a small smile. He said something in his language, too quiet for her to hear. "Will be close." He rose, towering above her. He stared down at her for a long moment but Lana refused to look up at him. She wrapped her arms around herself, closing herself to him. Eventually, he turned away and left her.

When the tub was filled, Lana stopped the water then carefully undressed. She removed the bandages from her arm and leg as well before dipping into the warm water, hissing in pain as the water licked her wounds. She laid back against the edge and curled into a ball once again, holding herself tight, feeling like a small, helpless child.

* * *

She wasn't sure how long she sat there in the tub, perhaps a few minutes, perhaps hours. Most of the time was spent just sitting there in shock, rocking back and forth but eventually she calmed down enough to make use of the water. She used a soap dispenser on the side of the wall to clean her skin and hair, scraping her fingers through her locks to untangle them. Scenes from barely a couple hours ago flashed through her mind. Fire and blood. Men sprawled out. Nicole lying on the ground. Lana's throat tightened at the thought of her friend now gone when only a few hours ago she had seemed just fine save for the broken leg.

But she hadn't been fine. Not in the slightest. Lana was still shaken up by the sudden change.

And now here she was, housed (or trapped?) with a lethal alien inside one of the most luxurious units on the base. It was too surreal to even believe.

Maybe if she had known everything from the start, known about the parasite, known Xerus wasn't dead, she would have left. And tried to warn others. Tried to get them to leave too. But she would never know. And it was too late now. If she had listened to Xerus and not been wrapped up by her emotions, things might have been different.

And now what? What did Xerus plan to do with her? Why did he come for her in the first place? she almost feared to ask.

When she was sick of sitting in the now filthy water, Lana slowly stepped out of the bath, pressing a button on the side to let it drain. The burns still throbbed and the scratches itched. She knew if she didn't disinfect them and wrap them up properly they could get infected. Limping, she went to one of the cabinets and took out a towel and wrapped it around herself. She would need new clothes too since her coveralls were toast.

She slipped back into the bedroom and saw it was empty. On the bed was a white robe laid out for her. Lana stood there staring at it as if she didn't even recognize what it was or how it got there. She went over to it and touched at the soft fabric and wondered if Xerus' kind wore robes. Or any clothes at all besides the thin armor pants. Or if they wore very little, their scales enough to protect them, and were unashamed of their nakedness.

Lana let her towel slip off her and drop to the ground, allowing herself a moment to stand there naked, letting the cool air touch her skin. She picked up the robe then looked down at her body, touching where the skin was tarnished by dark burn marks and slashes. The slash down her arm began to bleed lightly.

A low hiss made her jump and cover her front with the robe. Xerus stepped from the shadow of the hall into the bedroom, his eyes flickering down her body, focusing on her arm and leg.

"Sit." He nodded toward the bed.

Lana hesitated then put the robe on quickly and sat on the side of the bed, heat rising in her neck and face. She didn't look up at him but saw his movement from the corner of her eye. She tensed as he grasped her ankles and brought her around to the front of the bed then gestured for her to move back. Lana shifted up the bed, allowing her legs to stretch out on the mattress. She watched as Xerus picked up the case he had dropped on the ground and placed it on the bed next to her. He unlatched and opened it and took out several rolls of medical gauze and padding.

"Where did you get that?" Lana asked.

Xerus made a human-like shrug. "Around."

By around he likely meant found in one of the storage rooms. He pushed the case away and grasped one of her ankles again while his other hand went to the bottom of her robe. Lana pulled at her ankle and bent her knee, blocking his hand. "I can do it. I-is there any disin-fectant?"

Xerus gave her what she could guess was a confused look. "Diisssin...?"

"Like alcohol? Er...is there anything in the case that says hydrogen peroxide?" She pointed to the case. Xerus turned it over so she could see. "Ah, here!" she picked up the clear bottle. "I'll just use this." Even though it was going to hurt like no tomorrow.

Before she could uncap it, Xerus took it out of her hands and sniffed at it. His face contorted and he growled. "No."

Lana frowned. "What do you mean 'no'? This will help keep it clean." She went to grab for it but he kept it out of reach.

"*Leesha vixos,*" *Better method,* he said.

Lana let her arm drop. "What?"

Xerus tossed the bottle aside and quickly yanked up her robe before she could even react. Lana gasped as he bent his head down to her thigh and let his long tongue slip out between his teeth, the tip brushing against her burned skin. Lana cried out and struggled but he quickly pinned her in place, continuing his so-called 'better method'.

"How is that better?" Lana snapped.

"Heal...quicker," he said between licks.

Appalled, Lana groaned as his warm slick tongue grazed her skin, moving up her thigh to her waist. She clutched the robe to her tightly keeping it in place so nothing else could be exposed.

"How do I know your saliva won't just infect it more?" Lana said, eyeing him, heat rising and falling along her body mainly from embarrassment but also from something else she dared not think of.

Xerus lifted his head and licked his teeth, his mouth twitching. "Saliva is..." he seemed to think, trying to form the right words. "Is diissennfectint."

Lana wanted to laugh but could only stare at him. Dare she trust him anymore?

What choice did she have? And if he wanted her dead, it was highly doubtful he would use this method to do so. Lana grimaced but didn't fight him, instead she laid back on the bed and gazed up at the ceiling, trying her best not to move as he finished "cleaning" her wounds.

"So the parasite..." Lana finally spoke, trying to distract herself and break the awkward moment. "That was your mission all along... to destroy it."

Xerus lifted his head to gaze down at her. "Yes."

Lana glanced at him then looked away. "Why didn't you tell me? I could have warned the others, I could have...I don't know...done something."

Xerus shifted beside her and, when she peered, back he was looking out at the fake window. " Couldn't...rissk. *Veeris ni ix*...infected."

Lana sat up. "You didn't know who was infected...but you knew Dr. Grimmer was. You could sense it."

"He was...far gone. Was essy to tell. Others...not so much. Had to be...clossir."

Lana frowned. "And you didn't know if those who were infected might be listening to our conversations...you had to make it seem like you were just a prisoner." She shivered. "You deliberately let yourself get captured so you could follow Spectre here to kill it."

Xerus turned back to her and bowed his head. "It was...almost gone. On the dark planet. Had it cornered."

"Then my kind came," Lana said, her throat tightening. She closed her eyes. "And now that we brought it here..."

"I must destroy it."

Lana opened her eyes. "Does everyone...have to die?"

Xerus didn't say anything at first. He picked up one of the rolls of gauze and unraveled it, being careful not to tear it with his sharp nails. Lana reluctantly stretched out her arm so he could wrap it around her.

"I must...kill the parasite. At all costs. If a humin has it. I can't spare thim."

Death is the only way.

Lana felt her body go cold. "So if I have it..."

"You don't."

Lana blinked in surprise. "How do you...? Ah, you sensed it."

Xerus nodded. He tightened the wrap on her arm then moved to her leg. *"Rishi eris etz."*

Her brows furrowed. "Why won't I get it?"

Xerus finished with her leg then moved to bandage her burns.

"Xerus."

"You're staying with me," he responded.

Lana moved away, almost touching his hand to make him stop and look at her. "What do you plan to do?"

Xerus' eyes narrowed. "Finish my mission."

CHAPTER TWENTY-THREE

Lana was forced to rest despite her protests that she was fine even with the pain and injuries. She felt too on edge to sleep. Too tense to just lay there waiting around in this strange, fake paradise of a suite while outside was a living hell. It didn't help in the slightest that Xerus was planning to leave her to search around the base to hunt the parasite down. She wished she could say she wasn't worried for him but, as durable and powerful as he was, she still had her doubts.

"What if you get infected?" she asked as he was getting ready to leave. "If the blood gets on you..."

Xerus gave her an odd look. "I can't."

"What do you mean?"

"I'm immune," he said.

Lana stared at him in disbelief. "Your whole kind is immune?"

He grunted. "Iss why we fight it alone."

Lana shook her head. "But how?"

"It can't survive inside us. *Rexi ni viridu,*" *We are too strong,* he stated.

Lana crossed her arms and sat back on the bed, glaring. Was there nothing his kind couldn't survive? Were they immortal too?

As if understanding her thoughts, Xerus let out a low hiss of laughter. "We can die. Jist not essly."

"What about Galger and his men? They are looking for you and others that escaped," Lana said. "To take you down."

Xerus snorted. "*Sica ri nifas.*" *Let them try.*

Lana wanted to find some other excuse for him not to go but she had none. When he examined her once more and seemed satisfied, he went to leave.

"Be back," he said.

Lana lay silent. When he slipped from the room and she heard the door slide open and close, she waited for a moment longer then forced herself off the bed. Slowly she made her way over to the cabinets and then the wardrobe by the wall but they were mostly empty save for an extra robe. She wished she had at least asked Xerus to go looking for clothes.

She went back into the bathroom and found her discarded coveralls still lying on the ground. She bent down and examined it and saw it was no good to wear even if she did clean it. She picked it up to throw it away somewhere when she heard something clack against the floor. When she looked down, she saw her phone. Somchow it hadn't gotten lost. She picked it up and found the screen cracked and scratches marring the sides. She tried to turn it on but it was dead.

She threw the phone on the bedside table and stuffed the coveralls into a cabinet then made her way out to the hall. In the main entrance room, she stood looking around at the bizarre brilliance. The balcony at the back displayed an ocean view; everything was white and shiny and clean. She half expected room service to come knocking at the door any minute. The bar was even stocked despite not being in use. Lana studied the Scibot that sat by on a barstool, wondering what Xerus was using it for. Its head was bent back in a wrong way, its arms dangling lifelessly at its sides. She peered at the computer screen on its chest and saw it showed a map of Lazris.

Sitting down on a seat next to it, Lana poked at the screen. As she played around, checking out the various options, she realized the program had been hacked. She could go to a level and see a map of the various rooms like normal but the display also showed data within the rooms such as, to her great surprise, the number of lifeforms currently inhabiting the area. The program must have been switched over to a top security officer's account to access the extra information. She remembered learning about how they used infrared sensors and counters to mark certain areas so they could track people's whereabouts. The more she looked the bot over, in fact, the more she was convinced it was the same bot from the saferoom. After everyone had fled, Xerus must have stolen it. An easier plan than trying to hack one himself.

Lana pressed on a few more options until the bot began to speak in a grated, static tone. "Which data would you like me to summarize?" it said.

Lana pressed the option for all and the bot took a moment to gather the information.

"Currently there are...five thousand and seventeen active members. Six thousand three hundred and five are unaccounted for. Forty-eight are unidentifiable. Fifty-four percent are stationed in saferooms. Twenty percent within individual units. Twenty-six percent spread across levels."

Lana sat back. Though a good few were remaining in the saferooms, to have so many gone was alarming. And likely it was only going to get worse. There were still other assets on the loose. Asset T might be gone and few others because of Galger and his team but many others remained lurking in the dark. And there was still the matter of the parasite possibly hiding within others, ready to infect.

Lana leaned forward and closed out the data then went back to the map. She selected a level at random—level three—and the computer brought up the various rooms. There was one saferoom and only a few hundred inside. The other rooms showed no signs of life. On the side of the screen were several more options. Lana pressed through them until one with a camera icon brought up a secondary screen showing video feed. Lana stilled. She could see all the rooms through various angles.

Excitement building in her, Lana went through the different cameras. She found a few bots lurking about on three but no creatures yet. She switched to another level, going through each room, desperate to find anyone and anything.

Levels three, four, and five were vacant save for those in saferooms. Only the dead occupied five outside the saferoom as Galger's team had moved on, the fire mostly out. Four was where she was now and she had a feeling it remained empty because Xerus made it so. Whether by warning creatures off with his pheromones or blockading the level somehow, though that didn't mean someone still couldn't find a way in. Certainly Galger's team might but, to her relief, she found them occupied on level two where some of the raptors had somehow escaped along with a nasty tentacled creature that had gotten into one of the fish tanks in the farming sector.

She saw Asset C lurking on level seven, roaming the halls and sniffing around like a bloodhound on a hunt, though what he hunted for she wasn't sure. On Level six a few raptors remained and, to her surprise, a couple of people. Where they came from she wasn't sure but, as she watched them, she knew something wasn't right with them. They walked funny and didn't seem afraid of the raptors who, shockingly, didn't touch them. One man in particular, with bandages covering his face and head so she couldn't identify him, got on the elevator and made his way to another level.

When she got to levels eight through eleven, she began to see much more activity. Unidentifiable assets rushed down halls or lurked near rooms. A few people were either seen hiding, running, or just lumbering around. It was on level eight that she finally caught a glimpse of Xerus. Her eyes focused on him intently, her face close to the screen, watching as he stalked the rooms. He had a few items in his hand though she couldn't quite make out what they all were except for a couple of wires. The rest looked like metal pieces of some sort.

"What are you doing?" Lana whispered to herself as she observed his every movement. He was taking apart robots, going through spare parts, in search of specific items. She continued to watch him until she saw something sneak by the warehouse door. A large creature with long claws, a body similar to a monkey but with four eyes and a long snout. Lana cried out for Xerus as if he could hear her, watching in horror as the ape-like specimen ran behind Xerus and leaped up as if to catch on his back. Just in time, Xerus dodge and twisted around, whipping his tail out and slicing through the creature's stomach. The ape fell back and blood spurted on the ground, some hitting Xerus. The alien collapsed and Xerus bared his fangs at it, looking rather annoyed.

Lana let out a breath and placed a hand over her eyes, rubbing them. When she eventually looked back at the screen, Xerus was gone.

She went back to searching the other levels that were left. Twelve's cameras were black, likely damaged from the explosion. The last level was the city sector where she was surprised to see many people congregating near the front. Some she recognized from the saferoom she had first been in. Soldiers had their guns at the ready as people pushed to try to get on to the cars to take them up to the docks. They weren't letting anyone through.

Lana saw more guards stationed at the elevators on level one, those leading to any of the levels below, making sure nothing unwanted came up to greet them. She couldn't believe how many people were just sitting around the foyer instead of inside saferooms. But then she remembered she had been one of those people who had wanted to get to the docks instead of waiting around.

As she clicked through different angles, she saw one showing a clear view of the elevator doors. Without warning, one of the doors opened and the guards immediately went into action. They backed away and aimed their guns at the one who stepped out. Lana felt a chill run down her back as she saw it was the bandaged man who had been lumbering around on six, having made his way to one. Slowly he put up his hands, his mouth moving though she couldn't hear. The soldiers continued to aim their guns, gesturing for him to kneel on the ground. He did as they asked, placing his hands behind his head. One of the soldiers moved forward and carefully examined him. They seemed to talk things over for a moment until they picked him up and led him over to a group of people huddled by a wall.

"No...no!" Lana cried aloud. He was infected, he had to be. His mannerisms were all wrong, his eyes seemed off, soulless, black pupils with no shine. And they were putting him with others. They didn't know about Spectre. Galger and his damn group hadn't bothered to warn them, either too busy trying to gun down any of the specimens or not taking her and Nicole's warning to heart. Damn them. Damn them all!

She had to warn those on level one. There had to be some way to contact them. Lana hopped off her seat and began searching around for a phone. She carefully went through the other rooms, all just as pristine and unused, until she found an office. She went over to the computer and took up the phone beside it only to realize she didn't know or have a number to call. Cursing, she started up the computer instead. She went through the directories but the only numbers she could find were for various departments and warehouses which by now were empty. The city sector didn't exactly have its own number either. The closest thing she could try was the sector one security office but, no surprise at all, no one picked up. Feeling like she didn't have much left to lose and not seeing many other options, she dialed one of the few numbers she knew now by heart.

The line rang a few times. Then, to her delighted shock, she heard a click. "...Hello?"

"Jacob," Lana breathed.

There was a hiss of breath. "Lana?"

Lana's throat tightened and her face twisted but she dared not cry again. "Yes."

"Where are you? Nevermind, are you safe?"

Lana opened her mouth then closed it. Was she?

"I, um, yes...I think so," she said.

There was an exhale of breath. "That's good to hear. But, listen, I can't talk right now."

"Jacob, you need to hear this. There is a huge problem on base. Not just the specimens that got out as I'm guessing you already know."

"Right. The specimens are being taken care of as we speak. Galger and his team—"

"I know about that," she said. "But there is more. There is a parasite. It is infecting people and if we don't do something it will take over completely. You have to warn the officers on base somehow. Tell them people need to be separated and checked. When you arrive with reinforcements, you can't let any leave the planet until it is safe."

There was silence on the other end.

"Jacob? Do you understand? There is a—"

"I know, Lana. I know about the parasite. And as of right now orders are to stand by."

Lana froze, her hand tightening around the phone. "What do you mean?"

"We can't move in on the base. Just...stay hidden for now," he said.

Lana's hand shook. "You're not coming?"

There was a shifting sound and a cough. "Our orders are to wait. For security and safety purposes."

"If you don't come, then we are just sitting here waiting to die!" Lana snapped.

"As I said, Galger and his team are on the job..."

"They care only about taking out the assets. By the time they get through to them everyone could be infected," Lana stated. "Listen, Jacob, I have seen the parasite at work, I know the signs. Just now they let an infected into the city sector with a few hundred people. If you don't warn them, he will spread it to the others."

Jacob didn't speak for a long moment until he said, "Galger and his men will be taking care of that too. He called me and told me about the situation. I'm afraid we can't take any risks with regards to this parasite."

Lana felt her heart drop. "What are you saying?" she breathed.

"They have orders to take out any who...pose a threat."

"But they don't know who has it and who doesn't! How can they know which..." Lana paused. "They aren't going to check. They are just going to take out any they come across."

"I'm sorry, Lana."

Lana wished she could jump through the phone and throttle him. "There is a way to know! People can be spared!"

"If they deem someone isn't...sick. Then they will take the necessary measures. Otherwise, the parasite must be stopped. At all costs."

She knew that Spectre had to be stopped but not like this. Just when she thought Xerus' way was hard to swallow now she saw it was a hundred times better than what Jacob and the other generals were proposing. Jacob didn't know Galger and his team. They wouldn't spare anyone if they had to. And who would stop them? To them, the mission was the top priority. Take out all known and possible threats. And wipe out any information that the generals didn't want getting back to the rest of the population.

"You should have left," Jacob said. "I'm sorry, Lana, I really am. I have to go now." The line went dead before she could get in another word.

* * *

Lana sat there for a long time, too shocked to move.

A bad feeling finally forced her from the office. She limped back over to the Scibot at the bar and flipped through the feeds until she found Galger and his team. They were still on level two, taking produce and other food necessities for themselves from the food banks. A few raptor bodies were littering the floor. One soldier was ripping a few teeth out from a raptor's mouth as a souvenir. Lana's mouth went dry. She wanted to warn others but she wasn't sure how. All she could do was watch helplessly as the team moved on.

Frustrated, she went away from the bot for the time being and occupied herself instead with finding food. She had only water in the last few hours or so and, though her stomach turned and twisted from fear and anxiety and pain, she also felt empty and weak. She scoured the kitchen beside the bar not expecting to find much of anything. The commander probably only came to the base once a year, if even that, so they had no reason to stock up on any goods until he arrived. Thankfully, she did find a few cans of pears in the back of one cabinet. They were a little dated but they would have to do. She had no idea how Xerus was feeding himself but she would have to ask him to find food.

As she found a can opener in one of the drawers and was cutting the can open, a dark, but not entirely illogical, thought popped into her head.

Xerus could stop them. He could take out Galger and his team. The only issue was *would* he if she asked him. And was it right? After all, she knew full well if he were to stop them it would mean their deaths. And as deadly as he was he still could end up severely wounded in the fight. The team had a plethora of weapons at their disposal and were merciless and violent. Could she ask him to take such a risk?

Her feelings were a mixed bag of vague, murky indecisions and uncertainties. As she took out a fork and sat down on the couch to pick at the fruit she tried to keep her nerves level. But she knew she was running out of time and needed to decide soon. Once Galger's team was finished hunting specimens, they would move onto people if they weren't taking out those they came across already.

As she finished up the pears and threw the can away, she heard the front door opening. Tensing, she wrapped the robe tightly about her and stood motionless as Xerus came through the second door.

He paused as he saw her and they each stared at the other without saying a word. Xerus was covered with blood and what looked to be oil, likely from one of the bots he had been tinkering with. In one hand he carried a large bag. When he saw her eyeing it he dropped it before her.

"For you," he said.

Lana gave him a nervous glance then cautiously opened and peered into the bag. There she found a few pieces of clothing–uniform pants, a couple of simple t-shirts, and a pair of red coveralls–and some cans of food that he must have scavenged from somewhere.

"Thank you," she said softly.

He made an odd noise and she looked up to see him baring his fangs, giving her a strange grin.

"What?" Lana said, frowning. She didn't like that look.

"*Tika liss na visir*," he said.

Lana stared at him, confused. "Ready for a...favor?"

He bowed his head, his smile somehow widening.

It took Lana a minute to understand and when she did she grimaced. "I knew I would regret that," she said wearily. He grunted and she sighed. "Which one?" she asked.

When he gestured for her to follow into the bedroom and then pointed to the tub, she knew.

"You want me to bathe you?"

He nodded, his tail weaving behind him like a delighted puppy. Lana's face heated remembering that odd favor he had made after beating her at a game of chess. Never believing she would actually have to go through with it.

She felt her heart beginning to pound as she glanced over at the tub. "Right now?" she asked timidly.

Xerus let out an exasperated breath and gestured at his torso stained with blood and oil. Lana couldn't argue.

Clearing her throat she stepped over to the base. The tub was the size of a resort jacuzzi, large enough to seat at least five people. Or in Xerus' case, his whole body and maybe one other. Hesitantly she turned the knobs until hot water poured out. As the water rose she went to one of the cabinets, searching around for a scrubber and bars of soap. She knew there was a dispenser on the wall but that would require her to go into the tub which she wanted to avoid.

She heard Xerus shifting behind her but thought nothing of it. As dangerous as he was, she felt safe to turn her back. When she found one bar of soap and a small washcloth, she knew she would have to make do. As she grabbed the items and turned to face him, she let out a sharp gasp and immediately turned back around. Xerus had taken off his one pair of clothes—the scaly armored pants that she was so used to and practically thought were a part of him—and now stood fully naked before her.

She got a glimpse of the one part of him she had yet to see and was embarrassed by her reaction as well as the first thought being how surprised she was that he wasn't built like other species she had seen. Which should be obvious. She had seen her share of genitalia from a scientist's perspective and never thought anything of it, even when she was studying the Gyda. But with Xerus it just seemed different and she couldn't reason why.

It was strange of her to react as she did honestly, since there wasn't much there to see at first; just a hard layer of rimmed skin protruding upward in a v-like manner, surrounding a v-shaped slit at the center where likely his real member hid.

Shaking off her shock, she tried to keep her composure. She turned back around and moved to the bath, turning the hot water off. She backed away, allowing him to slip over the edge and into the steaming water. He settled in and positioned himself against the side, placing his elbows on top of the ledge, looking oddly human in his posture as he leaned back, spikes scraping the marble. Lana stood by, watching him as if fixated. He moved his tail slowly around, making ripples, his fingers dipping into the water, legs stretching out.

"Well?" he said. His head tilted toward her, amusement and anticipation gleaming his eyes. Lana chewed her lip then took up the soap and cloth then dipped them into the water. She scrubbed the bar against the cloth until it was soaped up, then moved to stand as close as she could to Xerus' back. She hesitated for a moment then touched at the nape of his neck with the cloth, being sure to carefully work around his sharp spikes. Xerus closed his eyes and didn't move, allowing her to gently clean the tiny, smooth scales around his neck and the tougher, harder ones at his shoulders. She washed in silence at first, scrubbing his back and horns then rinsing thoroughly until he shined.

"What were you doing out there?" Lana asked, wanting to break the awkwardness of her situation.

"Hm?" he grunted.

"You're covered in oil...and I saw you on eight going through the bots," Lana said.

Xerus tilted his head toward her, opening his eyes into narrow slits to leer at her. "You were to rest," he hissed.

Lana flushed. "I was restless. And the bot...I wanted to know what was happening."

Xerus let out a sharp breath and straightened back. His hands slipped to the edges of the tub and clung to the side, nails digging into the stone. He didn't respond at first and Lana thought he never would until he said, "looking fir parts."

"Parts for what?"

Xerus lifted himself out of the water to stand in the middle of the bath. Water trickled down his back and Lana had a sudden urge to wipe it away. "You'll see," he said. He twisted around and Lana made sure to only look at his face. He shifted closer to her until his legs hit the side of the tub. Lana forced herself not to move, only tilting her head up. She clutched the washcloth tightly in one hand to keep it from trembling. Xerus indicated for her to continue and Lana glanced down at his chest nearly unable to move. Slowly she reached out and pressed the cloth to his middle, letting the water drip down his scaley stomach. Heat rippled across her body, sweat forming along her nape as she lowered her hand.

Xerus didn't move nor speak as she cleaned the front of him

though she knew his eyes were on her. She assumed he wouldn't tell her any more about the bots so she wracked her brain for something else to say.

"You should know," she said after a pause, "I saw...I saw an infected go on to level one. But there are other people, not infected, there as well. I tried to find a way to warn them but I couldn't get contact."

Xerus grunted. "I will go soon then. When everything is ready."

Lana stopped washing. "You won't hurt the others. The ones not infected..." She didn't look up at him, too afraid to meet his eyes.

"I will spare those who are clean and defenseless."

Lana closed her eyes, thankful. "You must stay clear of Galger and his team. I have...information that they plan to take out any on sight. I don't know how you would be able to do it, but maybe you can somehow...I don't know...shepard the healthy ones somewhere hidden and safe...somewhere they can hide." Lana dared meet his gaze. "I know you don't exactly love the human race. But will you do this?"

Xerus raised his chin slightly as he glared at her. "I will...try."

Lana couldn't help the smile growing on her face from relief. Her smile fell, however, when she felt something slither and wrap around her ankle. Jumping, she glanced down and saw Xerus' tail caressing her leg. She hadn't noticed he had moved it out of the water.

Tensing, she dared not move as she felt it rise along her backside, pressing against her robe. Her breath caught in her throat and her heart hit harder in her chest. Not wanting him to see her reaction, she continued to clean him, trying to ignore his tail. She concentrated on his chest then his stomach, his shoulders then arms, trying to be done with it as quickly as possible. Trying not to think about how hard and powerful he felt under her hands. Xerus watched her again and she wondered what he saw. And what he was thinking. When she was finished with most of his upper body, she hesitated at his lower, her mouth going dry. Just as she touched at a section below his hip she found she couldn't go any further.

Lana opened her mouth to tell him that she was done when he reached out his hand toward her. As his fingers grazed against her neck, Lana went still as a rabbit in front of a hungry wolf. She dropped the cloth in the tub, her hands going to her sides.

"What was that thing you did when you saw my dead body?" he said slowly so that she understood each word. His hand wrapped tenderly around her throat, lifting her head so she would look at him. Lana stared wide-eyed. Though she understood the words she didn't get his meaning. "What thing?" she asked softly. Xerus tilted his head and his eyes flicked down to her mouth and Lana thought then she understood. He was talking about when she had kissed him after seeing his supposed corpse. As a way of goodbye. How he could have sensed or known it was her was unimaginable.

Lana's heart raced. She licked her lips, uncertain how to respond. "That was...I thought you were dead and..." Lana shook her head, heat building in her face. "It was a kiss," she said in a nearly inaudible whisper.

Of course Xerus heard her. "What does it mean?" tilting his head even more, eyes filled with a fiery curiosity. Lana let her lids fall, too embarrassed to meet his gaze.

"It's a form of..." oh, god, she didn't know how else to put it, "affection amongst humans."

"Affection?"

Lana felt like a child as she said, "I thought I'd never see you again. It was just my way of...saying goodbye."

Xerus didn't move for a long moment and neither did she. When his fingers slipped from her neck up to her jaw, brushing his thumb against her lips, Lana flinched away. Remembering her dream from many nights ago, her stomach did a violent flip and she backed away from the tub.

"I, um, I'm sorry if that had been rude," she said, stammering. "Anyway, I'm not feeling very well, I'm sorry you'll have to...finish without me." Before he could speak she pulled herself away from his tail and rushed out of the bathroom. She shut the door behind her then limped her way through to the other side of the large unit until she went into another spare bedroom far on the opposite end and shut the door soundly.

CHAPTER TWENTY-FOUR

Lana didn't leave the bedroom for the rest of the day and into the night. A new, inexplicable fear began to seep its way into her mind and she was uncertain how to respond save to stay away from the alien beyond the door.

It was when she finally fell asleep that the nightmares warped into something new and the fear revealed itself within her dreams. Ever since Xerus' supposed death, she had been having a new set of so-called nightmares. She was in a dark, wild forest racing through the trees. There was lightning lighting up the night sky but no rain. Just flashes of white and blue against a smokey backdrop. Though she didn't see it, she knew something was hunting her. The dreams usually ended with her stopping at the center of a rocky meadow, beside a large, murky pool; when she looked back, she saw the shadow of something giant and monstrous right at the edge of the darkness.

This time the dream didn't end. The shadow slipped from the darkness and there she saw Xerus in his raw, feral splendor, slowly coming towards her like a tiger stalking its prey. Lana drew her hands up as if to ward him off only to see that her hands were not her own.

They were alien to her; blue and sharp and scaled. A tail swayed beside her and when she looked back at the pool she did not see herself in the reflection but a reptilian creature with her face.

"Don't run," Xerus said. Lana looked back at him too frightened to speak, afraid she couldn't. He moved ever closer to her. "Don't run, Lana."

She stayed put like he asked though the fear still tugged at her, telling her to bolt. He came to stand beside her by the pool and they each looked down at it. He took her hand in his, intertwining their fingers.

"Vina sila. Kissala."

Lana's heart slammed in her chest but she stayed. His fingers slid to her throat, fingers pressing lightly. What happened after was a chaotic blur like the silent storm raging above them. She was on the ground, he was atop her. She hissed like a cat as his claws dug into her thighs. He moved violently against her but she didn't cry for him to stop. She felt primal and wild and alive.

When she woke up, she found herself slick between her thighs and sweating. Quickly, she rushed to her bathroom and turned on the shower making sure the water was ice cold. She didn't know how long she stayed in there, maybe hours, but Xerus never once came to check on her. She wasn't sure if she was relieved by that or disappointed.

When she came back into the room and sat down on the bed, she couldn't help thinking about the dream, analyzing its meaning. Of course, she could easily gather what it meant though she found it hard to admit to herself.

You're in love with him, aren't you?

Galger had said that to her and she thought nothing of it then, convincing herself that she only cared for Xerus, nothing more. But even she couldn't deny the intense emotions he was bringing out of her. More powerful than she had felt for any human man.

If she did admit it, the question she had to ask herself then was, was it right? It wasn't like interspecies coupling had ever been discussed in her academic years. It wasn't something anyone at the research base had ever considered. There were no rules or laws because society was still young in mingling with other species. Truly, if she was honest with herself, she cared little for what others thought. With the situation she was in, she had lost a lot of her faith in the human race, regardless.

So the issue was with herself alone. Insecurities about how they could be together. Would he even want her? She, who was so different from him, soft and small to his large, rough physique. And he was already chosen to be with another. A literal queen of his race. How could she compete with that?

What scared her the most was what would happen afterward. She had to believe that somehow they would come out of all this in the end, hopefully unscathed. Would she lose him again after he completed his mission? And could she bear it?

Lana closed her eyes and breathed deep. She had to face him. She couldn't remain locked in this room forever. Eventually she had to tell him the truth.

Slowly she rose from the bed and went to the door. Hesitant, she listened for any sound but didn't hear movement from outside. Regaining her composure, she opened the door and walked back out into the main room but found it empty.

"Xerus?" she called. She went through each room and hall but he was nowhere. He must have left while she was sleeping. She slipped back into the original bedroom then into the bathroom where he had bathed and found the water drained from the tub. Something shiny glittered on the surface at the very bottom. Frowning, Lana reached down and found a sharp, blood-red scale in her hand, a little smaller than her palm. It must have shed from Xerus when he bathed. She clasped it in her hand and found it oddly cool and smooth. Like a thin, yet hard gem. She flipped it in her fingers, realizing she still didn't know everything about him. Only the finest of details. Their sessions together had been cut short. But now, with her waiting for the parasite to be destroyed and for them to escape, she might still have her chance before he likely left her for good.

Lana squeezed the scale determinedly then left the bathroom. She put on a t-shirt and a pair of pants then hid the scale in one of the pockets before leaving the room.

* * *

"I just think since we are here for an unknowable amount of time we could continue where we left off," Lana said to Xerus as he dropped a few bags on the ground, searching through them. "And since it doesn't matter anymore, we could learn the things we didn't get to before."

Xerus huffed. "*Siv xia essira nika li.*" Something about how he didn't care to be studied anymore. Lana quickly protested.

"No, no nothing like that. I was only ordered to try to study you. I just want to talk, is all. I just want to know more."

"Why?" he asked.

"For...for personal reasons. Because I'm curious."

Xerus took out more cans of food and set them on the bar, then he brought out a set of tools from the bag and laid them on the ground, looking over them carefully. He didn't show any emotion about the other night. In fact, he barely looked at her.

"I'll tell you anything you want to know. Okay, maybe you don't care. But I'm saying you have no reason now to keep anything from me," she said, vying for his attention.

Xerus did look at her then. "What makes you so sure?"

Lana opened her mouth then closed it firmly. Xerus let out a short hiss of breath.

"*Reasi,* if you must know." He mumbled something about humans and their damn insatiable curiosity. Lana didn't care, she grinned from ear to ear.

"But one condition," he said. "You have to listen in my language."

* * *

They made a spot in the main room to settle. Xerus worked on the parts to some unrecognizable device she couldn't yet identify as he spoke slowly, answering her questions. Now with the newfound power to ask anything she liked, Lana took complete advantage, nearly bursting with questions, many she had since the beginning.

The first she asked was what his race was called.

"*Xil Vrisha*," he said.

"The Vrisha," Lana repeated. "Is that the name of your planet also?"

Xerus shook his head. "*Tryth.*"

Lana leaned forward. "And what's it like?"

Xerus stopped what he was doing for a moment to look over at the fake scenery at the back wall, still showing a luxurious ocean coastline.

"*Essa vi nek.*" Not like that, he said. He described a scene more like a tropical wilderness with deep caves and dark jungles. Black and red deserts and bottomless craters.

"Sounds...a little scary." Lana laughed. Xerus grunted.

"*Feela ni Vrisha.*" It fit his people. He then told her a story about a time when he was younger and he and his brothers went into the jungles to catch what he called a *Gris*. A giant, squid-like creature with tusks. Its deadly poison was one of the few things that could kill a Vrisha almost instantly. And for that they saw it as a formidable foe worth respect. They even gave it tribute at one of their festivals.

"You praise an enemy?" Lana asked, bewildered.

Xerus nodded. "Veradis taught to praise those with strength and power, especially if they nearly equaled our own. *Teris xi vreesha.*" Strength is survival.

"So you fought it and what?" Lana asked.

He told her they had found one after five days and killed it then brought it back home, turning its poisonous barbs into weapons. They then each fought in a ritual battle against others of their pack using the weapons. Those who lost died, those who won were given their first ranks.

'That's barbaric,' Lana thought, but kept her silence. She learned to keep her opinions to herself when studying other cultures. "And you would go up ranks from there?" she asked.

Xerus nodded once. Depending on our success in battles, missions, or other work, we would be placed accordingly. Only those worthy were given the highest ranks.

"Such as yourself," Lana smirked, aware of his arrogance even if he wasn't.

Xerus grunted. Lana's throat tightened at the next question. "And the queens, how are they determined?"

"*Reska nik lisha.*" They are usually chosen.

"Chosen?" Lana said. "Like in a voting system?"

Xerus shook his head. " By many factors. Strength, bravery, resolve..."

"But they don't go through the pack ritual?"

"*Nil,* they do."

Lana's eyes widened. "They are as strong as males?"

"No. But they can be more swift and cunning," Xerus said.

"Oh," Lana said. She looked down at her hands, hesitant to ask more, but too curious not to. "And, um, what then is the Predomis for? Just to guard them...and be their mate?"

When Lana glanced up, her eyes met his. He straightened, eyes narrowing. "They are the other half." He tilted his head when she let out a small laugh.

"Let me guess, for top offspring?" She knew she shouldn't assume or judge even if it hurt.

Xerus pupils dilated and he blinked several times. "Blood means little. Everyone must prove their worth. Even those sprung from Queen mothers and Predomis fathers have lost their battles."

Lana was surprised and a bit ashamed at her initial judgment. She looked around the room, thinking silently for a moment. "This place probably looks nothing like your home," she said softly.

Xerus grunted, looking around himself. "No. Our homes are

darker, more dome-shaped. Warmer too." He eyed the open door to the bedroom, Lana followed his gaze.

"And no beds?" she asked.

"Not like yours. Instead of raised, they are...hollow."

"Like a nest, or den?"

Xerus shrugged.

Lana thought some more. She was fascinated by all this until she realized that Xerus, for several months, had been completely out of his element. Worse, he had been locked in what was practically a box for most of it. She could imagine that he must miss his home and have a desire to be around familiar things.

She chewed on her lip, an idea forming. "I have a favor to ask you."

"Hm?"

"Next time you go out I want you to get a few things."

"Like what?" He looked at her suspiciously.

Lana glanced over at the cans of food along the bar, most of them things she would eat but not him. "Food," she said.

Xerus looked at her, exasperated. "Have I not gotten enough?"

"Special food. Found on level two," she said.

Xerus huffed. "Fine."

Lana smiled. She gave him a break with her questions and spent the remainder of time watching him in silence, a strange feeling warming her. Despite everything that was happening, she somehow felt an inkling of calm.

CHAPTER TWENTY-FIVE

Xerus went out several times for her, bringing back various items along with the requested food he would find on level two. She knew for the most part what he ate so didn't need to ask but she did inquire about the kinds of clothes his people wore and asked that he bring different pairs of clothing. He gave her odd looks at her requests but he said little and went in search without complaint, likely chalking up her strange wants for weird human habits.

Lana watched him on the video feeds as he gathered the items mostly without issue. Though part of level two was being guarded by security trying to keep wraps on all food storage, with a little distraction, Xerus was able to thwart them easily. Lana filtered through other feeds to keep up to date with everything happening on each level and found that things were currently at a standstill. Galger and his team were on level three hunkering down, their latest kill set in the center of their hub like a glorified trophy, a large, centipede-like creature with sharp green feelers. It looked like they were taking inventory of the rest of the armory while they rested from their hunt. On level one everyone was huddled together, some resting on mats, others sitting at pillars and walls, the infected man still with them.

All other levels seemed dead, even level six was empty of the raptors, most either killed off or hiding from Galger's team. The other safer-ooms remained locked.

When the food, clothes, and other items were gathered, Lana took stock of everything Xerus had found. Fresh meats, eggs, various fruit and veg, blankets, oil, lighters, along with different sets of clothes from armored vests to pajamas. She put most of the clothes with the wrong kind of fabric away while the rest she kept in a neat pile. Xerus mentioned that males and females of his species usually wore similar clothing albeit that females sometimes covered the top of their shoulders and chest and wore strips of cloth around their thighs and between their legs while males generally wore the armored pants and sometimes armored chest and stomach pads. The clothing was mostly just decorative or to protect the areas where their scales were thinnest but no one was required to wear a lot of gear. Xerus himself admitted he only ever wore his armored leggings.

The kind of fabric they used was thin yet extremely durable. Even without the use of a fallen's scales as the exterior. The closest thing she could find was under armor and bits of leather. They were nowhere near as good but they would do.

Thankfully there was a cloth printer in one of the rooms, a sort of advanced sewing machine that she had used a few times in her academic years. When Xerus was away, she quickly put pieces together, trying her best to make something close to what he described. Before he came back, she hid the clothing away.

"I need you to go out and get one last thing for me," Lana said to him on what was their fifth day locked in together. "It might be hard to find, it could take you a while."

Xerus crossed his arms, his tail tapping against the ground. "You are a demanding little thing aren't you. What is it?"

"I need you to find me a glass cutter and some silver wiring."

Xerus gave her a severe look. "That's two things." When Lana shrugged and smiled timidly he let out a breath. "What does the glass cutter look like?"

Lana drew him a picture. The object looked like a combination of a rod and an old-fashioned key. It wouldn't be easy to find and, in truth, she didn't really need it, she just needed to get him out of the unit for as long as possible for her plan to work. The silver wiring was for a different project and would be much easier.

"Likely you'll find such a tool on level eight or any of the various warehouses but I can't be sure," Lana said.

Xerus' mouth twitched. "*Ixa il vaas.*" Be back soon.

'Not too soon I hope,' Lana thought as Xerus left. As soon as he was gone, she went to work.

It took several hours but when her work was complete Lana looked around the main room with great satisfaction. The lights were dimmed low, the air was warm, the scenery on the back wall was changed to display a birdseye view of a vast jungle. Couches and chairs were pushed back to the walls wherein the center she had laid out a large dark blanket. On it were the various foods she had asked Xerus to find, cooked to his liking. Spiced meats sliced thin, seasoned boiled eggs, lightly baked mango slices along with grilled vegetables. In small metal bowls usually used for cooking, Lana poured in oil and lit it carefully, letting flames lick the bowl, the oil burning slowly. She placed them in various corners and along the bar to make the scene more genuine.

She went around the unit one last time making sure everything was right. She still limped a bit, her burns still stinging, but she had redressed the wounds earlier and found them healing quickly. The pain was of little issue though. If anything she felt more self-conscious as she stalked around the place wearing the scraps of clothing she had made to mimic Vrisha fashion as the cloth did nothing to hide her bandages. Because she didn't have scales to cover her, she used a two-piece bathing suit instead. She still felt exposed but, knowing she would look even more ridiculous if she put regular clothing on underneath, she shoved away her embarrassment for the time being. Thankfully the suit was dark like the cloth and so blended well enough.

She limped down one hallway on the left and entered a room down at the very end. She had been perplexed by the need for a pool in such a place but then they always went overboard with units such as these despite their rare use. The sauna and pool room had been well kept by small bots, the pool cleaned regularly, the water kept warm. The pool wasn't big by any means. About eight feet wide and just long enough for those using it to do short laps but nothing strenuous. The pool was made for leisurely use, nothing more.

It took Lana a solid hour and a half to empty it. Thankfully the controls weren't too complicated and the bots helped, using pumps and tanks to drain it completely. After, she had the bots clean it entirely. Once it was polished and dried she had pulled out every blanket, comforter, and pillow she could find and laid them out on the bottom. When she looked down on it now, it looked like a strange, albeit comfortable, in-ground bed. She had no idea if it was exactly how Xerus had described but she hoped it was close enough. The lights too were lowered inside the room, wall lamps set to display a deep, warm orange. Another makeshift window display at the back showed a separate jungle scene, looking out over a set of falls. Lana gave everything a quick glance-over and felt satisfied.

From down the hall she heard the sound of the door sliding open and then closing. Heart jumping in her chest, she left the pool and slowly made her way down the hall. In the main room, Xerus stood, his back slightly turned toward her. He was still as granite, frozen in place as he stared. Only his head turned down slightly to look at the blanket display on the floor.

Lana watched him for a moment then licked her lips and spoke softly, "I know it's probably nothing like your home but I thought maybe I could help..."

Xerus' head turned ever so slightly in her direction. His eyes gathered her in. He stared at her for so long Lana began to shift uncomfortably. She looked down at her self-made strips of clothing and felt her face heat up. "I...I hope I didn't offend you."

Xerus turned fully to face her. "I am not offended," he said in a low voice. Lana smiled, trying to calm her nerves. Clearing her throat, she went to step around him when he held up his arm. In his hand was a small sack. "For you," he said slowly.

Lana took it and opened it. The wiring and glass cutter were inside. "Thank you." She smiled and placed the bag by the bar. When she turned back, Xerus was looking her over.

"Ah, it's probably completely wrong." Lana laughed nervously, drawing a piece of long dark cloth from her leg through her fingers. "But it was the best I could do with what I had and–"

"It's closer than you think." Xerus tilted his head at her. "It suits you."

Lana laughed again, shying from his intense stare. She eyed the food on the ground and gestured toward it. "I hope you're hungry."

"*Rissinak*," Starving, he said as his eyes never left her.

Lana shivered and tried to hide it by making her way over to the blanket. She sat down on the left side, crossing her legs, waiting for him to join her. Xerus' mouth twitched and he carefully went to the right side and knelt.

"Is there anything you do before beginning a meal?" Lana asked carefully. She didn't want to do anything that was considered impolite by his people's standards.

Xerus' eyes finally left her as he looked the food over. With the end of his tail, he speared a piece of meat. "I wouldn't hold you to any of my people's rituals in this situation, *kissala*."

Lana tensed, heat licking up her neck. She had heard him use that word before towards her but never could translate it fully nor did he explain. But she was beginning to believe it was some form of endearment.

He took the meat in his sharp fingers then ripped off a piece with his fangs. Lana took it as a sign and carefully took a few pieces for her plate as well as some fruit and vegetables. She noticed he didn't use his plate and wondered if maybe his kind didn't bother with them.

"Always trying to figure me out," Xerus said. "I see you observing me still, don't look so shocked."

Lana glanced away, embarrassed. "I'm sorry."

"Don't be. I'm use to it by now." His mouth twitched and his eyes seemed more playful than angry. "But you will find," he said, picking up one of the eggs, "that I have curiossities of my own. And I hope you will...indulge me."

Lana eyed him seriously. "Like what?"

Xerus said nothing as he ate his egg in one bite, his eyes, full of amusement now, never leaving her. Lana could feel her pulse in her throat. "How do you like the setting? she asked.

Xerus gazed around. "It is like home...you did well." He looked back at her. "You have my thanks."

Lana smiled, bringing a mango slice to her lips and taking a slow bite. The juice hit her tongue and dripped down the corners of her mouth, tangy and sweet.

"There is one thing missing, however," Xerus said.

Lana swallowed and licked her lips. "Oh?"

"It is...too quiet."

Lana thought for a moment and then said the word herself, "*Esika.*" Music.

Xerus nodded once and Lana got up and turned to a sound system just under the TV screen on the wall behind her. She turned on the system and searched through the apps and their playlists on the screen. She found the type of music that Xerus had told her was like his own–sultry beats and low base instruments, the exotic music of her world–and pressed play.

They listened as they ate, Lana unable to keep the smile off her face. She closed her eyes for a brief moment, envisioning his world and her within it. She imagined the warm breeze on her skin, the scent of spices in the air. Though things were darker than usual, she imagined the sun, in its deep orange and red glow, hanging low in the sky. When she opened her eyes, she met Xerus' curiously sharp gaze.

They stared at each other like they did and Lana felt a warm feeling settle in her stomach. Once they had finished with most of the meal, she quickly wrapped up the leftovers and threw the bowls and plates in the sink.

"I didn't make any kind of dessert," she said. "As I know sweets aren't really your thing."

"What is dessert?" he asked.

"Usually an after dinner treat. But it is usually something very sweet."

Xerus grunted. "My kind have a drink called *Sivas* after a meal."

Lana raised her eyebrows. "Oh? What is it like?" Perhaps she could replicate it.

"A mixture of *Frasi* blood and *Leeki* milk."

Lana nearly gagged. "Oh," she choked. She heard Xerus let out a hiss of laughter.

"Not for everyone," he said.

Lana looked over at the bar and eyed the different bottles there. "Perhaps you try something of my kind?"

When she saw Xerus shrug she went over to the bottles and studied them carefully. There was mostly vodka and rum but when she looked down in the mini-fridge she found an unopened bottle of Merlot not too old. She took it out and uncorked it and tasted it herself. A little bitter but not sweet. Perfect. She took out two glasses and poured some in each. When she handed Xerus his glass he sniffed at it curiously.

"It's called wine. It is made from grapes. Another type of fruit on my planet," she said, sitting back down.

Xerus eyed it briefly then took a full swig, drinking the dark liquid down. Lana choked down a laugh and sipped at her own.

"You are supposed to savor it..." she mumbled.

Xerus licked his lips and teeth, mulling over the wine. His eyes lit up.

"You like it?" Lana said.

Xerus grunted, offering her back his glass, wanting more. Lana laughed quietly and poured him another glass. He again drank it down quickly.

"My brethren would greatly enjoy this," he said, staring down at his glass.

"Perhaps we have something to trade then?" Lana inquired, taking another sip of her own.

Xerus' mouth widened. "Perhaps."

"There are effects to drinking too much though," Lana warned as she saw him pour himself another glass, filling the cup almost to the brim. "It can make one feel a little off..."

"Off how?" Xerus asked.

"Like...dizzy. Or careless." She watched as he took another generous swig. "Maybe it won't affect your kind the same though..."

Xerus seemed to take the hint, taking slower gulps. Lana tried to contain her laughter as she finished her own. "I'll admit I'm not big on alcohol myself but, on special occasions, I like to indulge."

Xerus tapped his fingers along his knee, regarding her lazily. "This is a special occasion?"

Lana set her glass down and shrugged. "I think it is," she said timidly.

Xerus tilted his head. "How so?"

Lana chewed on her lip, already she was beginning to feel the effects of the wine. She had always been a lightweight. "Because we are together," she said.

She didn't even think before she said it, just blurted it out like it was some secret confession. Heat rose as she realized though that she might have given too much away. She thwarted his gaze, looking down at her hands, her glass, the ground, anything but him.

"You are...happy we are together?" he asked.

The room was beginning to feel a little too warm, Lana could feel sweat trickling down her neck and back. She clasped her hands tightly together. 'Can't take it back now. Just let it out, Lana,' she thought.

"I am," she said, closing her eyes. Then she laughed. "I'm happy you had lied and didn't decide to hunt me down and..." she couldn't finish the rest. Her heart pounded wildly in her chest. "I am glad things are back to how they were before because..."

Xerus bent his head forward. "Because...?"

Lana did look at him then, her gaze entrapped with his. "Because you are my friend." She said it as steady as she possibly could but the slight waver in her tone might have given her away.

Xerus' eyes narrowed, his mouth twitching. "Friend?"

For a moment Lana feared he would dispute that claim. His eyes flickered over her sharply.

"Are we not?" Lana's voice this time did waver and she cursed silently.

Xerus straightened, thinking. "I do not know."

A stab of pain hit her chest. "Oh. I thought maybe..."

"I don't think friends fear another," he said blatantly. "Unless that is some strange human trait."

Lana frowned. "I don't fear you."

Xerus bowed his head. "Your heartbeat says otherwise."

Lana stiffened. Xerus nodded then slowly rose. "You humans are a confusing breed, you know? You fear me yet you try to please me. You show affection when you think I am dead but when I am alive, you turn from me."

Lana stood. "It's not like that."

"You smile at me and say you are happy, but you shrink from my gaze and my touch." Xerus snorted. "It is confusing and frankly annoying."

Lana swallowed as her mouth went dry. "I just...it's complicated, Xerus."

Xerus turned, a low growl rumbling in his chest. "You know I don't wish to harm you. I never would." He twisted back toward her. "I have been struggling to understand you for some time. But also to understand why I hate that you shrink from me. That is the most confusing and annoying thing of all."

Lana's eyes widened. She stood frozen as he moved toward her, coming to stand before her. "Why do I care so much for the little human female? Why do I speak her language so she can understand? Why do I go out and get food and clothing for her and other useless trinkets to please her? Why do I protect her and care for her when I should be focusing only on my mission? Hm?" His face came close to hers. "It is beyond me, you know. It is unlike me. Yet I do it. Do you know why?"

Lana's lips trembled. "It's the same reason why I did all this for you," she confessed softly.

Xerus' eyes widened for a split second. "Then why do you hide from me?"

Lana closed her eyes then opened them slowly, uncertain what to say. Xerus lifted his hand and took a few strands of her long hair in his fingers, letting them slip through. Then he placed his hand again against her neck, wrapping his fingers lightly around.

"Is it only because you still fear me?"

Lana shook her head, her body trembling. "No."

His hand rose to cup her jaw, his sharp thumb grazing her lips yet again. "Prove it then. Kiss me again."

His demand was unbreakable. Lana stood on the edge for a moment. Cautiously, she gripped his wrist so that his hand fell to settle on her chest and then carefully placed her hands around the sides of his face, grazing his smooth scales. He watched her with such intensity that Lana feared she might burn up in his gaze. Feeling her pulse hammering in her head she acted before she became too afraid to. She lifted herself on her toes, stretching up to kiss the side of his jaw and neck, feeling his hard, smooth skin brush against her lips. Xerus remained still until she broke from him. She tried to step back and felt his tail wrap around her waist, pulling her closer to him. Without warning his head came down toward her and Lana stifled a gasp as his face pressed against her neck and nuzzled her.

"Vina sila. Kissala," He hissed softly.

Lana let out a small whimper, her hand trembling as she gripped his arms.

Be with me.

Lana could hardly breathe. She lifted her head, letting him in more. Whether from the confession or the wine, she couldn't be sure, she let all her fears and doubts slip away. Now there was only her and this lethal, terrifying, gorgeous alien that she wanted. Wanting him to take her and make her his until there was nothing but them together in the dark.

His tongue slipped between his teeth and grazed up her neck and Lana moaned uncontrollably. Like her dream, she felt wild and alive. She shivered as she felt his fangs nip her skin but didn't cry out, not wanting him to stop. It was a strange feeling at first, so different from a human man. But Lana let go of her cares, her hands gripping him tightly, wanting him closer.

His head rose and his warm hands slipped down on her waist, gripping her hips, bringing her against him. He let out a low growl and Lana felt something brush against her stomach. When she glanced down, she saw the bulge between his legs enlarged, only his armored pants keeping him in. Xerus' expression twisted as if in pain, his body shifting. His tail slipped from her to sway with impatience behind him.

"Xerus," Lana whispered. She kissed his chest and stomach and felt him tremble for the first time. A sharp hiss escaped him and, before she could even react, she was in his arms, being carried toward the bedroom.

"Wait, not there!" Lana said. She pointed to the hall with the pool room. "Down there. Trust me."

Xerus did as she asked and quickly made his way down the hall, pushing the door open with his foot. She felt his body tense as he took in the scene, similar to the main room with the inlaid bed instead of a pool.

Lana wrapped her arms around his neck. "I thought you would like–"

Xerus rushed for the pool bed, dropping down into it with little effort. As soon as he placed Lana on her back, he stripped off his armored pants and, with his talon-like fingers, gripped her bathing suit top and tore it off. Lana gasped as the clothing ripped in two and was tugged away from her. Though her body was on fire, goosebumps trailed along her legs and arms and her nipples tightened.

Xerus glared down at her naked upper torso as if transfixed. Slowly he knelt beside her and Lana saw him grimace as if in pain again. The slit between his legs opened and the head of him slipped out. A dark, pointed shape. Then the rest of him slid out. Deep red, long, thick, and rimmed, the tip curving up ever so slightly. Lana's heart did a little flip. Her scientist brain tried to push its way into full gear and Lana had to choke down an idiotic laugh, shoving the thoughts aside.

No, now wasn't the time for observing like that. Though she couldn't help the little fear growing at the thought of him entering her. She hadn't been with anyone since her college days. And he was large. It was likely going to hurt.

She didn't fear much else besides that. She had been treated a while ago to prevent disease and pregnancy, having her chip replaced when they asked for all her treatments to be up to date before coming to Lazris. And it wasn't like it was possible for him to get her pregnant. It couldn't be. Even if Xerus' race had odd ways of counteracting natural defenses.

Xerus licked his lips as if about to savor another delicious meal. He lowered his head and nuzzled her breasts and neck, nipping them. His fangs were so sharp, even with his lightest bite little beads of blood formed along her skin. He lapped at them and Lana let out a sharp little inhale.

He raised his head up to look at her again, his eyes swimming with liquid fire. "*Issina xi, Kissala,*" bare yourself to me, he said in a low voice.

Slowly Lana sat up and began to slide the suit bottom from her, the small strips of clothing coming off with it. She settled herself back, taking deep breaths, watching Xerus with nervous anticipation. Her body was wickedly hot and when his slick tongue stroked against her belly like licks of fire, she felt her lower core spasm and turn to liquid.

"Xerus," she whispered in a soft moan. She opened herself to him and he readily obliged, mounting on top of her. He lifted her legs, bending the knees so that her feet were around his stomach. With his arms on either side of her head, she gripped his wrists as if preparing herself, digging her nails into his skin. He didn't so much as flinch, his eyes only looking to her, searing and bright.

He bent his head and nuzzled the top of her head. "You are so small and soft, *kissala*. I can't promise I won't hurt you by accident. If I do..."

"I'm not worried," Lana said softly. "I'll be okay because it's you."

Xerus closed his eyes and she could feel a low rumble in his chest like a deep purr. He lifted his tail up, curving it above him, then pressed his hips against her. She felt the head of him push into her center and she tensed. She let out a small cry as the rest of him slid into her slowly. It did hurt at first just as she feared but she pushed through the pain until he was locked to her fully. He was so hot and hard and unimaginably different in the way he fit in her. Foreign. Alien. She let out a small laugh at that obvious thought and his eyes flickered over her face with concern.

"I'm okay," she said. "I'm alright."

Not totally convinced apparently, Xerus kept his head bent so that he could watch her every reaction carefully as he moved against her. He went excruciatingly slow at first, only the smallest of strokes. Lana could feel the tip of him hitting some secret place in her and her body reacted almost instantly. Loud moans escaped her throat and she writhed under him, her body desperate for more. Her hips moved and her back arched, her soft skin grazing against his scales, leaving small stinging cuts. Her bandages tore and ripped as they ground against his sharp skin. It didn't phase her. What she felt inside was more raw and intense than any small pain she might receive in return. It was a small price to pay for the pleasure.

Xerus barely moved on top of her, as if waiting for some sign from her. When she moaned again and called out his name in hungry desperation, he lowered his arms to lock around her waist, pinning her hard in place. His lip curled, showing the tips of his fangs, and a low growl escaped him, his eyes turning into glowing red slits. He brought his hips out then plunged back into her and Lana gasped, a blissful cry ripping from her throat.

He moved on her then with such a bestial urgency that Lana was forced to grip his arms to try to keep in place. The fire in her was reaching its peak, each spark shooting through her center with every stroke. She felt it from her core up to her belly, her heart about to burst. She clamped her teeth together despite each cry that tore through her lips. Xerus didn't slow as if he couldn't, already too lost in his own drive, too ravenous to stop. His hips slammed into her thighs and Lana winced, her grip tightening around his arms. The harder he moved the closer to her climax she got. There was a ripping sound as his nails dug into the sheets below them. They were both engulfed in their own inner flames.

As she shattered beneath him, Xerus still didn't slow. He was far gone in his wave of need. His growls grew louder, sharper, his fangs bared, eyes nothing but glowing slits. He looked like a savage beast above her.

Coming down from her high, Lana released one of his arms to place her hand on his chest. In response, Xerus shot his free hand out and cupped her jaw. A few more beats against her and he let out a long, sharp hiss. He moved inside her and Lana felt his liquid heat filling her. He released her face, panting hard, his body shuddering. It was the most Lana had seen his body react and it left her staring in shock.

"Xerus..." She could feel his heart beating against her palm, the same rhythm she felt in her core. Xerus huffed some more, his face twisting. He groaned and his body relaxed. He lowered himself on to her, sheltering her below his chest and stomach, making sure not to crush her under his weight. Breathless and sweating, Lana lay under him until his heart was back to its normal slow rhythm. She patted his side and he rose off her, slipping out of her. Instantly there was a gush of wet heat between her thighs and Lana tensed. Sitting up slowly, she looked down and quickly closed her legs.

"Oh." She looked away, a little embarrassed.

Xerus' mouth widened, looking pleased. He reached out his hand, stroking her cheek then curling a lock of damp hair behind her ears. When his eyes dropped down her body, his face fell.

"Ah, *cisa nifil, xi silla.* I have hurt you." His voice turned deep, angry with himself. His fingers slipped down to the cuts on her thighs and the bandages in shreds. Lana took his hand in hers.

"It's fine. I'm fine." She smiled. Though she knew she was going to be majorly sore.

Xerus said nothing as her other hand stroked his face tenderly. His eyes closed, still hungry for her touch. That low purr sounded deep in his chest as she caressed him.

"I wouldn't mind a shower though," she said finally, her hand dropping. "Seeing as..." Her legs shifted as she tried to keep from soiling the sheets more than they already were. Xerus' mouth twitched. He gathered her up and carried her out of the inlaid bed.

"A better idea," he said. "Another bath."

CHAPTER TWENTY-SIX

"There's nothing yet," Lana spoke through the headset, watching Xerus intently on the screen. "Though I'd be careful of the rooms on your right, I saw some odd movement."

A static-filled hiss of laughter sounded in her ear. "It's likely no threat." Xerus turned down one passage and Lana switched the feed so she could see him.

Lana smiled. "Not to you anyway. But I thought you should know."

There was a grunt in response and Xerus slipped into a large supply room. "I'm going to place one in here. Shouldn't take long."

"I'll keep my eye out," Lana said. She watched him briefly as he set the device in his hands to the nearby wall, connecting wires accordingly. She was still astounded by his ability to use the environment around him, even if unfamiliar, to his every advantage.

Though it wasn't like he hadn't had decades of experience training to utilize anything and everything around him or enough time to study "simple" human technology. Still, she couldn't help being impressed. Even she hadn't expected him to know how to construct bombs out of the machinery and bots scattering the whole base. When he had shown her, she could only stare at him in bewilderment. But now it seemed obvious and she scolded herself silently for her lack of observation.

"Almost done," Xerus said as he put the last wires in place, making sure the bomb was secured fully to the wall. Lana flipped through the feeds quickly to make sure there was nothing about to creep up on him. She had insisted on being Xerus' extra eyes, to make sure nothing tried to attack him by surprise while he concentrated on setting his bombs. Though he could easily defend himself, he needed complete focus to make sure the bombs were connected accordingly. When she saw the way was clear, she switched back to Xerus.

"Coast is clear."

Xerus looked over the bomb one last time. Then, when he seemed satisfied, he nodded and left the room. "I'll put the next one in a room on the opposite end," he said.

If a month before someone had told Lana she would be helping an alien to set bombs to destroy the entire base, she would think they needed to visit medical. Yet here she was and she still found it surreal. And honestly terrifying.

The night he had told her about the bombs after completing his first set from the wires, metal, and chemicals he had found from various bots on eight, she had been a little mortified to say the least.

"You told me you would try to save those who aren't infected," Lana had said.

"*Eti xi neesh,*" and I shall, he said.

Lana had crossed her arms, a hard set frown on her face. "Then how does destroying the whole base help exactly?"

"I will get to as many of the uninfected as I can once I set the bombs," he had said, placing each bomb next to the other on the table meant for dining, "but after, the base must be destroyed."

"Let me guess. In case you missed one?" Lana said.

Xerus nodded. "It will be easier too. Instead of having to go through every part of this place just to find each of the infected and destroy them. This way it can be done quicker."

Lana couldn't argue with that. And the quicker it was done the sooner they could get off the planet.

Xerus' plan was to set bombs on every floor starting with the lowest. With twelve already gone he hadn't bothered so he started with eleven. He had found the headset that allowed them to communicate while he placed the bombs on each level so she could help alert him to any "danger" as he went about his task. For now he only focused on the bombs, getting them ready for when the time came to detonate. Then, as he promised, he would look for those uninfected and lead them away.

Currently, he was on the lower levels which were mostly empty. The saferoom she had been in on ten was the lowest one and everyone from there was gone. The only possible life-forms left were any last surviving creatures that had yet to be obliterated by Galger's team.

"This is the last bomb here," Xerus said. "Eleven and ten are set. I'm coming back and will prepare the others for levels nine and eight." He took up his now empty bag and tied it around his neck.

"Alright. See you soon." Lana watched until he slipped out onto the emergency stairs then shut off her headset. She checked the feeds and found that most of the activity was on the upper levels per usual. Galger and his men had split up, some guarding their trove on level three, others back on level five for some reason, possibly looking for anything that made it in the destruction that they could salvage. Lana couldn't watch long, too sickened by the bodies still left all around. Many of them had burned but Lana still remembered and she shuddered thinking of her lost friend now nothing but ashes. She switched away when she saw nothing of value and flipped over to level one. Nothing was new. The people still huddled around, waiting, guards distributing food. The saferooms were still locked, although one did open briefly for scouts to go out and check the area. She watched them for a moment and was thankful when they returned quickly without incident.

She turned the feed off and placed her headset on the bar. Beside it, she picked up the scale Xerus had shed, now woven between bits of silver wire. She had thought to turn it into a necklace or bracelet but she had never been very good at arts and crafts. For now, it was just a red shard wrapped in a silvery cage. Before Xerus came through the door, she hid it in one of her pockets.

The door closed behind him and Xerus nodded toward her as he placed his bag on the ground. Smiling, Lana stood and greeted him.

"Nothing to report yet though there were a few sightings of stragglers, most everyone has kept to the upper levels," Lana said, wringing her hands as if somehow nervous.

Xerus grunted. "The rest of the bombs shouldn't take me long to assemble." He stepped around her to where he had left his tools and scraps of parts on the long table now pushed to the right wall in the main room. He went through the parts carefully. He picked up one particular device and showed her.

"This is the detonator. It is already paired with assembled bombs. The rest will follow suit." He gripped the narrow device firmly, the switch at the side meant to be pressed like a trigger. Xerus set it back down carefully. "When the time comes I will set it off. There will be about a three-second delay before the bombs go off."

Lana nodded, understanding. "I suppose we will be out of the base before they go off...if we can get to a ship."

Xerus' eyes flickered over to her. "I am not worried."

Lana wished she felt the same. But danger and fear still settled deep in her subconscious. As confident and assuring as Xerus was, anything could still go wrong.

"Will you go back out tonight?" Lana asked.

Xerus twisted to face her, his eyes glittering with something savage. "*Nil*," he said. He moved to stand close to her. "I will make the rest of the bombs. But first," his tail slipped around her back, bringing her against him, his clawed finger brushing the side of her face delicately, "*Xi na Essha*," I am hungry.

Lana suppressed a grin, her face heating. "I will fix you something," she said in a low voice, her eyes half-closed.

Xerus growled, showing off the tips of his fangs. His face came down and his tongue grazed the side of her neck. Lana shivered, her hands coming up to grip the sides of his arms. She craned her neck upward so that he was given better access, allowing his tongue to trail fire along the center of her throat up to her chin. A purr rumbled in his chest, vibrating against her.

Ever since their first night together Xerus had been much more needful in his wants. No longer suppressing his desire for her. And she never denied him even when she was sore. She wanted him too. In more ways than just physical. But she feared to voice those wants.

Even now that they were together she still feared the possibility of being tossed aside by his duty for his people and his right of passage to becoming a Predomis. And what that entailed. But now wasn't the time to think about that. At least that's what she told herself. She had him now and what was important was that they got out of Lazris alive.

Lana moaned as he nipped her skin and nuzzled her neck. "Was this morning not enough?" She laughed softly. Her body heated, remembering waking up curled against him in his newly made den. And of their early morning antics.

Xerus grumbled. *"Nisa vil shas."* It is never enough.

Lana breathed deep and gave in as she always did. She let him lead her down to the ground, too impatient now to make it to the den bed. The heat and power of him at her back was exquisite. She closed her eyes as he peeled off her shirt, feeling his warm hands graze her chest. As they undressed fully and he pressed himself behind her, sliding in deep, claiming her again, Lana's heart fluttered and dropped.

No, she couldn't think about what would happen afterward. Not yet.

CHAPTER TWENTY-SEVEN

Xerus successfully placed the next set of bombs, this time on all levels up to seven. A few incidents and mishaps had occurred along the way but Lana had been there at every step to warn him. A strange reptilian creature with quills on its back had found its way on level eight, spraying out thick, slimy layers of acid from its mouth. As it tried to target Xerus, who was able to dodge in time, the slime instead hit one of the bot-repairing machines with a set of pipes connected behind it, letting out a full layer of steam, making it hard for Lana to see in the room. Xerus took out the creature before it could do any more damage but the pipe was unfixable, belching out endless amounts of steam.

On level seven Xerus encountered a few lurkers. Some unfortunately infected. Lana didn't watch as he destroyed the bodies. Those who were clean he forced into a room and had them locked in. He promised her he'd go back for them later.

"I have one bomb left that I will place on six and will set the rest after my return," he told her as he made his way up to the medical bay.

"Okay, sounds good." Lana looked at the feed for six as well as the level's data. There was a small saferoom on six, one she hadn't noticed before as she had been too busy trying to save Nicole. There were at least a few dozen individuals inside. Those who were able to get in and lock the doors before the raptors got to them.

As Xerus made his way through the debris of six to set his bomb, Lana checked every passage and found it empty. Everything seemed still.

A rattling noise sounded from above her and Lana looked up at the ceiling with a frown. The noise was coming from level three. Curious, she switched over to three on the video as Xerus began to set his bomb.

Galger's team was drilling into the wall beside the saferoom's door on level three. Sparks flew as they drilled into the locking mechanism. Lana shook her head in confusion as she watched them. Why were they trying to get into the saferoom? And why with such force instead of asking those inside to open up?

They punctured a hole into the locking device then one of the soldiers set to fiddle with the wires within. As he went about pulling and connecting wires, several of Galger's men stood back and held their guns at the ready, aiming toward the door. Lana's heart raced and her eyes widened as they positioned themselves. "Oh, god, no," she whispered to herself.

She knew before the door even opened and when it did she jumped back, her chair falling to the ground as gunfire lit the feed and the noise drove downwards from level three into her room. Galger's men shot blindly, bullets spraying every which way into the safe room. The people nearest the door went down first, then those in the back trying to flee came after. A group of individuals, whether brave or stupid, came charging at the soldiers, flinging their arms and fly into the air, only to be flung to the ground, their bodies going limp. From their faces, Lana could see they hadn't been brave or stupid. They had been infected. Black blood flowing out of their dead lips.

Lana didn't think Galger and his men actually knew whether any of them had been infected or not. They had just planned to break into the room and open fire. And by the looks of it, that was completely true. A few still writhed on the ground in agony, tears spilling from their eyes, blood from their stomachs. They pleaded for their lives but the soldiers didn't respond. With cold stares they did as they were commanded, aimed their guns at the survivor's heads, and fired.

No one was spared. Though they had taken out only a handful of infected, the rest were ordered to die.

Lana watched with tears spilling from her eyes as the men dragged the corpses into a pile into the room, ready to set them ablaze. She fell to her knees, her hand covering her mouth. She barely registered the door opening and closing and the sharp hands dragging her up and encircling her.

"Are you hurt? What happened?" Xerus' face came into view.

Lana blinked up at him in surprise wondering how he had gotten to her so quickly. How he had known something was wrong. She shook in his grasp.

"I could hear your cries, *Kissala*. Tell me what's wrong?"

She had forgotten her headset was still on. Quickly she dragged it off, letting it fall to the floor. "They killed them," she choked. "They killed them all."

Xerus' face tilted and, when she gestured to the screen, Xerus saw what she meant. The bodies were now a pile of flames. Xerus' eyes narrowed. "You saw this?" he asked.

Lana nodded her head, more tears falling silently. "They opened the door and just started firing. They didn't even look, Xerus. Oh god, they didn't even look." Her body tried to slip down as her knees buckled but Xerus held her firmly.

"Were the people infected?" Xerus said, forcing her to look at him.

Lana gripped his shoulders, taking deep breaths. "Only a few were. The rest..." She shook her head unable to say more. Xerus crushed her to him.

She held on to him as her body trembled, his hand gripping the back of her head gently. "They are going to kill the rest, I know it," she said against his chest. "They will kill any they see because, unlike you, they cannot detect the parasite and are not going to save them."

A low growl rose in Xerus' throat. He muttered something in his language that she did not catch. He lifted her into his arms, carrying her out of the room, away from the video feed. Lana shivered, feeling cold despite his warmth against her.

"I'm scared, Xerus," she said, trying to keep her composure.

"I am here. Nothing will get to you."

Lana hugged his neck. "I know. But the others. What can we do?"

Xerus placed Lana back onto the ground. Finding herself in one of the bedrooms, Xerus led her into the bathroom adjacent, one with a large shower room.

"Come let me warm you, you are so cold and I need to clean."

Lana didn't fight or argue as Xerus turned on the shower using the controls by the wall. The water cascaded down from the ceiling overhead, hot rain on to black marble. Xerus slipped off Lana's clothes along with his own and, with one arm around her waist, he brought her with him into the steaming room.

If his plan was to ease her mind or at least distract her, it worked. Hot water poured onto her head and down her back, drenching her quickly. He held her tightly against him, his hand splayed firmly across her back. Lana curled into him, her tears melding with the spraying water.

"What can we do, Xerus?" Lana repeated more calmly after a moment.

Xerus brushed his hand down her spine. "I could kill them."

Lana closed her eyes. It was what she had had in mind for him before, only then she had been too afraid to ask.

"You could try. I had thought of the idea before. But I don't think I could bear the thought of possibly losing you again," Lana admitted.

Xerus snorted. "They are no threat."

Lana turned her head up to meet his gaze. "They are. I know you are well trained in combat and are more powerful. But they have something you don't. Numbers. And advance weapons that they could use with their eyes closed. They are one of the military's most trained men. A few might not be anything but there are at least two dozen of them. And I have seen the kind of weapons they are packing." Lana shook her head. "We can't risk it because I...my people need you."

Xerus' eyes bore deep into hers and Lana held his gaze. "If something happened, the others would be stuck. I would be left defenseless, unable to help," she said softly. She reached up and kissed his neck, trailing her lips upward, moving across his jaw. Xerus closed his eyes, groaning. He backed her against one of the walls, placing his arm against the black marble, leaning his body forward, sheltering her. She continued to kiss him gently, tasting droplets of water.

Xerus hissed. "I cannot avoid them forever."

"I know," Lana said between kisses. Then a thought lit up her mind. "I think I have an idea." She looked up at him. "We should send the uninfected straight to the docks right away. Though they can't leave until it is safe, it is better to have them all in one place, away from Galger's team. As soon as everyone is out, we keep Galger and his men from following. They either comply to set their weapons aside and be tied up or they remain and...we continue with the initial plan."

Xerus' eyes narrowed. "We set off the bombs."

Lana nodded.

"I would rather they were dead, but I assume your kind would wish them to face some sort of trial for their actions?"

"It would be the right thing," Lana said wearily. She had made sure the Scibot recorded all movement within the base so that every action was filed away into the main system. And every hour it sent those files into cloud storage which would be easy to access. Everyone would know once they got out and Galger and his men could face punishment for their crimes.

Xerus grumbled but didn't argue. "Very well. I assume then you will use the cargo elevators to get the rest of the people up to the docks?"

Lana's eyes widened. "How did you know?"

"I have seen the maps. I know the supply routes are the only ones capable of going from each level to the docks without having to stop at the city sector first. I was planning to use it myself when I first studied the map on level twelve."

"Ah, so that was the information you stole from the bot. I should have guessed..."

Xerus' mouth widened and he shrugged.

"Yes, that's the plan." Lana continued. "Right now there are a few waiting up on the docks now. Place the bombs then shepard those hiding or in saferooms and send them up. Galger and his team have been sticking to level three as their home base so we will go there last. Once it is highly unlikely that there is anyone left on those levels, we can just place the bombs and nothing more." Lana gripped Xerus and kissed his shoulder with excitement, her anger and fear subsiding temporarily. "It could work."

"I'll go back to the lower levels and get to the uninfected first that were left. Then make my way up once more," Xerus said. He pressed against her, nuzzling the side of her head. "It shouldn't be difficult. And quick. Once they see me, they will run faster than they ever have in their lives."

CHAPTER TWENTY-EIGHT

Xerus didn't have to go far down to find survivors. Based on the Scibot's readings, there was no one alive on any of the levels from eleven to ten. Just bodies. Some half-eaten by creatures lurking in the dark, others killed mysteriously in ways Lana didn't want to think about. Likely from those infected and hostile. Weeding out the weak. Lana had done her best to avoid looking or thinking about them when Xerus had been setting his bombs, but now it was all she could focus on and it made her stomach twist.

There was no one left on nine either as they had fled their units so Xerus made his way down to eight where, based on the data, there were a few hiding. Once he found them, Xerus made sure none were infected then drove the group out of the room they had blockaded and, with a little fear mongering, shepherded them into the warehouse, to the cargo elevator. They took it up and Xerus too made his way to the next level. He found the people he had left on seven and did the same with them as he did with those on eight. Their screams and cries of terror echoed through Lana's headset but she remained still and calm, knowing they were in no real danger. They had no way of knowing Xerus was helping them.

As he led them through the rooms, one did find an ounce of courage and took out his gun to fire toward Xerus. The alien dodged, the bullet barely missing his head, and quickly disarmed him. The man stumbled and fell then ran to catch up with the others.

"*Seci nix vi shaaves*," Xerus muttered. Something about humans being so ungrateful.

"They don't know you are trying to help," Lana reminded him.

"Still, it would be nice not to be shot at," Xerus sneered.

"I know, I'm sorry. Level six there is a group in the saferoom. They likely won't have guns."

Xerus hissed. "We shall see."

Lana's lips tightened, her heart pounding as she centered all her focus on the screen. She was nervous for him and for the others. Even if Xerus got them to run in the right direction toward the cargo elevator, there could still be other specimens or infected hiding, ready to attack.

Once those on seven were out, Xerus made his way through the debris-filled passages of the medical bay until he came up beside the saferoom door. He opened his jaws wide then shut his mouth as if setting it in a specific manner, his head bowed. He backed away to stand underneath an unlit corner, his eyes piercing the dark. He cleared his throat then lifted his tail to knock soundly on the door.

Minutes passed and there was no answer. Xerus went to knock again when a voice broke the silence.

"W-who's there?"

"This is Officer Galger. Me and my crew are looking for survivors." Xerus sounded exactly like him, giving Lana goosebumps. She would remind him never to use that voice while they were together. "The base is clear and safe and you can come out now."

There was another long pause. "We haven't heard anything. We were told we had to wait until we heard from the master officers and generals that the lockdown was lifted."

"Due to new safety measures they cannot contact you in the usual manner," Xerus said without hesitation. "They assigned us to get those in the saferooms out. If you open the door and make for the cargo elevator and take it up to the docks, there will be a ship ready."

A short pause and then, "Why are we taking the cargo elevator? Why not take us through to the city sector?"

Lana was grateful to see Xerus keeping his patience. "We want to get you out as quickly and as safely as possible and the main elevators are not in working order," Xerus said, making up excuses as he went. "Are you ready to comply?"

There was a murmur of noise on the other end as if they were arguing, then a clear voice said, "Okay, we are opening up."

Xerus backed farther into the shadows as the door slid open. Heads poked out looking all around.

"Nobody's there! Quick, close the door!" someone shouted within. As a man in a doctor's uniform went to press the button, Xerus revealed himself and strode into the room.

"Holy fuck!" someone yelled and the others screamed. Lana winced as she saw dozens scramble out of the room, Xerus having to block a few from running the wrong direction causing them to shrink back in terror.

It took a few attempts to get them to move the right way and lead them toward the level six warehouse. Once inside, Xerus trapped them within. He got them to flee into the cargo elevator then he stopped and grew still once they huddled inside.

"P-please," one of them begged. Xerus closed his eyes and sniffed the air.

"Xerus? What wrong?" Lana asked nervously.

Xerus opened his lids and narrowed his eyes on a pair of lab coats in the corner of the room. He growled and lunged for them, dragging them out of the elevator. "They are infected."

Before Lana could make a sound, Xerus snapped their necks quickly, their bodies falling to the ground. Lana gasped but kept silent though her stomach heaved and her mouth dried and she feared she might become sick. Xerus moved toward the rest of the group, now a whimpering bundle on the ground. He closed his eyes again then nodded. "The rest are safe." He moved away from the elevator and closed the doors.

Lana slumped in her chair and closed her eyes, trying to remain calm. The two had been infected and nothing could be done. She just had to be thankful the others were okay.

"I`m going to set more bombs on six then we will move forward," Xerus said sharply. He swung around the bag that had been resting at his back and made his way through the rooms to place his bombs.

Lana licked her lips and swallowed. "Alright," she said softly. Seeing Xerus kill the two men so swiftly and without thought scared her and reminded her what he was capable of. Silently she thanked whoever that Xerus had taken a liking to her and that she had never gotten the parasite.

As Xerus set his bombs, Lana brought up the data screen of the entire base. The numbers were so low it made her heart drop. Only a few hundred were left. Either some had found their way out—somehow making it to the docks—or many hadn't made it, succumbing to any number of threats. The level three saferoom had one of the largest populations inside and they were taken out in a matter of minutes by Galger's team. The largest population now was on level one and it was only a matter of time before the soldiers made their way up to finish the job.

Rubbing her forehead, Lana accessed the rest of the remaining data from the levels that were left. There was one remaining safe-room on level five along with a few readings of people in another room close by. Level three had activity but she knew it was only Galger and his men. Level four there was only her and level two was mostly empty save for a few guards protecting the food supply. Then there was level one with its several hundred or so.

"One last saferoom, Xerus, and then it's on to the top," Lana said. "There are people also in one of the rooms but they might be from Galger's team so be careful.

Xerus placed his last remaining bomb for six then headed for five. Lana checked the feeds to see for herself who was huddling in one of the rooms outside the saferoom on five. She flipped through the video until she found the room. To her surprise, it wasn't a group of Galger's soldiers as she feared. The group huddled together in a circle out in the open. They didn't have guns at their sides or any other weapons. They sat at the center with a bunch of equipment and what looked to be Scibots that were partially disassembled around them. The bots' wires spewed over the ground like a field of metal encompassing the group. Lana's eyes narrowed looking at them. Why were they just sitting there? And what were they doing with the bots? Were they too looking for parts? Lana hadn't seen anyone lurking around there before but perhaps they had come while she had slept or when she had been focused on helping Xerus. "There is another group," Lana said. "It isn't Galger's team."

Xerus grunted. He made his way into five and went for the saferoom first. As Lana switched over to watch him, she could see the saferoom was already unlocked even though the door was closed. Lana frowned and Xerus hesitated. He slipped over to the side of the door, readying himself. With his tail, he pressed the button and the door slid open. Lana braced herself.

The people inside had been sitting far from the door. When they saw Xerus they shot up and screamed. As they ran from him, Lana noticed some were badly injured. One person didn't even move from the room, clearly unconscious or dead.

Xerus checked the body then moved on after the group, indicating to Lana that the individual was indeed gone. Something bad had happened in the room and she feared one or more of them must have been infected.

The group was slow as so many were injured, making it easier for Xerus to catch up and keep them together. Once he got them to the cargo bay and into another elevator, he searched them over and, to Lana's shock, found none that were infected. As the elevator doors closed, Xerus went back for the last group.

'Maybe they are from the saferoom', Lana thought as she went back to the video of the room with the group huddled in the center.

'Maybe they were kicked out for attacking the others.' "Be careful, Xerus, these ones might be trouble," Lana said aloud.

When Xerus got to the entrance of the room, he hesitated a second to look inside. The group of men were bent over themselves, silent, with their eyes turned to the ground. They didn't even notice Xerus' presence as he stepped into the room. Xerus gazed at the disfigured bots and the wires on the ground curiously. As he slipped farther in, one of the men saw him. The man cried out and gestured to the others who saw the large alien and turned ashen. They screamed and did everything Lana expected them to do. Everything except run.

"Why aren't they moving?" Lana said, watching as the men cowered away and shouted curses but didn't attempt to flee. "Xerus...why aren't they–"

Then she saw and knew. They didn't run because they couldn't. They were chained to the floor.

Lana's heart jolted. "Oh my god, Xerus, get out of there!"

The Scibots turned on simultaneously and violent sparks of electricity shot down the wires into the floors. The room ignited. Electricity flashed through the room like a lightning storm, bathing the area in a brilliant white. The men died instantly, their bodies seizing then going limp. Xerus bent forward, letting out an ear-shattering roar.

Lana winced but kept the headset on her. "No," she cried. "Xerus!"

Sparks flew and the bots started going up in flames. When the electricity finally sizzled out, Xerus fell to the ground, unmoving.

"Xerus!" Lana called to him but he didn't respond. Panic spread through her body. She continued to call out to him because it was all that she could do.

Xerus didn't move no matter how much she pleaded. All she could do was sit and stare at the screen with horror, thinking he was dead. Her throat tightened, it was becoming hard to breathe.

"Xerus, please get up. Please!"

There was nothing.

A moment later a group of men stepped into the room, guns drawn, aimed right at Xerus. Lana couldn't make out what they were saying and she realized it was because Xerus' headset was fried. He wouldn't have heard her, anyway. Wide-eyed and cold as ice, Lana watched Galger's men enter the room. Galger and Torrence entered last.

They talked for a moment as Galger ordered his men to tie Xerus up, binding him with thick chains. Helpless, Lana watched as they stood over Xerus' body and wrapped his tail around him so that his spikes dug into his abdomen, using his own body against him. They cut the bag of bombs from his neck and, as they tied his tail to him and secured the binds, they took the ends of each chain and dragged Xerus from the room.

CHAPTER TWENTY-NINE

"Just remain calm, Lana. Don't panic. You can't lose control now," Lana said to herself as she paced the room, repeating the words over and over. But her voice cracked and her body shook because inside her head all she could think about was what they were going to do with her alien. Who risked his life and put aside part of his mission to help her save others. It was her fault. And now he was going to be...

Lana leaped for the Scibot's screen and switched through the feeds until she got to level three. Her breath quickened and her throat tightened as she searched the rooms. A tiny cry ripped from her throat as she found the team entering their hub with Xerus, dragging him over to the back wall and hooking his chains to a set of self-made handles, taken from spare metal parts and welded to the ground. Lana cursed herself. She should have been watching Galger and his team closer. She had every opportunity to observe them but she had been too busy with helping Xerus to take heed of what they had been doing. They knew Xerus was one of the last of the specimens left and had been planning all along to trap him. If she hadn't had him go out and look for others, he might have avoided them entirely. Tears stung her eyes as she now watched Xerus being tied to the ground and wall.

One of the soldiers then came forward and roughly slipped a sizable black cloth over Xerus' face to blind him.

They wouldn't have done all this if they thought he was dead so at least she had the small relief of knowing he must be alive only unconscious. It did little to ease her. Because deep down a horrible dread filled her. She had a very bad feeling she knew what they were planning.

Torrence and Galger talked among themselves, Torrence's face twisted with annoyance though he nodded his head, forced to comply with Galger's orders. The men drew away from Xerus, leaving him to hang. They seemed to be taking a moment to collect themselves, watching Xerus intently, waiting for him to wake up.

When he did finally awaken, their guns were instantly aimed at his head and torso. Xerus' body jerked, pulling at his chains. Lana couldn't hear it but, as his head bent forward and he went perfectly still, she imagined he growled low at them. The men moved closer and Galger came to the front. He gestured with his hands and Lana knew he was speaking, addressing Xerus in some sarcastic, demeaning way. Though she didn't know what he was saying, she could guess what his speech was about. They weren't going to kill him. Not yet. They wanted information as Galger promised General Vearez he would get. Xerus only had to answer and they might let him die quickly and painlessly. If he didn't, they would try to force him any way they could. And with Galger's method of torture, they wouldn't start gently.

Lana knew Xerus wouldn't give up any information easily. She was certain he would die before telling them a thing. As one of the men handed Galger a knife, he stepped forward to stand only a foot away from the alien and pressed the blade against Xerus' stomach. Lana cried out as he made to slice through Xerus' skin. As theorized, the blade didn't cut through and Lana wrapped a hand around her throat in relief. Galger was testing him. Experimenting in his own sick way. Which blades would be sharp enough to cut? What tool could pierce such skin?

Xerus' body was still. He didn't so much as flinch as the knife grazed against him. Galger traded the simple knife for a torchblade, a laser tipped knife that burned hotter than fire, used for cutting thick metal and stone. Lana tensed as he brought the glowing blade toward Xerus.

Lana wanted to do something, wanted to stop them. But how? If she went to level three, they would capture her and she would be forced to watch, only closer and tied up. Then they'd just kill her after. She tried to think fast, tried to form some semblance of a plan as Galger teased Xerus with the blade.

Xerus tensed as the blade went across his torso, leaving a black slash over his scales. His hands curled into tight fists but he moved little. Lana was glad now she couldn't hear because she didn't think she could take the sound of Xerus' roars of pain if he did make any sort of noise. Galger let the blade graze slowly against Xerus' side, leaving singed stripes. He would pause, say something and wait, then do another. Xerus wouldn't give in but his body wouldn't last forever. The tears that threatened to spill over finally did and Lana wept as she watched Xerus' skin go from a deep red to dark purplish-black, the dead scales falling to the ground, leaving a naked gash. Small trickles of blood fell from the wounds as the knife pierced the first layer of skin.

When Xerus still wouldn't answer even after Galger's assault, Galger waved at the men beside him. They took up the ends of the chains and pulled hard, dragging Xerus' head downward from a thick chain tied around his neck, forcing him to bend awkwardly. Then, with the torchblade, they began to cut at one of his horns.

"No," Lana moaned. "No. Dammit, Xerus, just tell them!" she screamed at the monitor. "Just tell them, don't let them do this." She hit her fist against the screen, no longer able to see clearly as her tears blinded her. She shut her eyes unable to watch, unable to think. There was no plan, only her despair. Xerus wouldn't give in. And they wouldn't stop.

* * *

Lana sat in silence, frozen and hollow, her throat sore, her eyes sunken pits as they stared at nothing. The torturing was over. For now. They'd kept at it for several hours before Galger finally stopped. What was left made Lana want to vomit.

Most of Xerus' beautiful scales were gone. In their place was charred, purplish skin. Some areas bled, others didn't. Several of his horns and spikes had been hacked off, leaving jagged stumps, the ends scattered all over the ground. Some of the men had taken them as souvenirs, playing with them and throwing them across the room. At one point Galger had torn the black cloth down from Xerus eyes, making sure to keep his mouth covered lest the alien try to bite him. Then he took the blade to Xerus' face, leaving a long black scar across his left eye. Whether he was blind in the eye was uncertain but it was closed shut.

The only places left untouched now were his mouth and tail. And only because they couldn't get to them without the possibility of getting attacked. His tail still remained firmly tied around him, the end cutting into his backside. If they tried to unravel it, Xerus would instantly try to use it so they didn't take their chances though it was known Torrence still wished to have the tail's tip.

In time he might just get his wish. Because once Galger was finished resting, he would go at the alien again. And next time they might try to find a way to get to the parts they couldn't.

Lana could hardly look at Xerus without wanting to burst into endless tears yet again. But tears were pointless and did nothing to save him or help her. Instead she sat, staring... thinking. Galger and his men looked like they were going to call it a night, some already finding places to lay around the gear and weapons. Galger had ordered some of his men to go back out and do some more "investigating". Just because he was in the process of torturing his prisoner didn't mean the rest of his mission would fall to the wayside. The men had gone out looking for others. And they had found their targets on level two. The guards were taken out before they could even speak, leaving the soldiers to take from the food supply what they wished just as they had before. They had come back not long after with everything they could need and their orders carried out perfectly. They would go out again in time to the other levels, not knowing yet that they were all empty save for level one thanks to her and Xerus.

Lana couldn't save those in the city sector now. Not without Xerus. Worse, most by now might be infected. The bandaged man had been there long enough now that some must be. But she couldn't think of it now. All she could think about was how she could save Xerus before it was too late.

Slowly Lana rose from her seat, her body shaking, feeling like she might collapse to the ground. She steadied herself then walked carefully toward the bathroom. She relieved herself then re-wrapped her bandages even though Xerus had already done it a day ago. She just needed to focus on something else to keep from losing it yet again. After, she came back to the main room and looked around. It was silent and she felt so alone. She shivered despite the warmth of the unit, the dim, calm lighting doing nothing to ease her.

She looked over at the dining table covered in Xerus' bombs and tools for making them. She wouldn't be able to place the rest of them either. She felt so useless, so hopeless. If Xerus died, his mission would fail and those with Spectre still inside them might get out of the base, spreading the parasite to other worlds. As much as she hated to think about it, she would rather let Galger take out the rest than have that happen if it was the only way to keep the parasite from spreading.

Lana closed her eyes. She wished then her father was still alive. He would find a way.

There's always a way through the storm no matter how bad.

He had always been a sailor at heart. But it was the sea that had taken him. His love for something so untamed, so wild, had been his undoing. Xerus was Lana's sea. And he might just be her undoing.

She could give herself up. She could go to them and be with Xerus one last time.

"No," she whispered. "No, don't think like that. There has to be a way."

Because she realized then if she didn't do something, eventually the team would make their way to the docks. All of her and Xerus' efforts would then be for nothing.

Lana opened her eyes and found herself staring at the table of bombs. The detonator sat firmly in the center next to a wrench and an unwired bomb. She stared for a long time until her eyes began to widen and her heart seemed to skip a beat.

She picked up the detonator carefully, making sure not to even touch the trigger. Because, as Xerus had said, it was active.

The bombs that were already set were active. Ready to be triggered.

When Galger and his men had taken Xerus, they had shucked aside the bag of bombs around his neck and left it on five. If they weren't all burned from the electricity, then they too were active.

Lana set the detonator down then rifled through the set of tools in the toolbag, her heart beginning to race. When she found the metal cutter, she squeezed it firmly in her hand. It was no torchblade, but it would do.

It was a crazy idea and it would give them little time to escape but it might be her only chance. With new purpose, Lana set down the tools and went back over to the monitor on the Scibot's chest. Xerus lay limp and unmoving in the center of the screen but he was alive. Lana touched her hand to the glass, touching her fingertips to Xerus' image.

"We aren't finished here yet," she said quietly, with a calm determination that was laced with anger. Letting her fingers slide from the screen she turned away and went to work.

CHAPTER THIRTY

Lana strapped the bag around her firmly, the metal cutter lying within. She checked the pockets of her red coveralls making sure everything was zipped tight. A gun lay strapped to her waist, one that Xerus had found in his many ventures outside the unit. She had very little practice with a gun and hoped she wouldn't have to use it. Most of her pockets were empty except for the one with the detonator and another holding her now most coveted item, Xerus' scale, still wrapped in silver wire, not yet finished but she told herself it would be someday. Because she was going to live and so would he. She padded the pocket down to be sure the object was still inside and making sure the detonator too was secure. When everything was in place, she stepped over to the door.

She hadn't been out of the unit for several days if not weeks. She hadn't been keeping track but she knew it had been a long while. Thankfully Lana knew what lay ahead of her. She had looked over the video feed one last time and saw that Galger's team was sleeping, only a small group keeping watch. Xerus was still the whole time, but she knew he must be awake. She only had to go up one level and there was no one around. She had mapped out the route in her head first, memorizing the turns she would make and passages she would go through. If all went well, it could be done quickly. She just had to go out the door and never stop.

Lana hesitated by the door and took a long, deep breath. She was scared shitless by what she was about to do but her desperation to help Xerus and the others overpowered her fear. "You can do this. You can do this." Lana hit the button for the door. It slid smoothly outward, revealing the small foyer and the secondary, outer door. Continuing to take deep breaths she moved to the door and hit the button. Darkness greeted her from the outside as the door slid open. Lana hesitated for only a second then shot out and ran down the corridor.

She didn't stop once. Making the necessary turns until she came to the emergency stairs. Flinging the door open, she flew upward, orange and red light bathing the stairway in ominous shades. When she got to the level three door, she flung it open as well and ran into the darkness. Only a few fluorescent lights touched the cemented walls overhead, some flickering, ready to go out. There was the scent of smoke in the air and something burnt. Lana didn't overthink what it was from; she could only guess. The closer she got, however, the more of the scent of dark coffee battled with the smell of fire.

"How much ya bettin' this time," a voice slipped out from the darkness. Lana slowed her pace then stopped just before the entrance of a rather large doorway. White lights beamed outward from within.

"Fuck, I don't know." Someone laughed low.

"I'll make it two thousand this time," came another. "Bettin it'll last a second round at least. Then give out on the third."

The men's voices echoed down the passage. Lana carefully peered around the corner to see the group of men sitting around near the door.

"I'll bet it dies in the second round," said one.

"Really? It's pretty tough. Made it this far without cracking."

"I know. I just want it to die already so we can get the fuck out of here."

Lana turned away and pressed herself against the wall. Xerus was at the very back, but there was another door to the side that was closer. The others were asleep for the most part though some merely laid out staring at the ceiling as if just waiting. Waiting to get back to the mission, to carry out orders. Torrence was one of the ones awake. Galger snored close by.

Lana backed away from the wall to hide better in the darkness. With cautious steps she went to sneak past the open door, her heart hammering in her chest, afraid any moment an alarm might sound. If there were any triggers, they probably would have sounded back at the stairs. Still, she needed to be careful. Thankfully the men must have lowered their guard, confident that nothing was going to ambush them when there was nothing left that could ambush. They seemed very certain they had caught and killed every specimen and any human they encountered wasn't a threat.

Lana barely breathed as she crept by the door, her eyes wide, one hand brushing the wall, the other clamped to the handle of the gun. The men talked in low murmurs and there was a dull buzz from the machines and lights within the room but very little sound otherwise. When she got to the other side, she rushed over to the door on the far end and dared to take another peek. Xerus was hanging, his arms above his head. She wouldn't be able to reach them but she could get to his feet and his tail.

They had placed the black cloth back over his eyes but Lana knew he could sense in other ways. He was completely still until his head lifted slightly and turned toward her. He let out a soft hiss and clenched his hands. He knew she was there.

Lana turned back to the darkness as the men fell silent.

"Did you hear that? Did that thing just hiss?" one of them said.

"Fucker gives me the creeps, man. How can these assholes sleep with that thing so close," another murmured.

Lana waited for a long moment until they focused on something else. Then, as quietly as she could, she took out the detonator. Her hands trembled slightly as she held it close to her. She tried to brace herself, knowing it was going to be loud. As her finger slipped to the trigger, she prayed it wouldn't collapse the entire base.

"Three," she whispered, licking her lips. "two..." she began to press down. "One."

The trigger clicked as she pressed it down fully. Nothing happened and Lana stood there in a stone-faced panic thinking it was broken. Then the wave hit. The booms from below made the ground tremble then turn into violent shaking. The blasts roared upward, bellowing up like a giant out of hell. Lana fell forward on to the ground just as shouts erupted from the men in the room. Lana fumbled back to her feet then another tremor shook the base making her catch herself on the wall. Without thinking, she lurched forward and stumbled to the doorway. Men were rushing everywhere, most going for their guns and others trying to brace themselves. Galger shouted to them, his gun in hand, face red, commanding them to not panic, telling them to focus on the outer doors and take positions. Those of his original team listened, others who were initiated recently were not so compliant. They argued and ducked by the crates as debris fell and the ground continued to shake. As the men turned toward the doors opposite her and went out into the dark halls to investigate, Lana flew into the room, heading straight for Xerus. She went for his tail first, hiding behind him so she could work at the binds.

Xerus said nothing as she worked the chains or maybe she just couldn't hear him over the blasts. Frantically she sawed at the metal, knowing she had little time. Her hands were sweating, slowing her progress, but she dared not pause to look around her, only to focus on freeing Xerus.

When the chain finally broke, she yanked them away, but Xerus' tail didn't unwrap from his abdomen right away as it was dug so deep into his skin. She didn't dare try to pull at it in fear she might injure him more. Instead, she went around to his front and started to work at the chains at his feet. Xerus squirmed to get her attention and Lana rose to pull the cloth from his face.

His face was twisted so much that she thought for a second Galger had damaged it more. In reality, he was furious with her.

"Are you trying to get yourself killed?" he nearly roared. "Damnable human woman! Get out of here before–"

Lana took hold of his face and kissed him. It was rough and hard, freezing him on the spot. Then without a word she released him and went for the chains at his feet, completely ignoring his curses and threats to her both in her language and in his.

She sawed at the bind when Xerus' shout caught her by surprise. She glanced up and was yanked back as someone grabbed a fist of her hair and pulled. The metal cutter dropped from her hand as she was flung to her back. When she started up, she saw the black eyes of Officer Torrence.

"You little bitch, I should have known," he said with a sneer. Lana crawled back and went for the gun at her side but Torrence was quicker. He took his gun out and aimed toward her. The bullet just missed her as Galger came up beside him and tugged back his arm as he fired.

"Step back, Officer Torrence," Galger shouted. "That's an order." Lana went for her gun again but was pulled up by one of the soldiers, her arms wrenched back, bending them till they hurt. Lana cried out as she arched her back and another hand tugged her gun from its holster. The blasts from each bomb started to subside and sirens cried out in response. The men argued as she stood, bent forward, waiting to feel a gun press against her or for a hand to make the final blow. She turned her head over to look at Xerus, to mouth she was sorry, when she caught him unraveling his tail from around him. In one swift movement, he stretched his tail outward and reached for the metal cutter.

A hand slipped to Lana's jaw and forced her head upward. Galger glared down at her. "Mrs. Hart, you really are full of surprises. What the hell did you just do?"

Lana tried to shake away his hand. "I did what I had to," she said through clenched teeth. "To stop you."

Galger frowned, for once not amused by her. "By destroying the whole base?" He shook his head. "You are one crazy bitch, aren't you?" He almost laughed. "Damn if Torrence hadn't been right. How did you even make it this far, eh?"

Lana struggled in his grip, betraying herself by once again looking to Xerus who had wrapped his tail back around him, his one eye on them both, burning bright with fury. Galger caught her gaze and cursed.

"You really were with that thing? Fuck me, you are one dirty girl. I didn't have a chance if I had to compete with that." He gestured toward Xerus.

"Enough of this, Galger," Torrence spat. "Let me take care of her."

Galger stared down at her, his eyes cold. He seemed to hesitate before releasing her, nodding his head. "Do it then. And make it quick. The rest of you get shit packed and head for the stairs. We're moving to level one," he shouted. The men complied and rushed to carry as much as they could. Torrence took Lana's arm in a painful grip, pulling her away.

"Hold on." Galger stopped him one last time. He brushed his fingers over Lana's cheek. "No hard feelings, eh?" He bent his head down and a violent roar escaped Xerus just before Galger's lips could make contact with Lana's.

"*Sipha ness vi,*" don't touch her, Xerus hissed sharply, baring his black fangs at them with deadly intent.

"Looks like your boyfriend has a jealous side." Galger laughed, but his smile didn't reach his eyes as usual. "You would have been a good lay. Too bad." He stepped back and didn't so much as glance at her again, moving away to help his men. "Oh, and I'll make sure to kill your boyfriend after you go, to save you from the heartache," he yelled back to her as Torrence tugged her away. Lana cried out, struggling in Torrence's tight grip, trying to look back at Xerus, to reach for him. Torrence backhanded her across the face, cutting her lip open, making her fall to the ground. In her blurred vision, she caught one last glance at Xerus' roaring face before being dragged from the room.

CHAPTER THIRTY-ONE

Lana continued to struggle in Torrence's grip, fighting him at every turn. She clawed and beat at his arms until Torrence lost his patience and smashed his fist in her face once more. Lana saw stars, her cheek throbbing, her lip already beginning to swell. He dragged her into a nearby room with empty crates and unused medical equipment, the doors open on either end, tempting her to run. If only she could.

Torrence flung her to the ground and stood over her, watching her try to sit up and crawl away from him. His black eyes shined bright, his mouth turned up ever so slightly as if he had been waiting for this moment for a long time.

"It's over, Ms. Hart," he said, taking out his gun and aiming to her head.

Lana turned her head up to look at him, raising her hand in front of her like it would somehow defend her. "They'll know what you did," she said. "Everyone will know you killed innocent people."

He lowered his gun only slightly, his smirk widening. "I doubt that, Ms. Hart."

"The cameras are recording everything this very moment. The video will get out." Lana tried to crawl back.

Torrence showed his teeth. "Even if it gets out, the generals will make sure it's covered. We were just doing our job. Everyone was infected and had to be exterminated." His gun rose back up to her head. "And you tried to sabotage our mission. You're not the hero in this, Ms. Hart. You are just a sad little woman who kept getting in the way." His finger tightened on the trigger.

A shadow slipped behind Torrence just as Lana braced herself. There was a loud whoosh followed by a sharp crack as something long and thin connected with Torrence's legs. The gun went off twice, releasing a blinding light and a deafening bang as the bullets pierced the metal walls beside Lana's head. Lana gasped and fell back as Torrence collapsed to the ground in front of her, his black eyes wide with confusion and shock. Blood spurted out from where his knees had once been, now shattered in half. A gurgling scream ripped from his throat just as the shadow behind him moved out from the darkness and slunk past a doorway.

Asset C looked back at Lana curiously, its tail swinging carelessly behind it, like a thick whip. It sniffed at her and bared its fangs before disappearing out into the passage beyond. Lana stared at where it had stayed hidden and saw one of the vents in the wall with an open gash big enough for the beast to slip through. Galger's men must have forgotten to check all the vents and so Asset C had used them to its advantage.

Torrence continued to scream in agony as blood gushed from his now two stumps for legs, his eyes filled with pain and fury as he looked at her and tried to drag himself toward her. Lana backed away further, toward the other door. She stumbled to her feet and tried to blindly run, only to fall to the ground once more as another tremor shook the base.

The levels below were collapsing and so too would the rest if they didn't get out soon. Lana crawled over to the wall and lifted herself once more as sirens continued to assault the level with a piercing noise, orange lights flashing, disorienting her even more.

Shouts and screams lifted above the sirens. Then so did the gunfire.

"Xerus," Lana whispered, thinking it must be him. She stumbled again down the passage back toward the hub only to come face to face with a group of Galger's men running the opposite direction.

"Where is Officer Torrence?" one yelled in her ear as he grabbed her, his gun focused on her chest. Before she could answer, Galger appeared from the doorway of the hub.

"Get the fuck out! Get to level one all of you!" he called. In his hands he fired a long assault weapon only instead of bullets it spilled fire.

"No!" Lana screamed as the flamethrower blasted out a torrent of fire into the room. Xerus must still be inside. She tried to tug away from the soldier but he caught her firmly and pulled her the opposite direction. He brought her back with the rest of the men who began making their way to a set of emergency stairs up to the city sector. The soldier touched his gun to Lana's back, forcing her to follow them.

* * *

As they broke through the doors into the city sector, the men quickly disarmed the guards stationed to watch the staircase and elevators. They too had felt the tremors and hadn't expected a full out attack in the wake of all the chaos. Galger's men walked into the foyer of the city sector with guns raised. The people who had been hunkering down in various areas between the fountain and the entrance now scrambled to their feet, eyes wide with terror as the men shouted for them to all come together in the middle of the still shiny, pristine foyer.

Lana squinted her eyes and kept her head bent, the skylights above so bright compared to all the darkness she had been used to below. The drones that usually floated overhead were now scattered around the floor, shutdown or shot down, Lana wasn't sure.

"Everybody on the ground now!" shouted the soldiers. They directed everyone to sit together in the very center of the large area near the fountain which no longer sprayed water, the Lazris star no longer floating but lying on its side in a pool of murky water.

Lana too was directed to sit with them but, as she moved closer, she saw the bandaged man sitting near the edge, his eyes a pupilless black with red around the edges. She looked over the others around him and saw that some of their eyes were the same. She shook her head and backed away.

"No, no, some are infected," she choked.

"I don't give a shit. They'll all be dead soon anyway," the soldier said low, shoving her toward the crowd of pale faces and red eyes.

As she knelt on the ground near the people, Galger came through the stairway entrance with the rest of his men, a pair of which were carrying a now bandaged up and gray-faced Officer Torrence. They sat him down against a pillar by the fountain and left him as Galger ordered his men to place the remaining guards with the rest of the people and to take positions at the stairs and the elevators.

As he twisted around toward her, their eyes met. Lana could see in his face his control slipping but still determined not to fail. He took up his gun and followed over to the elevators. Lana crept to the edge of the fountain so she could watch. They were preparing themselves for an attack and Lana knew who was coming. Her heart raced waiting for Xerus to burst through one of the many entrances.

A deep tremor rocked the base and small pieces of debris fell from the ceiling. A few of the people cried out, shielding their heads.

"We have to get out of here!" someone cried out. One man shot up and tried running for the exit when one of the soldiers gunned them down.

"No one goes anywhere!" he shouted.

The others cowered away and Lana's hands curled into fists but she dared not move. Her eyes flicked back to the elevators where the men stood at the ready, some hiding behind pillars.

Minutes passed but they felt like hours as they waited with more debris falling, cracks forming in the pillars, the skylight dimming.

Beyond the dull tremors, there was a tense stillness. Then one of the elevators turned on. Then another. And another. Until all eight were lit up.

The soldiers barely moved, their guns aimed and ready.

"Steady, boys, steady," Galger called.

Some of the cars didn't even come up, likely damaged from the explosions. But a few did and when they stopped on one, the men aimed their guns toward them.

As soon as the doors opened the guns went off, bullets piercing through the metal cars, destroying the lights within. The people around her covered their ears and bent their heads in agony. All except those under Spectre's sway, who merely watched, blood spilling from their mouths. Lana too covered her ears as the soldiers didn't stop their assault on the elevators.

When they finally did stop, the elevators were riddled with bullet holes. Nothing came out. Lana let out her breath, her hand curling around her throat.

Galger stepped over to the elevators to investigate closer and, when he saw they were empty, he cursed and kicked away a shard of metal.

The stairwell doors exploded outward and the men guarding it flew back. Xerus stepped out looking more menacing than Lana had ever seen him. Somehow more terrifying looking now with his gnarled flesh and jagged, asymmetrical horns. He was feral, wild. A destroyer ready to kill. Before those that had been guarding the stairwell could sit up, he was on them. With his teeth, he ripped into one soldier's flesh while with his tail he sliced through another.

"Get back all of you, ready your weapons!" Galger shouted. The men tried to comply as quickly as they could but Xerus was quicker. As they reloaded their guns and went to aim, Xerus flew at them. Slicing through the first few without issue, he swerved away as the other men still standing began firing again. As Galger and his men made their way back toward the fountain, the soldiers around Lana focused their attention on Xerus as well.

As their backs were turned, one of the infected rose. He lurched forward and went at one of the unsuspecting soldiers. Before Lana could shout a warning, the infected man latched on to the soldier, taking him down to the ground with him. The soldier screamed as the infected bit into his shoulder, his gun going off toward the ceiling, causing shards of the skylight to rain down. The people burst from the center. The infected flew at anyone they could get to while the others ran.

Lana crouched down beside the fountain uncertain what to do. All around her people were being attacked and bullets flew by. Xerus continued to evade and tear his way through Galger's men like an enraged beast, seeing nothing but enemies around him. Lana stood up and called to him, wanting to get his attention, to get him to stop and leave them so they could escape.

A piercing cry sounded beside her and she looked to see the bandaged man standing over Torrence who looked up at him with wide-eyed shock, blood pooling out of his mouth. His eyes fell and found hers just as his body went limp and fell to the side, a glass shard piercing his chest. The bandaged man straightened then slowly twisted around to see her. His soulless eyes glared at her and his jaw moved.

"You are strong. We could use you," he gurgled. He stepped toward her with uncanny movements and Lana tried to back away. "Don't be afraid, Ms. Hart. It won't hurt, I promise."

Lana stilled. That voice, so strange yet...

The bandaged man rushed at her and Lana tried to jump away only to trip over fallen debris. The man leaped on her and Lana screamed as he tried to pin her. Flailing under him, she attacked his face, trying to move him from her. She tore at his bandages, ripping at both the ones around his face and head until they revealed a dirty, unkempt face, one though that she still recognized.

Cole Kingsley smirked down at her, hardly moving as she

attacked him. It wasn't him anymore of course. He had been gone for a long time. Only Spectre remained.

Cole grabbed her shoulders in a tight, unnaturally strong grip, making her bones ache. Lana gasped at the sudden pain. She tried to struggle against him but he was too heavy, too strong. His head bent down towards her and a trickle of black blood fell down his mouth, to his chin. He released one of her shoulders to grasp her jaw to keep her in place. Lana wanted to cry out but she was struck with fear. This was it. She was about to be worse than dead. All she could think was Xerus would have to kill her after all. But no, she wouldn't allow it. She'd kill herself first to save him from such a choice. As he rampaged on, taking out Galger's men only a few yards away, he would never know. She just hoped he would finish off the rest and save himself.

As Cole's face neared closer to hers, a torrent of bullets went flying close by, a few catching Cole's back. He didn't even seem to notice. His grasp tightened and he continued to lower himself, his blood about to drip onto her.

A hand flew out and gripped Cole's collar, forcing him back. Galger pulled Cole away and took out his pistol and shot him in the head. The smile on Cole's face never left even as his body crumbled to the ground. Without hesitating, Galger lunged at Lana and dragged her to her feet, his pistol now against her temple.

"Enough!" he shouted so loud his voice cracked. Lana flinched as his hand tightened around her throat. The sound of gunfire ceased and Xerus dropped another soldier to the ground, the body a bloody mess. Xerus too was covered in blood, his teeth dripping with it as bodies lay all around him, torn and sliced.

"Enough," Galger said softly. "You're done." He shook Lana hard, making her teeth clack. Xerus straightened then stilled as his eye fell on her, his lip curling back. "One more move, asshole, and she dies," Galger warned.

Lana panted hard in his grip, digging her nails into the skin of his arm. Xerus slowly twisted his body toward them but dared not take a step as the gun pressed harder to Lana's temple. Lana inhaled sharply, raising her head, but her eyes never left Xerus.

"Good, now that I have your attention, eh," Galger said. "Why don't you start backing up slowly and we will do the same." Galger took a step back, taking Lana with him. "We will just leave together and you are going to stay right there."

Lana's face contorted, shaking her head as Xerus looked to her. His head bent low and he hissed softly but he didn't move. "That's it...good," Galger said. Lana didn't fight as he moved them closer to the exit where the elevator cars were. As she looked down, she saw bodies lying across the floor nearby. No one had made it past.

The base shook again but Galger kept his hold on her and his balance tight. If they left, Xerus might not make it. Cracks were already forming along the ground. Lana could do nothing. She would be forced to watch as they left him behind.

Trembling, Lana could barely watch. Once the base collapsed, there would be nothing left of him. Nothing except for the scale she still possessed in her pocket.

As the thought struck her, Lana froze, her heart skipping. With trembling fingers, she slipped her free hand to the side pocket and carefully unzipped it. As Galger came to the door at the end of the city sector, his attention fixed on opening it. Within that second, Lana slipped her hand into her pocket and took out the scale, gripping it tight.

As the door opened, Lana moved. She let her knees give out, dropping her weight, and simultaneously struck Galger with the sharp end of the scale, catching him in the eye. His gun went off, just barely missing her head. Lana dropped to the ground as he stumbled back, his hand spread across his face as blood gushed from his eye. He roared and went to shoot again but this time Xerus was on him. In one flawless motion, he sliced a hand across Galger's neck then threw him across the foyer until his body hit the end of the fountain, moving no more.

Breathless, Lana bent forward letting out a soft whimper of relief.

Xerus picked her up, cradling her to him. The base shook and the crack in the ground widened. Xerus turned and moved swiftly past the door, heading toward the elevator cars.

Lana wanted to weep but was still too scared they might not make it in time. As Xerus entered one of the cars and set her down carefully, he forced the doors closed then smashed the button that would take them up to the docks. The elevator car didn't move at first until it shuddered and slowly began to make its way upward.

Neither of them said a word as the car moved. Xerus went to Lana's side, crouching in front of her and she, in turn, took his face into her hands, her lips trembling as she formed a smile. She brushed her fingers over his eye then kissed it softly.

"It was my fault," Lana broke. "Oh, god, Xerus, I'm so sorry."

Xerus looked at her squarely and clasped her hands in his. "You have nothing to apologize for, *Kissala*," he said softly.

"But your scales and your horns."

Xerus placed her hands back against his face. "They can be mended in time."

The car stopped abruptly, flinging Lana against Xerus. The lights went out and the car ceased to move.

"*Ecisa va*," Xerus cursed. He went to the doors of the car and shoved them open. The car was stuck.

"What are we going to do?" Lana asked.

Xerus peered at her with his good eye. "You will climb on my back."

Xerus crawled up the darkness, his back muscles straining under her. She clung to him tightly, her arms wrapped around his neck, grateful that the way was slightly angled and not just a straight shoot down. When light broke from the top, Xerus quickened his pace, clambering for the pinpoint of light. When the light became larger and brighter,

Lana began to hear the voices of people; a dull echo, but there none-theless.

They didn't have a plan for what would happen when Xerus got to the top but Lana no longer cared as long as Xerus got out safe. She would take up a gun if she had to and point it at anyone who tried to stop him.

As Xerus made it to the end, he slid himself over the ledge then had Lana drop from his back. As he righted himself, he picked her up once more and carried her out of the station.

CHAPTER THIRTY-TWO

The people at the docks didn't run or scream. No guns were drawn, no orders shouted. They merely stared in wonder at Xerus with Lana still in his arms. Lana was shocked to be sure but also equally relieved. As the people backed away to give them space, Xerus set her down beside him.

Lana looked through the crowd of faces and saw Dahlia, Ben, and Sarah among them. They came to the front to hug and greet her.

"You made it, fuck, it's a damn miracle," Ben said.

"Everyone is okay?" Lana asked.

Dahlia nodded. "A few were injured, but we patched them up."

Lana looked at the faces of those watching them, most looking to Xerus with fear and awe. "Why don't they run?" Lana asked. "

"They saw you with him and got the hint," Ben said.

Dahlia smacked his shoulder lightly. "It was more than that. Once groups started coming up from the cargo elevators one after another we had a theory that someone was aiding them. When we asked, they each said it had been a great big red demon alien from hell." Dahlia shrugged as Xerus snorted and shook his head. "We knew it had to be Asset X. But what we didn't understand was why he did it and how everyone would come out alive. Since, let's be honest, there was no way they would."

"So we then theorized," Sarah said, "That he was actually helping. It took some time but we convinced them. Ben showed them the video recordings of all your sessions. Well, the good ones anyway." Sarah glanced at Xerus nervously. "We then told them to wait for others. Until we knew for sure everyone was out. But once the tremors started..."

"People have been itching real bad to leave," Ben finished. He pointed to the ships. "They are ready to go. No one is holding us back now that the officers stood down and the pilots are ready to fly them."

Lana nodded. "Let's get the hell out of here."

* * *

Xerus did one last round of scanning to be sure none held the parasite. To their relief, everyone was clean. A few volunteered to blockade the station entrance but Xerus was satisfied the infected were either all dead or still down in the earth ready to be buried. None would be able to make it out from the bottom to the top. And with all the ships taking off, there would be no way for Spectre to spread.

Lana stood out beyond the crowd where most were filing in line to get on one of the ships. She didn't know whether to join them or not. Now that she and Xerus had made it out, what she had avoided before could no longer be ignored. He had to go back to his home planet. Where he could get back to his kind and tell them he had completed his mission. Where he could be made Predomis and mated to a queen.

A sharp sting hit her chest at the thought and in that moment she fully considered forcing Xerus to take her with him.

But how could she force someone to go against their way of life, against their beliefs? They were from different worlds, no matter how much she loved him, she couldn't force him to go against his ways. Even if it broke her.

"They are getting ready to depart," Dahlia said beside her. "Better get on."

Lana swallowed hard, her throat tightening. "I..."

Dahlia's eyes widened at something behind her and she stepped back, bowing her head. Lana turned and saw Xerus behind her.

"We are taking this ship," he said, looking at Dahlia. "Since there is enough room for everyone on the others."

Dahlia glanced at Lana, her brows rising. Lana stared at Xerus. "We?"

Dahlia slipped a hand on Lana's shoulder reassuringly and gave her a small smile before returning with the others. They waved to her as they entered their ship. Lana waved back and turned to Xerus. "You want me to come with you?"

Xerus' eye narrowed on her as if annoyed. "Did you honestly think I would leave you?"

Lana opened her mouth then closed it, feeling ashamed. "I thought...you have to go back to your home planet to tell them you completed your mission."

"Yes..."

"And...to become a Predomis." Her eyes fell. "And..." Oh, to hell with it. "And I can't be there with you when that happens. I can't watch you be with another and be alone." Lana turned her eyes back to him. "I don't think I could take it. Because..."

Xerus nuzzled her neck then whispered in her ear, " Do you ever actually listen to me? Or do humans lack the ability to remember things clearly?"

Confused, Lana looked back at him and Xerus snorted. He took her hand in his. "I am not Predomis yet. But I already have a queen. Because she will be chosen as it is her right."

Lana blinked, staring at him. "I can be made a queen?" she said softly. "Even though I am not Vrisha?"

"A queen is chosen for her strength and bravery. For her cunning and ability to endure." Xerus stated. "That is the Vrisha way. You have proven this ten-times over. You who helped destroy our enemy and put your life at risk to save me." Xerus bowed his head. "The others will know as I will be the one to tell them. You will be made a queen and you will be mine."

Lana stared up at him, barely able to think. Not knowing what to say, only that a weight had vanished and she felt alive. She reached up and kissed his jaw, his neck, uncaring of the stares from people still waiting to board the other ships.

"Let's go home," Lana whispered, smiling.

Xerus grunted and lifted her in his arms. He took her to a ship at the very front, shutting the doors behind them.

At the front of the ship, Xerus placed her at a seat next to his then began working the controls. Lana watched in fascination as he started the ship.

"You really can fly this?" she asked nervously.

Xerus looked at her and his mouth twitched. "Your technology is rather simple."

Lana smiled then laughed.

The engine roared to life and, as it moved, the doors to the dock entrance opened. Light spilled out, the first natural light Lana had seen in months.

The ship sped up until Lana was pushed back by the force. They shot from the entrance then climbed to the clouds until the sky darkened and there was nothing but stars.

EPILOGUE

Xerus

They were close. At least if the readings were correct. Human tech always made him a little nervous as it was so susceptible to error. Or breaking at the most inconvenient times. But he could estimate enough that they were passing Airus, their third moon now, the farthest from Tryth. Already he could see in the distance the black-edged Vrisha ships in orbit. They would contact him soon.

Flicking a few switches and using his knuckle to tap at the screen before him, he placed the ship in auto and left his seat. Unhurried, he strode down the narrow passage behind the pilot's cabin until he reached a room at the back. Within, several dozen pods sat in rows of three from the ground to the top in a semi-circle around the room. He went to the one on the left closest to the door and peered down.

There his queen slept peacefully. How she could stand to be confined in such a space astounded him. Though she was so small he supposed it worked well for her race. At least he could feel assured that she was secure inside, only having to check on her every few hours.

The pods were barbaric. As were their ships. What space-traveling race in their right minds used such tech to get around? Clearly, they had been impatient to leave their homeworld even if it meant speeding through space in a ship slower than a Vrisha carrier on the Tryth seas. He'd wanted to tear the rest of his scales out just from the sheer frustration of it. But he forced himself to be patient. And grateful.

Only a few weeks ago they had escaped that toxic planet and the underground base within. Now gone and buried, his enemy with it. Xerus closed his eyes. Finally, the parasite that had destroyed so many other races was gone.

He didn't know if he could ever tell her how bad it really had been. He had kept so much from her in the beginning and even now he was uncertain. But then she would soon find out, regardless. The others would show her if he didn't. It was only good now that the parasite was gone. Even if the sacrifices had been great. Xerus curled his lip back as the memories of destruction flashed through his mind. Of the planets destroyed, of every living organism needing to be wiped out and exterminated. And he had been the enforcer.

He would have done it to her race too if it had come down to it. And he gave silent thanks to Veradis that it hadn't been so. It was the Vrisha way to place one's mission and duties above all else to complete their goal. But it did not leave out the agony or the despair or utter fear. Several times Lana had brought out those emotions within him when he thought he would have to end her life if it meant destroying the parasite. Even in the beginning he had felt oddly saddened at the thought, but once he understood what he was feeling towards her, he had been determined to save her at any cost.

This strange little human had made him more afraid than he had ever felt in many cycles. He didn't let it show, to keep her from worrying, but there had been more times than he cared to admit. When those human males had trapped him, all he could think about was what was going to happen to her.

He opened his eyes and let out a hiss of laughter. She had nearly sabotaged the mission and hadn't even known.

Maybe it would have been easier to have told her everything in the beginning. But he couldn't have risked it. Not when he didn't know who all was infected yet. Not when he suspected they were harboring the parasite. He had even feared at one point that they were working with it somehow. That they were planning to use it as a weapon. No, because he hadn't known for sure, he couldn't risk it. Even if he felt for Lana, wanted to protect her. He couldn't let slip his mission until he knew for sure they too weren't his enemy.

Xerus placed a hand against the pod's glass just above Lana's chest. He would never have believed in a thousand years that he would have found his mate in the middle of a war. He had fully come to terms with the idea that once his mission was complete, once the parasite was destroyed for good, he would come home and be given his queen as a reward. Never would have guessed that a strange earthling would be the one to move him. A soft-skinned, fragile-looking being, with an innocent face and fierce eyes. He had thought them strange looking at first, the humans, but the more he looked at his mate, the more he saw her loveliness. Her delicate beauty.

He imagined the others would be shocked, maybe even a little concerned for his mental stability for taking such a soft-looking crea ture as his queen. Tyrus certainly would have a laugh, as would Rysha, but he would put them out real quick. His mouth twitched in amusement at the thought of his brothers.

No, once they knew everything she had done, they would under-stand. She might not look it but she was worthy to be made queen. And knowing now that she would be by his side made his fiery soul swell and leap.

Letting his hand fall from the glass, Xerus moved to the controls beside the pod and activated the awakening cycle. The pod lit up from within, bathing his mate in a cool blue. The pod door opened, letting out wafts of cold air. Xerus shivered as he came around the front. Without his scales, the air nipped at him. If humans had wanted to learn anything useful about his kind, they would have known to use ice against him, not electricity. Though Vrisha could withstand any climate, icy atmosphere was the hardest for them to endure. They hated the cold.

Xerus leaned forward and grazed his fingers gently over his mate's soft cheek. She stirred, frowning, her eyes fluttering open.

"It's time, *Kissala*," he said softly. "We're almost home."

His mate looked up at him with her brilliant green eyes, staring up at him as if in awe. No more fear he noticed. And that was good. He never wanted to frighten her again.

She smiled at him and reached for him. He took her in his arms, bringing her close. He couldn't wait to have her in his home. In his bed. After the ceremonies were over, he would take her to every spot he loved, from Vilrak pass to the fire isles. He would have special clothing made for her, one from the scales of the fallen. And a crown of horns. He could envision it now and it made him growl with pleasure.

She looked at him with her confused stare. "What's wrong?"

He nuzzled her neck, nipping the delicate flesh, making her gasp. "Nothing is wrong...*Xevas nik kasa*."

She gave him a funny look. "You are...disappointed? About what?"

His eyes narrowed on her, forcing himself not to roll them. A decidedly human trait. "*Esca xi issa. Kasa*...impatient."

"Oh," she said, smiling sheepishly.

Xerus huffed. "You are too spoiled, you know. I have been too nice in speaking your tongue. And you are forgetting mine already." He shook his head. "You will need to understand mine more now than ever. As soon as we land, I won't speak human again."

Lana pouted but it seemed to be in jest. "Alright, fine. *Erssi*. I'm sorry."

Xerus tightened his hold around her. "That's better."

"How much farther are we?" she asked.

"We should be passing Syvi, our second moon, as we speak." He carried her out of the room of pods and started back down the passage. When they got to the pilot's cabin he placed her in the seat beside his.

A repetitive dinging sounded over the board and Xerus tapped the screen to confirm the call.

"*Risha nix vis na esya?*" came a low, guttural voice. They wanted to know who was in the strange ship.

"*Xi Vrisha Xerus xil riskna. Fina vese humin vishil,*" he responded.

There was a pause and then, "Xerus?" they said. They seemed in shock. They asked if he had completed his mission to which he responded yes.

Immediately they were escorted to Tryth, two Vrisha ships protecting their own from either side. They locked on with magnetic propulsion to take them onward at a quicker speed. In no time at all, Tryth, his homeworld, came into view. The brilliant red and purple planet was just as he remembered it.

"I can't wait to explore," his mate said beside him, staring out the window with unhidden fascination. Xerus grunted in agreement. She stood up to get a closer look and he couldn't help but bring her against him, wrapping his tail around her waist. He nuzzled her hair and she turned her face to kiss him on his jaw. "I want to see everything."

"And you will. But first, we must go through our ceremonies."

Lana's eyes fell as if she was in deep thought. "I hope the others accept me. It must be unusual to have an outsider become..."

"Maybe to humans. But to Vrisha it doesn't matter. If you prove yourself worthy, then you are accepted."

Lana gripped his hand. "What do we do after? Do we...rule?"

Xerus' mouth twitched. "In a way. We become part of a council of rulers and overseers. We will have missions and perform them together."

"Ah," Lana said, her mouth turning up slightly. "I would like to help in any way I can."

"But I will enforce that we are not given any missions in the first few months," he stated severely.

His mate looked up at him in surprise. "Why not?"

Xerus' eyes met hers. "Because you already have several of your own missions to perform. For me specifically." Lana looked at him in confusion and his mouth widened. "Or should I say favors that you still owe me."

When she finally understood, she groaned with agitated despair. "I knew I was going to regret those." She looked up at him and sighed, though her lips still curved ever so slightly. "All of them?"

Xerus twisted her around to face him then leaned down, brushing his mouth against hers. He tilted back and flashed his fangs. "All of them."

Sign up for Olivia Riley's Newsletter for updates on new releases, promotions, and bonus content.

Olivia's Newsletter

https://oliviarileyauthor.com

SERIES AND BOOKS BY OLIVIA

Dark World Mates

Heart's Prisoner
Dark's Savior
Shadow's Chosen
Heart's Keeper

Vrisha Warriors

Xora
Axrel
Vrexus
Xeda

Sidonions

Shade's Embrace
Draka's Heat

ABOUT THE AUTHOR

Olivia Riley loves the frightening possibilities of deep space, where dark heroes and brave heroines reside. She is also a gamer and film nut.

Instagram: oliviarileyauthor

Facebook: OliviarileySFR